MW00882445

INVINCIBLE

(ARK ROYAL, BOOK XII)

CHRISTOPHER G. NUTTALL

The characters and events portrayed in this book are fictitious. Any similarity to real persons, living or dead, is coincidental and not intended by the author.

Text copyright © 2018 Christopher G. Nuttall

All rights reserved.

Printed in the United States of America.

No part of this book may be reproduced, or stored in a retrieval system, or transmitted in any form or by any means, electronic, mechanical, photocopying, recording, or other-wise, without express written permission of the publisher.

ISBN: 1987607783

ISBN 13: 9781987607789

Cover by Justin Adams
http://www.variastudios.com/

http://www.chrishanger.net
http://chrishanger.wordpress.com/
http://www.facebook.com/ChristopherGNuttall

All Comments Welcome!

DEDICATION

To the men and women of the British armed forces.

AUTHOR'S NOTE

Invincible takes place roughly five years after *We Lead*, but draws on characters mentioned in *The Cruel Stars*.

As always, if you liked this book, please leave a review.

CONTENTS

PROLOGUE

IT WAS TRITE BUT TRUE, Doctor Dora Fayette had often thought, that in space no one could hear you scream. And yet, space *was* noisy to those with the right sort of ears. Stars, pulsars and even black holes produced radio noise, bursts of high-intensity energy that—once upon a time—had been mistaken for signs of intelligent life. It was hard, so hard, to pick out the faint hints of what *might* be radio signals from undiscovered civilisations against the towering waves of background noise, a task made harder by the radio signals put out by the ever-growing number of human colonies. And yet, it was a task that needed to be done.

Dora had never doubted it. Indeed, it was something of her calling, the only job she'd found that she'd ever considered remotely comfortable. She was a slight woman in her early thirties, although she looked younger, the result of a combination of rejuvenation treatments and a simple reluctance to take time away from her studies to eat. Living practically alone—there were five naval crewmen on Wensleydale Station, but they knew better than to disturb her—hadn't done much for her appearance, but she didn't care. She'd never liked being around other people anyway. Even videoconferencing was a strain.

There wasn't *much* to Wensleydale Station. It was nothing more than a handful of prefabricated modules that had been shipped to Wensleydale—a human-compatible planet on the edge of the Human Sphere—and put together to produce an orbital station and listening post. But then, there wasn't much to Wensleydale either. It would be a great colony one day, Dora had been assured, but right now there were only a couple of hundred colonists on the ground, breaking the soil and turning Wensleydale into a world that could actually host a far larger colony. Dora knew she wouldn't be around to see it. She'd be shipped further away from Earth well before the first large colony ship arrived.

She sat within her nest on the station and studied the latest set of read-outs. The combination of orbital and radio telescopes, long-range passive sensors and deep-space gravimetric monitors continued to insist that the Wensleydale System was as empty as her departmental head's brain, but she didn't care about local events. *That* was the Royal Navy's concern, although she'd been warned, when she first arrived, that if they did run into something they couldn't handle, they were in real trouble. Wensleydale Station was armed, technically, but it wouldn't take more than a single gunboat to turn the entire structure into vapour. It was one of the reasons Dora had been sent to Wensleydale in the first place. If there was a threat lurking in the unexplored regions further away from Earth, the Royal Navy wanted advance warning.

Dora rather suspected the Royal Navy was wasting its time, although she had no intention of pointing it out to them. Humanity had believed it was alone in the universe until it had encountered the Tadpoles and part of the *reason* humanity had believed it was alone was that a dazzling array of sensors had failed to pick up even the slightest hint that the Tadpoles existed. Dora had seen the exhaustive reports, compiled after the war. There hadn't been any clue, not in the official reports or buried somewhere in the raw data, that suggested the human race was not alone. Nor had humanity detected the Foxes or the Cows until their star system had been probed. And the Vesy hadn't developed technological civilisation by the time they were discovered. Dora might be wasting her time too...

...But she doubted it. Let the military worry about undiscovered threats. *She* was more interested in exploring the mysteries of the universe. And the equipment at her disposal was better than anything she'd used during her stint at the Luna Telescope. It was worth any discomfort, even having to share a station with five naval crewmen, to have access to the navy's tools. They might be largely wasted, but not completely.

A box blinked up in her headset. One of the naval crewmen had sent her a message, inviting her to dinner...such as it was. She shook her head, dismissing the note with a shrug. She was far too agoraphobic—and asexual—to risk spending time with any of them. Besides, didn't they have their own work to do? Little happened on Wensleydale Station—she knew that for a fact—but there was always *something* to do. The station required constant maintenance to keep it functioning...

...And then her console chimed an alert.

Dora leaned forward, puzzled. It wasn't the near-space proximity alarm. *That* would have set sirens howling all over the station. And it wasn't the alert she'd set to go off if there was even the slightest *hint* of alien transmissions, dozens of light-years away. It was...her lips thinned as she realised that the computers *hadn't* been able to neatly catalogue the signal. It was too close to be interesting to her, yet too far away to alarm the naval crew. Except...it was right at the edge of the system.

"Curious," she muttered. Wensleydale *had* been surveyed, although—reading between the lines—she had the feeling the naval crew who'd discovered the system had skimped on the survey. A human-compatible world was more interesting than the comets and asteroids lurking at the edge of the system. "What *is* it?"

She keyed a switch, unlocking the computer's free-association modules. She'd never trusted them—even the smartest computers couldn't *think* like humans, which meant they had a tendency to forget or ignore valuable pieces of data—but she had a feeling that they might be necessary. The computer hummed as it scanned the databanks while she scrutinised the live feed from the long-range sensors. It was odd, very odd. The...the *event*, whatever it was, was just over nineteen light days from Wensleydale. It almost looked like...

The computers blinked up an answer. *Fusion-drive flare.*

Dora stared. She'd studied the records. A number of asteroids had been converted into starships and launched into interstellar space before the tramlines had been discovered, over a hundred years ago. None of them had reached their destinations yet...come to think of it, none of them had aimed themselves at *Wensleydale*. The system's primary star would have been in their records, of course, but they hadn't had any reason to think they might have found a human-compatible planet at the far end. And even if they had, it would have taken them thousands of years to reach their destination. Ice ran down her spine. The ship—it had to be a ship— couldn't be human.

She took a long breath, then keyed her console, sending an alert to the naval crewmen. The ship—the slower-than-light ship—was still a very long way away, but it *was* heading directly towards Wensleydale. The aliens would know there was a planet, waiting for them. It was impossible to imagine a race that had fusion drives, but not basic telescopes. And yet...they might not realise that Wensleydale was already occupied. A society that had to rely on STL ships presumably didn't know anything about the tramlines.

A face blinked up in front of her. Dora fought down the urge to flinch away. Commander Haircloth wasn't a bad man—none of the naval crewmen were *bad*—but he was a person, intruding into her world. He looked to have let himself go, a little. Faint stubble lined his cheeks. He and his crew rarely bothered to make themselves look shipshape and Bristol fashion unless Wensleydale Station was having visitors.

His voice was sharp. "Is...is that thing real?"

"Yes," Dora said, turning her head so she wouldn't have to look at him. It was easier to pretend that he was just a voice if she couldn't see his face. "It's a genuine interstellar colony ship."

Haircloth took a long breath. "Where from?"

Dora checked her console. "Assuming a straight-line flight, it came from USS-38202," she said. "A G2 star, fifteen light-years away. There's no direct tramline route to that star."

"It might not have any tramlines at all," Haircloth mused.

"Perhaps," Dora said.

She considered it for a moment. Gravimetric science wasn't her field, but she was fairly sure that every star had at least one or two tramlines. But there was no guarantee that any tramline reaching USS-38202 would intersect with a tramline human starships could access. There *was* a way to create an artificial tramline, long enough for a starship to jump across interstellar space, but it had its limitations. Whoever they sent might find themselves trapped, unable to return.

Haircloth had his mind on more practical concerns. "How long until it enters orbit?"

Dora shrugged—interplanetary mechanics wasn't her field either—then keyed the computer console again, letting it do the work. It threw up a wide range of possible scenarios, ranging from several months to a year or two. Too much depended on just what the aliens could actually do. If they had drive fields, they might start deploying them once they entered the system. They'd reach Wensleydale in less than a month.

"It depends," she said, finally. She sent him the projections. "What now?"

"They won't have drive fields," Haircloth said. "They could have made the crossing far quicker if they had...unless they feared burning out the drive in interstellar space. That would be bad."

He cleared his throat. "I'll alert the crew, then pass a message up the chain," he said. "It'll be taking my career in my hands, but I'm sure the Admiralty will agree that launching the drone is necessary."

"No doubt," Dora agreed, dryly. The Royal Navy Admiralty and her former University's finance department had at least one thing in common. They were prepared to waste money on fripperies, while penny-pinching on important matters. Haircloth would be in real trouble if the Admiralty decided that launching an extremely expensive messenger drone up the tramline was a waste of money. It cost more than the average gunboat. "Good luck."

Haircloth smiled, rather wanly. "Thank you, Dora," he said. "Can you detail at least two of the sensor platforms to keep an eye on our visitors?"

Dora felt a hot flash of resentment, which she quickly suppressed. They already *had* answers, didn't they? The flare was artificial and therefore nowhere near as interesting as the quasar she'd been watching. But she knew it was a childish thought. That quasar wasn't going anywhere.

"Yes," she said. She ran her hand over the console. "Done."

"Very good," Haircloth said. His voice was tinged with excitement. "And now, we wait."

Dora sighed to herself as she closed the connection. She could understand why Haircloth would find the prospect of alien contact—*another* alien contact—exciting, but it wasn't an excitement she shared. It wouldn't be long before everything from naval gunships to Foreign Office First Contact teams started to arrive, probably followed by representatives from the other human and alien powers. And planetary developmental money would follow in their wake. Wensleydale would rapidly become as cramped and unbearable as Earth or Terra Nova. *She* would have to go somewhere else, if there *was* somewhere else. The Royal Navy might not be so obliging next time.

Joy, she thought. She looked at her consoles for a long moment. *But at least we just proved that the millions of pounds they spent on deep-space monitoring systems wasn't wasted.*

Shaking her head, she turned her attention back to the quasar. Commander Haircloth and his men could monitor their visitors as they made their final approach. She had better things to do with her time...

...And besides, she acknowledged quietly as she went back to work, if the visitors were hostile there was nothing she could do about it anyway.

CHAPTER ONE

"CAPTAIN ON THE BRIDGE!"

Captain Sir Stephen Shields stepped through the hatch and onto the bridge, taking time to note the crewmen who acknowledged his arrival and the crewmen who knew better than to take their eyes off their console, even to greet their commanding officer. Stephen had served under enough commanding officers who'd demanded respect from everyone—and left him with a complete lack of confidence in their leadership abilities—to know better than to demand such respect for himself. A helmsman should not look up from his console, whatever the reason.

He acknowledged Commander Daniel Newcomb's salute as the XO stood, vacating the command chair. Stephen sat down, sucking in his breath. HMS *Invincible* still *smelled* like a new ship, even though she had been on her shakedown cruise for the last six months. She wouldn't smell any better until she'd actually been to war. But then, he knew he should be grateful for the chance to work out the kinks in the assault carrier's design. *Invincible* was the first of her class and had had more than her fair share of problems. None of them had been anything more than mildly embarrassing—no ship ever went through her shakedown cruise without encountering problems—but they'd proven annoying.

And the press is being unusually pugnacious, he thought, crossly. The media was rarely openly friendly to the Royal Navy, but over the last year

1

they'd started to blow the navy's problems out of all proportion. *We have a backed-up toilet and they start saying the entire ship is a waste of money.*

It wasn't a pleasant thought. HMS *Invincible* was the first major combatant in the Royal Navy to put appearance before functionality, despite protests from both serving naval officers and shipyard engineers. The bridge looked to have been copied directly from one of the BBC's dramas on naval life, right down to the consoles that looked absurdly fragile, as if they would explode if someone looked at them funny. It wasn't *that* bad a design, he admitted privately, but it was annoying. Stephen would have preferred something that could be repaired on the fly if necessary.

He glanced at his XO. "Status report?"

"Enemy target has just come into range, sir," Newcomb reported. "She doesn't seem aware of our presence."

"Very good," Stephen said. A red icon glowed on the display, beating a steady path towards the nearest tramline. Text bubbles scrolled up beside the icon, calculating vectors and offering prospective interception windows. It looked very neat. "And the masking field?"

"Ready for activation, sir," Lieutenant-Commander David Arthur said. The tactical officer looked tanned, despite six months onboard ship. "We can slip under it at any moment."

"Then do so," Stephen ordered.

He sucked in his breath as the lights dimmed, slightly. The masking field wasn't a full cloaking device, not in the sense that it would hide *Invincible* from all sensors, but it would make it harder for any enemy ships to get a solid lock on her position. He hoped. The technology had been copied from the Foxes and Cows in the wake of the Second Interstellar War and, so far, it was proving hard to adapt to human ships. *Invincible* was the first starship *designed* to carry a masking field and even *she* had problems. The only saving grace was that the other Great Powers had the same issues with the system.

Or so we are assured, he reminded himself. Great Britain had plenty of secret installations, some in the Home System and some orbiting Britannia, where research could be conducted far from prying eyes. America, France, China and Russia had facilities of their own, he was sure. *They won't share any real breakthroughs with us unless we run into a third hostile alien power.*

"Field engaged, sir," Arthur said. "We should be beyond detection."

Stephen nodded, curtly. "Helm, move us into intercept position," he ordered. "Sensors, keep watching them. I want to know the *second* they detect us."

"Aye, sir."

The display updated rapidly, looking curiously bloodless as *Invincible* slipped after her lone target. It was easy to forget that the red icon represented a real starship, carrying real people...or that the distances between the ships were hard for groundpounders to comprehend. Or, for that matter, that appearances could be deceiving. Stephen hadn't been told the precise details, of course, but he was sure a surprise was waiting for him. The enemy wouldn't go down without a fight.

"Captain," Lieutenant Alison Adams said. The Sensor Officer looked perturbed. "I'm picking up a number of spacecraft leaving the asteroid belt and heading for Terra Nova."

Stephen's eyes narrowed as he keyed his private console, bringing up the live feed from the long-range passive sensors. There was a surprisingly large amount of traffic in the Terra Nova System, despite the simple fact that Terra Nova's Provisional Government was about as powerless as Earth's International Green Party. Perhaps that was *why* there was so much activity, he reflected wryly. Sol's asteroid belt was supervised by the Great Powers and the Belt Federation, but no one policed Terra Nova's outer system. The whole region was a lawless mess, populated by independent colonies, smugglers, and rogue political factions. He dreaded to think what would happen if Terra Nova ever developed the will to impose itself on the asteroid belt. It would be bloody.

He looked at Newcomb. "Assessment?"

Newcomb frowned. "It's odd, sir," he said. "There's no reason to take so many ships to the planet. Unless they're planning something."

Stephen nodded, slowly. Terra Nova had very little worth mentioning, certainly nothing that would attract independent shippers. A handful of shore leave facilities existed, he supposed, yet none of them could be considered *safe*. It wasn't as if it would be *difficult* to hop through Tramline Alpha and visit Sol. And there was enough orbiting firepower to make life dangerous for any merchant ship. Terra Nova's factions had often resorted to taking pot-shots at passing freighters when the world's politics became particularly nasty.

"Communications, pass the alert to the embassy," he ordered. "Warn them that they may have incoming."

He gritted his teeth in annoyance as *Invincible* closed in on her target, unsure what to do. If *something* was about to explode in the system, he had a responsibility to protect British interests...such as they were. It wasn't as if there *were* many, save for a handful of corporate-owned asteroid facilities. Britain had sold her shares in the Terra Nova Colonisation Consortium nearly a century ago. They'd gone for a song, to all intents and purposes. The seeds of disaster had already been clearly visible. And yet, he had a duty...

"Continue to monitor the situation," he ordered. "Tactical?"

"We will be in intercept position in two minutes, sir," Arthur reported. "The dropships and starfighters are primed and ready to go."

"Good," Stephen said. "Prepare to launch..."

The display flashed red. "They got us, sir," Alison reported. "I don't know how, but they got us. We just got swept!"

Stephen made a mental note to have a long *chat* with the boffins. The target ship had *known* she was being hunted, but still...they were, theoretically, too far from the target for the enemy to burn through the masking field. There must have been a flicker of turbulence, a faint glimmer of energy that had been unmistakably artificial against the inky blackness of space. Not, he supposed, that it mattered. Their target was already ramping up her drives.

Not that they have a hope of evading us, he thought. The target ship was smaller than *Invincible*, but there was no way her drives could produce enough speed to outrun the assault carrier. Even if they'd replaced her entire rear hull with drive nodes...he considered it for a moment, then shook his head. She'd rip herself to bits if she ever ramped her drives up to full power. *They let us get too close.*

"Drop the masking field," he ordered. His heart started to race. There was no point in trying to hide now. They'd been spotted. "Launch the starfighters, then the dropships. And then order our target to surrender."

"Fighters away, sir," Arthur reported. New icons appeared on the display: one squadron holding position near *Invincible*, just in case the carrier required support, while a second was racing towards its target. "Dropships deploying...now!"

"No response, sir," Lieutenant Thomas Morse said. The Communications Officer worked his console for a long moment. "They should be getting our signal."

"One would hope so," Stephen agreed, dryly. "Repeat the signal."

He waited, keeping his face under tight control, for the enemy ship to respond. Very few spacers allowed their communications systems to get broken. A working radio might make the difference between life and death if the ship ran into real trouble. He'd seen quite a few civilian ships where basic maintenance was deferred, for a time, but most of them had been heavily over-engineered. A crew too stupid to keep up with their maintenance in the long run would soon be a dead crew. Space was an unforgiving environment. It simply didn't tolerate carelessness.

And we have a squadron of starfighters bearing down on them, he thought. There was no way that even civilian-grade sensors could miss the starfighters. No one could hope to hide *their* power signature. *That should force them to pay attention...*

The display sparkled. New red icons flashed into existence, glowing with deadly purpose. Stephen cursed under his breath. Starfighters. Three *squadrons* of starfighters. The enemy ship was an escort carrier, then. And not a conventional design. Someone had gone to a great deal of trouble to disguise her true nature.

"Captain," Alison said. "The enemy starfighters are deploying in attack formation."

Ballsy, Stephen thought, feeling a flicker of wry admiration. Going on the offensive was about the only chance the enemy had, given just how badly *Invincible* outclassed their ship, but it still required nerve. *I wonder if they thought to load their starfighters with torpedoes?*

He pushed the thought to one side. "Launch the remaining starfighters," he ordered, "and then bring the point defence online."

"Aye, sir."

"The dropships are moving aside," Newcomb added. "Their CO is suggesting a forced-boarding."

Stephen shook his head. The Royal Marines had unlimited confidence in themselves—and he'd seen them in action enough to know that their confidence was justified—but he couldn't authorise a suicide mission. And it would be suicide. An escort carrier normally didn't have much in the way of point defence—it wasn't as if their hulls were designed to stand up to plasma fire or nuclear-tipped torpedoes—but he had a feeling that *this* escort carrier was cannoned to the gunwales. Whoever had designed her was a devious bastard. His sensor crews and tactical analysts had been completely fooled.

Something to analyse thoroughly later, he thought, as the enemy starfighters rocketed towards *Invincible*. *Right now, we have other concerns.*

"Charlie Squadron is out," Arthur reported. "Delta Squadron is launching now."

"The CSP is moving to intercept," Newcomb added. "Point defence is standing by."

Stephen braced himself as the enemy starfighters blew through the first squadron and continued their mad rush towards *Invincible*. A handful of starfighters on both sides greyed out, indicating that they'd been hit... the losses were bad, but better than he'd feared. The enemy might have enjoyed a slight numerical advantage, yet they were too smart to be lured into a dogfight. Crippling or destroying *Invincible* was their only hope.

"Enemy starfighters are entering point defence range," Newcomb reported. "Guns are engaging...now."

And they're smart enough to keep moving randomly, Stephen thought. It wasn't a surprise, not after the horrific losses during the early stages of the First Interstellar War, but it was still annoying. *We're not hitting many of them.*

"Incoming torpedoes," Alison snapped. "They're targeting our drives!"

"Switch point defence to concentrate on them," Stephen snapped. The enemy didn't seem to want to *destroy Invincible*, but they were sure as hell trying to cripple her. And the Royal Navy really didn't need the embarrassment of a multi-billion pound assault carrier being crippled by a ship that had probably been pulled out of a junkyard. "And order Alpha to target the enemy carrier."

"Aye, sir!"

Stephen gritted his teeth as the torpedoes rushed towards his ship. They flew straight-line courses, which were easy to track, but their penetrator warheads made it harder to get a solid lock on them. Sensor ghosts and shadows bedevilled his sensors, forcing him to expend thousands of plasma bolts on a single target. He was lucky, he supposed, that the enemy hadn't deployed many starfighters. A full barrage of torpedoes would have done serious damage.

And they would have practically been guaranteed to score a handful of hits, he thought, grimly. *The drive section is heavily armoured, but a couple of nukes could really mess us up.*

Red lights flared up on the status display. "Direct hit, lower drive node," Newcomb reported, sharply. "Damage control teams are on their way!"

"Order Charlie and Delta to join the attack on the enemy carrier," Stephen snapped. It was hard to keep his irritation under control. They'd been luckier than they deserved and he knew it. "Damage assessment?"

"The node is powering down now," Newcomb said. "But we can still make full speed."

Stephen allowed himself a sigh of relief. It wasn't good, but at least they were still alive and fighting. *Invincible* wasn't one of the fragile carriers that had been slaughtered during the Battle of New Russia. Her armour could absorb more damage than the legendary *Ark Royal*, while her drives could propel her forward at speeds that would have stunned Theodore Smith and his officers. *Invincible* couldn't go toe-to-toe with a battleship, or a dreadnaught, but she could outrun anything strong enough to tear her apart.

"We'll have to reassess the point defence programs," he said. The point defence systems hadn't done *badly*, but they could have done a great deal better. "And allow more room for random firing."

He shook his head in frustration. The boffins kept promising, but so far no one had been able to produce a piece of predictor software that actually did what it was *supposed* to do, at least when facing human opponents. There was just too much room for random decisions to interfere with the software's targeting matrix. The only real way to defend a starship against enemy starfighters was to fill space with plasma bolts and hope for the best. It wasn't ideal, but it would have to do.

"The enemy ship is engaging our starfighters," Arthur reported. "She's carrying quite a lot of point defence."

"Communications, repeat the surrender demand," Stephen ordered. The enemy CO had played his sole card and lost. It wasn't as if his crew were going to be executed the moment they surrendered. Nor, for that matter, were they being taken into captivity by aliens who might not have the slightest idea how to look after human prisoners. "And this time wide-band it."

"Aye, sir."

There was a long pause as the starfighters closed in on the enemy ship. Stephen braced himself, silently resolving not to attempt to force-board the escort carrier. There was too great a chance of the enemy CO simply waiting for the marines to dock, then hitting the self-destruct. It would break the laws of war, but no one had paid much attention to them since 2025. Even Theodore Smith had been unable to impose *real* change before his final desperate battle.

And aliens often have different ideas of what is acceptable in wartime, Stephen reminded himself. The Tadpoles had fought under one set of rules, the Foxes and Cows had fought under another. Their technology might be comparable to humanity's, but their mindsets were very different. *They might embrace suicide attacks with a will.*

"Picking up a signal from the enemy ship," Morse reported. "Sir, they're trying to surrender."

Stephen allowed himself a moment of relief. "Order them to power down—their starfighters too," he ordered. "And then tell the marines they can board."

"Aye, sir."

Newcomb grinned. "Can I resurrect the dead pilots now?"

"We may as well," Stephen said. The dropships had docked, allowing the marines to swarm the enemy ship. "Send the ENDEX signal."

"Aye, sir," Newcomb said.

Stephen leaned back in his chair as the 'dead' starfighters came back to life. The exercise had been relatively simple, but unscripted. There had been room—plenty of room—for surprises, and embarrassments. And there had been too many watching eyes in the system. An exercise designed to show the locals that the Royal Navy still had teeth—and a willingness to bite—could easily have ended badly.

"Contact the enemy ship," he ordered. "Invite Captain Crowe to dine with me before they return to Sol."

"Aye, sir," Morse said. "I..."

He broke off as his console chimed an alert. "Sir, I'm picking up a FLASH signal from Terra Nova," he said. "Sir...the embassy is under attack. All hell is breaking loose!"

Stephen swore. In hindsight, perhaps he should have terminated the exercise and set course for Terra Nova. It had been the right decision, given what he'd known at the time, but he was grimly aware that not everyone would agree with him. Hindsight was *always* clearer than foresight, particularly when applied by an armchair admiral twelve light years away.

He shook his head. "Helm, set course for Terra Nova," he ordered. The escort carrier would have to remain behind. He didn't think there was enough firepower orbiting the planet to stop him from entering orbit, if necessary, but he knew better than to take unnecessary risks. God alone knew what was going on down there. "And ramp up the drives as much as possible."

"Aye, sir."

CHAPTER TWO

"KEEP YOUR FUCKING HEAD DOWN!"

Captain Alice Campbell cursed under her breath as bullets—and the occasional plasma bolt—snapped over her head. It had been sheer dumb luck that they'd managed to vacate the convoy vehicles before the ambushers actually found their bearings and blasted them to flaming debris with plasma weapons. The diplomatic vehicles could drive through a hail of bullets without so much as a scratch, but plasma bolts could burn through their armour like a knife through butter. Alice gritted her teeth as she caught hold of Ambassador Rupert Crichton and dragged him towards the nearest alleyway. The Royal Marines had walked right into an ambush and, if they weren't careful, they were not going to walk out again.

She glanced from side to side, keeping her rifle raised and ready. The alley was apparently deserted, but that was meaningless. There simply wasn't any other cover within eyeshot. The enemy would have to be inept indeed to guess that the marines would go somewhere—anywhere—else. She might have risked it, if she and her platoon didn't have to babysit the ambassador, but now...she had to hole up and hope that someone would come to rescue them.

A dark shape appeared at one end of the alleyway, already raising a weapon. An insurgent, trying to catch the marines, or a civilian trying to defend his property? Alice didn't know, but the figure was clearly hostile.

There was no way she could take chances, not when Crichton wasn't wearing body armour. She shot him through the head and watched his body crumple, expecting to see more insurgents entering the alleyway. But the darkened passageway was clear.

"Captain," Corporal Glen Hammersmith snapped. "I can't get a link to the embassy!"

Alice felt the ambassador flinch next to her and sighed, inwardly. There was no shortage of Foreign Office diplomats who'd had genuine military experience, so why couldn't one of *them* have been assigned to Terra Nova? The wretched shithole rarely went a year or two without yet another round of the endless civil war. Surely, *someone* would have anticipated a diplomatic convoy being attacked. The Royal Navy would take a terrible revenge if insurgents attacked the embassy—it wouldn't be the first time some barbaric rogue state had been taught a sharp lesson—but that wasn't always enough to deter terrorists or religious fanatics. Or maybe even people who thought Terra Nova's odd position would be enough to keep the navy from carpet-bombing the attackers into dust.

"Keep trying," she snapped, trying to keep the dismay out of her voice. It wasn't her first combat engagement, not by a long chalk, but it *was* the first when she'd been in overall command. The platoon had expected a milk run, not a bloody ambush. Two of her subordinates were already dead. "And sweep for hostile communications."

She forced herself to think as the rest of the platoon secured the alleyway, Corporal Singh scrambling up a pipe to the roof while Sergeant Bert Radcliffe emplaced mines at the nearest end. They'd give anyone who came charging after the marines a nasty surprise, although Alice suspected they wouldn't be anything like as effective as she might wish. Terra Nova's various factions weren't short on manpower to absorb bullets. She'd seen human wave attacks before, in the Security Zone. There had been times when they'd come far too close to simply overrunning the defenders when they ran out of bullets.

If we can't get in touch with the embassy, we might not be able to summon help, she thought, grimly. *And that means we might have to beat feet out of here ourselves.*

Her mind raced. There was a company of Paras on permanent QRA within the embassy compound, but they wouldn't be sent out on spec. She'd sent an alert the moment the shooting started, yet she had no way of knowing if it had reached its destination. The plasma weapons had been a nasty surprise. It was quite possible that the enemy had modern jammers too. *That* was unusual—and worrying. Terra Nova's factions seemed to be quite capable of producing basic assault rifles and RPGs, but plasma weapons had to be shipped in from off-world. Someone was playing politics...

She shook her head as the sound of shooting grew louder. It *sounded* as though there were at least two factions fighting it out over the remains of the convoy, although she knew better than to take that for granted. Landing City was dominated by a multitude of factions, everything from political and religious movements to street gangs and thugs. It said a great deal about the former that the latter made better governors. The moment one of the political factions gained an advantage, it tried to enslave or exterminate its enemies. Terra Nova's history was one long endless liturgy of horror.

"Still nothing," Hammersmith said. "But I am picking up a modern drone overhead."

Alice looked up, scanning the sky through her visor. The drone would be invisible to the naked eye—either too small or too high to be easily visible—but her visor would probably pick it up. She sucked in her breath as she saw it, floating high overhead. There was no way *that* had come from Terra Nova. It was outdated, by modern standards, but still well ahead of anything that could be produced locally. The chances were good that it had either been purchased on the black market by an independent trader or, worse, supplied by one of the Great Powers in a bid for influence. She looked up and down the dark alley, silently noting the lack of maintenance and the signs of public urination. Terra Nova wasn't worth the effort.

The ground shook as one of the mines detonated. Alice cursed under her breath as she locked eyes with the sergeant. The enemy faction—or one of them—was starting to try to root the marines out of hiding. There was no way they could stay in the alleyway, particularly when there was no help on the way. They'd sell themselves dearly—there was no way she could surrender to a bunch of insurgents—but it would be ultimately meaningless. They had to move.

And that fucking drone is going to watch us, she thought, grimly. She'd seen enough drones in operation to know just how hard it was going to be to escape the robotic voyeur. Someone sitting in a trailer on the other side of the city—or the planet—was going to be directing the insurrectionists after them. The asshole had probably already played a major role in setting up the ambush. *We didn't tell anyone which route we planned to take, did we?*

"Roger, take the drone down," she snapped. It would be a diplomatic headache if she was wrong—if one of the other embassies had launched the drone to watch the city sink into chaos—but there was no choice. "Sergeant, take point. Dennis, take the ambassador!"

She motioned for them to hurry forward as she checked the man she'd shot. He was a dark-skinned man, probably South American rather than Arabic...although that meant nothing on Terra Nova. The different factions denied it, loudly, but there was quite a bit of interbreeding where two factions shared a city. His outfit was pretty clearly a paramilitary uniform—she couldn't help a flicker of amusement at just how little camouflage or protection it actually provided—yet he lacked anything that might identify him. She allowed herself a moment of relief—she hadn't shot a civilian, after all—then stripped his body of weapons, ammunition and ration bars. The marines might need them if the shit got deeper.

A second mine detonated. The wall shuddered. Alice *hoped* that meant it wasn't going to collapse. Terra Nova's building codes were substandard, where they had them at all. The constant fighting probably didn't help either. There were bullet holes in the wall that were probably older than her. God alone knew how many times the building had changed hands in the last fifty years. She shrugged, then nodded to the sergeant. He led the platoon down the alleyway and out into the street. Behind them, a third mine exploded. Alice heard someone scream, a noise that rose higher and higher as the victim realised just how badly he'd actually been hurt. Hopefully, the prospect of being crippled would slow his friends down. The planet's medical facilities were primitive, by modern standards. There was little hope of reconstructive surgery on Terra Nova.

"Street's clear," Radcliffe called. "Move out!"

Alice nodded, feeling a flicker of sympathy for the ambassador. *She'd* been in combat zones before, but *he* clearly hadn't. The marines raced down the street, weapons moving from side to side as they searched for threats. Shops had been closed, iron shutters slammed down to protect the shopkeepers from stray bullets. Not that it would be enough to save them if one faction seized undisputed control of the region, she knew. Their shops would be looted, their sons would be conscripted, their daughters claimed as war brides...she shuddered, despite herself. She'd often found Britain to be dull, but Terra Nova was worse. Who in their right mind would want to live in a war zone?

You decided to join the Royal Marines, she reminded herself, dryly. *Did you think you'd never be sent to war?*

The thought made her smile, even as she kept moving. It hadn't been *easy* to get into the Royal Marine Commando Training Program, not when she was both a woman *and* the daughter of a man who was both famous and infamous. She had the feeling, based on what she'd read when she'd finally managed to access her file, that there had been some pretty high-level discussions before she'd been allowed to sign up. And then she'd been put through absolute hell on the darkened moors and the trackless wastes of the lunar surface, just like the boys. It would have been easy to switch tracks and join the Royal Navy, or even the Home Guard, but she'd per-sisted. It was the only way to win respect.

And I figured a posting to Invincible *would be relaxing,* she reminded herself. *And we thought this was going to be nothing more than a dull deployment to provide cover while the local bootnecks got a rest.*

Singh loped up beside her. "Captain, there's smoke all over the city," he reported. "I think this is serious."

Alice nodded, calling up a map on her visor as the platoon paused for a moment. Landing City had never been mapped properly—it changed too frequently for anyone to bother—but it was clear they were quite some distance from the embassy. And there was no guarantee that the embassy would be safe, either. Singh was right. This was no simple exchange of fire between factions, but all-out war. Someone was risking everything in a desperate bid to secure control of the city.

The embassy is supposed to be secure, she thought. *But if modern weapons are involved...*

A burst of fire splattered over her head. Someone was on the rooftops, pouring fire down into their position. She ducked down, returning fire instinctively. The remainder of the platoon joined in, aiming a pair of grenades towards the enemy. Alice braced herself as the grenades exploded, then darted forward as the enemy fire fell silent. A body tumbled down, hitting the pavement hard enough to make her wince. The impact smashed the lower body, but the face was surprisingly intact. Chinese, she thought. They were some distance from the Chinese-dominated parts of the city, but that was meaningless. The various communities were also more intermingled than they cared to admit.

And the Chinese are the only Great Power who have a sizable presence on the ground, she reminded herself, as she checked the body. No weapons, no identification...nothing, but a grim awareness that the body was too fit to be a civilian. *They might have supplied the weapons to the faction.*

She took a handful of snapshots for later use—the various intelligence agencies would want to have a look at them—and then sneaked back to where the remainder of the platoon was waiting. The ambassador looked to have zoned out completely, not even noticing that he was practically hanging off Dennis's arm. Thankfully, the platoon seemed to be holding up alright. They'd taken a beating—and they would have to mourn their dead mates later—but they were still in high spirits. They hadn't given up hope of getting out before it was too late.

"I've still not been able to raise the embassy, Captain," Hammersmith said. "I even tried to call the Yanks and the Frogs. Nothing from either of them."

Alice nodded, curtly. It was hard to believe that *every* embassy had been overrun—she'd exercised with both the United States Marine Corps and the French Foreign Legion—but it was starting to look as though her platoon was on its own. And that meant...

We don't dare try to sneak back to the embassies, she thought. *And we can't stay in the city.*

She studied the map for a long moment, wishing—not for the first time—that the various intelligence services attached to the embassies had actually been able to keep track of which faction controlled which part of the city. Some parts were marked as Arabic or Mexican or Chinese, but others kept changing hands so frequently that the intelligence services hadn't been able to keep up. Not, she supposed, that it mattered. The Chinese *might* help the marines—at least until they could be repatriated to *Invincible*—but they were on the other side of the city. None of the *other* factions would help. The marines would be captured, then brutally murdered. *She* had certainly no intention of allowing herself to fall into enemy hands.

"We need to get out of the city," she said, catching the sergeant's eye. He had more experience than her...and, besides, she trusted his judgement. "If we get out of danger, we can hole up and wait for the ship to return."

Radcliffe nodded in agreement. "And how do you propose to get out?"

Alice checked the map, again. No close-protection team worthy of the name would risk escorting the person it was supposed to protect through a war zone, at least unless there was no other choice. But there was no way to avoid it, as far as she could see. Unless...she altered the map, noting the position of the Harmony River. If they could steal a boat, they could get onto the water and head downriver. It wasn't much of a plan, but it would have to do.

"We take the river," she said. There were risks, but...they were short on options. "Let's move."

The sound of shooting and explosions grew louder as they hurried towards the nearest dockyard, a tiny installation that looked more like a canal pier for barges than anything more formal. She felt sweat trickling down her back as she looked from side to side, expecting to be jumped at any moment. Waves of conflict were flowing over the city, yet they were leaving the marines untouched. She hoped the civilians were smart enough to keep their heads down and pray, although she doubted it would help. If one of the factions was making a real bid for power—and succeeded—the mass exterminations would begin shortly afterwards. There was too much hatred on Terra Nova for a peaceful resolution to their problems.

They should have just divided up into different countries, she thought, sourly. Surely, the problems with forcing different cultures to practically live in each other's pockets had been evident a hundred years ago. Had they forgotten the Troubles so quickly? *At least that might keep them from slaughtering each other.*

She winced as the river came into view. Harmony River—the name was bitterly ironic—was a sickly orange colour, thoroughly polluted. It stank so badly she had to force herself to breathe through her mouth, even though she shared a bunkroom with an entire platoon of Royal Marines. There were logging farms and factories upriver, according to the map, pouring their wastes into the river, but that wasn't the worst of it. What passed for a sewage system in Landing City poured its wastes into the water too.

They should be turning their shit into fuel, she thought, as they located a barge. It looked cumbersome, but they could handle it. *Instead, they're killing themselves.*

"Get the ambassador into the barge," she ordered. "And then try and raise the embassy again."

She scrambled onto the barge herself and stood on top of the cockpit. There were explosions—and plumes of smoke—all over the city, a number in the direction of the embassies. Singh had been right. This *was* serious. She hoped—prayed—that the countryside was quieter, although she suspected it would be just as dangerous. The communities might be more spread out—and centred on farms—but they were more inclined to shoot first and ask questions later. And she knew very little, beyond vague generalities, of just what she might expect to find outside the city.

But the ship should be on her way back now, she thought. She found it hard to believe that *Invincible's* crew wouldn't have realised that something was wrong. They had orders to keep a watchful eye on Terra Nova as long as they remained in the system. *They'll come pick us up.*

It wasn't much, she acknowledged as the barge was slowly pushed away from the pier. But it would have to do.

CHAPTER THREE

"CAPTAIN, I'M PICKING UP nine chinese warships holding position near the planet," Lieutenant Alison Adams reported. "Five destroyers, three cruisers and a single ship of indeterminate type."

Stephen sucked in his breath as the icons appeared on the display. Legally speaking, the Chinese had every right to deploy warships to Terra Nova. The system hardly belonged to anyone, not even the locals. But he couldn't help finding their presence ominous. The Chinese hadn't bothered to declare them to the other Great Powers. That too was legal, he knew, but it was a breach of unwritten convention. The Great Powers normally kept each other informed of warship deployments in open systems.

And the Chinese have a large presence on the ground, he reminded himself. The other Great Powers had abandoned Terra Nova once they'd located and claimed planets for their sole use, but the Chinese had kept their ties to their colonists. *They may be trying to help their fellows...or they may be up to something.*

"Keep an eye on them," he ordered. "Do we have any contact with the planet?"

"No, sir," Lieutenant Thomas Morse reported. "I'm picking up a lot of stray signals, but the main planetary net seems to have gone down and the direct link to the embassy has failed."

Stephen nodded, curtly. The direct link to the embassy was supposed to be unbreakable, which meant that...that something had happened to the embassy. Ambassador Crichton and his staff—including the marines Stephen had unloaded a week ago—might be fighting for their lives, or prisoners, or dead. Not knowing *precisely* what was going on made it impossible for him to decide what to do. And there were too many weapons platforms orbiting the planet—half of which seemed to be shooting at the other half—for him to risk taking *Invincible* closer.

"Launch two probes," he ordered. It was quite likely they'd be fired upon, if they were detected, but they *should* give him a clearer picture of what was going on. "And prepare to flash-launch our remaining starfighters."

He forced himself to think as the probes raced towards the planet, more and more details flashing up on the big scene. Orbital space was an absolute nightmare: freighters hurrying to get out of the firing line while the weapons platforms vaporised each other, giant habitats screaming for help as missiles and kinetic projectiles were fired in all directions, seemingly at random. It didn't look as though there would be anything left in an hour or two. Terra Nova's orbital guardians had exchanged fire before, but this was different. There was something oddly *final* about it.

"One of the probes got a look at the city," Alison said. "Captain, the embassy is a pile of rubble."

"Show me," Stephen said, harshly.

He leaned forward, grimly. The embassy had been smashed flat, a handful of figures poking through the debris while others held guns at the ready. It didn't *look* as though the attackers had managed to take any hostages, although he knew that could be an illusion. The embassy had a bunker buried under the ground for emergencies, one where the staff were meant to hide if the shit really *did* hit the fan. They could hide out for years, if necessary, but...the enemy would presumably try to dig them up.

And the other embassies are piles of rubble too, he thought, as the next set of images flickered up in front of him. *Even the Chinese embassy is a blackened ruin.*

Major Henry Parkinson's face appeared in the display. "Captain, we have to get down there," he said. "If they're already looking for the bunker..."

"I know," Stephen said. "Stand by."

He scowled at the images for a long moment, unsure what to do. He had every right to rescue British civilians caught in a war zone—and he wanted to try to rescue the other embassy staffs too, as there were no American or French ships in the system—but the Chinese ships worried him. So too did the weapons platforms and the fighting on the ground. He didn't want to plunge his men into a multi-sided war over a useless planet.

There's no choice, he told himself, firmly. *We have to save our people.*

"Communications, send a wide-band message," he ordered. "I want everyone in the system to hear it. We are mounting a rescue mission to recover our people and the rest of the embassy staffers. Anyone who so much as looks at us funny will be fired on without further warning."

"Aye, sir."

Stephen keyed his console. "Launch aerospace fighters, then follow up with the dropships," he added. "Rules of engagement are alpha-delta-three. Anything that looks hostile is to be vaporised before it can pose a threat."

"Aye, sir."

He leaned back in his chair, eying the Chinese ships. They were the only force in the system that might be able to oppose him, although the Chinese would have to be insane to try. The destruction of the embassies was quite bad enough. Firing on a British carrier would be worse. No one would fault them for backing their people on the ground—there was a case to be made that Chinese rule would be better for Terra Nova than the constant insurrections and civil wars—but there were limits. Picking a fight with *Invincible* would mean war.

"Captain, a handful of the weapons platforms are targeting us," Lieutenant-Commander David Arthur said. The Tactical Officer worked his console for a long moment. "They're locking missiles on our hull."

Stephen winced. Terra Nova's defences were old—some of them dated all the way back to the First Interstellar War—but that didn't mean they weren't dangerous. An old-style missile could still do considerable damage if it hit the right—or rather the wrong—place. And a barrage of thousands of missiles would be damn near unstoppable. Terra Nova didn't have nuclear weapons, if Naval Intelligence was to be believed, but he wasn't sure he trusted their assessment. It wouldn't be *that* hard for one of the factions to set up a breeder reactor somewhere nicely isolated. The belters had been doing it for years.

"Take them out," he ordered. "Any platform that lights us up, kill it."

And hope to hell I'm not making a mistake, he added, silently. *If we leave the other platforms alone, they'll be in a perfect position to fire on our ships as they enter the atmosphere.*

Newcomb glanced up. "The dropships are launching now," he reported. "They'll be entering the atmosphere in five minutes."

"Very good," Stephen said. "Keep me informed."

• • •

Wing Commander Richard Redbird wasn't entirely sure what to make of the British Aerospace Tornado Starfighter, even though he'd been flying the oversized craft for the last six months. The Tornado was designed, according to the boffins, to actually enter a planetary atmosphere and fight there, something previous starfighters had never been able to do. He'd certainly made enough atmospheric entries to know it could be done. And yet, the Tornado was also heavy, lacking the agility of a Spitfire, Hurricane or Lightning. He had the nasty feeling that the design was a jack of all trades, thus master of none.

But at least we don't have to worry about taking a beachhead, he reminded himself, as the starfighter raced towards the planet. *We can carry out precision strikes without having to land ground-based aircraft first.*

He sucked in his breath as he peered through his cockpit, keeping a wary eye on his scanners for potential threats. The planet's orbital defences were cheerfully banging away at each other, seemingly ignoring the British starfighters. *That* wouldn't last. Richard had flown over countries where the locals had fired in all directions, seemingly at random. Besides, the locals *also* had good reason to know what *Invincible* could do to their defences. They might want to get their retaliation in first.

Terra Nova looked pristine, he thought. It was hard to believe that the beautiful blue-green orb was a constant war zone, where people were routinely slaughtered for following the wrong religion, or having the wrong skin colour, or even just because someone else wanted to take their land. He couldn't help thinking, as they flashed closer, that it was a shame that such follies hadn't been left behind on Earth. But then, too many people had been deported to Terra Nova because their governments had decided that it would be more politic than killing them. Perhaps the governments would have done better to move themselves and leave the extremists behind.

His threat receiver shrilled. "Incoming fire!"

"Break and attack," Richard snapped. An orbital weapons platform was spitting antistarfighter missiles in all directions. They looked to be over fifty years old, dating back to the days when humanity had thought it was alone in the universe, but that wouldn't keep them from being dangerous if they actually scored a hit. Starfighters were fragile. A single warhead would be more than enough to vaporise them. "Weapons free. I say again, weapons free!"

He yanked his starfighter to one side as his plasma guns started firing automatically, picking off the missiles before they could enter attack range. Their targeting wasn't good—they certainly didn't have modern seeker heads—but the enemy CO was trying to compensate through sheer weight of numbers. Normally, Richard knew, it wouldn't be a serious problem unless the enemy was using nukes. The odds of a stray unpowered missile striking a starfighter were minimal. But with so many starfighters and dropships passing through the same general area, the odds of a collision were considerably higher.

"Direct hit," Flight Lieutenant Monica Smith shouted, as a weapons platform vanished from the display. "I *got* the bastard!"

"Don't get cocky," Richard reminded her. Monica *had* scored a direct hit, but she'd done it with a modern penetrator warhead. Terra Nova was pretty much defenceless against modern weapons. The Chinese ships would be *much* tougher targets, if they got off their arses and engaged the British starfighters. "We're not playing the big boys here."

He ignored her snort of disgust and concentrated on his display. The starfighters were clearing a path through the defences, firing on anything that even *looked* hostile. He breathed out a sigh of relief as he realised the orbital habitats were being very careful not to do anything that looked remotely threatening. Slamming a penetrator into a weapons platform was one thing, but firing on an orbital habitat was quite another. He'd seen enough footage from the Battle of Earth to know he didn't want to take the risk of killing thousands of civilians.

Idiots shouldn't have dragged those asteroids into orbit, he thought, as he vaporised another weapons platform. His plasma guns picked off a handful of targets that might have been anything from pieces of debris to stealthed mines. *They should have stayed in the belt, where it was safe. Instead, they came here.*

"Stand by for atmospheric insertion," he ordered, bracing himself. His heart started to pound, so loudly he was surprised no one else could hear it. "Everyone ready?"

His pilots didn't sound nervous as they replied, one by one, although he'd never met a serving pilot who'd ever admitted to fear. And yet, they'd all trained extensively, in and out of the simulators. They knew the dangers. They would be vulnerable for a handful of minutes, a very brief window of opportunity for anyone with hostile intentions. Every starfighter pilot who lasted more than a week in basic training knew better than to fly a predictable course, particularly so close to enemy installations, but it couldn't be helped. The drive fields simply wouldn't allow them to treat a planetary atmosphere—and a gravity well—as if they were somewhere in the middle of interstellar space.

He glanced at the marine dropships, following behind, then nodded to himself. "Here we go..."

The hand of God slapped his starfighter as it struck the planetary atmosphere, the drive field automatically adjusting itself to compensate. He gritted his teeth as the gravity field seemed to tighten around him, the compensators whining loudly as they struggled to hold the starfighter together. It was easy to believe that he was leaving a trail a blind man could see as he plummeted down, a line that any planetary defence system worthy of the name could use to project his course and blow him into dust. The cockpit darkened, automatically, as the drive field flared red and white. It felt like hours before the shaking lessened and he resumed control. The first thing he did was alter course. No one had fired at them, but it was only a matter of time.

"Sound off," he ordered, as the squadron descended. "Did we lose anyone?"

He breathed a sigh of relief as it became clear the entire squadron had survived the entry manoeuvre. Their threat receivers picked up dozens of anti-aircraft facilities, although none of them seemed to be taking any interest in the British starfighters. Not that it mattered, he reminded himself, sharply. A single sensor mounted some distance from the weapons could easily track the starfighters, then direct the antiaircraft fire. There didn't seem to be any local aircraft in the skies either, save for a couple of helicopters following the river. He couldn't tell which side they were on, but they weren't doing anything to impede his pilots.

"That's Landing City in the distance," Monica said, cheerfully. "Buckle your seatbelts and prepare for landing. Thank you for flying with Hostile Airways."

"More like a crash-landing," Flight Lieutenant Ryan Loyn commented. He snickered, rudely. "Have you *seen* their airports? Even the stewardesses wear bullet-proof jackets over their tits."

"I wouldn't trust their aircraft, either," Monica said. "They have bullet holes in their wings."

Richard rolled his eyes as the starfighters closed in on the city. Landing City was immense, easily bigger than London even though it was over two *thousand* years younger, but it was a mess. Originally, the plans had been for the prefabricated buildings to be replaced within the first few decades by local construction—galvanising the construction sector—but it hadn't worked out. Instead, the locals had built row after row of buildings around the *original* colony, absorbing smaller towns as their city grew bigger. There was no charm or elegance to Landing City, even under the best circumstances. Now, with smoke rising all over the city, it was clear that it was on the verge of a total collapse.

The starfighters passed over the embassies, sensors probing for signs of life. A handful of emergency beacons popped up, all very low-power. Dozens of insurgents were swarming the site, no doubt looking for the emergency bunkers. Richard doubted they could break in, unless they had power tools and plenty of time, but they had to be stopped. The marine dropships were bare seconds away.

"Engage firing patterns," Richard ordered, as the insurgents started shooting at his starfighters. It was unlikely they'd score a hit, but he knew better than to give them a chance to get lucky. A targeting display popped up in front of him, allowing him to select the best targets for antipersonnel weapons. "And...fire!"

The starfighter lurched as it unleashed the missiles, firing them straight down into the hostile crowd. The missiles detonated a metre or two from the ground, sending waves of flame in all directions. Anyone caught in the open would be killed instantly, he'd been assured, but the blasts wouldn't do any damage to the bunkers. He felt a flicker of pity for the dead, mingled with the grim awareness that they *had* attacked the embassies and, in doing so, put themselves beyond the pale. There could be no mercy.

"Ground clear," Monica reported. She paused. "I'm picking up antiaircraft emissions to the north."

"Kill them," Richard ordered. They couldn't afford to wait for someone to take a shot at the starfighters before deeming them hostile. The starfighters weren't as nimble as they should be and the dropships were even worse. A ground-based HVM could blow a platoon of marines out of the sky before they even knew they were under attack. "And then watch the city."

He flipped his starfighter over as the dropships began their approach, slamming down beside the shattered embassies. Landing City was burning, mobs battling it out even as their home was consumed by the flames. It was impossible to tell who was on what side, let alone who was winning. The fog of war had enveloped the city from one end to the other. But it didn't really matter. Whoever won would find themselves in charge of a shithole.

They really should have just evacuated the whole wretched planet and started again, he thought, sourly. Someone had *clearly* been asleep at the switch when the first colonists were landed. *Was it really that hard to vet the newcomers before it was too late?*

He lifted his starfighter into the air and watched as the marines swarmed the embassy compound, smaller detachments heading out to secure the streets leading to Embassy Row. The bootnecks probably didn't need fire support, but he kept a wary eye on the live feed just in case. If they needed fire support, they'd *really* need it. He couldn't help wondering just *what* had happened when the fighting actually began. Losing one embassy was bad enough, but losing *all* of them was careless...

A new voice broke into his deliberations. "Richard, we're picking up an emergency beacon from the marine detachment," Lieutenant-Commander Rebecca Wycliffe said. The CAG sounded tense. "They broke out of the city and headed downriver, but they're in trouble."

"Understood," Richard said. He remembered the helicopters and swore. Perhaps they *should* have blown them out of the air after all. "We're on our way."

CHAPTER FOUR

"CAPTAIN?"

Alice opened her eyes, one hand reaching for the pistol she'd placed by her side when she'd found a place for a quick nap. The barge had made it out of the city, thankfully without drawing more than a little fire from one or more of the factions, allowing her a chance to make sure the entire platoon got some rest. She was used to taking catnaps, whenever she had the opportunity to close her eyes for an hour or so, but she didn't feel any better as she stood upright. It felt as if she hadn't slept for very long at all.

She rubbed her eyes, looking from side to side. The barge's interior was stained with *something* that was clearly more than a little corrosive, although that could just have been the river. It was a minor miracle that the barge was *watertight*, she thought. The hull was rusty and decrepit, so weakened that she thought one good kick would shatter what little integrity it had left. Perhaps there was a perfectly good reason the barge hadn't been stolen and used to escape the city before the marines got to the dock. It wasn't safe at all.

Neither is staying in the city, she reminded herself, wryly. *And someone might have a chance to survive if they fell into the river.*

"Sergeant," she said. Her body *hurt.* The barge was vibrating, the dull roar of the engine echoing through the hull. "Report?"

"The river is growing choppier," Radcliffe said. He sounded worried. "I think we should get off the water."

Alice nodded. "Probably a good idea," she said, picking up her helmet and buckling it into place. There was a nasty mark on the side where a bullet had hit her and bounced off. She wondered, as she snapped her visor over her eyes, when that had happened. She'd certainly never *noticed* the Angel of Death brushing her with his wings. "Let's go."

The smell lessened, barely, as she led the way up the steps and into the cockpit. Singh stood at the wheel, his dark face lined with concern. Alice nodded to him, assuming command, then peered through the open window. The river was darkening, the water splashing in all directions...she couldn't help wondering if they were about to run into the rapids. Or, more likely, someone had emplaced hidden traps below the waterline to sink any boat foolish enough to try to break through and run down to the sea.

She sucked in her breath as she looked at the bank. Greenish vegetation, a strange mixture of earthly and alien plants, seemed to infest the riverside. It looked to be rotting, yet somehow alive...it almost seemed to be *thriving* on whatever chemicals were present in the water, even though she thought it was an illusion. There didn't seem to be any place they could dock or even pull alongside, just for a moment, and jump off. They might be trapped on the barge.

A dull quiver ran through the barge. Alice exchanged a look with Radcliffe. They'd hit something below the waterline, which meant...what? A piece of wood or something designed to slow them down. She wished, not for the first time, that she had a man who knew the river like the back of his hand. She'd boated over many of Britain's rivers as part of her training, learning to read the waters like a book, but this was Terra Nova. Her training might be actively misleading.

"As soon as you see somewhere we can pull in, take us there," she said, as she checked her visor. The maps of Terra Nova outside Landing City were useless. "We'll find a place to hole up for a few days."

And hope that's long enough for the ship to return, she thought, as she eyed the murky waters. Their ration packs could be stretched out that long, if necessary, but afterwards they were going to be in dangerous territory. Everyone outside the city was armed—and presumably trigger-happy. They would have problems trading for food and problems stealing it. *After that, we may be in some trouble.*

A hooting sound echoed through the air. She looked up, just in time to see an immense paddle steamer appear further down the river. For a moment, she could hardly believe her eyes. She'd known that such primitive ships had been used, back during the early days of settlement, but the reports insisted that they'd all been decommissioned after Terra Nova developed its industrial base. Now...she gritted her teeth as she saw the armed men, standing at the prow of the steamer. *That* was no pleasure cruise.

"Try to avoid contact," she ordered, glancing at the riverbank. Unbroken vegetation ran in all directions. "And tell the rest of the platoon to stand by."

Radcliffe spat into the water. "We're not going to be able to avoid contact."

Alice suspected he was right. The barge was about as manoeuvrable as a flatbed truck, while the paddle steamer was agile enough to put itself right alongside the barge and—presumably—tough enough to simply ram the barge without suffering serious damage. Singh was doing the best he could to steer the barge out of the steamer's way, but it didn't look as though the steamer was going to let them go. Alice had no way to know if this was a planned ambush or a chance encounter, yet it didn't matter. Either way, they were in trouble.

"They're moving to block us," Singh snapped. "I can't evade them!"

"I see," Alice said. She glanced at Radcliffe. Surrender was still not an option. Nor was abandoning ship. Even if the water was harmless, their BDUs would get waterlogged and drag them under very quickly. She wouldn't panic—she'd had worse, during training—but the ambassador had probably only swum in the embassy's pool. "Get the grenade launchers ready."

"Aye, Captain."

Alice gritted her teeth as the steamer rotated again. Whoever was in command was a decent sailor, even if he wasn't a decent man. The steamer was going to pass close enough to the barge for a boarding party to hop across and take control. She could see them getting ready to move, half of them covering the barge with assault rifles while the other half readied themselves to jump. They looked practiced enough, she had to admit. Perhaps they'd encountered pirates, rather than insurrectionists. She wondered, idly, just how much of the original steamer had been replaced over the years. The polluted waters had to be particularly bad for the immense paddle wheels.

Not that it matters, she told herself. She briefly considered trying to seize the steamer herself, but there were too many hostiles on the boat. *That ship isn't going to be around for much longer.*

A voice boomed over the water, a language she didn't recognise. "That's Mexican," Singh said. "They're ordering us to turn off the engine and keep our hands in sight."

Alice nodded. "Grenades. Now!"

Radcliffe appeared from behind the cockpit and fired a grenade into the steamer. Chesterton followed a second later, aiming a grenade into the giant paddle wheel. The first explosion shattered the uppermost level of the boat, the second smashed the wheel and tore a hole in the hull. Slowly, agonisingly slowly, the steamer started to heel over and capsize. Alice lifted her rifle, ready to repel anyone desperate enough to try to scramble onto the barge, but it was unnecessary. The steamer disintegrated, pieces of debris crashing into the barge's hull as it sank beneath the waves. A handful of survivors, desperately swimming towards the nearest bank, showed no interest in trying to engage the marines.

"I think we got it," Singh said. The barge shook, again. "And I think we really need to get off this ship."

"Understood," Alice said. If the steamer had managed to send a distress call—or even if someone up the river was expecting the steamer to show—someone might come looking to see what had happened. She didn't think it had been a planned encounter, but there was no way to be sure. "Get us into shore as soon as..."

"Captain," Hammersmith shouted. "I got a link to the ship!"

Alice allowed herself a moment of relief, even though she didn't let it show on her face. "What did they say?"

"They're entering orbit and sending help," Hammersmith said. "They want us to find a place to wait for pickup."

"Understood," Alice said. The marines weren't in any immediate danger. Captain Shields and Major Parkinson would be more concerned with the embassy bunkers, as long as Alice didn't need help. "We'll keep moving until we find a place to stay."

The barge groaned, worryingly. Alice eyed the waters, then the riverbank. They had a couple of thermal grenades which they could use, in theory, to clear the vegetation away, but she had literally no idea what lay on the far side. She'd done enough jungle exercises to know they didn't want to have to hack their way through the foliage, probably getting lost as they headed away from the river. And yet, she was starting to think they didn't have a choice.

"There," Singh said. "A little place to get up."

Alice followed his gaze. There was a small gap in the vegetation, barely large enough for a car. It looked as though someone had used chemicals to clear the ground, killing everything so thoroughly that the vegetation had never managed to grow back. She peered through her visor, trying to see what might be lurking under the trees. Her instincts insisted that the gap wasn't natural.

Radcliffe sucked in his breath, sharply. "Captain, can you hear that?"

Alice listened. Terra Nova was quieter than Earth, save for the ever-present sound of running water. No birds sang in the trees, no small animals moved in the undergrowth...she couldn't help feeling that the polluted waters had killed every animal in the vicinity. And yet, there was a faint sound in the distance, slowly growing louder. A human sound...

"Choppers," she said. The helicopters were upriver, but coming towards the marines. "Shit!"

She looked at Singh. "Get us into the bank," she ordered. "Ram the shore, if necessary. Ken, grab the ambassador and get ready to jump."

"Aye, Captain."

"They'll be on us in two minutes," Radcliffe said, as the barge slowly turned towards the bank. "If they know we're here..."

"I understand," Alice said. Caught out in the open, with only a single plasma rifle to defend themselves, the marines would be sitting ducks. The helicopters might not realise the marines had plasma weapons, but—perversely—that would actually work in their favour if they were hostile. She'd hesitate to fire until it was too late. "Send a message to the ship. Tell them we need help."

"Aye, Captain," Hammersmith said.

The barge hit the riverbank and bounced. Alice was moving before her conscious mind had realised that the groaning sound was the barge finally reaching the end of its life. The other marines joined her, racing for the edge of the boat and jumping a moment before the barge slowly started to sink under the filthy waters. Alice landed hard, scrambling up the muddy bank and down a path someone had marked out years ago. The faint, but unmistakable signs of new growth suggested that the pathway had been abandoned for quite some time.

"I..." Ambassador Crichton coughed and started again. "What...what's happening?"

Alice hesitated. The ambassador looked like a drowned and drugged rat. He'd fallen asleep almost as soon as they'd boarded the barge, but it clearly hadn't done him much good. She wondered, grimly, if he'd taken something he shouldn't. Her marines knew better than to give their medical supplies to civilians, but the ambassador might have obtained something from the embassy medical room or...she sighed, dismissing the thought. Some men—and women—just weren't cut out for combat.

"We're being hunted," she said, as the sound of helicopters grew louder. "Keep your voice down."

She glanced from side to side as the marines slipped down the path towards an ancient and decaying hut. It had been a farm, once upon a time, before it had been abandoned...probably a few years ago, if she was any judge. The fields, far smaller than any she'd seen on Earth, were heavily overgrown, corn and potatoes competing with alien plants for supremacy. A few more years, she thought, and it would be impossible to tell that the farm had ever been there in the first place. She felt a lump in her throat as she eyed the farmhouse. Someone's hopes and dreams had been invested in that structure, only to be lost over the years...

The helicopters flew overhead, their blades clattering loudly. Alice held herself still, hardly even daring to breathe. Modern sensors would have no trouble picking them—or at least the ambassador—out from the background...even older sensors would probably be able to give the pilots a good idea where to find their prey. But if the locals didn't have such sensors...she silently timed the flights as the helicopters turned back to fly over the abandoned farmstead once again. There was no way she could believe their appearance was a coincidence now.

"If they open fire," she hissed to Corporal Roger Tindal, "take them both out!"

Time seemed to slow down as the helicopters floated overhead. Alice kept a wary eye on them, unable to understand the enemy tactics. If they were armed, they should have opened fire by now. Spraying the trees with bullets was a simple way to flush out their prey. But if they weren't...what were they doing? Leading other forces to the marines...?

Her blood ran cold. She'd been wrong. The enemy knew *precisely* who they were chasing and they'd tracked the marines ever since they'd boarded the barge. Perhaps earlier, too. Roger had shot down one drone, but there might have been others...or even watching satellites, high overhead.

Terra Nova's satellites weren't designed to spy on the planet's surface, but it wouldn't have been hard for them to obtain something to fill the gap. She'd thought they were hiding. She'd been wrong.

"Take them out," she ordered. "Now!"

Corporal Tindal opened fire. A plasma bolt flashed upwards and burnt through the closest helicopter's armour. It exploded a second later, pieces of flaming debris raining down. The second helicopter started to bank away, too late. Tindal killed it too. This time, the wreckage crashed into the river.

"We need to move," she snapped. If there *was* a large enemy infantry force closing in on them, and she could hear faint sounds of people moving through the undergrowth, she and her men were in trouble. Trapped against the river, they wouldn't have much room to manoeuvre. "Sergeant, take point..."

A hail of fire crashed through the trees over her head. She hit the ground instinctively, cursing the mud as she searched for targets. The enemy was flitting through the trees, snapping off shots towards the marines; she fired back a handful of shots, grimly aware that she probably hadn't hit anyone. It was only a matter of time until they ran out of bullets.

And then we get shot in the head, she thought. The marines weren't important, not in the grand scheme of things, but the ambassador *was*. Whoever was backing the insurrectionists needed to kill him, along with anyone else who could testify against them. *There's no getting out alive.*

"Help is coming," Hammersmith said. "We just have to hold out for another few minutes."

Alice nodded as she fired at a shadow, which vanished before she could tell if she'd hit anything or not. The people they were fighting weren't professionals, she thought, but they weren't unskilled either. They certainly seemed to have been given some training. She'd heard stories of units that had once specialised in training irregular forces, teaching the peaceful villagers how to oppose the communists or religious fanatics who would tear their lives apart. There hadn't been much of *that* over the last hundred years or so, but if someone had resurrected the concept...

"Here they come," Hammersmith said.

A deafening roar split the sky as a squadron of starfighters rocketed overhead, so low she felt she could reach up and touch them. Their plasma guns yammered loudly as they strafed the ground, systematically wiping out the enemy force. Alice let out a long breath, then forced herself to stay low as the fighters made another pass. Of all the ways to go, a blue-on-blue—being accidentally killed by one's own side—would be the worst.

"The dropship is inbound," Hammersmith said. "I think we made it."

Alice said nothing as the dropship slowly landed in what remained of the fields. She thought she'd made it too, but she wasn't fool enough to say it out loud. Hammersmith was already getting dirty looks from the other bootnecks for jinxing them. The mission wasn't over until they were back on the ship and the ambassador was in sickbay, probably being treated for shock. And then there would be a shower, an extensive debriefing and—probably—some comments on her leadership from armchair generals. Major Parkinson knew better than to micromanage his subordinates, particularly someone who had been on her own, but a REMF back on Earth would make it his business to ask questions.

Particularly someone who thinks that women have no place in the Royal Marines, she thought, as she scrambled to her feet. *And thinks he can win the argument by making me look a fool.*

"Come on," she said. There was no point in worrying about it now. "Let's go."

CHAPTER FIVE

"CAPTAIN," ALISON SAID. "The Chinese ships are moving."

Stephen glanced up, sharply. "Going where?"

"The planet," Alison said. "They're bringing their targeting sensors online now."

"The orbital defences aren't moving to counter them, either," Newcomb added. "Sir, they may be battered too badly to offer resistance..."

Or the Chinese might have subverted them already, Stephen thought. The majority of crews on the defence platforms were Chinese, according to the reports. They could have taken over most of the platforms in a single move, then attacked the platforms that couldn't be taken by stealth. *What is going on?*

He studied the display for a long moment. "Are the dropships ready to take off?"

"Aye, sir," Newcomb said. "They've recovered seventy people in total, twenty-nine of them ours. The remainder are largely French and American with a handful of other Europeans."

Stephen winced. There had been over three hundred people assigned to the British embassy alone. He doubted the other Great Powers had assigned any *less*. The losses had been staggering, all the more so as it had been a long time since *anyone* had dared attack an embassy. There *would* be punishment.

And the Chinese and Russian staffers were completely wiped out, he thought. *Or at least we weren't able to locate any survivors.*

His eyes narrowed. He'd grown up amongst the aristocracy, and the Old Boy Network had smoothed his path to command, but that didn't mean he was *stupid*. There was a sizable Chinese population on the surface, a handful of undeclared Chinese ships approaching the planet, and the Chinese embassy had been blown to bits, apparently taking its entire staff with it. No one would bother to lodge more than a token protest—let alone do anything effective—if the Chinese pounded Terra Nova into submission, then installed a government that would pay whatever reparations the other Great Powers demanded. And that meant...

He cursed under his breath. It was no longer a strictly military matter, not any longer. It was a political and diplomatic matter, one that would need to be settled at a far higher level than a mere *captain*. He did have some authority, when he was operating far from Sol, but not enough to settle matters on Terra Nova. It would only take a couple of hours to get a message from Terra Nova to Sol.

But that won't be quick enough, he thought, grimly. *By then, the Chinese will have taken the high orbitals.*

He glanced at the simulations the analysts had worked out for him. *Invincible* could take the Chinese ships in a long-range engagement, but a close-range encounter near the planet could go either way...all the more so, he figured, if the Chinese were in complete control of the planetary defences. And, whatever the outcome, it would mean war. The rules of engagement were clear. He could engage insurrectionists and terrorists—and even pirates, as rare as they were—at will, but not fire on another spacefaring power unless he had very good reason to believe that his ship and crew were in imminent danger.

"Launch our remaining starfighters, but hold them in position nearby," he ordered. He didn't *think* the Chinese would fire on the dropships as they returned to *Invincible*, but if they did he'd be ready. "And then order Major Parkinson to expedite."

"Aye, sir."

Stephen leaned back in his chair, then hastily composed a message for the Admiralty. The FTL communications network was cranky at the best of times—the combination of human and alien technology didn't always work well—but it was so much better than anything humanity had had before that everyone was delighted. Stephen wasn't so sure—the Admiralty had shown a disturbing tendency to micromanage when it actually *could* dictate events in real time—yet he had to admit the flicker network had its advantages. Perhaps, just perhaps, the Admiralty actually *could* get some orders to him in time.

But they'll probably have to relay it to the PM first, he thought. He glanced at the chronometer. It was nearly midnight, London time. *They'll probably have to wake half the government up and pour coffee down their throats before they can make a decision.*

He shook his head. If he was right—if the whole insurrection was cover for a Chinese land grab—the politicians would have to decide what to do. They might just shrug and let it pass. Terra Nova had been a thorn in humanity's collective side for quite long enough. If the Chinese wanted to batter the factions into submission, why not let them? What was the worst that could happen? It wasn't as if the Chinese would be expending fleet carriers and battleships on Terra Nova.

Unless we're missing something, he thought. *The Chinese Government isn't noted for doing things out of the goodness of its heart.*

It was a sobering thought. Chinese politics were such a strange mixture of communism and capitalism, aristocracy and meritocracy, that it was difficult to know which way the Chinese would jump. They'd fought beside the other Great Powers during the First and Second Interstellar Wars—and fought bravely—but otherwise they dominated East Asia and limited their obligations to the rest of the world. There was no shortage of horror stories about what happened to groups that refused to accept Beijing's dominance.

And just because I can't think of a reason for them to intervene on Terra Nova, he thought, *doesn't mean that they can't think of a reason.*

He finished the message and uploaded it into the communications queue, then looked at Morse. "Encrypt the message," he said, "then transmit it to the flicker station."

"Aye, sir," Morse said. He worked his console for a long moment. "Message sent."

"Good," Stephen said. "One hopes the Chinese will not be able to *read* the message."

"Yes, sir," Morse said.

Stephen sighed, inwardly. The Great Powers refrained from waging open warfare on each other, but espionage was still a fact of life. GCHQ claimed that the latest encryption protocols were unbreakable, yet they'd made that claim before...and then discovered that the other Great Powers *had* broken their codes. There was a quiet, but none-the-less savage contest between the Great Powers to alternatively devise a genuinely unbreakable encryption system and break everyone *else's* encryption systems. The Chinese might well be able to read his message, if they intercepted it.

But there's nothing in the message they don't already know, he thought. He would be astonished if Beijing wasn't already well aware of what was going on. *It's the answer that comes back that should concern them.*

"Captain," Newcomb said. "The dropships are taking off now."

Stephen let out a sigh of relief. "We'll move away from the planet as soon as they are recovered," he said, firmly. "And then we'll wait for orders."

"Yes, sir."

• • •

"They're not trying to light us up again," Monica said, as the starfighters swooped over the city again. "Do you think they've learnt their lesson?"

"Probably," Richard said. The marines had been attacked several times, although they'd seemed to believe that the attackers had been roving gangs rather than insurgents. He and his pilots had provided fire support, raining down plasma bolts from high overhead to obliterate anyone foolish enough to attack the marines. "Or they might be preparing for something *really* bad."

He frowned at the darkening sky. It was high summer and the days were long, yet this particular day of terror was finally coming to an end. He felt a stab of pity for the locals, cowering in their homes and waiting to see what terrors tomorrow would bring. Richard doubted it would be anything pleasant. He'd flown over enough mobs—looting, raping and killing—to know that it would be a long time before Terra Nova settled down, if it ever did.

The only peace that can be imposed on this planet is the peace of the grave, he thought morbidly, as the dropships began to take off. *No one cares enough to do anything else.*

The marine dropships rose quickly, scattering chaff and ECM decoys to confuse any watching sensors. Richard braced himself, half-expecting a hidden antiaircraft battery to open fire now it had a chance to do some real damage, but nothing happened. Monica was probably right. The starfighters *had* taught anyone with access to *real* hardware that they should probably keep it hidden, at least until the marines had withdrawn. There was nothing to be gained by calling down the wrath of *Invincible*.

Or at least more wrath, Richard thought. He had a feeling the assault carrier would be carrying out punitive strikes, either exterminating whatever faction was responsible for attacking the embassies or punishing the entire population. It didn't seem a very effective idea to him, but it had been a long time since anyone had dared offer sympathy for enemy populations. *The Great Powers will want revenge for the attacks.*

He pushed the thought aside as he guided his starfighter upwards. Darkness was falling rapidly across the land, a darkness broken only by fires that the locals were unable or unwilling to quench. Landing City looked to be on the verge of burning down, flames moving from house to house as the population fled in all directions. The remainder of the continent wasn't much better. His eyes couldn't pick out a single light, while his sensors couldn't detect a single emission. Terra Nova had blown itself back into the Dark Ages.

Or maybe they're just keeping their heads down and hoping not to be noticed, he thought. It was unlikely that any community could remain undetected in Britain, but here…an entire town might manage to keep itself off the grid. *There might be all sorts of settlements hidden away in odd places.*

"The Chinese ships are coming," Monica said. Her voice was scornful. "Apparently, we're to give them a wide berth."

Richard nodded in understanding, although he knew he'd have to reprimand her later. Starfighter pilots were given a great deal of latitude—it was still the most dangerous job in the Royal Navy—but there were limits. He understood precisely why she disliked the thought of avoiding the Chinese, yet he also understood that they didn't want to find themselves accidentally starting a war after playing chicken with the Chinese ships. His lips quirked. Starting a war was probably a court-martial offence.

And it might give the Chinese diplomatic leverage over us, later, he reminded himself. *The government would not be pleased.*

The starfighter shook as it forced its way out of the atmosphere. Richard braced himself, but the shaking stopped almost as soon as it had started. Leaving atmosphere—thankfully—was easier than entering, although he knew that might change if *Invincible* ever had to hit a heavily-defended planet. The proliferation of PDCs and ground-based weapons systems that posed a real threat to orbiting starships threatened to change the face of war once again. It was quite possible that they'd find themselves flying down to a planetary surface and carrying out bombing raids that would have felt very familiar to some of his ancestors, the ones who'd fought in the Battle of Britain…

"I see them," Loyn said. "Nine Chinese ships, inbound."

"Alter course to evade," Richard ordered. The Chinese ships didn't look to be targeting the starfighters and dropships, although he would have been surprised if their crews weren't running firing solutions. Tactical crews were taught to regard anything moving near their ships as a potential target—and threat. "Are the planetary defences tracking them?"

"Negative," Monica said. "I bet they've already overwhelmed the defences."

Richard nodded. He had a nasty feeling she was right. No defenders worthy of the name would allow a hostile force into orbit without making *some* attempt to stop it. Terra Nova was in deep shit. The Chinese had every right to seek revenge for the destruction of their embassy and the slaughter of their people. And they had to know it, too.

He studied the Chinese ships warily, silently trying to gauge their power. Their energy signatures were very similar to their British counterparts, unsurprisingly. The Great Powers had worked hard to ensure that most of their starship components and weapons systems were standardized, even though it meant sharing technology with potential competitors—or enemies. It was impossible to tell just what weapons they were carrying—cruisers and destroyers were modular, allowing their crews to outfit them with whatever they required for a particular operation—but they'd be formidable. No one would risk flying such ships into a warzone unless they were able to defend themselves.

The Chinese made no hostile moves. They didn't even track the British starfighters and dropships with active sensors. Richard frowned, telling himself—again—that the Chinese would have to be insane to fire on his craft. In space, there was no way it could have been passed off as an accident. But his back still itched as they made their closest approach to the Chinese ships and rocketed past, heading straight for *Invincible*. He didn't allow himself to relax until the starfighters were approaching their mothership.

Invincible slowly came into view, a floating city hanging against the darkness of interplanetary space. She was immense, compared to the starfighters, but regular fleet carriers were a third again her size; she was flatter, with only two launch tubes clearly visible to prying eyes. Her hull was studded with weapons, sensor blisters and docking points for a small fleet of assault shuttles and dropships. She looked formidable, Richard thought, even though a civilian might have thought her fragile. The layers of armour covering her hull made her strong enough to survive blows that would kill a fleet carrier.

Although that has never been tested, Richard reminded himself, as the starfighters fell into landing formation. *The battleships went to war, but the assault carriers have not yet tasted combat.*

He shook his head. He'd joined the navy as soon as he could—his parents had refused to allow him to join at sixteen, forcing him to wait another two years—but he hadn't qualified in time to see action in the Second Interstellar War. Five years a starfighter pilot, eventually rising to squadron command...and yet, he'd never seen real action, never matched himself against another starfighter pilot. Simulations just didn't cut it. The worst anyone could expect from a particularly bad performance in the simulators was being chewed out by the CAG afterwards. There was no risk of death.

The marines probably feel differently, he thought, dryly. Flying a support mission might not feel particularly exciting, or risky, but that didn't mean it was unimportant. *And there are people on the ground who are trapped in hell.*

The starfighter landed neatly on the flight deck. Richard unbuckled his helmet as the automated systems took control, dragging the craft through an airlock and into the hangar bay. The ground crews were already moving into position, readying themselves to replenish the starfighters and return them to the launch tubes. Richard glanced at his display—he was surprised to see *just* how many weapons he'd expended over the last few hours—and then opened the cockpit. There was no point in waiting for the ladder. He jumped down and landed neatly on the deck.

"Sir," Monica said, as she fell in beside him. "I think you need a shower."

Richard had to laugh as he caught sight of his own reflection. He was a healthy young man, his brown hair cropped close to his scalp, but he looked like something the cat had dragged in. Monica didn't look much better. Flying starfighters was the greatest job in the Royal Navy, but it was very wearing. It was funny how those details were never mentioned during recruitment tours.

"So do you," he said. "So do you."

. . .

"Captain," Newcomb said. "All the starfighters have returned to the ship. The dropships are being unloaded now."

"Send the evacuees to sickbay, then assign them quarters," Stephen ordered, curtly. It wouldn't be very comfortable, and he was sure there would be quite a few complaints, but at least the evacuees wouldn't be in any danger. "Tell the doctor I want a full medical check done on each and every one of them."

"Aye, sir."

Stephen looked at the helmsman. "Lieutenant Michelle, move us to Point Alpha," he ordered. "Best possible speed."

"Aye, sir."

The tactical console bleeped an alarm. "Captain, the Chinese have opened fire on the planet!"

"Show me," Stephen snapped.

He grimaced as the display shifted, focusing on the planet. The Chinese ships were unleashing one hell of a bombardment, launching over five *hundred* KEWs in a matter of minutes. Their targeting seemed scattered, as if they were firing at random…no, he realised grimly, they were blasting the various factions from orbit. A sizable number of KEWs seemed to be targeted on Landing City itself. He wouldn't have given much for the fate of anyone underneath when the projectiles landed. Nothing short of a concealed—and very deep—bunker could survive a direct hit.

"They're flattening the entire planet," Newcomb breathed.

"It certainly looks that way," Stephen agreed. The Chinese were presumably working their way down a targeting list, instead of firing on targets of opportunity. Their people on the surface had certainly had plenty of time to compile one. It was local night, too. The locals wouldn't have any time to realise they were under attack before it was too late. "And no one is in any position to stop them."

He shook his head. "We'll continue on our current course and leave the wretched planet behind," he added. "Unless, of course, the Admiralty wants us to do something else."

"Yes, sir."

CHAPTER SIX

RANK, ALICE CAMPBELL had once been told, might have had its privileges...but not in the Royal Marines. Bootneck officers were expected to share the privations of their men, at least while they were on deployment. The handful of senior officers deemed too important to risk in combat might not be expected to sleep in the barracks or share showers with their subordinates, but they weren't allowed to issue orders in the field either. She wasn't sure, if she was honest with herself, if she wanted to ever climb to such a level. It wouldn't be quite so easy to say she was a marine.

And there's a good chance I will never be allowed to climb so high anyway, she thought, without heat. The first woman to join the Royal Marines *and* pass Commando Training *might* be in line for a later promotion, but her lack of connections—and her father's reputation—presumably worked against her. *It's not easy to promote someone who has to earn her right to be there again and again.*

It was a frustrating thought, but one she'd come to terms with long ago. The Royal Marines—and the military in general—encouraged a realism that civilians would probably consider a little harsh. Male soldiers suspected that female soldiers weren't up to the task, a legacy from the era before the Troubles. She might have passed Commando Training, where some of her instructors had openly looked for reasons to fail her, but she still needed to prove herself in the field time and time again. It was the way of the world.

She undressed rapidly, placing her sweaty uniform in the basket as she walked into the communal showers. She'd grown used to sharing the showers with the men long ago, even though her elder sister had been horrified at the mere thought. It helped that she'd gone to boarding school—where she'd discovered that girls could be worse than boys—and that, in training, most of them had been too tired to even *consider* hanky-panky. Now, she was one of the men.

A man with tits, she thought wryly, as she looked down at herself. She wasn't exactly a bodybuilder, or one of the weirder human augmentations from the belt, but she wasn't exactly anyone's idea of *feminine* either. Her arms were muscular, her head was shaved and her breasts were so flat that they were practically non-existent. *And people take me for a man, too, as long as they don't see between my legs.*

She scrubbed herself down rapidly, then hurried out of the shower and scooped up a clean duty uniform. There would be debriefings before she could sleep, probably with intelligence staff as well as Major Parkinson. Hopefully, she'd have a chance to catch something to eat before she finally collapsed into her bunk. She'd eaten a pair of ration bars in the dropship, but they weren't *real* food.

Sergeant Radcliffe met her as she left the showers. "The Major wants to see you in his office," he said. "I'm to take over the platoon."

"Understood," Alice said. She resisted the urge to remind him to ensure that the debriefings were carried out before the bootnecks started forgetting important details. The sergeant had been doing his job for years. He'd forgotten more than she'd ever learnt. "I'll see you this evening."

She took a long breath as she hurried down the passageway. It was possible—unlikely, but possible—that she might be in trouble. Manhandling an ambassador was the sort of thing that tended to look bad on one's service jacket, even if it had been fully justified. Or...she had driven right into an ambush, after all, which had cost her the lives of two men. She'd have to answer for their deaths at some point too. Some jackass REMF would be bound to insist that she could have done *something*...

There were no guards outside the Major's office, something that had amused her when she'd first boarded *Invincible*. There was little *point* in guarding the office—they were on a starship, not a military base in the security zone—but it was tradition. Major Parkinson didn't hold with tradition, it seemed, although even *he* couldn't keep a pair of marines from being detailed to guard the bridge hatch. She smiled at the memory, then pressed the buzzer. The airlock hissed open a moment later, revealing a tiny cubbyhole. Major Parkinson's office was smaller than the bedroom she'd had to endure at school.

Just because you were a little brat to the grandparents, she thought, as she marched across the deck and came to a halt in front of the desk. *They simply couldn't cope with you.*

Major Parkinson looked up, his eyes meeting hers. He looked...weathered, as if he'd seen it all before and hadn't been impressed the first time. His blond hair was cut close to his scalp, like most of the men, but his face looked older. Alice was privately surprised he hadn't been offered a promotion that would take him off active duty, although she suspected he would have declined the promotion if it had been offered. Major Parkinson loved his job too much.

"Alice," Parkinson said. His voice held traces of a Welsh accent, buried under the firm tones drilled into marines during training. "Pour yourself a cup of coffee, then sit down."

Alice relaxed, slightly, as she did as she was told. She wasn't in trouble, then. Traditionally, tea or coffee was offered as a way to put the discussion on slightly less formal terms. If she had been in trouble, she would have been bracing the bulkhead while Parkinson explained her mistakes in excruciating detail. Instead...she sat down, silently wondering why Parkinson had installed a pair of folding chairs in his office. They—and the desk—gave the entire office a feeling of impermanence. But then, Parkinson knew better than to get too comfortable. He might wind up commanding a military operation from a requisitioned civilian house, a tent, or a foxhole in the middle of nowhere. The Royal Marines prided themselves on travelling light. *They* didn't need a dozen men in the rear to support one man at the front.

She took a sip of her coffee. It tasted ghastly. Parkinson was clearly one of the officers who actually *liked* military-issued coffee grains. Her last CO had used his luggage allocation to transport several boxes of premium blend from Earth. She didn't really blame him either, although a case could be made that he'd bent the rules. Military-grade coffee didn't *really* corrode the decks, but it had a damn good try.

Parkinson leaned forward. "There'll be questions about the ambush," he said. "What happened?"

Alice took a breath. "We departed in three vehicles: two escort AFVs and the ambassador's limo. I put myself in the limo, along with two others; the remainder of the platoon were distributed over the AFVs. The route we took was randomised, known only to the driver of the lead AFV and myself. I made certain that it would not leak out ahead of time.

"Despite that, we ran into an ambush including at least one plasma weapon," she said. "I believe they were watching us from a high-altitude drone, as we shot one of them down later. The first we knew of the actual ambush was a plasma blast striking the lead AFV, turning it into a fireball. Corporal Yammer and Corporal Taylor were both killed instantly."

A shadow crossed Parkinson's face. He knew—they both knew—just what would happen if a superhot plasma bolt burnt through armour and exploded inside a vehicle. If they were lucky, the two corporals would have died instantly. The alternative—that they would have been aware of their injuries before their deaths—was far worse. Alice could tell that he was considering what she'd said, turning it over and over in his mind as he tried to decide if she'd made a mistake. Two men were dead. If anyone had played a role—even accidentally—in their deaths, Parkinson would stop at nothing to make sure they were punished.

She forced herself to continue. "I judged that a weapon capable of killing an AFV would also be capable of burning through the limo," she said. "Accordingly, I ordered an immediate evacuation of both the limo and the remaining AFV. In hindsight..."—she paused for a moment—"I believe that the insurgents intended to capture the ambassador, as they passed up at least one opportunity to kill the limo too. We moved into the nearest alleyway, then tried to contact the embassy. When it became clear that we'd lost contact with the embassy, and that Landing City had turned into a war zone, I decided it would be best to get out of the city before we were overwhelmed."

"An interesting choice," Parkinson said. "You didn't think it would be better to head back to the embassy?"

Alice kept her voice under tight control. "There was a sizable enemy force, perhaps more than one, between us and the embassy, sir," she said. She knew it was his job to second-guess her, but...she didn't like it. "I did not believe that we could get the ambassador to safety, sir, and given what happened to the embassy, I think I made the right call."

Parkinson nodded. "I tend to agree," he said. "There will probably be *someone* who will try to argue that you should have waited for pickup, but you had no way of knowing when the ship would return."

He stood and poured himself a cup of coffee. "Why did you agree to escort the ambassador?"

Alice looked at him, evenly. "I was under the impression that our orders were to reinforce the embassy's security forces and give their overworked men a rest," she said. "I rather assumed that providing an escort force was part of the job."

"True enough," Parkinson said. "And you *did* save his life."

"At a cost," Alice said. "Has he got around to filing a complaint yet?"

"He's currently under sedation," Parkinson told her. "I dare say he'll recover, sooner or later, to hear that most of his staff was killed when the embassy was bombed. He'll be grateful once he realises that you're the only reason he's still alive."

Alice had her doubts. She'd met a handful of diplomats in her time and some had been little better than spoilt brats. The ones who'd been in the military weren't too bad—and the ones who had served in the army knew how the world worked—but the ones who came out of Eton or Cambridge and went straight into the Foreign Service were appalling. It took far too long for them to grasp that the world didn't care one jot for their theories, no matter how appealing they were. She was privately surprised that some of the overqualified idiots had survived their first encounter with the real world.

She sighed, then dismissed the thought. Parkinson was probably right. And, even if he wasn't, it was unlikely that too many people would take the ambassador's complaints seriously. But it only took one or two people in high places to ruin a career. Too many senior officers were adamantly against allowing women to join the Royal Marines. The hell of it was that she knew, from studying military history, that they had a point.

"Overall, you did fine," Parkinson said. "It's unfortunate that we probably won't be able to recover the bodies, but...no one will fault you for getting the ambassador out of the line of fire as quickly as possible."

Alice felt a pang of guilt. Corporal Yammer and Corporal Taylor had both been experienced men, experienced enough that she'd had no qualms about putting them on point. And it had gotten them killed. Their bodies would be little more than ash, if anything had survived at all. It wasn't the first time a funeral had been held with nothing in the casket, but...it tore at her, more than she cared to admit. She might as well have signed their death warrants herself.

"Thank you, sir," she said, careful not to allow any trace of her feelings to show on her face. Weakness would get her in trouble. "You did pretty fine, too."

Parkinson laughed. "We crashed into the city, shot a number of idiots who tried to test us, dug up the survivors, and crashed out again," he said. "It wasn't *that* hard a deployment."

Alice smiled, then sobered. "Sir...someone was supplying the insurgents with advanced technology. That plasma gun and the drone didn't come from local factories."

"It looks that way," Parkinson said. "Make sure you mention it in your report."

"If someone did," Alice said, "what are we going to do about it?"

Parkinson grimaced. "That's above our pay grade," he told her. There was a hint of frustration in his tone. No one would think twice about dropping KEWs on insurgents, but insurgents backed by a Great Power was something else again. "But attacking an embassy...that's a pretty serious declaration of intent."

"Yes, sir," Alice said. She asked the question she knew her men would want answered, sooner rather than later. "Are we going to go back and secure the site?"

"I don't know," Parkinson said. "Right now, the Chinese are battering the planet into submission. It may be some time before we can return to recover the bodies."

If we can, Alice thought. *The bodies may already have been removed from the embassies and dumped in a mass grave.*

She felt a flicker of sympathy for the planet's population. She had no love for insurgents and terrorists—she'd seen how they terrorised entire communities into supporting them—but the rest of the planet was a different story. They'd been trapped in a nightmare of religious and ethnic violence, unable to resist or escape. And now it looked as though the Chinese were taking control of the entire world. It might be better for the Chinese population, but it wouldn't be much of an improvement for everyone else. None of the Great Powers—and the Chinese least of all—were particularly interested in winning hearts and minds these days.

Parkinson smiled. "Go write your report, then get some sleep," he ordered. "We'll be continuing our drills tomorrow."

Alice nodded as she stood. Of *course* they'd be continuing as normal. Two marines were dead, but they couldn't allow that to stop them from going on. There would be a service for Yammer and Taylor, then...then they'd be going straight back to work. She knew better than to expect anything else, even when she died, but it still hurt. It would be a long time before she was entirely used to the idea of losing men under her command.

"Thank you, sir," she said.

She saluted, then walked through the hatch and down to the barracks. They were dark, a handful of men snoring loudly as they lay in their bunks. She stepped past the guard at the hatch and walked to her bunk, right at the end of the compartment. It was the only real luxury afforded to her, at least when she was on active duty. She got a few more seconds of sleep every day.

Damn it, she thought, as she recovered her datapad and headed out again. *There'll be no time for anything, but writing.*

She walked into the common room and sat down. A handful of marines were sitting in front of the display, watching a Stellar Star movie that had been three or four years old when Alice had been a baby. She rolled her eyes at the main character's ample assets, then sat down in a corner and keyed the datapad. It lit up, showing a picture of her family when she'd been a child...her family as it had been, before it had been torn apart. Alan and Judith Campbell looked to be very much in love, their arms wrapped around each other as they held their young daughters. She felt a lump rise in her throat as she remembered when the photograph had been taken, a year before her father had murdered her mother. She'd thought she'd been happy...

Idiot, she told herself, sharply. *You just have to bring up the past.*

The memories refused to go away. Her mother, buried quickly after some dispute with the local church wardens; her father, locked in a prison cell on the other side of the country. Her grandparents, alternatively indulgent and strict; her teachers, urging her to develop her mind even as they struggled to cope with her tantrums. The boarding school had been very much a last resort. She'd been warned, when she'd been admitted, that if she was expelled she'd spend the rest of her childhood in a borstal. The threat had been enough to keep her in line.

Her eyes lingered on her father's face. Jeanette had forgiven their father, more or less, but Alice never had. Her father had been hurting, true, yet that didn't justify murder. He'd had plenty of options, starting with divorce. And he'd torn their small family apart. Alice understood, now, that her grandparents had only wanted the best for her, but at the time she'd been a nightmare. It was a miracle they'd never given up on her.

Be practical, she told herself, sharply. There was no point in dwelling on the past. Perhaps she should have just changed her name by deed poll, ensuring that no one connected her to a murderer's daughter. *Be practical and get back to work.*

Taking a deep breath, she brought up the typing screen and began to tap out her report.

CHAPTER SEVEN

"THE CHINESE HAVE DEFINITELY secured the planet," Commander Felix Jackson said, as he displayed a set of maps. "They've taken almost every location of importance."

"Ah," Newcomb said. He took a sip of his tea as he sat on the recliner. The Ready Room was surprisingly luxurious for a warship. "And I thought there were *no* positions of importance on Terra Nova."

Stephen had to smile, although he knew it was a serious point. The Chinese didn't seem to be getting much out of the whole affair, save for Terra Nova itself. He could understand why someone might want to capture a planet's infrastructure, but Terra Nova's industrial base was barely advanced enough to build petrol-driven engines. The planet's main export was people who wanted to go somewhere—anywhere—else.

"Positions they need to take control of the planetary infrastructure, then," Jackson said, patiently. His face darkened. "Right now, Chinese militias are firmly established right across the continent. Resistance has been brutally crushed. There appears to be some low-level fighting still going on, sir, but overall they seem to have won. As long as they are prepared to call in the KEWs as soon as fighting heats up, and there's no sign they'll start holding back in future, they should remain firmly in control."

"Understood," Stephen said. He was morbidly impressed. The Chinese had seized a whole planet in four days. "And the provisional government?"

"Nothing has been heard from the former provisional government," Jackson said. "The Government House—the one built during the founding years—was destroyed at the same time as the embassies. The *new* government—Chinese-dominated, of course—insists that it is now the sole representative of Terra Nova. They certainly seem to fit the basic requirements for a recognised government."

"But no one has recognised them yet," Stephen mused. "Or has that changed?"

"So far, no," Jackson said. "But I think it's only a matter of time before the Chinese recognise them. They may be waiting to see how the other Great Powers react before they decide to annex Terra Nova or merely support a puppet government."

"And our government may simply decide to do nothing," Stephen said. He met Jackson's eyes. "How does this affect *us*?"

Jackson frowned. "For the moment, sir, the new provisional government hasn't attempted to order us out of the system," he said. "That may change, if they become a recognised government. They may also attempt to extend their control over the entire system, which *will* provoke resistance. There is a good chance of another Rock War—a potentially more *serious* Rock War—breaking out. And with British civilians in the asteroids here, we might be dragged into the mess."

Newcomb swore. "And if they secure control over the system, they will also secure the tramlines. Right?"

Stephen sucked in his breath. Terra Nova had been an open system for nearly a century, simply because the planetary government had never been able to project power outside the planet's atmosphere. Unlike Britannia or New Washington, there were no fees for using the system's tramlines. But if the Chinese annexed the system—or worked to build up their puppet government—that could change. It would cause all sorts of problems. The Chinese might just start levying transit fees, which none of the Great Powers could reasonably oppose without calling the fees they levied themselves into question. And they might just get away with it too.

"That's one concern," Jackson said.

"There's no way anyone will go along with it," Newcomb said. "Nearly two-thirds of interstellar shipping goes through Terra Nova!"

"Yes, sir," Jackson said. "And if we refuse to pay Chinese fees here, they'll start refusing to pay *our* fees."

He leaned forward. "There's also the problem of reversing the damage the Chinese did to Terra Nova," he added. "Even if we backed one of the other factions, sir, they'd have real problems fighting back. The Chinese have crushed their opponents pretty thoroughly."

"And it would unleash mass slaughter," Stephen said.

"*More* mass slaughter," Newcomb said. "The Chinese colonists are probably already settling scores."

"I'm afraid so, sir," Jackson said. "We've picked up chatter from the surface. The Chinese have already started driving other groups into the wilderness, away from their settlements. I don't think it will be long before they start machine gunning them instead."

"Fuck," Stephen said.

Newcomb's voice was bleak. "Is anyone on Earth going to care?"

Stephen rather doubted it, if the tramlines issue could be settled to everyone's satisfaction. No one on Earth gave much of a damn about a failed colony, particularly when the failure owed more to human stupidity than natural disaster. Terra Nova was good for nothing, beyond providing a lesson in the limits of diversity. The average man or woman in the street, he suspected, would see no harm in letting the Chinese have the colony. Either they sorted Terra Nova out, which would be good for the colonists, or they wound up getting dragged into a quagmire, which would keep them from causing trouble elsewhere. And besides, the costs of reversing the near-annexation would be staggeringly high.

And if they lead to a general war, he thought, *they would be insurmountable.*

His wristcom chimed. "Captain?"

"Go ahead, Mr. Morse," Stephen said.

"We just picked up a message from the flicker network," Morse said. "It's encrypted, sir, with your personal key."

"Forward it to my terminal," Stephen ordered. He placed his hand against the terminal's scanner, allowing it to verify his identity. The message unlocked a second later. "Excuse me a moment."

He frowned as he read the message. *Invincible* was to withdraw from the Terra Nova system immediately and proceed directly to Earth. There was little else, not even permission to attempt to recover the bodies from the planet. He couldn't tell if that was because the Admiralty believed there was little hope of recovering anything, which might well be true, or the politicians had ordered it in a bid to reduce tensions. There was no political briefing attached to the message, but it didn't take a genius to realise that the Terra Nova Crisis could easily lead to war.

"We're to go back home," he said, shortly. "And it doesn't suggest that another ship will be detailed to watch the system."

"There *are* facilities in the asteroid belt, sir," Jackson pointed out. "And we can leave drones behind when we do."

"Yes, but they're not *warships*," Newcomb countered. "If the Chinese get uppity…"

Stephen held up a hand. "Mr. XO, prepare the ship for departure," he said, before the argument could get out of hand. Newcomb and Jackson had the same rank, although the regulations clearly stated that intelligence officers were not in the chain of command and therefore Newcomb was Jackson's superior. "Mr. Jackson, I want you to concentrate on gathering all the intelligence we can as we leave. We'll give the Admiralty a detailed report when we arrive."

"It won't tell them anything really useful," Jackson warned. "We still don't know what the Chinese are *thinking*, for one thing."

Stephen nodded, reluctantly. The Chinese were formidable, deploying a significant force of carriers and battleships, although they probably weren't a match for a British-French-American alliance. They wouldn't *want* to get into a shooting match with three of the four other Great Powers, no matter which way the Russians jumped. Russia had been well behind the other Great Powers for the last fifteen years. It was unlikely that China *and* Russia would want to pick a fight with Britain, France and America.

But they might assume we wouldn't want to fight, he thought, as his two subordinates left the Ready Room. *And they might be right.*

It was a bitter thought. The Great Powers had resolved, nearly two hundred years ago, that the world—and later the Solar System—was big enough for all five of them. A major war within the system would be utterly devastating, no matter what happened outside. The Anglo-Indian War— spat, really—hadn't been allowed to affect Sol itself. Far too many people remembered what had happened when the Tadpoles had attacked Earth directly. The devastation had been immense.

And the Chinese might be counting on our reluctance to push them against the wall, he reminded himself. *We'd have plenty of reason not to risk pressing them too hard. If we beat them outside the Sol System, they might take the war into* the system.

Stephen puzzled over the question of which way the government would jump for a long moment, then decided there was no point in worrying about it. There was no way he could answer the question. The Prime Minister and his cabinet would have to devise a response, although *that* wouldn't be easy. The government's majority in the Houses of Parliament was very slim. It ensured that their backbenchers had more influence—and power over government policy—than was normally the case. There was no way to know which way they would jump either.

He leaned back in his chair for a long moment, feeling old. He knew how to deal with hostile ships, or how to provide assistance if someone was in trouble; he even knew what to do if *Invincible* encountered a fourth spacefaring alien race. But politics? He didn't understand politics, even though politics were the lifeblood of his family. And here, where the right tactical decision could easily be the wrong *strategic* decision, he wasn't sure which way to jump himself. There was no doubt that the wrong decision could plunge the Human Sphere into war, yet that made it impossible for him to do *anything*. The Chinese had gambled and, for the moment, won.

It wasn't a pleasant thought, he reflected, as he stood and looked around the compartment. It was bare, save for a handful of photographs he'd hung on one of the bulkheads. He'd served under officers who'd turned their Ready Rooms into shrines to themselves, or covered the bulkheads in artworks that cost more than their subordinates made in a year, but he'd never seen the point. The Ready Room wasn't his cabin, even though he'd been known to kip in it for a few hours. And besides, it wouldn't be his forever. He loved *Invincible* with all his heart, but she would outlast him. Her next commanding officer would probably change all the decor as soon as he took command.

He picked up his datapad and glanced at it, without seeing a single word of the exhaustive reports his officers had prepared. There had been no doubt what *he* would do with his life, as the second son. A military career had been decided for him before he'd even managed to take his first steps. He'd gone to the Luna Academy almost as soon as he'd left school and had been warned, in no uncertain terms, that he had better make his family proud. He still couldn't decide if command of *Invincible* was a reward or a punishment. Officers who commanded the first vessel of a new class tended to discover that it overshadowed them for the rest of their lives.

A dull quiver ran through the hull. He put the datapad down and walked out of the Ready Room, pasting a calm expression on his face. The bridge was alive with activity, the display glowing with icons as it tracked the Chinese warships orbiting the planet. It looked as though the Chinese were trying to lure the interplanetary freighters back to the habitats, although they didn't seem to be having much luck. Stephen wasn't surprised. The freighter crews loved their independence almost as much as they loved their ships. Going to work for a Great Power would be their idea of hell.

"Captain on the bridge," Newcomb said.

"Mr. XO," Stephen said. He sat down in the command chair. "Status report?"

"Drives are online, sir," Newcomb said. "We can leave as soon as you give the command."

Stephen wondered, sourly, if he should inform the Chinese that he planned to leave. They *were* the *de facto* planetary government now, damn it. But they hadn't announced that they'd annexed the planet yet, let alone laid claim to the entire system. They'd certainly done nothing to make it clear that they *expected* everyone else to inform them before making a move. It would be a while before they did, whatever they had in mind. They wouldn't want to get everyone else's back up before their position was absolutely solid.

"Very good," he said. "Helm, take us to Tramline Alpha. Best possible speed."

"Aye, sir," Sonia said.

Stephen watched the displays, warily, as *Invincible* slowly moved away from Terra Nova and set course for the tramline. His ship had performed well, under the circumstances, but he was all too aware that the shakedown cruise had shifted from peace to war in the fraction of a second. It would be easy for something to go wrong now...he let out his breath as it became clear that nothing was about to go spectacularly wrong. Embarrassing the Royal Navy in front of the Chinese wouldn't get him court-martialled, probably, but it would put an end to any hope of further promotion. The Admiralty wouldn't forget.

"Captain," Sonia said. "We will cross the tramline in seven hours."

"Take us across as soon as we reach the tramline," Stephen ordered. "And then set course for Earth."

"Aye, sir."

Stephen leaned back in his chair and watched the in-system display. Traffic had really slowed down over the last few days. Hundreds of independent freighters had crossed the tramlines in hopes of finding somewhere safer to ply their trade, while asteroid colonies had either gone dark or started preparing for war. He didn't envy the Chinese, if they found themselves forced to fight another Rock War. Belters rarely had access to top-of-the-line military gear, but they were often revoltingly ingenious *and* knew how to get the best from what they *did* have. And while there was no Belt Federation in the Terra Nova System, it wouldn't be long before one formed, if the belters had to fight for their freedom. They understood the value of working together too.

He smiled at the thought, then reached for his console and started to work his way through the reports. The CAG had written a careful set of reports detailing precisely how the Tornado starfighters had performed during the orbital insertion, although it was notable that some of the pilots *really* didn't like their starfighters. Stephen didn't blame them, either. He was no starfighter pilot, but it was obvious that a craft designed for operating in and out of a planetary atmosphere wouldn't be perfectly adapted to *either* environment. And besides, point defence did better against Tornados than Lightnings. The pilots probably should be taken seriously.

We might need to reduce the Tornado squadrons, he thought, planning his report to the Admiralty. *Or try to find a way to store more Lightnings onboard ship.*

He passed command to his XO and headed back to his cabin for a nap. It felt like he hadn't slept at all by the time the alarm rung, reminding him that he wanted to be on the bridge for the jump. He checked the status display as he pulled on his jacket and drank a mug of hot coffee, wondering if anything significant had happened while he'd been asleep. But *Invincible* was practically alone in space. The Chinese hadn't even bothered to dispatch a cruiser to escort her home.

Which could easily have backfired on them, if they did it too early, he reminded himself as he walked back onto the bridge. *The politicians are going to have fun sorting out this mess.*

He sat down. "Helm?"

"We will cross the tramline in five minutes," Sonia said. "Puller Drive is powered up and ready."

"No contacts detected," Lieutenant Alison Adams added. "Local space is clear."

Stephen nodded, feeling a flicker of irritation. The odds of one starship accidentally crashing into another while crossing the tramline were so low that they were literally inconceivable; indeed, the odds of hitting an asteroid while flying through an asteroid field were considerably higher. But it was well to check. They *were* on a least-time course between Terra Nova and Tramline Alpha, after all. Everyone else who wanted to get from one to the other would be on a similar course.

"Then jump as soon as we can," he ordered.

He forced himself to relax as the tramline came closer and closer. The boffins swore blind that there was no sensation when a starship jumped, but experienced spacers felt something anyway. It felt...it felt indescribably wrong. And then...it hadn't been *that* long since HMS *Warspite* had suffered a catastrophic power failure during her first jump. The ship had been very lucky to survive.

Sonia tapped her console. "Jumping...now!"

Stephen felt, just for a second, as though the entire universe was preparing to sneeze...and then the feeling was gone, as if it had never existed. The display blanked, then hastily started to reboot itself as new data flowed into the computers. Sol was a very busy system, the busiest system in the Human Sphere. Thousands of starships came and went every day. It was hard to believe that, only two hundred years ago, there hadn't been any interplanetary or interstellar starships at all. Now, the entire system was settled and humanity was spreading itself across the universe.

Because we got very serious about putting our eggs in as many different baskets as possible after the war, he thought. He could see a handful of colonist-carriers within detection range, heading straight for the tramline. *And because we now know we have non-human competition.*

"Jump completed, Captain," Sonia said. "Puller Drive is powering down."

"Very good," Stephen said. "Set course for Earth. It's time to go home."

CHAPTER EIGHT

"CAPTAIN SHIELDS," Admiral Sir John Naiser said. The First Space Lord stood. "Welcome back to Nelson Base."

"Thank you, sir," Stephen said. A hovering midshipwoman passed him a cup of tea. "It's good to be back."

He studied Naiser for a long moment. The First Space Lord hadn't changed much in the last five years, save for his brown hair slowly starting to turn grey. Naiser was a commoner, if Stephen recalled correctly: a man who'd been promoted through merit, rather than blood or connections. And he'd deserved promotion too. Naiser had commanded the fleet that won the final battle of the Second Interstellar War. His office reflected his birth, too. It was bare, save for a giant painting of a small starship blasting a larger one and a handful of photos of Naiser's adopted children. Stephen found it somewhat refreshing.

"Your shakedown cruise was rather more exciting than we would have wished," Naiser added, wryly. "We weren't *expecting* you to become entangled in a shooting war."

"No, sir," Stephen said. He cocked his head. "What's going to happen to Terra Nova?"

Naiser frowned. "That's up to the politicians," he said. He sounded like a man distracted by a far greater thought. "Right now, Captain, no one gives a damn about the people on the ground, but they are *very* concerned with the Chinese—or a Chinese-backed planetary government—having a claim to the tramlines. Not to mention the sheer number of independent settlements within the system...it could get nasty, I think, unless the diplomats work out a solution. Too many starships pass through Terra Nova for us to be sanguine about the Chinese sitting atop the tramlines."

"They'd have trouble preventing us from *using* the tramlines, sir," Stephen pointed out. "It isn't as if they're single points. We could cross a tramline a few light-hours from the primary and the odds of detection would be minimal."

"True," Naiser agreed. He still looked distracted. "The politicians will have to hammer out *some* kind of solution, but for the moment"—he shrugged—"the Chinese appear to have taken control of a planet and got away with it. We will see."

His gaze sharpened. "Now, I've read your official reports, Captain, and those of your subordinates. But I would still like your unofficial opinion. How did *Invincible* perform over the last six months?"

Stephen took a moment to marshal his thoughts. "We had the normal headaches of any shakedown cruise, sir," he said, carefully. "There were all sorts of minor problems, but nothing that threatened the integrity of the ship or the lives of the crew. Smoothing out launch and recovery procedures took a little longer—in hindsight, it might have been better to assign officers who weren't so familiar with fleet carriers—but we made it. The crew shook down well too, once we were underway. There were no major disciplinary issues."

"You must have kept them busy," Naiser commented, amused. "They didn't even find time for a concealed still?"

"Apparently not," Stephen said. By tradition, an illicit still somewhere in the bowels of the ship would be ignored unless it got out of hand. "The only real problem, sir, lay with the Tornados. They're nowhere near as agile as either starfighters or jet fighters and we might end up paying a steep price if we ever have to send them into a *real* war zone."

Naiser's eyebrow lifted. "Terra Nova wasn't a *real* war zone?"

"The vast majority of the antiaircraft weapons on the surface were older than the colony itself," Stephen said. He had no idea why *anyone* had shipped such primitive weapons to Terra Nova, although he did have to admit that one could be killed by a slingshot as easily as by a laser. "Their tracking systems were poor and their reaction time was weak. I think their crews were poorly trained, if they were trained at all. But a modern air-defence zone will be a far tougher target."

He met the First Space Lord's eyes. "The *concept* behind the Tornados is a fine one, sir," he said. "And yes, I agree we need it. But I don't think the tech has caught up with the requirement just yet. In space or in the air, the Tornados are going to take heavy losses."

Naiser grimaced. He'd been a starfighter pilot, Stephen recalled, before transferring to command track. He wouldn't take the concept of starfighter losses lightly. Starfighter pilots might be deemed expendable, on the grounds that starfighters were cheaper than starships, but no one was particularly happy with it. Anything that helped keep British pilots alive while making enemy pilots dead would be warmly welcomed.

"I see," Naiser said. "The politicians are not going to be pleased."

"No, sir," Stephen agreed.

It was hard to keep his face expressionless. He hadn't been privy to the high-level discussions between Britain, America and France, but he knew a lot was riding on the Tornado program. A failure that brought down the joint project would have embarrassing diplomatic repercussions, although that would be preferable to heavy losses in wartime. The Royal Navy couldn't afford to find itself unprepared for a sustained period of high-intensity combat. They knew how close they'd come to complete disaster in the First Interstellar War.

"But that is my problem, not yours," the First Space Lord added. He tapped his terminal. A holographic image sprung into existence, floating over the desk. "What do you make of this?"

Stephen frowned. He wasn't sure *what* to make of it. It *looked* like a deep-space tracking report, perhaps an image taken from an optical sensor that had been reprocessed for a holographic display, but...he felt his frown deepen as he puzzled it out. Something moving in deep space...*very* deep space? A rogue settlement? Or something more unusual?

He looked up. "Sir?"

The First Space Lord's voice was very crisp. "Two weeks ago, long-range sensors on Wensleydale Station detected an extremely powerful fusion burn at the very edge of the system. They instantly focused all their monitoring gear on the burn and discovered a starship—an STL starship—reducing speed before it entered the system. The latest projections are that it will reach Wensleydale in two and a half months, assuming they don't have drive fields."

Stephen stared at him. "An STL ship?"

"Yes," Naiser said. "According to our readings—you can download the full report for yourself later—the ship is over a hundred kilometres long, big enough to carry over a million people. So far, there has been no attempt to communicate—as far as we know, of course."

"Yes, sir," Stephen said, automatically. Wensleydale was a *long* way away, right on the edge of the Human Sphere. It would take two weeks to get a message from Earth to Wensleydale even with the flicker network. Events might have moved on. "If it's an STL ship...they don't know about the tramlines?"

"It's possible," Naiser agreed. "We've seen nothing suggesting any understanding of gravity technology at all. But they may just have been very unlucky and evolved in a system where there were *no* tramlines."

"I thought that was impossible," Stephen said.

"Very little is completely impossible," Naiser reminded him. "There *are* star systems that are functionally inaccessible, at least until we find a link between our tramline network and theirs. But these are questions that can only be asked and answered once we make contact with our new visitors."

Stephen studied the image for a long moment. He'd heard plenty of *stories* about life on an STL colony ship, but he'd never seen one. The brief period when humanity had launched converted asteroids into the interstellar void had ended when the first tramline had been discovered, over a century ago. Why spend hundreds of years in transit when you could just jump through the tramline? Whoever had launched that ship into interstellar space had to be brave...or desperate.

His eyes narrowed. "They're not visitors, sir," he said. "They're colonists."

"That's the majority viewpoint, down in the analysis office," Naiser said, jerking a finger down at the deck. "There's a very good chance they don't know that we got to Wensleydale first, Captain. They may not even have the *concept* of alien life. There certainly haven't been any radio signals spilling out from Wensleydale, telling the universe that the planet is inhabited. They're in for a surprise."

He looked up. "There's no sign that they have any particularly advanced technology," he added, slowly. "However, the government would like to make sure that we are in a position to stomp on them if they are hostile."

"Yes, sir," Stephen said. "It seems hard to believe that they come to us in the spirit of war and hostility, though."

He frowned. He found it hard to imagine interstellar warfare *without* the tramlines. Even with modern technology, it would take fifteen years to get a ship from Earth to the nearest star...assuming the drive nodes didn't burn out during the voyage. Fifteen years...and another five for Earth to find out what had happened to the invasion fleet. There was no way an STL ship could match the resources of an entire star system. The logistics would be horrific and the costs would be nightmarish. He couldn't imagine Parliament okaying the expense.

"An ounce of prevention is better than an pound of cure," Naiser said. "Given the...ah...political situation at the moment, it has been deemed that a small flotilla of ships will be dispatched to Wensleydale and make first contact. *Invincible* will be lead ship of Task Force Leinster"—his lips twitched—"as you may already have guessed. Ideally, you'll make peaceful contact and find out what they want before they reach our settled worlds. If not...give them hell."

"If possible," Stephen said. It was *vaguely* possible that the aliens might have preferred a fusion drive for crossing the interstellar void. Slow it might be, but it would be a great deal more reliable than drive fields. And *that* meant the alien ship might be a supersized carrier, ferrying capital ships from star to star. How many *Invincible*-sized ships could he fit into such a hull? "They may have everything we have, save for the tramlines."

"It's a possibility," Naiser agreed. "A team of analysts dug up an old book series that featured something along those lines."

He smiled, rather wanly. "But every one of *our* plans to build a hundred-kilometre-long carrier foundered in the face of political opposition."

"Yes, sir," Stephen said.

"We're assembling the rest of the flotilla now," Naiser informed him. "You and your crew should have at least a week of shore leave before preparations start in earnest, although I'm afraid the remainder of the promised leave is going to have to be cut short. We'll be the lead power, as the system is ours, but diplomats are currently talking to the other powers about sending representatives. You may find yourself accompanied by a Chinese or Russian starship."

Stephen winced. "*That* could be awkward."

"I expect you to be professional," Naiser said, firmly. "The diplomats will sort out the mess on Terra Nova."

"Sir, I lost good men on the surface," Stephen said. "If one of the Great Powers was backing the insurgents..."

Naiser held up a hand. "I understand the problem," he said. "*However,* I also understand that it may be difficult to prove it, let alone demand recompense. China is *not* a warlord state in the middle of nowhere. We cannot bomb them back to the Stone Age without retaliation, even if we had solid proof that a Chinese intelligence officer gave the order to target your people deliberately. And we do *not* have that proof! The Chinese can simply claim that your men ran into insurgents and it will be impossible to prove them wrong."

He shrugged. "They may even insist that they killed the insurgents for us, during their bombardment. And they may be right."

"Someone *was* selling advanced technology to the insurgents, sir," Stephen said. He clamped down, hard, on his anger. "We have proof of *that*."

"Not enough to point the finger at anyone," Naiser told him. He made a face. "As much as we hate to admit it, Captain, a *lot* of technology has leaked over the past ten years. The Great Powers are not in a position to keep the lesser powers from innovating, let alone the Belt and the other independent settlements. It's quite possible that the Chinese didn't sell any advanced tech."

Stephen met his eyes. "Do you believe that, sir?"

Naiser looked back at him, evenly. "No," he said. "But being *sure* of something isn't enough to satisfy a court of law. The World Court will take the coward's way out, Captain, and declare the charges unproven. And even if they didn't...the Chinese would pay compensation or refuse to accept the verdict, which would force us to either *make* them accept the verdict or let them get away with it. I don't think the politicians *want* to risk opening that particular can of worms when there's a general election coming up."

"Yes, sir," Stephen said. He looked down. "I'm just not...I'm just not very happy with it."

"None of us are," Naiser said. "Life was a great deal simpler when I was on *Warspite's* bridge, and we were sneaking up on the Indian carrier, even though I knew *precisely* how poor our chances of survival were if the Indians saw us. Now..."

He shook his head. "But that's not something we need to worry about, not right now," he said. "You have *alien* concerns."

"Yes, sir," Stephen said.

"It's funny how...*blasé* we've become about alien life," Naiser added, after a moment. "I was a young man when the Tadpoles announced them-selves by attacking Vera Cruz. We were all shocked, back then. We'd encountered aliens and they were hostile. And then...we encountered the

Vesy, who were no threat to us, and the Foxes, who very definitely *were* a threat. The entire galaxy suddenly seems to be teeming with life. And politicians look at this"—he nodded to the display—"and feel nothing, because they have problems at home."

"It'll take us at least a month to reach Wensleydale," Stephen observed. "And, without the tramlines, there's no way the newcomers can reach Sol before we find a way of dealing with them. The politicians probably don't see any danger."

"No, they don't," Naiser agreed. "And that may not be a good thing. They may be settlers, some alien counterpart to the Belters who fled Sol a hundred years ago, or they may be fleeing something worse. The Foxes did it, didn't they? They fled their original home system. The analysts have come up with all sorts of possibilities. One of them involves the aliens running from a greater threat, one that *does* use the tramlines."

Stephen considered it. "That ship must have been in transit for generations," he said. It was hard to imagine. His longest deployment had never taken him out of contact with the rest of humanity. Even someone assigned to a remote base would still be able to send and receive messages. "Surely, anyone following them—anyone who did have access to the tramlines—would have crossed our path by now."

"Perhaps," Naiser said. "Or perhaps they didn't think there was any reason to push further towards us. They might not have suspected our existence. We were planning, originally, to expand further in their direction, but we wasted a decade because we had to fortify the systems between Earth and Tadpole Prime. First Contact with the Foxes and the Indian War only made it harder to return to pure expansion. They may have had similar problems."

He smiled. "Or we may be completely wrong," he added. "And the newcomers are nothing more than simple colonists."

"Yes, sir," Stephen said. STL colonists, at least, wouldn't be *dangerous*. But they would bring other issues in their wake. "Sir...what if they want the planet?"

Naiser sighed, heavily. "That's a political issue," he said. "On one hand, it isn't as if we *need* Wensleydale. We have nine other planets in various stages of development. But, on the other hand, we can't be seen to abandon our claim too easily. They'd need to offer us something in exchange for the planet and...well, what do they have? Perhaps nothing, Captain."

"But they don't have anywhere else to go," Stephen pointed out. "They may not even be *able* to go."

"Perhaps not," Naiser agreed. "I don't mind admitting, Captain, that this could cause all sorts of political problems. There will be people who will insist that we got there first, which is true, while there will also be others who will claim that ordering STL colonists back into interstellar space at gunpoint is wrong. That will bring the people who will drag up historical precedent out of the woodwork; they will insist that allowing immigration from alien societies will cause all sorts of problems, even though the newcomers will be restricted to a single planet..."

He shrugged. "And all of this may be academic, seeing we don't know what is heading towards us," he concluded. "Captain, whatever happens, I expect you and your crew to handle it in the finest traditions of the Royal Navy."

"Yes, sir," Stephen said. It was a challenge, but...it was one he could handle. A peaceful First Contact would look good on his resume, particularly as there hadn't *been* a peaceful first contact in human history. At worst, if the aliens *did* turn out to be hostile, they could lay down covering fire long enough to get the civilians out. "We won't let you down."

"I have no doubt of it," Naiser said. "Dismissed."

CHAPTER NINE

ALICE CHANGED INTO a standard uniform before leaving the spaceport.

It was something she didn't care to do, but there was no choice. The days when British servicemen had been scared—or forbidden—to wear their uniforms on the streets were long gone, along with the terrorists and traitors who'd thought themselves above the law, yet *someone* would notice she was wearing a Royal Marine uniform and call the police. She had a perfect right to wear it, as the police could easily confirm, but it wasn't worth the hassle of explaining herself again and again. Too many people believed that any woman wearing a marine uniform had to be a Walt.

She took the monorail south to Tunbridge Wells, then hired a manual car and drove down the motorway to Mayfield. There were some very definite advantages to wearing a uniform—servicemen always had priority, even when they were off-duty—but she would have preferred not to attract attention. She'd been asked, more than once, to speak at her old school about life in the military, yet she'd turned every request down. She just didn't want the attention it would have brought her. And besides, if she'd told the young kids the truth, *none* of them would have wanted to join the marines.

The three-lane motorway was crowded, but the lane reserved for manual vehicles was nearly empty. Alice couldn't help a sniff of contempt for the civilians, utterly dependent on computers to drive them from place to place. Had they forgotten the lessons of the Longest Night so quickly? How many people had wound up stranded because the traffic control network had simply deactivated their cars when the aliens attacked Earth? It was safe enough, she had been told, as long as the system remained foolproof. But, in her experience, there were a number of very ingenious fools. It was just a matter of time before someone hacked the system and caused havoc.

And it might be someone from the other side of the world, she thought, as she drove onto the slip road. The automatic cars recognised that she was driving a manual and gave her plenty of room, something that irritated more than pleased her. *There are plenty of links between Britain and the global datanet these days.*

She pushed the thought out of her mind as she took a turning onto a country road and slowly drove down it, watching for tractors and small vans. It was hard to believe that the road was new, even though it was lined with hedgerows that made it difficult to see the farmlands on the other side. But the entire region had been devastated after the alien bombardment. The tidal waves might not have made it so far north, but the rain had caused floods which had done no end of damage. It had been sheer luck, Alice knew, that her grandparents had survived. Their home had been designed for a different era, but they hadn't predicted such great floods.

The gate was firmly closed and locked. Alice pulled up beside the gate and climbed out, digging through her pockets for the key. Her grandparents hadn't held with newfangled biometric locks, even though the technology had entered the mainstream long before *they'd* been toddlers. Instead, they used a padlock that could have come from a hundred years in the past—or Terra Nova. Alice opened the lock and the gate, then drove the car through before closing the gate behind her. There was no sign of Jeanette. Alice wasn't surprised. Her older sister would be late for her own funeral.

Which isn't such a bad thing, Alice thought, as she looked up at the farmhouse. *She wouldn't want to die too soon.*

She sucked in her breath, feeling a confusing mix of emotions. Her maternal grandparents hadn't *really* been farmers, even though they'd owned a farm. They'd quietly let most of the fields go fallow, save for a couple they'd turned into herbal gardens. They *had* offered to give the farm to their daughter—and her husband—but that had come to nothing. Alice couldn't help wondering, as she walked around the old building, just how different her life would have been if her father had tried to work the farm. He would certainly have been around a lot more.

It would have been a fine place to grow up, she thought, if a shadow hadn't hung over their lives. She'd enjoyed running and playing in the fields—and helping her grandmother to potter around the farmhouse, fiddling with little things for the sake of fiddling—but she'd always known it could never last. And then she'd been sent away to boarding school...she shook her head. She didn't really blame her grandparents, but...she did. They hadn't been able to cope as Alice grew into her teens.

She heard the sound of an engine behind her, but paid it no heed. Hardly anyone came to the farmhouse, save for Alice and her sister. If it wasn't Jeanette...she'd see, soon enough. It was the sort of region where everyone kept everyone else's business, something she liked and detested in equal measure. The person who came to check on her grandparents after the rainstorms might also be spreading gossip to the neighbourhood. Alice hadn't needed the marines to teach her about OPSEC. She'd learnt that growing up in the countryside.

The grave stood in the centre of the overgrown flower garden, the memorial stone half-hidden under a dozen different types of flowers. Her grandmother had been exceedingly pleased with her roses, growing several different types in hopes of creating a new variety for herself. She'd never succeeded, but she *had* created a unique resting place for her daughter's body. Alice felt a tear prickling at the corner of her eye and brushed it away, sharply. She was not going to cry. Not now.

Her hand dropped to her holster as she heard footsteps crunching around the house. She turned slowly, readying herself for trouble. The countryside was safer than the city, she knew, but it was also harder to get help. Quite a few crimes had gone undetected for years because the police were a very long way away. Farmers carried guns to protect themselves because they knew no one else would do the job.

Jeanette walked around the corner, her high heels crunching oddly on the rocky path. Alice nodded to herself and let go of the gun, hoping that Jeanette hadn't noticed. Their relationship was difficult enough without her sister realising that Alice had been ready to draw the gun if necessary. But then, Jeanette hadn't shown any interest in the Combined Cadet Force, let alone a military career. She had gone straight into business, then marriage...

She was lucky to avoid conscription, Alice thought, remembering the handful of conscripts she'd seen on the monorail. *But at least she found a job she wanted and a guy she liked.*

"Alice," Jeanette said. She sounded more of a Londoner than ever. "Did you have a good flight?"

Alice studied her sister for a long moment. Jeanette was tall and thin, wearing a suit that was carefully tailored to show off her figure—and her long red hair—without actually revealing anything below the neckline. Her face was strikingly feminine, but—at the same time—there was something businesslike about it. Alice had no idea why Jeanette had chosen to wear high heels—it wasn't as if this was her first visit to the farm—yet she had to admit that Jeanette made them work. Perhaps she'd had to drive down from London herself.

"I had the usual Military Airlines experience," Alice said, finally. There were times when she wondered what Jeanette thought her sister actually *did*. Alice hadn't *lied* to her, but...her words just seemed to slip into one of Jeanette's ears and come out the other. "Cramped, smelly and bumpy."

"Ouch," Jeanette said. She looked past Alice. "Is the grave okay?"

"Yeah," Alice said. It had often struck her as odd that Jeanette, who was older than her by five years, seemed to be more accepting of their mother's death. Alice herself had been a great deal younger at the time. "No one desecrated it."

She turned back to the grave, smiling in relief. Their mother had committed adultery, which was bad enough, but cheating on a serviceman was worse. The local pastor had refused to bury her, despite an offer of a substantial bribe. Alice's grandparents had had to bury their daughter within their lands, knowing that some drunken idiot might decide to express his patriotism by trying to desecrate the grave. Hardly anyone knew that Judith Campbell was buried at the farm and that was how it needed to stay.

I'm sorry, Mum, she thought, as she looked at the grave. *I wish...*

Jeanette let out a long sigh. "I'll go put the kettle on," she said. "Come inside when you're done."

Alice glowered at her retreating back, then turned her attention to the grave. It wasn't fair, somehow, that her memories were patchy as hell. Judith Campbell had been pretty enough, but...how many of her memories were real and how many came from photographs and videos her grandparents had shown her before their deaths? She had never really known her mother, not really. Her grandmother and the school matron had been more motherly to her than her *biological* mother. But then, her mother was dead.

She didn't abandon us, she told herself, firmly. *She was murdered.*

It was a bitter thought. She'd seen young men torn apart by 'Dear John' letters, young men who'd done nothing to deserve their sweethearts finding someone else while they'd been on deployment. And she'd been dumped herself...*that* had hurt too, more than she cared to admit. And yet... it didn't excuse murder. Her father could have divorced his wife, cutting her off without a penny to her name. Instead, he'd killed her.

And destroyed his life and career at the same time, she reminded herself. It seemed hugely unfair that her father should be cursed as an irredeemable monster and feted as a hero in the same breath. To the public, he was a hero; to Alice, he was the father who'd betrayed her and her sister. *If the war hadn't broken out...*

She rose slowly, taking one last look at the grave. It was sheer luck she'd been able to make it, after word had come down from on high. Shore leave hadn't been cancelled, but it *had* been sharply reduced. She wouldn't have time to paint the town red or do anything *fun*...she shook her head as she turned and walked back to the house. It wasn't as if she'd been planning a trip to Sin City in any case.

The house felt eerie as she stepped inside. Her grandparents had turned it into a monument to themselves, lining one wall with bookshelves and another with shelves holding dozens of trinkets from their global wanderings. They really had been quite wealthy—and lucky. If they'd been a little closer to the coast, they would probably have lost everything when the waters rose sharply. As it was, their home had escaped serious damage. Her hand twitched as she heard someone moving in the kitchen, even though she knew it was only Jeanette. It was suddenly very hard to escape the sense that her grandmother was in the very next room...

Jeanette walked into the living room, holding a mug of tea. "Here," she said, passing it to Alice and turning back to recover her own. "It's just the way you like it."

"Thanks," Alice said. She didn't have the heart to tell her sister that she'd grown used to military tea over the last decade. Civilian tea always tasted a little weak. "I...how have you been?"

"Well enough," Jeanette said. She sat down on the sofa, crossing her long legs. "Alex is getting a promotion, so he's been working extra hours...not good for Christopher or Clive, I fear. But it will be worth it."

Alice nodded, shortly. She'd never really approved of Alex—her sister's husband had always given her the impression that he was looking down his nose at her—but she had to admit that he was nothing like their father. And besides, Jeanette's sons had always been pleased to see him when he came home. Alice thought that was a good sign. They were usually pleased to see her too.

"And yourself?" Jeanette asked. "Shuffled any good pieces of paper lately?"

"In a manner of speaking," Alice said, dryly. Did she *look* like a paper-pusher? "I've been having some good times and some bad ones. I was on Terra Nova when the shit hit the fan."

Jeanette didn't look impressed. "And was it as bad as the media made it sound?"

"Oh, *probably*," Alice said. She'd caught a couple of media shows during the flight to London. Their basic take seemed to be that everyone on Terra Nova deserved the thrashing the Chinese were handing out to them. "It was pretty bad."

"I'm sure you were safely on base," Jeanette said. "You could have been in the embassies instead."

Alice opened her mouth to make a sharp reply, then thought better of it. "Yeah," she said, instead. "I could have been in the embassies instead."

They sat together for a long moment, drinking their tea. It was hard to believe, sometimes, that they were sisters. Jeanette had rejected the military entirely, while Alice had embraced it. They didn't even look alike. But then, they never had. Alice took after their father, while Jeanette looked more like their mother. No wonder, the dark part of her mind muttered, that their grandparents had liked Jeanette more.

"I heard from Dad," Jeanette said, softly. "He's still in the Belt."

Alice felt her fingers tighten around the cup. She loved her father and she hated him. She understood him and yet she couldn't forgive him. And... she wanted to hug him and she wanted to kill him. Their grandparents had stopped trying to force her to visit her father, after he was released from hospital. Alice would have been happier—so much happier—if their father had died in the war. She could have mourned him and then got on with her life.

"Fine," she said. She knew she sounded like a petulant teenager, but she didn't particularly care. "And what is he and that...hussy...doing in the Belt?"

"Running a ship, it seems," Jeanette said. "He wants to see us."

"No," Alice said, flatly. "Go see him yourself, if you want. I'm not going to see him."

Jeanette met her eyes. "He's your—our—father."

"He murdered our mother," Alice reminded her. Her voice hardened. It had taken a long time for the truth to sink in, but when it had sunk in she had resolved never to forget. "And I do not forgive."

They stared at each other for a long moment. Alice had never really understood why Jeanette had been so attached to their father, not after he'd killed their mother. Perhaps Jeanette was old enough to imprint on him, to see him as a father figure in fact as well as name, while Alice had been too young. *Her* father figures had been the Cadet Force Colonel and, later, her sergeants. She was damned if she was embracing a murderer. Bio-dad he might be, but he wasn't her *father*. Not in any way she cared to recognise.

"He wants to see us both," Jeanette said. "Alice..."

"No," Alice repeated. "I wouldn't go even if he was offering us a million-pound legacy in his will. And you shouldn't go either."

"He'll be down here," Jeanette said. Her voice grew challenging. "Or are you scared of meeting him?"

Alice swallowed several nasty retorts. Jeanette had always been able to get under her skin, even after going through basic training. It seemed to be a common superpower for elder siblings. Jeanette could probably remember Alice in diapers. She'd certainly helped look after her younger sister when the shit had hit the fan.

And yet, meeting Jeanette brings out the child in me, Alice thought. She'd endured far worse insults from her fellow boots during training, but Jeanette irritated her in ways none of them had been able to match. *She makes me be immature again.*

"He killed our mother," she reminded Jeanette. "So no, I am not going to go."

Jeanette let out a heavy sigh. "As you wish," she said. "When do you have to be back in space?"

"Tuesday," Alice said. She didn't really have any plans for the next couple of days. Sign in at one of the transit barracks, perhaps, or find a hotel in Central London. It would be pricy, but it would be worth it just to be away from the others for a little bit. "I was just going to stay in London."

"Then come back for dinner with me," Jeanette said. "I can drop you off at the spaceport on Tuesday, if you like."

Alice hesitated. It would be nice to see her young nephews again—and make sure Alex was treating Jeanette all right—but...she wasn't sure she wanted to spend any more time with *Jeanette*. She simply couldn't take very much of her sister without wanting to scream—or worse. But she couldn't politely back out either.

"If you'll have me," she said, finally.

"Of course I'll have you," Jeanette said. She took the empty mug and stood. "You're my sister."

"I know." Alice stood. She'd have to check upstairs before they closed the farmhouse down again. The building had looked undisturbed, but it was well to be sure. "You never let me forget it."

CHAPTER TEN

"IT SEEMS THAT THE SYSTEM gets busier every month," Commander Daniel Newcomb commented, as he took a sip of his tea. The holographic display showed hundreds of starships leaving Earth and heading to the tramlines. "How many colonist-carriers are we flying now?"

"Two hundred, I believe," Major Henry Parkinson said. He sprawled on the sofa, somehow managing to look alert even when technically off-duty. "Each one carries upwards of a hundred-thousand colonists."

"And Britannia has plenty of space for them," Stephen said. He dismissed the steward with a nod, then glanced around the Ready Room. "Have you read the briefing notes?"

"Yes, sir," Newcomb said. "An STL ship...pretty fascinating, if you ask me."

"And also potentially dangerous," Parkinson said. "Their tech may be crude, but that won't stop it being lethal."

"They're not going to be *hostile*, not if they've crossed dozens of light years to reach us," Newcomb said. "And if they are...a single missile will cripple that ship."

"Or so we believe," Parkinson said. He looked at Stephen. "They may not have the tramlines, sir, but that doesn't mean they're not dangerous."

Stephen nodded. "We'll be very careful," he agreed. "And besides, something could be chasing them."

"Perhaps," Newcomb said. "But really...I don't know *what* those analysts were smoking."

Stephen was tempted to agree. The analysts had managed to put together so many possible scenarios that he was inclined to wonder if they were paid by the word, particularly as there was so little hard data. If the aliens really *weren't* that advanced, they'd reasoned, it wouldn't be hard to establish communications...but the mere sight of *Invincible* and the rest of the flotilla might cause a staggering culture shock. The newcomers were far more advanced than the Vesy, the analysts had pointed out, yet they would still find it hard to come to grips with the concept of *one* star-spanning race, let alone four. It would be tricky to tell them that they had to find another planet.

And then there were the *other* scenarios, where the aliens possessed equal technology—save for the tramlines—or even superior technology. If they were friendly, they'd have something to trade...but if they weren't friendly, they would become an instant threat. And even if they *were* inclined to be peaceful, the analysts had pointed out, they might feel pressured into waging war on humanity anyway. There weren't any other habitable planets within reach.

At least their reach, Stephen told himself. *And that will last until they develop or reverse-engineer the Puller Drive for themselves.*

He held up a hand. "There's no way to know what we'll face, so we'll prepare for the worst while hoping for the best," he said. "The more serious matter, right now, is preparing the ship for departure. Mr. XO?"

Newcomb steepled his fingers. "Ship-wise, we have a handful of components that need replaced, but nothing serious. Ted"—Chief Engineer Theodore Rutgers—"implemented the program as soon as we entered orbit, so I'm hopeful that it will be completed in the next couple of days. Replenishing our expended ammunition is also underway. I have no doubt that we will be ready to depart on schedule.

"Morale-wise, things could be better. Obviously, the crew was anticipating a month of doing bugger-all on shore leave, so the announcement that there would only be a few days of staggered leave didn't please them. I don't think it will go beyond grumbling, Captain, but there *will* be grumbling."

"Which is better left ignored unless it gets out of hand," Parkinson said. "I'm sure the crew will not let their feelings interfere with their professionalism."

"We can operate on reduced crews for a week as we travel to Wensleydale," Stephen said, seriously. "It won't be much, but it will be *something.*"

"Yes, sir," Newcomb said. "I've given orders to prepare the guest cabins for the ambassador and his staff. They should be ready for his arrival."

Parkinson frowned. "Not Ambassador Crichton, I hope."

"The government hasn't picked an ambassador yet," Stephen said. "I don't think it'll be anyone assigned to Terra Nova, though."

"They'd want a xenospecialist," Newcomb agreed. "Prince Henry has retired now, hasn't he?"

"I believe so," Parkinson said.

"We'll also be taking a staff of xenospecialists and contact crews," Stephen reminded them, dryly. "Make sure there are quarters for them too. Turn out a couple of the labs if necessary so they have space to work."

"Aye, sir," Newcomb said. "I'll check the biohazard seals too. Ideally, we'd seal off the entire section—or put the bio-labs on another ship—but that might not be possible. Perhaps we should go through the biological warfare drills again, too. I don't want to risk someone opening the wrong door by accident."

"Good thinking," Stephen said. He looked at Parkinson. "Do you see any security issues?"

"It depends," Parkinson said. "If the contact team is entirely British, then no. I wouldn't expect them to cause problems. But if we have to take representatives from another power or two onboard...well, I'd expect them to include a spy in their ranks. And that could be awkward."

"Make sure they stay out of the classified sections," Stephen ordered. A civilian might not be able to tell his handlers anything useful from a brief walk through the ship, but a trained spy might pick up on a minor detail that would allow his handlers to put the whole puzzle together. "If worse comes to worst, we can distract any spies who might be attached to the ship."

"Yes, sir," Parkinson said. "That said, we know nothing about alien capabilities. They may pose a threat, simply because we don't know what they can do. I would recommend extreme caution when—if—we invite them onboard ship."

"There's nothing to suggest they have some sort of superweapon capable of blowing us out of space with a single shot," Newcomb pointed out.

"There's nothing to suggest they *don't* have one either," Parkinson countered. "We know *nothing* about them, sir. For all we know, tramline shock kills them...but they still have everything else we have and more besides. It's my job to be paranoid."

"I understand," Stephen said. "We will take every precaution."

He looked at Newcomb. "Once we know how many ships are joining us, we'll start running some war games too," he added. "It's been too long since we fought side-by-side with the other Great Powers. We need to be ready in case the aliens *do* turn hostile."

"That will mean telling them too much about *our* capabilities," Parkinson said. "They *will* be keeping one eye on the brand new carrier..."

"They'll have seen too much at Terra Nova, anyway," Stephen said. He understood the concern—he even shared it—but there was no point in trying to hide what they could do. Any Great Power worthy of the name would have the records from Terra Nova by now. "And besides, if it does come down to a direct clash, they'll need to know what we can do."

"As long as it's a two-way street," Newcomb grumbled. He brightened. "But then, first contact! We'll get an entry in the history texts."

Stephen smiled. "As long as it doesn't come under the heading of *what not to do*," he said, dryly. "We'd better not count our chickens before they've hatched."

He sighed as yet another datapacket blinked up in his display. "I'll see you both later," he said, tiredly. The Admiralty never seemed to run out of reports and paperwork. No doubt he'd just been sent something else he had to read, yet had no practical relevance to him whatsoever. "Dismissed."

"Aye, sir," Parkinson said.

Stephen watched them go, then looked at his console. Five messages were waiting for him, three of them little more than junk. It would be worse, he told himself severely, when the media *finally* heard about the new aliens. An STL ship might not be as exciting as the prospect of war over Terra Nova, but still...he was surprised the news hadn't leaked yet. All the Great Powers knew about the alien ship now. *Someone* would have leaked it...

Be glad, he thought. *The last thing you need is the media peering over your shoulder.*

He frowned as he read the last two messages. One was from the First Space Lord, clearing him for a private briefing at the Admiralty in London. It puzzled him. The First Space Lord *knew* Stephen shouldn't be leaving his command, not for a flight to Earth. Nelson Base was only a shuttle flight away, if they needed to confer. The second message solved the mystery, but created a new one. His elder brother, Lord Shields, wanted a chat.

He must have convinced the First Space Lord to allow me to visit London, Stephen thought, crossly. He wasn't pleased. Duncan, Lord Shields, wasn't a bad person—or at least he didn't *mean* to be a bad person—but he *was* a major headache. Stephen's career had been both helped and hindered by his relationship to a senior member of the House of Lords. *And who knows what he wants to talk about?*

His fingers rested on the terminal for a long moment as he considered his options. There was no easy way to get out of it. He'd have to go to London anyway, for the briefing, which meant he'd have time afterwards to meet his brother. There would be no polite way to escape. And that meant...he cursed his brother under his breath. Duncan might have thought that leaning on the First Space Lord was a good idea, but it was *Stephen* who'd pay for it. If the First Space Lord thought that *Stephen* had requested the meeting...

"I can give him a piece of my mind, at least," Stephen muttered, as he tapped a quick acknowledgement into the terminal. "And then I can find out what he wants."

• • •

"It's a damn shame, what?"

Wing Commander Richard Redbird did his best to ignore the grumbling as his pilots returned to the squadron room and started to unpack. He didn't really blame them for grumbling, even though they'd been first on the list for a couple of days of shore leave. They'd been promised a whole month of glorious freedom after *Invincible* returned to Earth and the sudden change had been disorienting. At least one pilot had devised complicated travel arrangements that would let him see a whole string of girlfriends, one after the other, that had had to be cancelled on short notice. The bloodsucking travel firms had been understandably reluctant to return his money.

"Yeah," Monica said. "And I had a weekend of debauchery lined up."

Richard rolled his eyes. He doubted *Monica* had had any trouble finding company for the last two days. She was young, pretty and came with no strings attached...hell, none of the pilots would have had any trouble finding a date for the night. Their uniforms guaranteed a great deal of attention from men and women alike. London might not be Sin City—perish the thought—but it was hardly Dubai either.

"We should have stayed down there," Flight Lieutenant Ryan Loyn insisted. "No one would have noticed if we'd missed the flight back to the ship..."

Richard straightened up. "That will do," he said, in a tone that made them all snap to attention. "Or do you want to spend the rest of the afternoon cleaning the deck?"

His eyes moved from face to face, daring them to challenge him. One by one, they lowered their eyes. Richard didn't really blame them for grumbling—he wasn't very pleased himself- but there were limits. He wasn't sure what was going on—no one had bothered to tell him the *reason* for the sudden change of plans—yet the Old Man wouldn't have done it without a very good reason. Richard had had worse commanding officers.

"You knew what you were getting into when you signed up," he said, into the silence. "I know; you all had plans, plans that had to be altered or cancelled on short notice. But being in the military sometimes means that your plans have to be changed at short notice. Two days of shore leave are better than none."

He made a show of looking displeased. "So tell me," he asked. "Are you mature and understanding young men and women...or are you just immature kids?"

Monica leaned forward. "I don't recall being told that I had to be *mature* when I joined the navy."

"I think it was taken for granted," Richard said, dryly. Starfighter pilots definitely weren't the most mature people in the navy, for sure. "Now, get ready for inspection at 1900. I don't want to see a single *sock* out of place."

He surveyed the squadron room with a growing feeling of dismay. If the inspection had been held now, the squadron would have been in hot water. Bags lay everywhere, their contents spilling out as his subordinates hastily changed into their shipsuits; pieces of loose clothing were scattered on the deck, ranging from a dress uniform shirt to a pair of knickers that someone had dropped while they changed. He reminded himself, once again, that he hadn't been much better when *he'd* been a lowly flying officer. His commanding officers had probably felt like booting him out the airlock too from time to time.

"Sir," Monica said. She started to undress as she talked. "What do *you* think it is?"

Richard shrugged. "They may expect us to go back to Terra Nova," he said. "Someone has to show the flag, if nothing else."

"But the Chinese are already in firm possession of the planet," Ryan said. "We'll need a handful of *fleet* carriers to evict them."

"Don't let the CO hear you say that," Richard advised. "I don't think we'll actually be waging war on the Chinese."

"Then why bother to show the flag?" Monica asked. She removed her shirt, then snapped her navy-issue bra into place. "They're not going to be intimidated if we're cruising around doing nothing."

"There are a few colonies in the outer system that'll need protection," Flight Lieutenant Anders Parham pointed out. "The Chinese will probably try to grab them if we're not in a position to intercept."

"Could be," Monica said. "But do we have a *commitment* to guard the system?"

"It doesn't matter," Ryan said. "Now the whole system is up for grabs... well, what you get is what you grab."

"Very philosophical," Monica said, dryly.

Richard tuned out the ensuing argument as he finished changing, then placed his knapsack in his drawer. The shore leave hadn't been *that* great. He'd met up with his girlfriend, only to be told that she'd found someone else...someone who was actually there for her on the weekends. Richard had stamped off in a rage, then found another girl in a bar who'd been quite happy to help him get over his ex. *She*, at least, hadn't expected much from him. It shouldn't really hurt, he told himself. God knew that most long-distance relationships ended badly.

But it does hurt, he thought. *It just isn't fair.*

He snorted at his own thought. It wasn't fair...that was a child's argument. A *toddler's* argument. Life wasn't fair. Only an idiot would believe otherwise. He was a starfighter pilot, after all: live fast, die young, leave an expanding cloud of vapour. The navy might have deemed him responsible enough to command other starfighter pilots in combat, but...he was still a starfighter pilot. He really shouldn't be thinking about anything *perma-nent* until his tour of duty came to an end.

Monica glanced at him. "More simulations tonight?"

"We'll start tomorrow morning," Richard said. He *still* had no idea why their shore leave had been so drastically curtailed, although he *was* fairly sure it wasn't an *immediate* emergency. The entire navy would have been placed on alert if an alien fleet from Andromeda had suddenly arrived in the Sol System and demanded to be taken to Earth's leader. "And yes, we'll be flying against simulated Chinese targets."

"I see," Monica said. She shot him a mischievous look. "Have you heard something?"

"No," Richard said. He doubted Britain and China would come to blows, unless there was an accident that turned into a shooting war. But the diplomats would surely pour water on the fire before the Solar Treaty disintegrated into war...surely? The Solar Treaty had survived the Anglo-Indian War, after all. It would survive a clash with China. "I just feel they're our most likely opponents right now."

Monica looked disappointed. "The odds favour a skirmish with China."

"You'd be better off saving your money," Richard advised. Betting was technically forbidden, but senior officers would turn a blind eye as long as it didn't get too far out of hand. "There's no way to know what we'll encounter."

He turned to survey the compartment. "Pick up your clothes," he said, raising his voice to be heard over the babble. "I want this floor so clean, this evening, that I could eat my dinner off it."

"Yes, Dad," Ryan said.

Richard gave him a sharp look. "And I want you all to be ready for training, tomorrow morning," he added. "If you brought anything you shouldn't have up from the surface, get rid of it. I do *not* want to find one of you out of his mind on dust or something equally obnoxious. Do I make myself clear?"

Ryan paled. "Yes, sir."

"Good," Richard said. He didn't care what his subordinates did on shore leave, but they were back onboard ship now. If the inspection wound up embarrassing him, he'd take it out on them. "Get to work."

CHAPTER ELEVEN

AMBASSADOR TIARA O'NEIL knew, without a shadow of a doubt, that she was not what most reasonable people expected to see when they thought of an ambassador. She was short and slight, her dark hair cut in a fashion that made her look young for her age—and more than a little nerdy. Her slanted brown eyes told of a heritage that wasn't fully British, something that had given her some hard times at school; her spectacles, which she didn't really need, gave her an air of absent-mindedness. She was not a conventional ambassador. But, as an expert in human-alien contact, she was at the top of her field.

It wasn't a very big field, even though four alien races had been discovered over the past fifteen years. The vast majority of human ambassadors concentrated on mastering the skills needed to either negotiate with or dictate to the other human powers. Human-alien contact was a tricky field to master, full of pitfalls for the unwary. The aliens were different from humans, but they were different from each other too. One race's friendly greeting was another race's declaration of war. Tiara had cut her teeth on talking to the Tadpoles—humanity's first alien enemy and later ally—but she'd never been allowed to forget that the Tadpoles didn't have the same priorities as the other known races. It was sheer luck that the Tadpoles were well-aware of the limitations of the translation software. They made allowances for humans, just as humans made allowances for them. The Foxes were less forgiving.

She glanced down at her datapad as the shuttle docked with the carrier, fighting down a flicker of nervousness. The Tadpoles hadn't cared one jot for her appearance—all humans looked alike to them and vice versa—but the newcomers might expect someone who looked more formidable. Tiara was all too aware that she'd been chosen because she didn't present an obvious threat, yet there was no way to know what the *aliens* would consider an obvious threat. The Tadpoles might not be able to tell the difference between her and a genetically-enhanced super-soldier twice her size, but the Foxes would regard the latter as a very clear threat. For all she knew, the newcomers were going to think that humans smelt funny...or the mere act of wearing clothes was a sign of distrust. Tiara had attended enough naked discussions to know that they weren't a joke.

A hand touched her shoulder. "Madam Ambassador," Ken Walworth said. "We have arrived."

Tiara nodded and slowly unstrapped herself. The shuttle flight had been too long and too short; long enough for the truth to sink in, but too short for her to come to grips with the fact that *she* was now the designated speaker for humanity. Her datapad held a set of instructions that had—mostly—been hashed out while she was still in school, giving her a list of objectives that had to be accomplished before relations with the newcomers were normalised and a larger group of diplomats arrived. Some of them were fairly simple—she was to make sure that the newcomers didn't learn anything about the internal astrography of the Human Sphere before humanity was sure they could be trusted—and others were complex, likely to cause problems in the future. The Great Powers wanted to make sure the newcomers weren't carrying any biological hazards before open contact could begin. Tiara understood the logic, but she also understood that the newcomers weren't likely to be pleased. *She* wouldn't want to hand over biological data either.

She stood, slung her knapsack over her shoulder and slowly made her way to the hatch, silently thanking all the saints that she'd managed to make it clear she didn't want a welcoming party. The military did love its ceremonies, but she'd never been particularly comfortable, either as a participant or an observer. Besides, it was better to remember that she was the ambassador, not a military officer. She couldn't afford to start thinking of the military as the solution to everything when dealing with aliens of unknown power.

The gravity fluctuated, just slightly, as she stepped through the airlock. It wasn't bad, not compared to a couple of civilian ships she'd used in the Belt, but it was just bad enough to be a little disconcerting. She made a mental note to check her health bracelet later, just in case she needed medical intervention. Space had always discomforted her and she'd never been able to figure out why. It was more than a little frustrating, particularly as she would be expected to visit more alien homeworlds in the future. The thought of being a natural-born groundhog terrified her.

I suppose I could find work communicating with the Tadpole colony on Earth, she thought, wryly. She was a strong swimmer—it was a requirement for service on Tadpole Prime—and she could have gills spliced into her body, if she wanted to commit herself. *But that wouldn't be the same.*

"Madam Ambassador," a calm voice said. "Welcome onboard."

Tiara looked up, fighting down the surge of sudden panic at something *unexpected.* She knew better than to think the aliens would be understandable, but...she controlled as much as she could, just to make it easier to cope with the things she couldn't. The military would have understood that, she'd thought. But then, the ship's captain could hardly let her board without greeting her in some way. It would be taken as an insult. Tiara wouldn't care, but she knew her superiors *would.* The Foreign Office and the Ministry of Defence often spent more time engaged in bureaucratic infighting than doing their jobs.

"Thank you," she said, holding out a hand. "It's good to finally be on the move."

Captain Sir Stephen Shields was handsome, she supposed, in a bland kind of way. He'd probably had some genetic enhancements spliced into his DNA during his childhood, as he looked to be in his early twenties rather than his mid-thirties. Only a faint sense of *age*—something she couldn't quite put her finger on—spoilt the effect. His blond hair shone under the light, his uniform was clean and freshly-pressed...she couldn't help thinking that he might have stepped out of a recruiting poster and gone straight to work. And yet, there was something *common* about his looks. There was no point in being handsome if anyone could be handsome with a few hours in the rejuvenation tank.

"We'll be departing in two days," Captain Shields said, shaking her hand. His grip was firm, with none of the dominance games she'd seen from other officers. "Are you and your staff ready to depart?"

"The ambassadorial staff accompanied me," Tiara assured him. "I believe the xenospecialists will be boarding later today. At that point, we can depart."

She smiled up at him, hiding her amusement. A competent commanding officer would already know the answer to that question, although he might be interested in hearing *her* answer. She was a passenger onboard his ship, but a passenger with considerable authority...even though he was, by right and law, the ship's master. She'd read the briefing papers, time and time again. Captain Shields had practically unlimited authority while the ship was away from Earth. He could order the entire mission abandoned on a whim, if he wished.

"Perhaps we can convince the Admiralty to let us depart early," Captain Shields said. He gestured. A pair of crewmen appeared from a side hatch. "My crew will assist your staff to transfer your supplies to your suite. I'll show you to your cabin personally."

"As you wish, Captain," Tiara said, politely. The captain wanted to talk to her in private, obviously. She wasn't disposed to object. "It will be my pleasure."

She looked around with interest as Captain Shields led her down a long corridor. It wasn't the first time she'd been onboard a naval ship, but *Invincible* was considerably larger than the destroyer that had ferried her to Vesy or the courier boat that had transported her home from Tadpole Prime. *Invincible* was practically a city in her own right: hundreds of crewmen walked her decks, opening compartments in the bulkheads and carrying out tasks that were completely beyond her understanding. Captain Shields nodded politely to his crew as they passed, returning salutes or simply saying a few words. Tiara couldn't help wondering if he was showing off or merely taking the long way to her cabin. But then, his ship was *big*.

"We set aside this whole section for the diplomatic staff," Captain Shields said, as they passed through a large hatch. The interior looked very similar to the exterior corridors. "You have a private mess—ah, dining room—and a conference room as well as nine cabins. I'm afraid that some of your junior staff will have to double up."

"That's quite all right," Tiara assured him. "I did my fair share of hot-bunking when I was a junior too."

Captain Shields smiled, as if her words had reminded him of something. "We may be able to reassign space later, depending on how things shake out, but right now I'm afraid we have no choice."

Tiara nodded. She hadn't been lying when she'd told him she'd shared a bunk with her fellows, back when she'd been a junior herself. Comfort was important, as far as she was concerned, but it couldn't be allowed to overshadow the mission. Besides, there was very little comfort on Tadpole Prime. The heat pervaded everything. Going to work in bikinis and shorts had seemed normal. It hadn't been until she'd been promoted a couple of times that she'd become entitled to her own room.

They stopped in front of another hatch. The captain pressed his palm against the sensor, opening the door. "We've already entered your bio-print into the ship's systems," he said, as he led the way into the cabin. "You have permission to add users, then remove them yourself later if you wish. There are low-level security sensors within the suite, and the rest of the compartment. If you want privacy, you'll have to go to one of the privacy tubes."

Tiara nodded, unsurprised. There was very little privacy within an embassy and none whatsoever during a first contact mission. *Everything* was recorded, from diplomatic remarks at the dinner table to sly asides and vague remarks that might—might—allow future generations to put together an accurate picture of what had happened. The prospect of a first contact mission going horrifically wrong had terrified the diplomatic staff. Tiara didn't *like* the idea of her superiors watching everything she did, even when she was off-duty, but she was used to it. It was just part of the job.

"It would be better to remind everyone of that," she said, as she unslung her knapsack and dumped it on the deck. "Too many juniors make indiscreet remarks when they forget they're being recorded."

"Of course," Captain Shields said.

Tiara made a face. It was easy to forget, at least after the first few days. No one wanted to *think* about their superiors watching them, after all. But an indiscreet remark could end a career, if it was discovered by the wrong person. It didn't have to do any harm, either, to bring the wrath of the media down on the Foreign Office. Shit rolled downhill...and a junior who couldn't watch his mouth might find himself buried under a mountain before he realised what had gone wrong.

She looked around the cabin, silently admiring its smooth lines. The lounge was a combination of a comfortable sitting room and an office—there was a desk in the corner—while the bedroom was larger than she'd expected and the bathroom carefully arranged for maximum functionality. It was just like living in a hotel, although she expected there would be a slight lack of room service. She had a feeling she could get used to it.

"There's a coffeemaker in that cupboard," Captain Shields said. "And a handful of snacks in the drawers underneath. You can call the mess for food, if you like, although I'm afraid the quality isn't great. We won't be carrying fresh foodstuffs for very long."

Because it's going to be eaten very quickly, Tiara thought. *And then we'll be stuck eating reprocessed protein.*

She pushed the thought aside—wise spacers were careful not to think too much about where their food came from—and looked up at the captain. He looked back at her, evenly. She was fairly sure she would have pegged him for an aristocrat, even if he hadn't been knighted at some point in his career. There was a *confidence,* perhaps even an *arrogance,* about his movements that suggested he knew himself to be amongst the elite. It wasn't something she could allow herself to share. A mistake when dealing with humans was bad enough, but a mistake when dealing with aliens was far worse. The Foreign Office was dreading the day a simple diplomatic mistake led to all-out war with a race that possessed an insurmountable technological superiority.

"I am aware that we will probably be treading on each other's toes a bit," she said, keeping her voice calm. There was no point in putting on airs and graces, not when the captain outranked her. "However, please rest assured that I have no intention of making your job harder."

"I don't intend to make yours harder either," the captain answered, after a moment. He was *good* at keeping his face under control. She couldn't tell *how* he felt about her words. But then, someone who'd endured an aristocratic boarding school would be very good at self-control. "However, the safety of this ship and her crew are my first priority."

"I understand," Tiara assured him. "I have no doubt that you can handle whatever the newcomers throw at you."

The captain looked rueful. "It's what we don't know that'll kill us," he said. "If they're as primitive as they seem, by our standards, they won't pose any challenge to us. But if they have a secret weapon up their sleeves... well, we may be in for a surprise."

"They may not even wear sleeves," Tiara said, tossing the line out to see what the captain made of it. "They may not even wear clothes."

Captain Shields's lips twitched, as if he thought she'd made a weak joke. "The point remains, Madam Ambassador, that we have no idea what we're facing. Can we even *talk* to them?"

"My team is very practiced at developing communications and translation programs," Tiara assured him. She was fairly sure that just about *every* race would want to develop a way to communicate, if only to keep from having to fight a series of endless wars. Even the Tadpoles had managed to come up with a translation program, despite the glitches that still plagued the system. "We should be able to build up a common vocabulary unless they are truly alien."

"Which is the problem," Captain Shields said. "What if they are *truly* alien?"

He smiled, humourlessly. "What if they refuse to talk to us? Or simply *can't* talk to us? What if they just keep flying until they enter orbit and start landing settlers? At what point do we try to warn them off—with warning shots, if necessary?"

"Opening fire on someone is *also* a way to communicate," Tiara pointed out. "And they might reply in a much louder voice."

"If they *can* reply," Captain Shields countered. "Do we let them land on the planet—our planet? Or do we blow their ship apart to keep them from landing without permission?"

Tiara grimaced. Her orders were clear. Britain wasn't against allowing the newcomers to settle on Wensleydale, particularly if they had technology or something else that might prove useful to trade. *But* she also had orders to make sure the aliens didn't pose any real threat before they were allowed to land. If the aliens just kept moving towards the planet, what was she supposed to do? Let them land...or commit mass murder, perhaps even genocide? She didn't think she could live with herself, afterwards, if she gave the order to slaughter millions of helpless aliens.

Particularly if they don't have anywhere else to go, she thought, numbly. *Should we drive them back into interstellar space?*

"I think we will have to confront that when it happens," she said, carefully. "I find it hard to believe they're not going to want to talk to us."

"I hope you're right," the captain said. "If nothing else, they *will* be seeing starships performing impossible manoeuvres."

"Yes, Captain," Tiara said. "But if they don't have the concept of alien life, they may need time to get over the shock."

The Captain's wristcom bleeped. He lifted it to his ear, sending Tiara an apologetic look. She nodded in understanding, then turned her attention to the bathroom while he spoke quietly to whoever was on the far end. Technically, it was rude to allow someone to interrupt, but they *were* onboard a starship. The captain could never be out of contact with his crew.

"Thank you," the captain said. He keyed his wristcom, closing the connection. "Madam Ambassador?"

Tiara looked up. "Yes?"

"I've been called away," the captain said. "I probably won't be back for at least a day, but my XO will be happy to make sure you have everything you need. And we will have a formal dinner once we depart."

"Thank you, Captain," Tiara said. She disliked formal dinners—they were rarely nothing more than a few hours of awkwardness, where guests guarded their mouths so carefully that they rarely said anything at all— but they were unavoidable. Thankfully, there wouldn't be many foreign guests. "I look forward to it."

CHAPTER TWELVE

"YOU TOOK YOUR TIME," Duncan Shields said, as Stephen was shown into the private dining room. "I was starting to think you'd jumped into a black hole."

Stephen sighed as he glanced around the room. It looked like an idealised hunting lodge, with a roaring fire, stuffed animals mounted over the mantelpiece and historical weapons hanging on the walls. The fact that very few of the club's members had ever hunted anything more dangerous than a fox, or that the club itself was situated in London and thus well away from the hunting fields, hadn't stopped the staff from turning it into a paean to an England that had never really existed. But then, the club's members believed in exclusivity. No one was allowed to pass through its doors unless they had a title, the older the better.

"Please, sit down," Duncan said. "It's been too long."

"Longer for you than for me," Stephen said. He sat down at the table, trying to conceal his annoyance. The briefing had been a pointless waste of time, covering nothing he hadn't already known. "You do realise that I'm very busy at the moment?"

"I believe you have a staff to handle the little details," Duncan said, in a languid voice that had never failed to get under his younger brother's skin. "You have a day before your planned departure date, do you not?"

"Unless it gets put back," Stephen said, tartly. "What do you *want*, Duncan?"

A waiter—a *human* waiter—materialised at his elbow before Duncan could say a word, holding out a pair of menus. Stephen took his and scanned it, somehow unsurprised to see that there was nothing that wasn't authentically English, save perhaps for a curry that might have originated somewhere in Britain. Fish and chips, steak and kidney pie, game stew and dumplings. It was a change from navy food, he supposed, but it came with a price. His brother hadn't pulled strings to get Stephen down to the surface for nothing.

"I'll have the roast lamb," he decided, handing the menu back to the waiter. "And a glass of water."

The waiter bowed, took Duncan's order and retreated. Stephen frowned, unsure if they were really in a secure environment. The staff would have been thoroughly vetted, of course, and they'd be in deep shit if they broke their NDAs, but that wouldn't be enough to stop word getting out if an opportunistic reporter managed to bribe the waiter. So much official business and backroom dealings were conducted in the club—and the dozen other such clubs—that a particularly cunning reporter might get the scoop of a lifetime. And even Duncan's position might not be enough to save him if the Prime Minister wanted a scalp.

"Politics has been quite interesting over the last few days," Duncan said. "I had to whip a couple of MPs to make sure they attended parliament."

"I hope you're talking figuratively," Stephen said, dryly. The thought of Duncan chasing the MPs with a real whip was amusing, but it could easily go too far. "Why didn't they want to attend?"

"They wanted to stay out of the discussions so they could switch sides, if necessary," Duncan said. He frowned as he took a sip of his glass. "They didn't want to commit themselves before they forced the PM to make concessions to the backbenchers."

"Ouch," Stephen said, dryly. "I'm glad *I'm* not the firstborn son."

Duncan scowled. "You benefited hugely from being the *second* son," he said. He pointed a finger at Stephen. "I'd suggest that you muted your complaints to a dull roar."

Stephen inclined his head, acknowledging the hit. He *had* been lucky. The second son went into the military, with the family name smoothing his path to command. And he *enjoyed* the military. He wasn't sure Duncan enjoyed playing politics in the House of Lords. But *someone* had to make sure the family's interests were protected.

And besides, he got most of the inheritance, Stephen thought, wryly. The family's possessions were entailed, passed down from Lord Shields to Lord Shields. *I only got a small amount of money and a name.*

"Very well," he said, flatly. "Let me ask again. What do you *want*?"

Duncan let out a heavy sigh. "Politics has been getting more than merely *interesting* over the last year or two," he said. "The government's majority has been cut to the bone recently, thanks to the defection of a couple of senior MPs. That means, Stephen, that one bad day could see the opposition forcing a vote of no confidence. And if the Prime Minister *loses* that vote of no confidence, we'll have another general election unless the political parties can hammer out a coalition to govern the nation until their term runs out."

"That's bad," Stephen said. "Why should *I* care?"

"Spending has been a major issue recently," Duncan said. "Do you know how much of the country's budget has been spent on the military over the last few years? Or the colonisation program? And it's happening at a time when the economy is entering a minor recession, which isn't good for our tax base. People are saying, Stephen, that perhaps it's time to cut back a little."

Stephen leaned forward, alarmed. "But we *need* the military."

"I agree," Duncan said. "Not least, I must admit, because the family owns a sizable percentage of the country's space-based industry. *However*, cracks in the edifice are finally starting to break open. The government approved emergency spending bills to pay for the reconstruction, as well as assisting the displaced persons to find transport to Britannia or one of the other colony worlds, but we're running out of ready cash. Right now, we're robbing Peter to pay Paul. The economy needs time to breathe."

He shook his head. "There was a proposal on the table for a warship holiday, an agreement between the Great Powers that none of us would build any new warship designs for five to ten years. We thought we could convince the minor powers to agree, if we offered a mixture of carrot and sticks. But this...this *thing* on Terra Nova, and the Chinese involvement, may have blown that proposal out of the water before it even got started."

"Good," Stephen said. "If we—humanity—stops building new ships, will the Tadpoles? Or the Foxes? Or...how long will it before we're suddenly outgunned?"

Duncan looked down at the table. "I know the risks," he said. "And the Prime Minister knows them too. But we *are* running out of money. It wasn't easy to get agreement on funding for the NGW program. The only reason we managed to get that through the gate was an understanding that elements of the program would be cleared for public release as soon as possible."

He shook his head. "That's why your mission to Wensleydale must not fail," he added. "We cannot afford another war."

Stephen frowned. His elder brother was a pompous ass, but Stephen had never doubted Duncan's political instincts. Duncan had been going to the House of Lords as an observer—and, later, as their father's assistant—for *years*. Duncan might be unimaginative, by Stephen's standards, but he was very far from stupid. He knew politics like the back of his hand.

"I see," he said. "Just how bad is it likely to be?"

"I don't know," Duncan said. "The extreme left-wing wants to scrap the navy, of course, but they won't get any support for *that*. I dare say the moderates will do everything in their power to push the extremists out before they have to stand for election, if there *is* a general election. However, even the moderate leftists want to make major budget cuts. The hell of it is that they have a point. In times of peace, the military is nothing more than a money sink."

"And, in times of war, the military is all that stands between you and death," Stephen said, quietly. "The Royal Navy is an insurance policy. If you don't need it, fine; if you do need it, you'll *really* need it.

"I know that," Duncan snapped. He made an effort to calm himself. "I dare say the Navy League will fight tooth and nail to prevent any budget cuts, particularly ones that dig into muscle and bone, but...funding may be cut to a great many programs. It was very hard to get permission to turn *Invincible's* conceptual outline into a complete design, let alone actually turn the plans into reality. Your ship may remain unique."

Stephen winced. "I thought there were plans to build five more *Invincibles*."

"That was before it was decided that it would be more cost-effective to budget for two fleet carriers and a lone battleship instead," Duncan said. "At least those are proven technologies, with all the glitches worked out. And believe me, Stephen, getting the funding for *those* was hellish."

"They're also harder to deploy," Stephen said, quietly. "And considerably more costly to replace."

"Yes," Duncan said. "Now tell me...how many people on the Naval Oversight Committee have actually served in the military? There are nine committee members"—he went on without waiting for an answer—"and only three of them have any actual military service. And only *one* of them was actually in the navy. And do you know what? They took what little they could get."

He sighed. "I'm telling you, Stephen," he said. "If the government loses its majority completely, expect massive and painful budget cuts."

"Shit," Stephen said. "I...fuck it."

The waiter returned before Duncan could reply, pushing a silver trolley into the room. Stephen's stomach rumbled at the smell of lamb, cooked to perfection and accompanied by roast potatoes, vegetables, a large jug of gravy and a jar of homemade mint sauce. The government might encourage people to cook carefully, recycling their leftovers into later meals, but the upper crust had never had to worry about *that*. Stephen rather suspected that the cooks and their staffs would take any leftovers home, rather than allow them to go to waste. It wasn't as if anyone was going to stop them.

"Just like we used to have at home," Duncan said. He quirked an eyebrow as the waiter withdrew, as silently as he'd come. "Do you miss it?"

Stephen shrugged. Growing up on the estate had been interesting, although his father had hired a succession of tutors who actually expected him to *learn*. He hadn't realised just how lucky he'd been until he'd gone to boarding school, where the teachers had all believed—quite firmly—that sparing the rod was spoiling the child. He'd done well at school, but it wasn't something he remembered with much fondness. His kids, assuming he ever had any, would be homeschooled.

And I could have been one of the poor bastards who lost everything after the war, he thought, slowly. *I was luckier than I realised at the time.*

"It had its moments," he said. "Do *you* miss it?"

Duncan snorted. "I think that Dad would have known what to do," he said. "Right now, all I can do is keep the party together and hope for the best."

"Quite," Stephen agreed. "Do you have any plans to become Prime Minister yourself?"

"There are times when I think I could do a better job," Duncan said. "And times when I feel I don't want to step any further into the spotlight."

Stephen nodded, curtly. They'd both been in the spotlight from birth, but their parents had been good about keeping the media away from the estate. Some poor aristocratic kids were expected to be miniature adults, growing up in a goldfish bowl as they were paraded around by their doting parents. He'd always felt there was something deeply weird about those children, as if they were both spoilt rotten and afraid to say or do anything that might upset listening ears. It was a relief that *he'd* never been expected to go in front of the camera and pretend to be normal.

"You probably could do a better job," Stephen said. "You'd have to put the title aside for a while, though."

Duncan made a rude sound. "I'd survive."

He shrugged. "Right now, Stephen, the navy *needs* something to boost its reputation before the next budget debate. Try not to fuck up."

Stephen nodded, curtly. "Is it really that bad?"

"Yes," Duncan said. He attacked his meat savagely for a long moment. "What were you doing when you heard about Vera Cruz?"

"I...I was probably standing outside the headmaster's office, waiting to be caned," Stephen said, after a moment's thought. He'd been going through a very bad adolescence. His tutors had used the cane frequently, but there were limits. If he hadn't been an aristocratic brat, he would probably have been expelled. "What about you?"

Duncan ignored the question. "Vera Cruz taught us that there were other intelligent races in the universe, Stephen, and that some of them were hostile. Billions of humans are killed before we managed to convince the Tadpoles to come to terms with us. Five or so years later, we cross swords with the Indians; five years after *that*, we stumble over another alien race that attacks us on sight. And so we are dragged into another war."

"We weren't exactly offered a choice," Stephen pointed out. "If we hadn't made a treaty with the Tadpoles..."

"Exactly," Duncan said. "And now we have *another* alien contact on the edge of explored space. There are people, people not more than a mile or two away, who are saying that perhaps it's time to *stop* expanding and consolidate our gains. That perhaps we should continue the settlement program, and fortify the tramlines, before we consider poking our noses into another anthill. And the hell of it is that they have a point. We came far too close to anarchy after the Longest Night. What if the *next* attack leaves Earth in ruins?"

"There's no reason to think the newcomers are hostile," Stephen said. His brother's words were more than a little disturbing. "We don't know *anything* about them."

"No, we don't," Duncan agreed. "But they're yet another factor that we can't afford to ignore."

Stephen took a piece of lamb, covered it with mint sauce and took a bite. It tasted heavenly.

"I see," he said, once he'd swallowed. "And what do you want me to do?"

"Don't fuck up," Duncan said. "Whatever it takes, Stephen. Don't fuck up."

"Fine," Stephen said. "I won't fuck up."

He met his brother's eyes. "Any luck on finding a suitable *debutante* for a wife?"

Duncan flushed. "Not as yet," he said. "It's hard to enter negotiations when you're so busy."

"You'd better get on with it," Stephen said. "You're what? Fifty?"

"I'm forty-one," Duncan snapped. "As you know perfectly well, baby brother."

Stephen smiled, although there was little real humour in the expression. Their parents had died shortly after the Longest Night, yet they'd both been adults at the time. Duncan had tried to be a father figure of sorts, but Stephen had been careful to draw boundaries to keep his elder brother from trying to overshadow him. It helped that Duncan had gone straight into the House of Lords while Stephen had joined the navy. They simply hadn't had much contact.

Although that didn't stop him from interfering in my career, Stephen reflected, as he finished his dinner. *And nothing I could say would deter him.*

He declined the offer of dessert and stood, collecting his coat from the doorman before striding out onto the streets of London. Duncan would have been quite happy to share his flat, at least for one night, or pay for a hotel, but Stephen saw no point in staying any longer than strictly necessary. No one would notice—or at least no one would make a fuss—if Stephen didn't head straight back to *Invincible*, yet Stephen himself would know. He'd disliked too many officers who'd been derelict in their duties to want to fall into the same pattern himself.

It was strange to see how *bright* London was, even after dark. The streetlamps were bright, driving back the shadows; thousands of revellers were pouring out of the theatres, chatting and laughing as they hailed cabs to go home or looked for somewhere to eat. Stephen couldn't help thinking that the crowd was *safe,* safe and happy. Central London was one of the safest places in the world, thanks to the military and the police. Did these people really want to throw it away?

He shivered. It didn't seem believable, but it was easy—all too easy— to forget that the world was red in tooth and claw. Mother Nature wasn't a soft, caring figure. The only thing allowing the civilians to sleep well was the presence of rough men, willing to visit violence on the enemies of civilisation. Winston Churchill, Stephen reflected as he hailed a cab himself, had known a thing or two. *And* he was nowhere near as controversial as Sir Charles Hanover. What could one say about a man who had been both good and evil?

A black cab pulled up beside him. Stephen stepped inside and sat down, hoping that the cabbie wasn't going to be in a chatty mood. London was the only city in Britain where the cabs were still driven by real humans, even though automation was much more efficient. It was tradition and tradition was not to be gainsaid, not by mere mortals. The cabs were part of London's charm.

The cabby's accent was so cockney that Stephen was *sure* it was an act. "Where to, sir?"

"Heathrow military spaceport, please," Stephen said. There were flights to Nelson Base, every hour on the hour. He could catch a shuttle from there that would take him back to his ship. "And don't spare the horses."

"Right you are, sir," the driver said. The cab hummed to life. "We'll be there before you know it."

CHAPTER THIRTEEN

"THEY'RE COMING THROUGH the bulkheads," someone snapped. The transmission fuzzed out in a hail of static. "Section nine-three-omega..."

Alice cursed under her breath as the transmission vanished again, this time for good. The enemy had landed on the hull and were trying to cut their way through...successfully, it seemed. She snapped her mask into place as she pounded down the corridor, snapping orders at her subordinates. An enemy boarding party could *not* be allowed to get comfortable, let alone start striking towards the bridge or main engineering. Or, for that matter, given time to set up a nuke. *Invincible* was tough, but even *she* would have trouble coping if a nuke detonated *inside* her armour.

She felt sweat trickling down her back as they stopped in front of a hatch and checked the telltales. There was atmosphere on the other side, apparently. She used hand signals to move the marines into position, ready to react if the enemy was waiting for them, then nodded to the sergeant. He opened the hatch, allowing them to see into the next compartment. It was empty. Alice breathed a sigh of mingled relief and disappointment, then led the marines forward. The enemy *had* to be close.

New alerts flashed up in front of her as the other squads hastily sealed off their sections, hopefully trapping the enemy within a relatively small section of the ship. Alice knew better than to take that for granted, if only because the enemy boarders knew *Invincible* as well as her crew. They could have made their way into the Jefferies Tubes by now, throwing themselves deeper into the ship before the hatches were closed. She'd long since given up wondering why the naval designers had ensured that the hatches could be opened relatively easy by someone with the right tools. Even the assurances that someone couldn't open a couple of hatches and vent the entire ship seemed hollow. *She* knew she could do a great deal of damage with a multitool and bad intentions.

"We're moving into Section nine-one-omega now," she said, as she reached the next hatch and paused. The marines fell into combat position, two of them readying stun grenades. "Going in hot."

She nodded to the sergeant, who keyed the switch. The hatch opened slowly, too slowly to suit her. Corporal Lewis lobbed a stun grenade under the hatch as soon as it was wide enough, the grenade detonating a second later. Flashes of blue light filled the corridor, just for a second. Her mask darkened automatically, keeping it from affecting her. She didn't presume to understand the theory behind the grenades, but she'd experienced their effects during training. An unprotected person who took the full brunt of the blast would be on the ground, twitching helplessly, for hours. Even catching a glimpse of the light could be thoroughly unpleasant.

The marines lunged forward, to be greeted by a hail of fire. Alice dropped to the deck, throwing a portable sensor ahead of her. The boarders had protective suits too! A handful of them were stumbling to the deck—they'd clearly caught at least *some* of the blast—but the others were unharmed. She shot one with grim efficiency, cursing the enemy under her breath. They'd secured a defensive point and made it theirs. *And* she didn't have time to dig them out the old-fashioned way.

"Fuck," Corporal Lewis snapped. "I'm hit!"

"Grenades," Alice ordered. There would be time to mourn later. If there *was* a later. "Clear the decks!"

She took cover behind the hatch, an instant before the grenades exploded. The enemy firing slacked off, sharply. Alice gritted her teeth, then ran forward. A dozen bodies lay in the corridor, all apparently dead. They'd taken the worst of the blast. Two more were in the nearest cabin, bending over...*something*. Alice shot them both, hoping it wouldn't trigger the nuke. If it *was* a nuke. She waved a portable sensor over the device, trying to figure out what it actually was. The sensor insisted that it was just a standard penetrator cutter. Alice didn't relax. Under the right circumstances, a cutter could make one hell of a weapon.

"Grabbed the other room, Captain," Sergeant Bert Radcliffe reported. "They had a nuke."

"Smash it," Alice snapped. There was no time for half-measures. If the enemy's superiors realised they'd been wiped out, they might try to trigger the nuke remotely. It was particularly ruthless, but understandable. "Do we have any prisoners?"

"I don't think so," Radcliffe said. "But we *did* manage to wipe them all out before it was too late."

Major Parkinson's voice echoed over the command link. "ENDEX," he said. "I say again, ENDEX."

Alice let out a long breath, then undid her mask and took a breath of fresh air. The 'dead' bodies were already getting up, looking somewhat the worse for wear. Concussion grenades weren't as bad as high-explosive grenades, but anyone caught in the blast would be thoroughly banged up, even if they wore armour. She looked down at the two men she'd shot, then shook her head. They were already getting to their feet.

"Senior officers, report to the briefing compartment," Parkinson added. "Sergeants, take command."

Alice nodded to Radcliffe, then turned and walked down the corridor. It hadn't been *that* intense an drill, compared to some of the extensive exercises she'd endured on Salisbury Plain and later on Britannia, but it had been trickier than she'd expected. And the timing had come as a surprise.

Boarding actions were relatively rare, yet they had to be planned for. Who knew what the *next* set of enemies would consider acceptable tactics?

She slung her rifle over her shoulder as she walked into the briefing compartment. Captain Janus was already there, studying the replay with an air of immense concentration; Captain Furthermore joined them a moment later, his pale face badly scratched. Colonel Parkinson entered a second later, looking grim. Alice snapped out a salute, wondering just how the colonel was going to react to the exercise. They'd done well, but she knew they could have done better.

"Stand at ease," Parkinson ordered, once Janus and Furthermore had saluted. "Take a mug of coffee and sit down."

Alice nodded and poured herself a mug, then found a seat on one of the folding chairs while Parkinson brought up the exercise results. He'd watched everything from the office, carefully noting what had worked and what happened. Alice didn't envy him. They were due to depart in a few hours. If one of the replacement marines wasn't up to the task, replacing him would be difficult. The beancounters would throw a fit.

Though we could probably knock someone into shape, if we had to, Alice said. She found it hard to believe anyone could go through Commando Training without being able to tie his bootlaces, but there were some people who just never learnt to think outside the box. At least she could read a map! *It would just be a problem if we actually had to go to war.*

"So," Parkinson said. "Impressions?"

"We expected them to come through the airlocks," Janus said. "That caught us by surprise."

Alice nodded in rueful agreement. Technically, she shouldn't have been leading the charge, not when their communications network was in disarray. Sergeant Radcliffe or Corporal Hammersmith should have assumed command. But she'd had no choice. Her platoon had been meant to be part of the reserves, not on the front line. There had been no time to make changes when the shit hit the fan.

"We didn't clear and seal the section quickly enough, either," she added, after a moment. It would reflect badly on her, but there was no point in trying to hide it. "They spread too far for us to counter easily."

"And they managed to get a nuke onboard," Parkinson said. "If they'd managed to detonate it..."

Alice made a face. Theoretically, *Invincible's* internal armour should have been able to deflect the brunt of the blast into space. Theoretically. No one in their right mind wanted to actually *test* the concept. And even if it worked as designed, the ship would be immensely damaged afterwards. The enemy warships would have a perfect opportunity to pour fire into her hull. They might not kill *Invincible* with the first wave of missiles, but the second or third would be enough to put an end to her.

And the damage would be enough to put us out of the fight long before we were actually blown to atoms, she told herself. *We'd be thoroughly screwed.*

"We need to work on our deployments," Janus said. "And we probably also need to arm the crew."

Parkinson nodded. "I'll discuss the latter with the captain," he said. "He'll have to make the final call. But you're right—we should insist that the crew be armed, particularly when we reach our destination."

Alice wasn't so sure. She'd been using guns since she joined the CCF, years ago, but it was rare for naval crewmen to do more than pass the basic course. They tended not to bother using the shooting range, even though it was open to all comers. In her opinion, armed crewmembers would know just enough to be dangerous and not enough to be actually helpful. She found it hard to believe they could delay trained soldiers for more than a few seconds. But the crew might just slow down enemy boarders long enough for the marines to react.

"We need more practice," Alice said, when Parkinson looked at her. "We were surprised this time, but next time...who knows *what* we'll face?"

"We'll be running *far* more drills," Parkinson assured her. "We have a *lot* of ground to cover."

Alice nodded, curtly, as Parkinson started outlining the engagement and pointing to a number of problems. He wasn't being unreasonable—anyone with any real experience would know that most emergency drills left out the emergency—but he was being nit-picky. She didn't really blame him. Exercises were *designed* to let the marines make mistakes that could be studied, without actually getting anyone killed. But, at the same time, there was such a thing as being *too* nit-picky. The marines knew as well as she did that mistakes and screw-ups happened. And when they did, there was no point in placing blame until *after* the shooting had stopped.

"We still don't know what we're facing," Furthermore said. "Has there been no update?"

"None," Parkinson said. "Do you really expect one?"

Alice shook her head, wordlessly. She didn't *think* the Admiralty would deliberately hide vital data from its subordinates, particularly the ones who were going to make First Contact with a new alien race, but it wouldn't be the first time some pen-pusher in high office had tried to keep a monopoly on vital information. And even if everyone was being rational...she knew, all too well, that the situation was evolving slowly. There would be no updates until they actually reached Wensleydale.

Unless the situation really does go to hell, she thought. *And we have to make a jump into a combat zone.*

• • •

"This is the latest xenoanalysis and translation system," Doctor Percy Ganymede said, waving to a boxy structure on his table. "This beauty can build up a common language even *without* help from the other side."

Ambassador Tiara O'Neil eyed it warily. In her experience, that meant it would make mistakes faster than humanly possible. "Shouldn't it be connected to the ship's datanet?"

"Not at all, Madam Ambassador," Ganymede said. "Ideally, we'd be establishing a datalink to an alien computer and building up a vocabulary from there. It shouldn't be *that* hard to establish a solid link if their computer technology is a hundred years or so behind ours. But we can't risk tying the translator into the main datanet if we do. Someone might send us a computer virus."

Tiara frowned. "And what if we can't?"

"It will be a little harder," Ganymede said. "But we devised this system with help from both the Tadpoles and the Foxes. It is stripped of all the underlying assumptions that made it so hard to establish early communications with them."

"Not being in the middle of a shooting war will probably help too," Tiara commented. She admired Ganymede's enthusiasm, but she mistrusted his judgement. In her experience, aliens were aliens and couldn't be treated as humans. "And the remainder of the system?"

Ganymede waved a hand towards the far bulkhead. "We set up a biological containment lab, as planned," he assured her. "Any face-to-face discussions will be held within the chamber, with a complete decontaminating program for anyone who wants to go in and out. I don't think that anything could get out of the chamber and into the ship, not without being detected and destroyed. We'll also be able to carry out non-invasive scans of alien entities who enter the chamber. I think we'll learn a great deal about their bodies without having to...ah, ask to examine them."

"I don't want to know the gory details," Tiara said. Alien exhalations would be analysed endlessly, along with alien biological wastes. It wasn't something she intended to discuss at the table. "Are you ready to equip the chamber for all known forms of life?"

"Yes, Madam Ambassador," Ganymede said. "If they're water-breathers, we can fiddle with the chamber to give them a tank. If they need a particular air mix, we can reproduce it—at worst, we can ask them for a supply. We have ways to feed you oxygen even if their atmosphere is poisonous to us. The only real problem would come if they were completely incompatible with us—gas giant dwellers, for example."

"Which may not even exist," Tiara said. She'd seen projections suggesting that gas giants *could* give birth to spacefaring civilisations, but they seemed to rely on an awful lot of things going just right. Humanity had had to pass through a few bottlenecks to become a spacefaring civilisation, yet any hypothetical gas giant civilisation would have far worse problems. "You seem to have covered everything."

"I like to think so," Ganymede said. He glanced around the room. "The real problem, of course, is the lack of hard data. All of our precautions could be useless."

"As I am constantly reminded," Tiara said. "We may wind up having to improvise."

"The media should be onboard too," Ganymede said. "Why have they been reassigned to the transport ship?"

Tiara considered several answers, then decided on brutal honesty. "I felt it would be better if the media was kept at arm's length, at least until we established communications with the newcomers," she said. "The last thing we need is the media pressuring us to do things one way or the other...at least for a while. They simply don't understand the realities of interstellar diplomacy."

Ganymede looked displeased. "They also need to see that our office does useful work."

"They will," Tiara assured him. She'd heard plenty of horror stories about budget cuts. The Foreign Office was a favourite target. "But right now, we really *don't* need them getting in the way."

She eyed him for a long moment until he nodded, reluctantly. Tiara allowed herself a flicker of relief, mingled with concern. Ganymede was unlikely to have another chance to demonstrate his office's importance in front of the entire Human Sphere. He presumably didn't want to miss it. But, at the same time, there were more important concerns. She didn't have time to deal with bureaucratic infighting when she was trying to make contact with a whole new alien race.

"I'll speak to your staff later," she said, firmly. "Before then, I hope you'll have time to update the proposed scenarios...perhaps even rule out some of the more unlikely possibilities."

"My predecessors didn't believe that a water-breathing race could ever turn into an interstellar civilisation," Ganymede said. "I think we are pushing the definition of *unlikely* as far as it will go and yet, I wouldn't rule anything out until we had hard data. There are just too many things we considered *unlikely* before they became all too real."

"True," Tiara agreed. She forced herself to smile. "I do wonder what some of the analysts were smoking, when they came up with their lists."

"Probably something illegal in most places," Ganymede said.

Tiara bid him farewell, then walked down the corridor, trying to ignore the cold feeling in her heart. There were limits to how much she could prepare for a diplomatic meeting, even if the people she was meeting were *human*. She could no more keep preparing until zero hour than a child could revise right up until the moment of the exam. And yet, and yet, she *wanted* to prepare. She just didn't know how.

Because we have no idea what's waiting for us out there, she thought. An STL ship was a unique problem, even if humanity really *did* have a technological advantage. *And who knows why they crossed interstellar space on a whim and a prayer?*

She passed a line of marines as she walked onwards, lost in thought. The entire ship was preparing for war, even as her crew hoped for peace. Tiara didn't really blame them. It was better to be ready for trouble and not encounter it than meet trouble without being ready. But they knew so little about what was coming...

Years ago, Earth had been shocked when news of Vera Cruz had slowly leaked onto the datanets. An alien power...a *hostile* alien power. Everything the human race had thought it had known about the cosmos had been turned upside down. Space was suddenly dangerous, a threat of utter destruction as well as a promise of species immortality. Now, humanity was almost unconcerned about the prospect of a *fifth* alien race. The news had been leaked, followed by a formal announcement...

...And no one seemed to care.

I care, Tiara told herself, firmly.

A dull quiver ran through the ship. She checked her wristcom, then sucked in her breath. It was time. *Invincible* was about to depart...

...And who knew what she'd encounter when she reached her destination?

CHAPTER FOURTEEN

STEPHEN SAT IN HIS COMMAND CHAIR and tried to project an image of calm as he studied the in-system display. There was no reason to be nervous, not when *Invincible* had already undergone her shakedown cruise, but still...he felt a lump of cold ice in his heart. War was one thing—he understood war—yet...this time, they were going into the unknown. There was no way to be sure what they might encounter. Even the worst-case scenarios might be nothing more than pathetic underestimates...

He cleared his throat. "Mr. Morse," he said. "Have the other ships checked in?"

"Yes, Captain," Morse said. "They're standing by."

Stephen smiled to himself, although the lump of ice refused to melt. Squadron command at such a young age was nothing to sniff at, even though the 'squadron' was only a handful of ships. It would look very good on his resume, assuming everything went well. And yet, he couldn't keep himself from worrying. An assault carrier and five destroyers—two of them foreign—might not be anything like enough to put a lid on the situation if the aliens turned out to be hostile. There were just too many wretched unknowns.

"Send a signal to System Command," he ordered. "Inform them that we are ready to depart."

He leaned back in his chair and studied the display, trying to project an air of calm. It wasn't easy. Earth was surrounded by starships, interplanetary ships and massive defences, but he could see the weaknesses. Duncan had been right, he suspected. The funding to continually expand the defences simply wasn't there. It wouldn't be long before the Great Powers would have to cut back or merge the defences into one, which would cause all sorts of long-term problems. The transnational institutions that had tried to dominate the world, before the Troubles and the Age of Unrest, had started to grow out of control long before the world was thrown into chaos. No one wanted to repeat *that* experience.

But we might not have a choice, he thought. *The universe grows smaller with every passing day.*

His eyes tracked a colonist-carrier, heading for the nearest tramline. The Americans, like everyone else, were trying to get as many people off Earth as possible. Humanity could no longer afford to put all its eggs in one basket, not when there was no way to know when the *next* alien threat would materialise out of the darkness. And yet, the sheer cost of the colonist program was also threatening a financial meltdown. Stephen had read the latest government paper with a cynical eye, carefully noting what *wasn't* said. Britain was pushing its economy to the brink. The only saving grace was that the other Great Powers were in the same boat.

Sure, he told himself. *And she's the* Titanic.

"Captain," Morse said. "We are cleared to depart."

"Inform the task force," Stephen said. He hadn't had much time to get to know his new subordinates, but there would be time for that during the voyage. The upside of having so few ships was that he'd have a chance to speak with all the commanding officers individually, rather than merely host awkward dinners. "And then..."

He felt a sudden thrill of anticipation. *This* was no shakedown cruise. *This* was a mission. A deployment to the very edge of explored space. Who knew *what* might be waiting for them on the far end? He was nervous, but he was excited too. The endless reaches of interstellar space seemed to be calling to him. Perhaps he should have gone into Survey instead.

"Helm, bring up the drives," he ordered. "And then take us out."

A dull quiver ran through the ship as the drives came online, the engineers running a final set of checks before giving the final okay. Stephen released a breath he hadn't realised he was holding, even though there hadn't been any reason to be concerned. A catastrophic drive failure so close to Earth would be embarrassing and probably fatal to his career. But nothing went wrong. His eye traced the power curves as the drive field built up, slowly pushing *Invincible* into interplanetary space. Everything was nominal. The engineers had done a *very* good job tuning the drive.

"Course laid in, Captain," Morse said. "We'll cross the tramline in nine hours."

Stephen nodded, shortly. *Invincible* and the destroyers could ramp up their speed, if necessary—*Invincible* had an impressive and classified top speed—but RFA *Wanderlust* and SS *Silver Star* couldn't keep up. The nasty part of his mind was tempted to leave the *Silver Star* behind—the media had sent a small army of reporters, all of whom were on the interstellar liner—yet it would cause too many problems. Reporters, in his experience, were almost always ignorant of military realities, but they'd probably notice if they'd been left behind. It was going to be bad enough keeping them away from the aliens until peaceful contact had been made. One of them would probably start a war by shoving a recorder in an alien face and demanding a quote.

Which is how Stellar Star found herself fighting yet another interstellar war, he reminded himself, wryly. *At least her scriptwriters were a little bit more imaginative than blaming everything on the military.*

"Captain," Newcomb said. "All decks have reported in. All stations are nominal. We are good to go."

Stephen nodded. He'd done everything in his power to ensure they'd leave on time, but...he dismissed the thought, silently reassuring himself that they *had* left on time. There was some slippage built into the schedule, but not much. The alien STL ship presumably *couldn't* slow down very quickly, let alone turn on a dime or come to a dead stop. She would enter orbit on a fixed timetable unless she had some drive technology no one had ever heard of, hidden away inside her massive hull. Stephen had seen the projections. A drive field capable of slowing a ship larger than most asteroids would be hellishly inefficient.

And they haven't even tried to communicate with the station, he thought. Everything they knew was out of date, but still...it worried him. *Do they even know the station is there? Do they care?*

"Keep us on course," he ordered, turning his attention back to the display. *Invincible* was designed for solo operations, but it still bothered him that so few escort ships had been assigned to the squadron. The Terra Nova crisis was forcing the Royal Navy to keep its deployable units close to home. "And take us across the tramline as soon as we arrive."

"Aye, Captain," Lieutenant Sonia Michelle said.

Stephen nodded to himself. "We'll resume active drills as soon as we cross the tramline," he added. "Tell the beta, delta and gamma crews to get a rest. They're going to need it."

"Aye, Captain," Newcomb said.

Invincible shivered, again, as she picked up speed. Stephen kept a wary eye on the power curves for a long moment, then turned his attention to the in-system display. The remainder of the flotilla was keeping pace with the carrier, *Wanderlust* and *Silver Star* bringing up the rear. Their commanders had strict orders to run for their lives if the shit hit the fan, no matter how they felt about it. *Wanderlust* had some point defence, but not enough to make a difference if someone really wanted her dead. And *Silver Star* was completely unarmed. She probably hadn't flown into disputed space in her entire career.

Although space pirates are a reality now, Stephen thought, as he studied the liner's striking curves. *Perhaps we should be more concerned about arming civilian ships.*

He shook his head, wondering why whoever had designed *Silver Star* hadn't been fired for gross incompetence. She looked elegant, he had to admit, but she had been designed for looks rather than practicality. He couldn't help thinking that she was staggeringly inefficient, compared to a military ship. And her owners *had* to be operating her at a loss. Very few people could afford a third-class cabin, let alone a first-class suite. No wonder they'd leapt at the chance to volunteer her for the contact mission. The reporters would be living in luxury while they wrote stories for their rags.

His gaze wandered over the remainder of the system. Thousands of beacons were clearly visible, each one representing an asteroid settlement or a mining station...Mars was surrounded by a small halo of her own, even though Mars was no longer as attractive a destination as she'd been a century ago. The Great Powers had even talked about conceding independence, or at least autonomy, to their settlements on Mars. There was just little to gain by keeping the world. Venus, unsurprisingly, had the same problems. But then, Venus had never been an attractive destination. The terraforming program was incredibly speculative.

And they're still talking about blowing up Mercury, he reminded himself. *As if we didn't already have an inexhaustible asteroid belt!*

Dismissing the thought, he turned to his XO. "Start putting together the exercise schedule," he told him. "I want to review it before we jump."

"Aye, Captain."

• • •

It was a long-established naval tradition that crewmen on a starship heading for Tramline Alpha would be given a short break to allow them to compose a final message to their families before the ship jumped out of the solar system, although there was rarely any time for a reply. Alice hadn't really expected a break—she'd spent the last two days drilling endlessly, trying to prepare for contingencies that no one could really clarify—but Major Parkinson had ordered everyone to take advantage of the final chance to write to their families. She'd reluctantly booked herself into a private cabin—little more than a closet, really—and keyed her ID code into the terminal.

A handful of messages popped up in front of her. Three were worthless, little more than spam; she deleted them without bothering to reply. Two more were short notes from friends she'd made at her last posting, inviting her to meet up with them sometime over the next fortnight. They must not have realised that her shore leave had been cut short so dramatically. Her lips twitched in bitter amusement as she tapped out a quick note, then sent it back. They were military personnel, thankfully. They knew the score.

The final message was from her sister. Alice's eyes narrowed. A text-mail was relatively rare, amongst family. V-mail was considered much more intimate, although Alice rather suspected it also made it harder to compose messages. She certainly preferred to draft out her reports first, *then* submit them. Nothing she said out loud was quite as polished as the written word. But then, she'd also been forced to defend herself in front of a promotions board. They'd been more interested in what she'd said on the fly, rather than any pre-prepared remarks.

She scanned the message quickly, then sat back in her chair, unsure what to feel. Jeanette wanted to sell the farm. Alice wasn't too surprised—neither sister really had the time or inclination to turn the farm into a going concern again—but it still felt as through Jeanette was throwing away a piece of the past. *Their* past. The farm was *theirs*. Jeanette had limited powers of attorney, simply because she lived relatively close to the area, but she couldn't *sell* the land without Alice's signature on the dotted line.

She should have bloody mentioned it when we were at the farm, Alice thought. She'd gone to dinner with her sister, for fuck's sake. *It wouldn't have been hard to open her goddamned mouth.*

Gritting her teeth, she forced herself to read the text-mail again. The basic argument was fairly simple, even understandable. Jeanette couldn't maintain the farm, nor could Alice. And there was a decent offer too...

enough money to ensure a nest egg for both sides of the family. Jeanette's children would be able to go to any university they wished; Alice's future children, assuming she ever had any, would have enough money to choose their own path through life. Alice couldn't fault the logic. She'd never really wanted children, but she'd never ruled the possibility out either.

And yet...she closed her eyes for a long moment, feeling as though she'd been punched in the chest. Their grandparents had loved the farm. Selling it to some worthless property developer would be a betrayal. And their mother had been *buried* on the farm. What would happen to her grave? There was no way to be sure they could move the body to a proper cemetery. God knew they hadn't been able to get permission to bury her in church grounds...

Fuck, she thought. *She really should have mentioned it to me.*

There was no time limit mentioned on the text-mail, no suggestion that Alice had to agree immediately. And yet, she suspected there *was* a time limit. Jeanette had always been a sneaky bitch, even though she'd never been as remorselessly physical—and willing to throw punches—as her younger sister. She might well be trying to bounce Alice into making a hasty decision. Alice had seen it before, during exercises. Trying to push one's enemy into making a mistake was a very old-fashioned tactic.

Damn it, she thought. *What the fuck do I do?*

She took a deep breath. There was no need to hurry, based on the email. Jeanette could hardly blame her for not replying immediately. There had been a very good chance that the message would go into a buffer for later transmission to a courier boat, rather than being forwarded directly to *Invincible*. Jeanette had plenty of good reasons not to expect an immediate response. If she'd needed a quick answer...well, she'd had plenty of time to address the issue while they'd been together.

And she can't sell the farm without my permission, Alice told herself, firmly. Their grandparents hadn't designated either of their grandchildren as the senior partner. *And she hasn't given me any reason to hurry.*

But still, it bothered her. Jeanette wasn't normally so...so *hasty*. She knew how much her mother's grave meant to Alice. Had something happened? Something that forced Jeanette to make a desperate bid for funds? But...she could have simply *told* Alice. It wasn't as if Alice would have laughed in her older sister's face. She was torn between cutting herself free of the farm, and leaving the past firmly where it belonged, and hanging onto it tooth and nail. It was *hers* too, damn it. Jeanette had no right to even *consider* a sale without discussing it with her first.

Although if I don't come back, the point is moot, Alice thought, soberly. Jeanette and her children were the only family she had left—or, at least, the only family she cared to acknowledge. Her father was dead to her, as far as she was concerned. *Jeanette would inherit the farm anyway.*

She thought for a long moment, then tapped out a brief reply. She'd consider the matter, if Jeanette forwarded the details of the offer to her. It would be interesting to see what she said and—she glanced at the chronometer—to see if Jeanette managed to get a reply to her before *Invincible* crossed the tramline. Alice was no spacer, but...she had no real trouble calculating communications times between *Invincible* and Earth. Jeanette would have to reply within the hour to have even a *slight* hope of getting back to her before it was too late.

Unless she pays to send a message up the flicker network, Alice told herself, as she sent the message. Governments and corporations did it all the time, but civilians? The cost would be noticeable. Nothing short of a serious problem would convince Jeanette to pay for a message, not when there would be no guarantee that she'd receive a positive answer. *That would be interesting.*

She leaned back in her chair, staring at nothing. Her sister was up to something, which meant...what? She didn't know. Part of her didn't really care, either. They'd spent most of their lives in the shadow of their father, pushed together by a world that was either voyeuristic or judgmental. Their grandparents had been decent people, but...but they'd been too old to raise a pair of teenage girls. No wonder she and her sister had had problems, as they grew to adulthood. And no wonder they'd grown apart too.

The terminal bleeped. A new message had arrived. Alice stared at it in utter disbelief. Jeanette couldn't have answered that quickly, could she? It was impossible. Alice's reply was still winging its way to Earth. Jeanette wouldn't see it for at least another forty minutes.

She keyed the console. The message opened up in front of her. It was from her father.

Alice stared at it for a long moment, feeling a surge of rage. How *dare* her father try to contact her? Hadn't she made her feelings clear? She'd cut him out of her life! She wasn't some teenage orphan looking for a father-figure and, even if she *had* been, he would have been right at the bottom of the list of candidates. She'd sooner look up to one of the arseholes who'd sneered at her for daring to even *think* about becoming a marine than the man who'd murdered her mother. They, at least, hadn't pretended to give a damn about her.

I am an orphan, she told herself. Jeanette could try to make nice with their father, if she wished. Alice was much less forgiving. *And that isn't going to change.*

Shaking her head, she deleted the message. It definitely wasn't going to change. She'd made a life of her own, without him. Their father could rot in hell for all she cared. And besides, she had plenty of work to do. She wasn't going to waste time telling him to stay out of her life when someone else probably needed the cabin. It wouldn't be *that* long before the ship jumped.

And he probably won't listen to me either, she thought, as she left the cabin. *He was never very good at hearing things he didn't want to hear.*

CHAPTER FIFTEEN

"TO HUMANITY," STEPHEN SAID.

He smiled to himself as the assembled officers—the commanding officers of the squadron's ships and a handful of his senior officers—echoed the toast. It was nicely uncontroversial, something that couldn't be said for drinking the health of various political leaders. There was no room for political debates and international quarrels when the squadron would have to work together if the newcomers turned hostile. It was bad enough that they didn't have anything like enough escort units to please him, although *that* was no surprise. He would have been happier making first contact if he had every warship in the Human Sphere a lone jump away.

And yet, there's no reason to think we need them, he reminded himself, as the guests started to form small groups. *We haven't seen anything to suggest they have drive fields, let alone modern missiles and starfighters.*

He surveyed the dining room with a practiced eye. The designers were *good* at making the compartment seem large, although it was only half the size of the dining room on HMS *Theodore Smith*. A single long table, chairs that seemed to date all the way back to the pre-space era, a handful of candles that *looked* real even though he knew they weren't...the stewards had done a good job. And the food was good too. He told himself to enjoy it while he had the chance. It wouldn't be long before they were eating processed algae and drinking recycled water.

Ambassador Tiara O'Neil appeared to be having fun, he noted; she was chatting in Russian to Captain Semyon Danilovich. The grim-faced officer seemed to be lightening up a little, although he didn't look very happy. Stephen didn't really blame him. The Russian was alone, surrounded by British and American officers. And while the Royal Navy and the USN worked together regularly, the Russians were practically isolated. Stephen didn't know why the other Great Powers were reluctant to treat the Russians as equals—he hadn't even heard a single creditable rumour—but he couldn't help feeling that it was going to bite them in the arse sooner rather than later. Russia had taken a battering in the First Interstellar War, yet she was still a Great Power. Her sheer immensity worked in her favour.

Stephen made a mental note to have a private chat with Danilovich, then turned his attention to the destroyer captains. Captain West and Captain Baldwin were swapping lies about their role in the last set of fleet exercises, while Captain Corcoran was looking down his long nose at them. There had been some sort of scandal revolving around Corcoran's daughter, Stephen recalled, although few of the details had been leaked. The man was probably pleased to be heading away from Earth. God knew his career had stalled. Stephen hadn't bothered to check, but he was pretty sure that Corcoran was the oldest destroyer captain in the navy. It was a young man's game.

He shook his head as he caught Captain Andrew Robbins's eye. The cruise ship captain looked out of place, wearing a uniform that made him look like an admiral in one of the more unstable Third World countries. Civilians liked gold braid, it seemed; indeed, there was something about the uniform that captured the eye. It was hard to see the man's face inside the uniform, making it hard to form any kind of judgement. British Interstellar wouldn't have given a starship to a man who wasn't up to the task, but civilians had odd priorities. They might have chosen a commander who was more photogenic than competent. Robbins had to look good as well as be good.

Captain Corcoran caught his eye. "Establishing a whole new branch of the flicker network is quite expensive, is it not?"

"Yes," Stephen said. Technically, he was the senior officer; practically, it was better to maintain a pretence they were equals. "But the long-term payoff should be quite spectacular."

"Assuming we get *anything* out of establishing diplomatic relationships with a bunch of primitives," Corcoran commented. "The cost might bankrupt us."

Stephen considered it for a long moment. The flicker network *was* expensive. It was why so many governments had clubbed together to pay for it, rather than establish a dozen separate networks. And no one had bothered to establish a flicker chain running all the way to Wensleydale. The system was at the ass-end of nowhere. Until recently, no one had seen any point.

"But it will pay off in the very long run," Stephen commented. Britain had laid the main chain, which meant that messages to a dozen colonies and offshoot worlds would go through the British systems. "Unless the other powers decide to pay for some of the costs."

"Unless," Corcoran said. "There's really too many unknowns here."

Ambassador O'Neil joined them. "The aliens might have nothing useful to teach us, tech-wise, although the Vesy *have* given us quite a few insights into how our civilisation developed over the centuries. However, their mindset—and what they make of our technology—may offer us quite a few promising angles for development. This ship"—she waved a hand at the nearest bulkhead—"wouldn't have been possible twenty years ago. The drive system is derived from a mingling of human and alien technology."

"True," Stephen agreed. In the background, he could see the Russian CO speaking rapidly to the American. "But the Tadpole tech base was more advanced than ours. The gaps in their tech tree came from their...ah, physical limitations, rather than the inability to produce functional hardware. They weren't interested in solving problems that have bedevilled us since the dawn of time."

"That didn't stop us using some of their tech to solve *our* problems," Tiara said. "And they used some of our tech to solve *their* problems. The back-and-forth trade in tech and ideas—concepts—was quite enlightening. I dare say that the synergy between us and the other alien races will produce their own advantages, given time."

"They built an STL ship," Corcoran said. "What does that tell us about them?"

"That they were able to construct such a ship and keep it functional for a voyage that must have lasted well over a century," Tiara said, with the air of someone reading from a position paper. "Can we do as well?"

"Yes," Corcoran said. "But *would* we?"

Stephen allowed himself a smile. The crews had been discussing—and laying bets—on what the squadron was going to find ever since the files had been uploaded to the ship's datanet and made available to everyone. So far, there was little hard data...but that hadn't stopped his crew competing to see who could come up with the craziest idea. One faction was sure the aliens were actually rogue machines—AIs could survive a century-long voyage without going mad—while another was insisting that the aliens were actually dead and the ship was really a tomb. It explained why the aliens hadn't tried to communicate with the station, they'd pointed out. The automatic systems might be trying to bring the ship into orbit without any awareness that the planet was already inhabited.

"Perhaps we would, if we were desperate," Tiara said. "Or if we saw no other choice."

"Or just wanted a homeworld light years from everywhere else," Stephen put in. "A number of belters *did* set off for interstellar space."

"And they're going to be in for one hell of a shock when they reach their destinations," Corcoran said. "The systems are already inhabited." He shook his head. "But it's hard to believe that the newcomers can teach us anything worth knowing."

"You might be surprised," Tiara told him. "Humanity was planning the conquest of space long before flights to the moon, let alone anywhere else, became practical. We were imagining all kinds of super-advanced materials and technologies...and plotting how they might be used, when they were finally invented. Even this ship was partly designed before anything larger than a shuttlecraft was launched into space. I believe that spacefaring carriers were practically invented *before* manned spaceflight."

"They didn't understand how starfighters fly in space," Corcoran said. "And their designs were more like jet fighters than anything else."

"True," Tiara agreed. "But they also came up with quite a few concepts that are actually workable. And more and more of them become practical every year. The NGW program is supposed to be mining old science-fiction, searching for ideas."

She smiled. "The aliens might have come up with hundreds of concepts that would be workable, if they had the technology," she added. "And if *we* have the technology...well, there's a payoff right there."

"Assuming we haven't thought of them already," Corcoran said. "How many ideas haven't worked out because the real life got in the way?"

Stephen opened his mouth to point out that history was full of false starts, some of which had actually been revisited as the technology improved, then saw Captain Robbins trying to catch his eye. "Excuse me," he said. "Duty calls."

He took a wine glass from the table and walked over to Robbins. Up close, the civilian captain looked more than a little absurd. His gold braid was truly ridiculous, as if he'd stepped out of a fantasy from the days of sail. Stephen had grumbled about his dress uniform—it was something he had in common with every other naval officer—but none of the admirals he'd met had worn anything so ornate. He couldn't help thinking that Robbins would be a prime target for any sniper searching for officers...

Not that he goes onto the battlefield, of course, Stephen reminded himself. *He's a civilian.*

"Captain," he said. "I trust you are enjoying the voyage?"

"It's been an interesting and quite fascinating cruise," Robbins said, in a tone that suggested it was anything but. "Can you believe the reporters expect my crew to wait on them hand and foot?"

"I find it *very* easy to believe," Stephen said, seriously. "How are you coping with the other ambassadors and representatives?"

"They're hanging back and enjoying the voyage," Robbins said. "They won't have anything *real* to do until they reach the far end."

Stephen nodded in wry agreement. He'd kept his crew busy, running them through drill after drill until they could do it in their sleep, but the ambassadors didn't have so many duties. Hell, most of them were nothing more than advisors—whatever their titles—until formal relations were established. He didn't think much of the corporate representatives. Most of *them* had probably been sent out in the hopes that they'd find something marketable once the newcomers talked to humanity. Or in the hopes they *wouldn't* return. The couple he'd met had struck him as slimier than the average politician.

"It's putting quite a strain on my stockpiles, let me tell you," Robbins said, a glint in his eye suggesting he wasn't entirely serious. "They're eating me out of house and home."

"It must be terrible," Stephen said. He'd read *Silver Star's* brochure. For the low—low—price of a million pounds per person, first-class guests were flown directly to the cruise liner and pampered mercilessly during a voyage that touched on a dozen planets and asteroid settlements. There was no processed food or recycled water on *Silver Star*. Everything was natural, save for the gravity. "When do you start the shift to processed food?"

Robbins winked. "We've already started," he said. "But our chefs are very good. So far, no one has noticed."

Stephen had to smile. Royal Navy crewmen were *used* to processed food, although the gallery chefs were good at hiding the flavour and there was a roaring trade in various condiments. The chefs bragged that they *could* hide the taste if they wished...maybe they were right. He'd never bothered to wonder why they *didn't*. Eating recycled crap—sometimes

146

literally—was just part of being in the navy. It was better not to think about the details.

"I'd bet they'll never notice," he said. "Are you keeping some of the real food in reserve?"

"We were going to host a wedding before we were hastily redeployed out here," Robbins said. "Someone's probably pissed, down on Earth, that their chocolate fountain has vanished into deep space."

"Oh dear," Stephen said. "Will they be *very* unhappy?"

"They'll have a new one by now," Robbins said. "Although we have dealt with some real bridezillas over the last two years. You'd think that having enough money to afford our services would come with some *class*, wouldn't you? And probably some taste as well."

Stephen had to smile. He'd been forced to attend more weddings than he'd wished as a young man, although it had been easier to find excuses after he'd joined the navy. High Society demanded perfection, with weddings carefully choreographed for months before the happy couple tied the knot. He didn't really blame Duncan for hesitating about finding a bride, not when she would come with all sorts of social expectations. She'd have to be someone who was willing to marry the entire family—and the estate—as well as Duncan himself. It wouldn't be easy for her.

And the newly-rich are often worse, he thought. *They're the ones who'll think nothing about blowing an entire fortune on a fancy wedding when the marriage won't last two years.*

"Class takes a generation," he said, recalling some of the commoners who'd married into the aristocracy. They were welcomed for their achievements, but they never quite mastered the manners of one born into High Society. Their children, however, were a different story. "And taste is never universal."

He met Robbins's eyes. "How are you coping with the unusual demands?"

Robins shrugged. "It's different, but we *did* plan for a long-range deployment if necessary," he said. "I was expecting to have to tear out all the fittings so I could transport troops and supplies from Earth to some godforsaken rock in the middle of nowhere, to be honest. I didn't think I'd be playing host to high-class ambassadors and low-class reporters, but it is a bit of a break. There's no real danger of having to halt the ship because some little brat left her teddy in the shuttle."

"Ouch," Stephen said. He knew exactly what the *navy* would say if a midshipman left something behind in *his* shuttle. It wouldn't be very polite. "Does that happen often?"

"Often enough that we make sure to search the shuttle from top to bottom once the passengers are disembarked," Robbins said. He smirked. "I bet you don't get a lot of petty pointless complaints. I once had a man complain he couldn't get laid in the casino."

"I have *never* had that complaint," Stephen said. He shook his head. "You must find this *very* relaxing."

"It does have its moments," Robbins agreed. "The only *real* problem is what we'll find at the far end."

"Hopefully, peaceful contact," Stephen said. "Did you read through the contingency plans?"

"Turn and run as though the hounds of hell are after us." Robbins nodded. "It's very basic, Captain, but understandable. I don't want to be anywhere near the aliens if they turn hostile."

"Very good," Stephen agreed.

He turned and surveyed the room. The party was starting to wind down, although—by long custom—none of the guests could leave until he did. It was hard to tell if they'd actually enjoyed themselves. He wasn't sure he'd bet on it. But at least they had gotten to know each other a little better. It was a relief to know that Robbins wasn't a *prima donna*, unlike some of the other civilian captains he'd met, or that he wasn't going to listen to sense when he heard it. Stephen had heard too many horror stories about starship commanders who had ignored obvious danger signs to be sanguine about how his civilian subordinates would react to alien threats.

As long as he turns tail and runs when the shit hits the fan, I don't mind, he told himself, firmly. It was hardly heroic, but Robbins wasn't being paid to be a hero. He needed to get out of the danger zone with his cargo of ambassadors, reporters and representatives while the military bought him time. *We'll see what happens when we reach our destination.*

He nodded politely to the ambassador, flicked a telling glance at Newcomb, then turned and walked through the hatch. The XO would handle the closing moments, ensuring that everyone got back to their shuttles without any trouble. Stephen didn't envy Newcomb—or the shuttle pilots, waiting for their senior officers to return. He didn't think anyone was actually drunk, but a couple of officers were definitely tipsy.

"Captain," Tiara said, from behind. "That was a very good party."

"Thank you," Stephen said. She *was* quick. Stephen hadn't even heard her coming up behind him. "It would be a great deal less pleasant if we had more ships."

The ambassador shot him a smile. "But you'd be glad of it if you *did* have more ships, would you not?"

"Yes," Stephen said. He'd had his doubts about Tiara—the ambassador didn't *look* like an ambassador—but he had to admit she was good at her job. The aliens presumably wouldn't care *what* she looked like, as long as she could talk to them. "We still don't know what we're going to meet."

Tiara nodded. "Are you still planning a combat jump into Wensleydale?"

"Yes," Stephen said. "I don't see any choice."

"Even paranoids have enemies," Tiara agreed. "And it *will* give you a chance to test your crew before we meet the aliens."

"Yes," Stephen said. Being paranoid, particularly when aliens of unknown power were involved, was a survival trait. "And if the situation has changed radically in the time before our arrival, which it might have done, we will be ready."

CHAPTER SIXTEEN

"THE LAST FLICKER NODE is in place, captain," Newcomb reported. "We are ready to jump."

Stephen nodded, torn between relief that the long voyage was finally over and a grim awareness that he had no idea what was lurking on the other side of the tramline. Passive sensors had revealed no hint that there was *any* presence, human or alien, in the Falkirk System, but that proved nothing. Space was so vast, so mind-bogglingly vast, that the combined navies of all known interstellar powers could be concealed within a single star system and, as long as they were careful, nosy observers wouldn't have the slightest clue they were there. It was all too easy to imagine a stealthed recon platform tracking the squadron as it crawled from one tramline to another, sending signals back to its compatriots on the far side. Someone might be plotting an ambush.

We really shouldn't have brought a civilian ship with us, he told himself. It was funny how no one at the Admiralty had raised the obvious concern. *Silver Star* didn't have a stealth mode, let alone a masking field or a cloaking device. *Or we should have left her in the last system.*

He sucked in his breath, bracing himself. There was nothing of interest within the Falkirk System, save for three tramlines. Britain hadn't bothered to lodge a claim to the system, although *that* policy might need to be reassessed. The Chinese plan to lay claim to Terra Nova might force

Britain—and the other Great Powers—to lay claim to every uninhabited system between Earth and their colony worlds. But...who knew what was on the other side of the tramline? Wensleydale Station didn't have any more drones, didn't even have a starship capable of crossing the tramline. The station could have been blown to atoms weeks ago and no one would be any the wiser...

His mouth was dry. He had to swallow before issuing orders. "Order *Pinafore* to hop through the tramline, as planned," he said. "And stand ready to activate point defence."

Pinafore's icon vanished from the display. A timer started counting automatically, telling him just how long it had been since *Pinafore* had jumped into the system. If she didn't come back in ten minutes, perhaps less, he'd know that she'd run into trouble. His heart started pounding in his chest as the timer ticked mercilessly on. It would be easier, so much easier, if he *knew* the system was hostile. Instead, he could only wait and see if *Pinafore* returned.

The odds of being ambushed are extremely low, he told himself. There had only been a handful of cases where a ship had been jumped as it crossed the tramlines and they'd all been a matter of luck as much as judgement. Tramlines were *lines*, after all. It was very hard to predict where a ship would appear, particularly when a tiny little course change could throw one's projections off by thousands of kilometres. *She'll be back before we know it.*

He forced himself to remain still, his face showing no trace of his inner concern as the seconds counted upwards. If *Pinafore* didn't return...he'd have to find another place to jump through and send a second destroyer into Wensleydale. And if that ship didn't return...

An icon flashed to life on the display. "*Pinafore* has jumped back through the tramline," Lieutenant Alison Adams reported. "No sign of hostile contact."

"Beginning data download now," Morse added. "No trace of hostile activity."

"Put it on the main display," Stephen ordered.

He nodded to himself as the Wensleydale System appeared in front of him. It was fairly typical: a G2 star, a handful of planets in the habitable zone and a couple of gas giants, further out from the system primary. Wensleydale itself was further away from the tramline than he'd expected—he made a mental note to go back over the records and find out why he'd been wrong—but the alien ship was clearly visible. She'd evidently been slowing down over the last two weeks, her movements dictated by the iron laws of physics and orbital motions rather than drive fields. It looked as though she would enter orbit within a week.

"There wasn't time to get a download from the station," Newcomb said. "But the station is clearly intact. Their beacon is functional."

"Good," Stephen said. There was no sign of anything particularly dangerous. "Helm...take us through."

He braced himself as *Invincible* moved forward, the destroyers fanning out in front of her while the two transports brought up the rear. Space seemed to darken, just for a second, a moment before everything snapped back to normal. The display blanked, then hastily rebooted itself. Stephen let out a sigh of relief as he spotted the alien ship—and the station, orbiting the planet. It definitely looked intact.

"Communications, send a standard greeting to the station," he ordered. "Helm, take us to the planet. Best possible speed."

"Aye, sir."

Stephen settled back in his chair, feeling an unaccustomed sense of relief. The aliens *hadn't* blown Wensleydale Station to bits with a concealed superweapon after all. It certainly *looked* as though their tech was a hundred years behind humanity's, which meant that humanity could greet the aliens from a position of strength. Stephen was too mature to believe that might made right, but he was all too aware that might tended to determine what happened, even if it wasn't *right*. There was something comforting about holding a big stick and being prepared to use it.

"Launch stealth probes," he added. "I want to see their hull and any surprises they might have before we go too close."

"Aye, Captain."

He watched, calmly, as data slowly flowed into the display. The alien ship was immense, a fantastic piece of technology even if she was—technically—primitive. Her hull was scarred and pitted with the detritus of interstellar travel; fusion lights flickered over her dark mass as her operators slowly cancelled her spin. She actually *spun* to create gravity, rather than relying on a simple gravity generator...Stephen was torn between amused contempt and a genuine sense of wonder. The aliens had apparently built their ship from scratch, instead of hollowing out an asteroid and converting it into a starship. Humanity had never built anything so large.

"If she has weapons, Captain, I can't see them," Lieutenant-Commander David Arthur said, slowly. "She *is* carrying a number of smaller craft, but I can't tell if they pose a danger."

Stephen nodded, slowly. The aliens didn't seem to have internal launch tubes for starfighters or shuttlecraft. Instead, a number of parasite ships were docked to their outer hull, ready for immediate launch. None of them looked particularly advanced, certainly no match for the squadron, but he couldn't help thinking there was something a little ominous about them. He just couldn't put his finger on it.

They're alien, he told himself, sharply. *Their sense of the aesthetic might be different from ours.*

He sucked in his breath as the squadron approached Wensleydale, wondering what the aliens were thinking. Had they *seen* the squadron as they crossed the tramline? They weren't using active sensors and there was no way to know what passive sensors they carried...they might not even be able to *see* the squadron. And yet, if they could...he wondered what they'd make of what they were seeing. *Invincible* was tiny, compared to their giant mothership, but she was clearly far more powerful. He couldn't help wondering if his alien counterpart was panicking right now.

Too many officers panicked after the Battle of New Russia, he thought. The shock of watching so many fleet carriers die in a handful of minutes had terrified them. *And some of them never quite recovered.*

His console chimed. "Captain, this is the ambassador," Tiara said. "I would be grateful if you could meet with me at your earliest convenience."

"Understood," Stephen said. "I'll be down in a moment."

He looked at Newcomb. "Take us into orbit, but continue to monitor the aliens," he ordered. "If they do anything that strikes you as even remotely dangerous, call me at once."

"Aye, sir," Newcomb said.

Stephen rose. "You have the bridge."

• • •

Ambassador Tiara O'Neil barely paid any attention to the babbling from the analyst deck, where they were happily pointing out the different aspects of the alien ship and comparing them to designs real or imagined. It made little difference to *her* if the alien parasite ships helped to propel the mothership or not, or if they had lasers that could slice a warship in two before it could retaliate. What mattered was how the aliens *thought* and, so far, data was somewhat limited.

"That ship was deliberately designed for interstellar travel," one of the analysts insisted, loudly. His voice was uncomfortably loud even through the intercom. "They're expanding, even though they'd doing it very slowly."

"But the hull is incredibly pitted," another analyst snapped. "They could have used an ice shield when they crossed interstellar space."

"Perhaps they did," the first analyst said. "And they simply discarded the remains in interstellar space."

"They should have used a ramjet," a third analyst said. "But where is it?"

The hatch bell rang before someone could think of a reply. Tiara muted the sound, then ordered the hatch to open. Captain Shields stepped into the room, looking as calm and composed as always. Seeing the alien ship had probably been something of a relief, Tiara judged. The military liked knowing it held the whip hand. Tiara had no intention of pushing the aliens around, but...she wanted to be very sure any threat could be contained, if necessary. Who knew what the aliens *really* wanted?

"Captain," she said. She indicated a chair, then turned her attention back to the holographic display. The aliens didn't seem to have noticed the stealth probes, which wasn't entirely surprising. They were designed to evade far more capable sensors. "What do you make of our visitors?"

"I don't think they can go anywhere else," Captain Shields said. He sat down, his face blurred behind the hologram. "It's a minor miracle their hull has survived so long without eroding completely. I'm unconvinced that that ship was *really* designed for interstellar travel."

Tiara narrowed her eyes. "What makes you say that?"

"A handful of things," Captain Shields said. "The aliens don't seem to have cared much about protecting their hull, even though they were cut off from all possible help. No protective coating, for example. And the design is quite odd. It's more like a massively scaled-up bridge ship than a generation ship."

"True," Tiara said. There was no point in arguing over the technical details with him. "And what does that tell you about them?"

"Nothing certain," the captain said. "And I'm reluctant to make too many guesses."

Tiara nodded. The aliens might have a different approach to risk than humanity. They might see nothing wrong with setting out on an interstellar voyage with a leaky and somewhat insecure starship. Or they might have been desperate. She'd read horror stories about stranded spacecraft where the crew had done everything in their power just to survive one more day. Back in the days before drive fields, a single failure—even a relatively *small* failure—could mean total catastrophe. The aliens had taken one hell of a risk.

And that ship has to represent a major investment, she thought. She'd seen the economic projections. It was hard to be sure, of course, but building such a starship would require a sizable percentage of the planet's GNP. The bridge ships had been vast investments, back in their heyday. And *they'd* been far smaller than the alien ship. *How much did it cost them to build?*

She put the thought aside for later consideration and deactivated the display, allowing her to see him properly. "Do you believe the ship poses any threat?"

"Not immediately," Captain Shields said, slowly. "It is still possible"—he held up a hand to forestall any objections—"that she does have a hidden stash of advanced technology, but I would expect to see some traces of it by now. I don't think she poses any *military* threat to us. However, I also don't think they can go elsewhere. They have pretty much committed themselves to entering orbit and...and, presumably, landing colonists."

Tiara pressed her fingers against the tabletop. "Can they land their mothership?"

"Not unless their gravity-manipulation technology is an order of magnitude more powerful than ours," the captain said. "There is no way we could land *Invincible* on a planetary surface without causing a global disaster. And that ship"- he nodded at where the hologram had been—"is far larger. My guess is that their parasites are designed for shuttling between the mothership and the planet. They certainly *look* capable of making it down to the ground."

"I see," Tiara said. She took a long breath. It was starting to look as though they had no choice, but to let the aliens enter orbit. "Do you have any objections to making contact?"

"No," Captain Shields said. "The only thing that puzzles me, Madam Ambassador, is that they haven't made any attempt to contact the station themselves. Commander Haircloth was quite clear on that point. The aliens haven't tried to contact them. And yet, they *must* be able to see the station. A simple telescope would be quite enough to detect it."

Tiara let out a long breath. "And what does that tell you?"

"Nothing useful," Captain Shields admitted, ruefully. "That *might* be a dead ship, Madam Ambassador, or one where the organic crew is still in suspension. Their automatics might not be programmed to recognise the existence of alien life, let alone wake the crew if the ship runs into something the automatics can't handle. Or...the aliens may think that the station and her crew are *native* to Wensleydale, in which case they presumably want to speak directly to their superiors. Or...there are too many possibilities."

"And we really need answers before that ship enters orbit," Tiara said. A hundred-kilometre-long ship crashing into a planet would do immense damage, even if the ship was technically primitive. "What happens if we don't get an answer?"

"We try to board her," Captain Shields said. "But really, we're running out of options."

"Then we start trying to make contact now," Tiara said. "And hope for the best."

"Very good, Madam Ambassador," the Captain said. "Do you wish to watch from the bridge?"

"I'll monitor from here," Tiara said. She didn't dislike the military, but she preferred to keep her distance. "And I'll be online if necessary."

Captain Shields nodded. "Understood."

• • •

"They should be able to see us, sir," Alison said. "A blind man could see us between the mothership and the planet."

Stephen nodded. He was feeling rather naked. Even his growing certainty that the aliens had literally nothing that could hurt his ship didn't help. The alien mothership *must* have seen the squadron by now—Stephen had made sure to turn on their beacons, just in case the drive fields were screwing with the alien sensors—and yet, they had made no attempt to make contact. He had a nasty feeling that a ghost ship was barrelling down on him. The alien ship might have to be destroyed to save the planet.

"Establish a datalink to the flicker network," he ordered. If something went badly wrong, the Royal Navy would know about it. And then...who knew? A new threat might be enough to convince the Great Powers to put their petty posturing aside and unite against the common foe. "And then run the preliminary First Contact package."

"Aye, Captain," Morse said. There was a long chilling pause. "First Contact Package Alpha running now."

Stephen braced himself. The First Contact package had never been *really* tested. There hadn't been a chance. And what worked for one alien race might not work for another...

A red light flashed across the display. "Report!"

"They swept us with a radar system," Lieutenant-Commander David Arthur snapped. "It's primitive, but they got us. They know we're here!"

"Finally," Stephen said. "Communications?"

"No response, sir," Morse said. "The package is still running."

Stephen braced himself. Mathematics was supposed to be universal, right? But the aliens might not understand what they were seeing...or the aliens might be still in suspension or dead or...his imagination provided too many other possibilities. The radar sweep might just have been a simple anti-collision alarm. But surely the aliens wouldn't expect a dumb rock to be emanating radio signals. Radio was meant to be universal too.

And they can't stop, he thought. *What will they do if they think we have to be pushed out of their way?*

"No response as yet," Morse reported, a moment later. "But they may need some time to untangle the package."

"Keep us a steady distance from them," Stephen ordered. What if they *were* dealing with dumb robots? Or a society that thought vacuum tubes were the height of computer technology. "We don't want them trying to remove us."

"Aye, sir," Sonia said.

"Picking up a response," Morse said. "They're unpacking the package!"

Stephen allowed himself a sigh of relief. The aliens were still faceless, but at least they'd made progress. "Send the second package," he ordered. They'd have to build up a common language before they could start *talking*, but at least they were on the way. Compared to the previous first contacts with spacefaring powers, it was going remarkably well. "And then send the third when they're ready."

"Aye, Captain."

They're not shooting at us, Stephen thought, as the two ships continued to exchange messages. It looked as though the aliens were as determined to establish contact as the humans themselves. *That's a good thing, right?*

CHAPTER SEVENTEEN

ALICE COULDN'T HELP FEELING nervous as the shuttle slowly flew towards the alien ship.

It wasn't something she should have felt, not after more combat insertions—real or simulated—than she cared to remember. The alien starship was primitive, the crew unable even to scratch *Invincible's* paint. There was no sign of a superweapon that might be able to blast the carrier out of space, let alone the technology that might hint at its existence. And yet, her instincts were nagging at her. Something was badly wrong.

She accessed the live feed from the drones, flicking through them one by one. There was something almost *obscene* about being able to deploy so much surveillance technology without running into enemy counter-measures, countermeasures that were practically off-the-shelf technology back home. Even terrorist fuckers had anti-surveillance tech in their lairs, jamming miniaturised probes that might otherwise reveal their existence. But the aliens were as naked as newborn children. They didn't seem to be capable of tracking the probes, let alone countering them. Their ship was nothing more than a sitting duck if *Invincible* opened fire.

And yet, something just kept nagging at her.

She scowled behind her visor as the pilot altered course, directing the shuttle towards a collection of lights on the alien hull. The massive star-ship was practically a cylinder, rotating to provide gravity at the outer hull, although—with the spin cancelled—she assumed that the entire ship was in zero-g. It probably made it easier to steer, she thought. The aliens were going to have enough trouble entering orbit without rogue gravity fields screwing up their calculations. She'd heard horror stories of ships that had destroyed themselves when the gravity fields went wonky.

"We'll be latching ourselves to the deck," the pilot said, as the shuttle entered the alien shuttlebay. "I can confirm there's no gravity field within the ship."

"Then deactivate our gravity," the ambassador said. She didn't look like much, Alice had thought during their brief meeting, but there was a surprising amount of steel in her voice. "And put us down where they want us."

Alice tensed, despite herself, as the gravity field slowly faded away. She was used to operations in zero-g, but she'd never liked them. A couple of her subordinates swallowed hard, but she carefully didn't look back. Her men had enough sense to inform her if they couldn't cope with the environment. Besides, they had more than enough time to accustom themselves to the absence of gravity. They certainly had the training to cope.

Unless some of them go into alien shock, she thought. She'd never seen it, but she'd heard stories. Men and women who simply could not cope with the existence of aliens. They practically went catatonic when they came face-to-face with a living alien. It wasn't something the navy could test for, not really. She hoped the Foreign Office had had better luck. *If I lose a couple of my men...*

A low *thump* echoed through the shuttle as it settled onto the deck. Alice frowned as she realised the aliens were closing the outer door, even though she'd expected it. The aliens would have to pump atmosphere into the chamber before they could enter, unless they wore spacesuits. Alice wouldn't have blamed them if they had. The humans came in peace, but their bacteria might have different ideas. She kept a wary eye on the pressure gauges and waited.

"We've still got a direct feed to the Old Lady," Corporal Glen Hammersmith whispered. He didn't have to keep his voice down, but there was something about their situation that forced them to be quiet. "They're not trying to jam us."

Sergeant Radcliffe coughed. "Are you picking up any of their transmissions?"

"Very few, mainly low-level radio tech," Hammersmith said. "I've been in terrorist training camps with more advanced communications arrays."

"They'll probably be using an onboard datanet rather than radios," Alice commented. "It won't make *that* much difference as long as the system remains intact."

"The atmosphere is breathable," the pilot called. "Some odd biological particles, according to the scanners, but nothing harmful."

He raised his voice. "Got some movement too," he added. "Aliens. Entering the chamber from the far wall."

"Understood," Alice said. "Put the bio-scanners on alert, then open the hatch. It's time to meet our new friends."

The ambassador had wanted to be the first to leave the shuttle, but Alice had firmly vetoed the idea. She was expendable, while the ambassador was nothing of the sort. The ambassador, thankfully, hadn't known enough to point out that the entire shuttle was trapped inside the alien ship. If the aliens were hostile, Alice would merely be the first to die. But *Invincible* would take a terrible revenge.

She checked her mask and shipsuit as she unbuckled herself from the seat and glided over to the hatch. She felt uneasily naked, even though a handful of weapons had been woven into the suit. Telltales flickered up in her HUD, warning her that her concealed weapons were ready to fire on command. She had no idea if the aliens would realise they were there, let alone take them seriously. A standard-issue rifle was *much* more intimidating—and very much a universal threat. It was better to deter trouble than have to waste time and resources squashing it.

Bracing herself, she stepped through the inner hatch and checked the telltales again, an instant before the outer hatch started to hiss open. The alien shuttlebay was weird, somehow both strikingly primitive and staggeringly advanced. It was huge, yet barren; she couldn't help thinking that it was large enough to take one of the parasite craft, perhaps even a destroyer or two. She triggered her jetpack as she searched around for the aliens, gliding away from the shuttle. Her telltales insisted the air was safe to breathe.

"Here we go," she said.

She unsnapped her mask and took a long breath. If there was anything poisonous in the atmosphere, anything the scanners had missed, she was in deep shit. A rush of alien air cascaded into her lungs, a faint taste of something acidic and unpleasant tickling the back of her throat. She'd been in places that smelt worse, places that were so foul that the marines had joked their mere existence violated the taboo on biological warfare, but never anywhere that smelt so *alien*. She couldn't put a name to the smell. It was simply *there*.

"You're not dead, Captain," Hammersmith commented. "How do you feel?"

"The air smells odd," Alice said, taking another breath. The scent of decay—and age—assailed her nostrils. The alien craft was *old*, very old. She looked down at the metal deck and saw traces that suggested it had been repaired time and time again. "I think they're having problems with their recyclers."

"Or maybe it's the sort of environment they find comfortable," Sergeant Radcliffe offered, dryly. "Look up, Captain. They're coming."

Alice looked up. The aliens were...*alien*. They were so strange that she actually had trouble forcing her eyes to focus on them. The aliens were humanoid, but they were so tall and thin and spindly that she couldn't help thinking of walking trees. Their limbs moved in jerky motions, each one so fast that they seemed to shift position every time she blinked. Up close, their skin was brown, almost reptilian; their eyes seemingly scattered randomly over their heads. They didn't seem to have hairs on their heads, or noses...their mouths were so hard to spot that it took her several seconds to see them. A shiver of fear ran down her spine, despite her training. She was face-to-face with entities that had originated very far from Earth. And there was something fundamentally *wrong* about them.

They're aliens, she reminded herself, sharply. Her heart was pounding so loudly that she half-feared the aliens could hear it. *They're not human.*

The lead alien came to a halt in front of her. She could see veins—or something she assumed to be veins—pulsing under its head. It was hard, so hard, to focus on its eyes. There was something eerie about the way its eyes seemed to have been randomly placed on its head. It was impossible to tell if the alien was male or female. The alien was naked—she thought— but she couldn't see any trace of sexual organs. Perhaps they were hidden. Or perhaps the aliens were so different from humanity that they didn't even have sex. She had no way to know.

She keyed her voder. "I greet you," she said, trusting the computer could produce an acceptable translation. The boffins swore blind that they had the basics of a common language after two days of swapping various first contact packages. But she was all too aware that something could go spectacularly wrong. "We come in peace."

The alien raised a hand. It was *just* human enough for her to feel that it was very *definitely* wrong. She heard a chattering sound, an instant before the translator went to work.

"We greet you," the alien said. Alice's telltales flickered, warning her that the translator wasn't as confident in its work as the boffins had claimed. "We request your help."

• • •

Tiara was torn between admiring the alien ship—it really was a fantastic piece of work, even if the technology behind it was primitive—and wondering just how desperate the aliens had been to risk crossing the interstellar void on such a piece of junk. The constant flow of information from the probes had allowed the analysts to update or revise their projections, confirming Tiara's belief that the aliens had been incredibly lucky to make the crossing without serious incident. It was clear, as the aliens gave them a tour of the ship that seemed to last for hours, that they were desperate. They were practically throwing themselves on humanity's mercy.

Which may have been a mistake on their part, Tiara thought, as they walked through a network of cryogenic cylinders. Hundreds of thousands of aliens were frozen, held in suspension until they reached their new world. *We have bad memories of refugees who outstayed their welcome.*

She forced herself to put aside her concern as the analysts wittered in her ear, providing a commentary that underlined the seriousness of the situation. The alien craft was on her last legs, practically on the verge of total failure. God alone knew how many of the frozen aliens would survive being unfrozen. Humanity had never been *quite* able to work the bugs out of cryogenics, despite a considerably more advanced technological base and a lack of time pressure. There was a good chance that a number of the aliens were already dead. And the ship's drives weren't any better off.

"They should be able to make it into orbit," one of the analysts said. "But if they don't start offloading people soon, their life support system is going to collapse."

Tiara nodded to herself, silently grateful that her training had included a great deal of physical education. She was no marine—the marines had fanned out around her, watching the aliens as if they expected an attack at any moment—but at least the aliens weren't exhausting her as they moved from chamber to chamber. The lack of gravity helped, she supposed. She didn't have to do more than pull herself along lines the aliens had rigged up to speed their transit from compartment to compartment. Even so, it was a relief when the aliens finally showed her to a conference room.

Some things are universal, she thought, as she surveyed the chamber. The furniture had been designed for alien bodies, rather than humans, and it looked a little odd to her eyes, but it was recognisably a conference room. She perched on an alien chair, declined the offer of water and checked her recorder. *And now the real task begins.*

"I am Speaker," the alien said. The translator seemed to hesitate, unsure if 'Speaker' was a name or a title. "I speak for my people."

"I am Ambassador, I speak for my people," Tiara answered, carefully. "Why have you come to our system?"

The alien studied her for a long moment. Tiara looked back, wondering if the alien thought she was being rude. It wasn't something she would have said to a *human* diplomat, although a *human* diplomat wouldn't have needed an unreliable translator to get the point across. She'd been told it was better to keep it simple, where aliens were concerned. They didn't understand the subtleties of human communication, any more than humanity understood theirs. But hopefully they'd understand the point. The analysts had already noted that the aliens seemed to be surprisingly adept at reading and understanding the first contact packages. They'd clearly given the prospect of alien contact some thought.

"We need a new home," the alien said, finally. "Our old one was lost."

Tiara's eyes narrowed. "Lost?"

"It was taken," the alien told her. "We were"—the translator stumbled for a moment—"*invaded*. We were forced to run."

They were invaded by another alien race, Tiara thought grimly. She supposed *that* explained why the aliens had prepared so diligently for another first contact. They must have been terrified when they'd spotted *Invincible* and her escorts. There was no way they could turn tail and run. *And if they're fleeing from an unknown enemy, did that enemy come after them?*

• • •

"It's hard to be entirely certain that we understood them perfectly," Tiara said, two hours after she'd met the alien leader. "But, if we *are* understanding them perfectly, they are fleeing another alien race."

Stephen's eyes narrowed. "Another alien race? Not a faction of their own people?"

"Apparently not," Tiara said. Her hologram was tiny, yet somehow she still managed to look reproving. "They were very clear that their system was attacked by aliens. The defeat was so total that the only thing they could do was adapt an in-system ship for interstellar travel and flee."

"I see," Stephen said. Interstellar refugees...it *had* been one of the scenarios the analysts had drawn up, although they hadn't considered it very likely. "And do they know anything useful about these new aliens?"

"They've given us copies of their records," Tiara told him. "My staff and your analysts are working on them now, but...Captain, their ship is a mess. They're very lucky to have made it across seven light years without something going badly wrong."

Stephen nodded, thoughtfully. He'd been unwilling to risk his chief engineer, but the chief's deputy had volunteered to join the contact party. His report had made extremely interesting reading. The alien ship was primitive, allowing for a degree of in-flight repair that he'd deemed quite impressive, but it was clear that the aliens were at the end of their tether. Their ship was on the verge of coming apart at the seams. There was no way they could alter course and try to reach another star system.

And they're the only ones who know anything about this new threat, he thought. He brought up a starchart and studied the projected tramlines. If the alien invaders knew anything about the tramlines, they could reach Wensleydale within a handful of weeks. And yet...his brow furrowed. *Surely we would have seen something of them by now.*

He shook his head. "How long were they in transit?"

"Around a century, we think," Tiara said. "We're not quite sure we understand time, as they reckon it, but we think they were in space for around a century. That's consistent with our projections."

"I know," Stephen said. A century...humanity should *definitely* have encountered an expanding alien race by now. Unless the second race was under attack by a *third* race...he sighed, dismissing the thought. There was no proof there even was a second race, let alone a third. "Do you think we should let them land?"

"I think we have no choice, unless we want to be responsible for indirect genocide," Tiara said, bluntly. "They've already started waking up some of their settlers for the planned landings, putting an intolerable strain on their resources...our projections say they have a month, at most, before they start suffering crippling shortages. And there are half a million *more* aliens in suspension. They really *do* need help."

Stephen frowned. "It could be tricky," he pointed out. "The government won't thank us for letting refugees land."

"Stuff and nonsense," Tiara snapped. "They're no threat to *us*, Captain. It isn't as if we're planning to settle them in Central London or even on Britannia or Nova Scotia! This planet is a *very* long way from Earth, even with the tramlines. We don't lose anything by letting the aliens have the bloody place!"

The Colonial Office would disagree, Stephen said. There was no way there *wouldn't* be a political firestorm at home, no matter what decision Tiara and he made. *If nothing else, there would be questions asked in Parliament about the planned settlement program...*

He shook his head as he glanced at the engineer's report. Forcing the aliens to stay in orbit would be tantamount to genocide. No, not tantamount. *Identical.* There was no way the squadron could provide enough support to keep the aliens alive...even with help from the colonists, it was going to be tight. The aliens simply hadn't had the time to plan a proper settlement. They'd had to set sail with whatever they'd been able to assemble at short notice.

"Tell them they can land, as long as they acknowledge British dominance of the system," he said, finally. That *might* convince some of the doubters that Britain hadn't given up anything really important. "And then tell them to enter orbit as quickly as possible. It won't be long before word reaches home."

"Understood, Captain," Tiara said. "If nothing else, we *have* learnt something useful from them."

Stephen looked back at the starchart. "Yes," he said. "We have."

CHAPTER EIGHTEEN

"THAT'S A PRETTY IMPRESSIVE bit of handling, captain," Lieutenant Sonia Michelle said, as the alien ship slowly slid into orbit. "They've got a very good crew."

Stephen nodded, curtly. The alien ship might be old and ungainly, but her crew had an instinctive understanding of ballistics and gravity wells he couldn't help thinking that the Royal Navy had lost long ago. The days when Earth-Mars convoys sought out gravity wells for manoeuvring were long gone. There was no *need* to worry about ballistics when drive fields produced all the momentum a ship could possibly require. The alien ship, on the other hand, had to be extremely careful. A single error in their calculations could send them straight into the planet's atmosphere or spinning off helplessly into space.

"Continue to monitor them," he ordered. He was convinced—now—that the alien ship was no military threat, although he feared it was the harbinger of another interstellar conflict. Wensleydale Station had been scanning for alien transmissions—or other STL ships crossing the void in hot pursuit—and found nothing, but Stephen was all too aware that that *proved* nothing. "And keep scanning local space for possible threats."

I'm probably being paranoid, he thought. *But even paranoids have enemies.*

He glanced at his console. They'd sent a message to the Admiralty, outlining what they'd discovered *and* what they intended to do, but there'd been no reply. Stephen suspected that *that* meant the Admiralty—and the British Government—hadn't been able to decide what orders to send back, even though they'd had four days to think about it. They'd probably decided to consult with the other Great Powers, hoping to put together a united response. It was hard to believe that they'd come up with something quickly enough to make a difference.

And they seem to have forgotten how to micromanage, Stephen thought. The flicker network allowed the Admiralty unprecedented power to peer over a captain's shoulder and issue orders from a safe distance. He'd heard the grumbling from his fellow captains about senior officers who didn't really know what was going on butting in and issuing orders that made no sense, but now...the one time he could have used orders from someone higher up the food chain and they didn't come. *They're probably waiting to see what happens...*

"Captain," Sonia said. "They've entered a stable orbit."

"Very good," Stephen said. "Inform them that they can begin settlement at once."

He looked at Newcomb. "Mr. XO, please coordinate our shuttle flights to ensure that they don't get in the way," he said. "We'll help them get as many people down as possible."

"Aye, sir," Newcomb said.

Stephen settled back in his chair and watched as the alien starship launched a small fleet of parasite ships. A number looked odd, too stubby to make it through the atmosphere unless they had drive fields...no, he realised as the tactical display updated, they were using lasers to land on the planetary surface. It wasn't something *humanity* had ever done—drive fields had rendered such technology obsolete before it had ever been truly deployed—but he had to admit the aliens had made it work. They'd have to set up laser launching stations on the surface if they wanted the ships to take off again, he reminded himself, yet that was nothing more than a matter of logistics. Given time, there was no reason the alien parasite ships couldn't be fitted with drive fields.

Once we decide we can trust them, Stephen thought. It would be a long time before the aliens established a tech base of their own—the engineers reported that the mothership didn't have a particularly large industrial capability—but they would. A race that could cross interstellar space on a generation ship wasn't one to take lightly. *And who knows what will happen if we decide we can't?*

He looked at the latest set of reports from the contact team. The aliens were being...odd, a mixture of approachable and standoffish. They were quite happy to talk about the threat that had driven them into the interstellar void, but less happy to talk about themselves. They'd flatly refused to let their people be examined by the xenospecialists, even though they *had* to know that *Invincible* could block their landing with ease. Stephen wasn't sure how he felt about that, although he had to admit that *he* wouldn't be very keen on having his people be examined by alien xenospecialists either. Besides, the aliens *had* let human observers inspect their ship. Not *one* of them had discovered anything out of place.

"I'd like to try to fly one of their ships, sir," Sonia said. "They *have* to be pretty interesting to fly."

"Ask them for a ride, once they've settled in," Stephen said, absently. The aliens seemed to have followed the same basic concept as humanity when it came to getting a lot of hardware—and settlement tools—down to the surface as quickly as possible. They were already launching heavily-armoured colony pods into the atmosphere. "I'm sure they'll be happy to accommodate you."

His intercom chimed. "Captain?"

"Go ahead, doctor," Stephen said.

"Maris and Steward completed their quarantine period," Doctor Isabella Hausa reported, stiffly. "There were no issues of concern, sir: no biohazards, no apparent risk of cross-species infection, nothing that might lead to disaster. I'd prefer to keep Level Two quarantine procedures in place for a while longer, as the alien atmosphere does seem to include a considerable amount of biological matter, but I don't think it poses a threat."

She paused. "That said, anyone who suffers from hay fever may have some problems if they breathe the alien air," she added. "We should be careful."

Stephen nodded. "Do you have any theories about the biological matter?"

"None," Isabella said. "It appears to be dead, as far as we can tell. It's possible the aliens shed skin flakes constantly, like dandruff...it's equally possible that it's part of the alien atmosphere, something they need to stay healthy. All I can really tell you, now, is that it appears to be harmless."

And if you're wrong about that, we may be in some trouble, Stephen thought. *But as long as it's inert, it shouldn't pose a threat.*

"Keep an eye on it," he said, slowly. "Do you believe they pose any threat to the colony?"

"No, sir," Isabella assured him. "Certainly not a biological threat, at least. Right now, I'd be more worried about how their biochemistry will handle Wensleydale. They might not be able to eat anything native to the planet—or to Earth, for that matter. They'll have to set up something akin to our algae farms very quickly."

"We can help them with that," Stephen said. "If they need it, that is. They do seem to have most of what they need to set up a colony."

"Yes," Isabella said. "We do need more information on their biology, Captain. Right now, I'd be afraid to carry out any medical procedures on them. Even something as minor as setting a bone could prove lethal. We have no idea how to *sedate* them, let alone how to treat them. And while I'm fairly sure that the risks of cross-species infection are minimal, there's no way to be entirely sure. We have to be very careful."

"I'll raise the issue with the ambassador," Stephen said. "But it might be a while before you get your answers."

"I know, Captain," Isabella said. "But if any of the aliens die—and we could have prevented it—we might find ourselves facing all kinds of diplomatic repercussions."

• • •

"This would be a nice place to spend a few days," Hammersmith observed, as the marines found a vantage point and settled down to watch. "Climbing hills with a pretty girl, swimming through cold waters with a pretty girl... cuddling together to stay warm because it's bloody cold after our swim..."

"That probably explains why you don't have a girlfriend," Sergeant Radcliffe growled, crossly. "Keep your eyes on our new neighbours."

Alice barely heard him. She was too busy watching as the alien colonist pod fell out of the sky, retrorockets firing just in time to save the pod from a violent landing. Even so, she felt the ground shake when it landed. Two more followed, a third losing control and spilling over to crash into the ground with immense force. The aliens didn't seem to be deterred by the sudden disaster. If anything, it forced them to move faster.

"Impressive," she muttered, as a giant alien ship flew overhead. It looked like a *Thunderbird*-class heavy shuttle, with tiny wings that didn't seem anything like large enough to help it fly, but somehow it made it down to the ground and landed gently. Hundreds of aliens spilled out of the hatches, heading towards the colonist pods. "We couldn't have done it better."

"We would certainly not be treating this as a beachhead on a hostile world," Radcliffe said, as the aliens unloaded the cargo pods. "Look at them, Captain. They're treating this as a forced landing."

Alice narrowed her eyes as she swept her binoculars over the scene. The alien landing zone *did* look like a beachhead, right down to the organised chaos and unspoken disdain for minor accidents that would have been catastrophes everywhere else. She half-expected to see tanks rolling out of the cargo pods, followed by ATVs and self-propelled guns. Instead, the aliens unloaded prefabricated buildings and handed out tools to their people. A dozen alien woodsmen were already attacking the nearby trees, cutting them down to make room for landing strips. It wouldn't be long before they started cutting the wood into planks, then turning them into huts. They wouldn't be very impressive, not at first, but they would do.

Better to be sheltered than to be exposed to the elements, she thought. One of her instructors had told her that happiness consisted of being warm and dry. She hadn't appreciated what he'd meant until her first exercise, where she'd squelched through enough mud to drown an elephant. *They've got their priorities right.*

And yet, she couldn't help thinking that it *did* look like a beachhead. She told herself that she was being silly, that the handful of human settlers were literally on the other side of the planet, but the impression refused to go away. The aliens *moved* like a military crew, rather than a bunch of civilians. And yet...maybe that was normal for them. She'd seen enough alien movements to know they seemed to move faster, on average, than humans. She wouldn't care to have to shoot one if he had a head start.

The hours ticked past slowly, very slowly. Alice passed her binoculars to a couple of other observers, but kept an eye on the alien settlement. It grew with astonishing speed, even though the majority of the buildings were prefabricated. And more and more aliens arrived, every hour on the hour. She couldn't help feeling a flicker of admiration, mingled with unease. How different would first contact have been, she asked herself, if the aliens had possessed advanced technology?

It wasn't a comfortable thought. She was a firm believer in nipping threats in the bud, no matter how harmless they seemed. The Trojan Horse should have been a firm reminder to dozens of long-gone human civilisations that something that *looked* harmless might not actually *be* harmless. Would it have been better if the alien ship had suffered a catastrophic failure in deep space, leaving an empty hulk to drift into the system? Or would humanity need to keep the aliens confined to their new homeworld to ensure they didn't pose a threat?

And Pure Humanity might have a point after all, she thought, darkly. *This race might be a real threat.*

She shook her head, irritated, as she strode towards her bedroll. She was being silly. The newcomers—no one seemed to have agreed on a nickname yet—were energetic, but they were trapped on a single world. They hadn't done *anything* to humanity, unlike the Tadpoles or the Foxes. She was being paranoid, uncomfortably paranoid. And yet, all her instincts kept telling her she was missing something.

"Wake me if something happens," she ordered, curtly. "And be alert for them coming towards us."

"Aye, Captain."

• • •

The water smelled funny.

Tiara tried not to gag as the warm liquid splashed over her naked body, reminding herself—again—that it was probably unwise to swallow the water. It had been treated with disinfectants and a dozen other chemicals to eliminate any possibility of alien biological matter passing through the quarantine and getting onto *Invincible*. Tiara was pretty sure the military officers were being uncomfortably paranoid, but there was no point in arguing. The protocols had been devised long before humanity had *known* it wasn't alone in the universe.

The water cut off. Tiara barely had a moment to run her fingers through her short hair before warm air poured into the chamber, drying her with ruthless efficiency. The inner hatch clicked open a second later, allowing her to step into the next room. A shipsuit and a small collection of underwear sat on the bench, waiting for her. Tiara dressed rapidly, checked her appearance in the mirror and then stepped through the final door. There was no danger. She wouldn't have been allowed through the inner door if there had been even the *slightest* hint of a biohazard.

"Welcome back, Madam Ambassador," Ken Walworth said. Her aide held out a military datapad. "The scanners insist that you're clean."

Tiara glanced at it. The scanners had analysed everything from blood, stool and urine samples to the very air she breathed, as well as any residue from the shower. She had her doubts about the point of *that* procedure—the chemicals should have destroyed anything that might have been remotely dangerous—but it was better to be careful than dead. And yet, Walworth was right. She was clean.

"Very good," she said, taking a long breath. *Invincible's* air felt cool and dry after the alien ship. "Did you arrange a meeting with the captain?"

"Yes, Madam Ambassador," Walworth said. "He said he'd be happy to see you after your return."

Tiara felt her stomach rumble. She was tempted to go straight to her cabin and order food—or do whatever it took to get something to eat—but duty called.

"I'll see him now," she said, reaching for her wristcom before remembering she'd left it in her cabin. There had been no point in taking it to the alien ship. "Can you inform him?"

"Of course, Madam Ambassador," Walworth said. He spoke briefly into his wristcom, listened to the reply, then nodded. "He'll see you in his cabin."

Invincible definitely felt odd after the alien ship, although returning to her was a little like coming home. Tiara couldn't help feeling a little uneasy. The gravity field was pulling at her, tugging her down...she told herself, firmly, that she hadn't been in zero-g long enough for her muscles to start to waste away. Hell, they shouldn't have wasted away at all. She'd had the latest genemods during her last rejuvenation cycle. She nodded politely to the crew—the human crew—as she walked past them, then dismissed her aide when she reached the captain's cabin. The door opened when she tapped the buzzer.

"Captain," she said, stepping inside. Captain Shields was sitting on a comfortable chair, reading a datapad. "Thank you for seeing me."

"You are more than welcome," the captain said, dryly. He put the datapad to one side and stood. "What do you make of our guests?"

"I think they're going to be our *very* long-term guests," Tiara said. She sat on the sofa and waited while he poured them both tea. "They literally can't go anywhere else."

"So it would seem," the captain said, as he passed her a mug of tea. "Earth has yet to give me any actual *orders*, Madam Ambassador, and the longer they take to say something...the harder it will be to change course. Our guests are unloading with frantic speed."

"It's hard to blame them," Tiara said. "That ship of theirs is very definitely on its last legs."

"So the engineers keep saying," Captain Shields said. His lips twitched into a smile. "My Chief Engineer wants to keep the ship as a museum. He thinks it'll be a tourist draw."

"Captain Robbins may have something to say about that," Tiara replied. They shared a faint smile. "We really are *quite* some distance from Earth."

"I know," Captain Shields said. "The real question, of course, is simple. Where are their enemies?"

Tiara frowned. "If they don't have access to the tramlines either," she said, "they wouldn't be able to reach us without crossing the interstellar void..."

Captain Shields leaned forward. "There's no precedent for two intelligent races sharing the same star system," he said. "Even the Foxes and the Cows didn't evolve in the same system. And that means that our mystery invaders either crossed the interstellar void on an STL ship themselves, or they used the tramlines."

"I thought there was a way to generate an artificial tramline," Tiara said. She wasn't an expert, but she'd read the briefing notes carefully. "It was used in the war."

"Yes," Captain Shields agreed. "But *that* technology was derived from the Puller Drive, which can only be used on a tramline. I don't think you can build a jump-line generator without knowing about the tramlines. There's no reason to research gravimetric technology unless you think you can get something practical out of it. And *that* raises a very obvious question, Madam Ambassador."

He met her eyes. "If there *is* a threat out there," he said, nodding to the bulkhead, "where is it now?"

CHAPTER NINETEEN

IF I HAD REALISED *just how much politicking I would have to do when I accepted the post of First Space Lord,* Admiral Sir John Naiser told himself as he stepped into the COBRA briefing room, *I would have resigned on the spot.*

He took his seat in the small conference room and waited, impatiently, for the principals to join him. COBRA—the British Government's emergency crisis response committee—was perhaps the single most important institution in government, as far as he was concerned, but it was a constant frustration that the politicians seemed to feel differently. It might sound good to tell the press that COBRA had been convened—the absence of any media presence ensured that the committee was shrouded in mystique—but it didn't mean the government was actually going to do anything about the latest crisis. The lack of an immediate threat to Britain—or the world—didn't help.

It was hard to keep his face under control as the room filled, even though five years in the job had taught him the value of patience—and humouring politicians. There were times, too many times, when he wished he'd had the sense to stay on the command deck, rather than let the Admiralty cover him in gold braid. It was important to have someone with actual experience in fighting a war—as a starfighter pilot, as a starship captain, as a fleet admiral—to be in a position to give the politicians useful advice, but at the same time...why him? He wasn't the only officer who met the requirements for the post.

But then, I also know when a starship designer is trying to pull the wool over my eyes, he reminded himself, as the door was closed and locked. *And when someone is suggesting an operation that doesn't have a snowball's chance in hell of succeeding.*

The Prime Minister tapped the table, once. "COBRA is called to order," he said. "Sir John, you have the floor."

John nodded. Normally, the Admiralty—or the MOD—would have supplied a dedicated briefing officer, but wallflowers—aides and subordinate officers—were rarely allowed entry to COBRA. He didn't mind giving the briefing himself, although he'd heard that a number of politicians and civil servants considered it to be beneath their dignity. He'd given a number of high-level briefings during his stint in the shipyards and it had always been worthwhile.

He rose, allowing his gaze to sweep the room. Prime Minister Sheldon Henderson looked tired, tired and worn. The Conservative Unionist Party was in trouble; everyone knew the knives were already being sharpened. It wouldn't be long before one of the Prime Minister's Cabinet officers decided to plunge a metaphorical knife into the Prime Minister's back, either out of a belief that new leadership would make a difference or—more likely—personal ambition. John wondered, absently, just who'd strike first.

And the Leader of the Opposition is probably asking himself the same question, he thought, as he activated the display. *A catfight within the CUP will be enough to shatter the government's grip on power.*

"Ladies and Gentlemen," he said. "Five days ago, as you know, Task Force Leinster made contact with the alien ship approaching Wensleydale. A common language was quickly developed, allowing the aliens to request permission to land. Given the...ah...technical problems facing the aliens, Captain Shields made the decision to allow them to settle on Wensleydale."

"Without bothering to consult with us," the Secretary of State growled. Beside him, the Colonial Secretary nodded. "That's *our* planet!"

"It was within his orders," John reminded them, gently. "The aliens literally did not have anywhere else to go."

He paused to see if anyone else wanted to object, then continued. "That alone would be a relatively minor matter," he said. "However, in the course of discussions with the alien newcomers, we have discovered that they were forced to flee their homeworld by another alien race. That race may be a significant threat to humanity."

"And one that happens to be umpteen thousand light years away," the Secretary of State said, coldly. "Can they cross the interstellar gulf to reach us?"

"There are *seven* light years between Wensleydale and the alien homeworld," John said. It wasn't easy to keep his voice calm, but he managed it. "However, there is a very good chance that the alien invaders can use the tramlines."

The Foreign Secretary coughed. "If they can use the tramlines," he said, "surely we should have seen them by now."

"That's a good point," John conceded. "We don't know why they haven't continued to expand in our direction. However, the alien records—once decrypted—suggested that the invaders literally materialised out of nowhere. Cloaking technology...or jumping through a tramline? We just don't know."

"We don't seem to have enough proof to draw any conclusions," the Secretary of State said, carefully. "Do you *know* they're telling the truth?"

"The evidence, such as it is, upholds their story," John told him. "It *is* possible that there's been a massive translation error, Mr. Secretary, but the boffins don't think it likely. The aliens we detected appear to be refugees, refugees fleeing an alien force of unknown power and motivations. That race may be aware of our existence."

"Or they may not even exist," the Colonial Secretary said. "Losing Wensleydale is going to play havoc with our budgets."

"We could simply cancel the settlement plans and reroute the settlers to Albion or even Britannia itself," the Prime Minister said. "Wensleydale was always a long-term project."

"And not one we can give up without getting *something* in return," the Colonial Secretary said. "It will make us look weak."

"It *is* unlikely that we will get anything worth having from the newcomers," the Foreign Secretary said, coolly. "But, on the other hand, we never intended to ship millions of people to Wensleydale. As long as we hold clear title to the system itself, we can proceed more or less as planned."

"We can't," the Secretary of Defence said, flatly. "There's a hostile alien power on our border."

"Which is the *last* thing we need right now," the Prime Minister said. "They may stay away the next hundred years..."

"...Or they might be planning the invasion right now," the Secretary of Defence said. "If they are aware of us, Prime Minister, they have to view us as a potential threat."

He looked at John. "Admiral, I assume you have a plan...?"

John nodded. "We have completed our analysis of the local tramlines," he said, as he altered the display. "As you can see"—he indicated a set of tramlines—"a minimum of four jumps would take a ship from Wensleydale or Falkirk to the alien homeworld. I don't need to add, I think, that none of the systems beyond Wensleydale have been properly surveyed. We simply don't know what's there.

"I propose that we redeploy a task force, probably based around a fleet carrier or a battleship, to Wensleydale, then deploy *Invincible* to scout out the alien homeworld. If we are lucky, she will be able to survey the system from cloak and determine what—if any—threat we actually face, then withdraw as silently as she arrived. If she is detected, on the other hand, she will have a first contact team on board, which will give us at least a *reasonable* chance of opening communications."

"And she can look after herself long enough to break contact and escape," the Secretary of Defence said. "It has promise."

"We might also be able to round up international support for the task force," the Foreign Secretary said. "If nothing else the crisis *might* give us a chance to pour cold water on international disputes."

John winced, inwardly. The timing of the new threat—if, indeed, it *was* a new threat—was appalling. It had been hard enough to get permission to deploy a relatively small task force to Wensleydale...and only the certainty that the STL ship couldn't stop had spurred the politicians into action. Now...humanity might be too preoccupied with its internal concerns to worry about a prospective new threat until it was far too late.

"It's certainly worth looking into," he said, neutrally. "I'd suggest we invoke the Solar Treaty."

"Over a threat that might not even *exist*," the Secretary of State said. "I'm sure *that* will go down well."

"It might," John said. "We have proof, sir, that *something* happened to the aliens. Now, it's vaguely possible that they had a civil war, instead of a full-scale invasion from interstellar space, but *something* definitely happened. And the prospect of a Third Interstellar War might *just* provide enough impetus to come up with a face-saving solution to the Terra Nova crisis."

The Prime Minister nodded. "We can always repeat the proposal to concede Terra Nova to the Chinese, on the grounds they have the wretched planet already, but not the rest of the system or the tramlines," he said. "The Chinese might well accept it if there was a very real possibility of a third major war."

Let us hope so, John thought. He had to admire the Chinese official who'd dreamt up the scheme. Trigger a major war between the factions, then step in to occupy the planet under the guise of avenging the dead ambassadors. And they'd had good reason to believe that no one else cared one whit for Terra Nova. *They'd definitely be able to save some face if they were allowed to keep the planet.*

"It's risky," the Secretary of State said.

"And we will be ceding a planet to aliens," the Colonial Secretary said. "Somehow, I don't think the other Great Powers are going to compensate us for that!"

John took a long breath. "First, the aliens literally have nowhere else to go," he said, sharply. "That ship of theirs was breaking down long before it reached its destination. And second, these are not invaders or migrants in the guise of refugees. It's quite possible that they're the last of their kind. Do you really want to commit genocide? Because that's the only way we're going to get them off Wensleydale unless we care to provide transport to another world."

The Prime Minister held up a hand. "Half a million or so aliens are unlikely to challenge our control of the system itself," he said. "And it wouldn't be the first time we've put a system in international control."

"Vesy was never *ours*," the Secretary of State said. "And the Vesy are no threat."

"Nor are the newcomers," John said. "Their technology is *well* behind ours."

"That might change," the Colonial Secretary insisted.

"We can't go around committing genocide because a primitive race *might* become a threat," John said. "What would you have us do?"

He held the older man's eyes. It was impossible to hide his disgust. The Colonial Secretary wanted something to be done, but he wasn't about to say *what*. And he certainly wasn't going to get his hands dirty. No, he'd expect the military to commit genocide—and it *would* be genocide—while he hid behind interdepartmental memos and concealed his involvement through a series of cut-outs. John was no stranger to making hard choices—and he wouldn't hesitate to do whatever it took to exterminate a real threat to human survival—but the newcomers were no danger. There was no need to drop a hammer on them because the Colonial Office found their presence inconvenient.

"We can survive without Wensleydale, if necessary," the Prime Minister said. "And sharing ideas with the newcomers might give us some newer and better concepts...don't you think?"

"Yes, Prime Minister," the Foreign Secretary said. "Our technology has advanced in leaps and bounds since we started sharing concepts with the Tadpoles."

"So did theirs," the Secretary of State said. "And they *are* a potential threat."

The Prime Minister ignored him. "I'll call for a Great Power conference this evening," he said. "I'll tell them what we've discovered—if they don't already know—and then outline the Admiral's proposal. If they go for it, we can assemble an international task force to cover *Invincible* when she sneaks into enemy space."

"*Prospective* enemy space," the Colonial Secretary said. "And perhaps even *empty* space."

"Perhaps," the Prime Minister said, with the air of a man humouring a fool. "If the other Great Powers refuse to provide support, we may be in some trouble. Can we spare enough ships to provide a covering force without denuding our defences here?"

John took a moment to consider his answer. Theoretically, the Solar Treaty prevented any hostilities within the Solar System itself, but he'd never placed any great faith in treaties. The Indians hadn't broken the Solar Treaty, yet the Indians had had every incentive to play by the rules. The Chinese, on the other hand, might believe they could win a war fought within the Solar System itself...or, more likely, be determined to claw the other powers as much as possible before they went down. He shuddered at the thought. Every simulation of a full-scale war between the Great Powers ended in mutual destruction. The 'winner' might be the only power with a handful of ships left.

And they wouldn't be able to support their ships for long, he told himself. *The shipyards and industrial nodes would be blown to hell.*

"I believe we could spare a fleet carrier and a handful of escorts," he said. "Victorious is completing her refit at the moment, sir; we pushed the work forward as fast as possible after it became clear we might need her. We could dispatch Impervious or Formidable now and replace whoever

187

we sent with Victorious, once she leaves the yard. However, a single fleet carrier is unlikely to deter a full-scale attack. We simply have no idea what we're facing."

"If anything," the Colonial Secretary muttered.

He cleared his throat. "Let's assume, for the moment, that there really is a hostile alien power on the far side of that tramline chain," he said, nodding to the display. "Is it really worth poking the hornet's nest? I assume there's no sign of any immediate threat?"

John frowned. "With all due respect, sir, the unknown is always threatening," he answered, carefully. "We really *do* need to know what might be lurking in unexplored space, even if it isn't posing an immediate threat. Our defence plans may need to be adjusted to cope with a new threat..."

The Colonial Secretary scowled. "Do you always see alien powers in terms of *threats*?"

"Yes," John said, flatly. "It doesn't matter, sir, if we care to admit it or not. A power that *can* threaten us is a power that might *want* to threaten us, one day. They may see us as weak, and weakness invites attack. Or... they may feel that they are so superior to us that they can bully us, or simply refuse to take our considerations into account. It's possible that the aliens may be friendly, that their religion or whatever prohibits them from striking the first blow, but we still have to evaluate them in terms of potential threat."

He looked up at the display for a long moment. "It's possible that we can open communications with the aliens and establish a set of mutually-acceptable borders," he told them. "And we should certainly *try* to open communications. We need to see if we can talk to them, if we can learn about their society and what's likely to trigger them...for all we know, the war started by accident. Perhaps we can avoid another such accident.

"But I don't really believe it did, not if the second group of unknowns have access to the tramlines. They could have avoided combat entirely, if they outmatched the first group so completely. I think we're dealing with a powerful and hostile alien race—or, at least, a race that was powerful and hostile a hundred or so years ago. They may have turned their eyes towards other targets, sir, or they may be gathering their forces for a drive into our territory."

"You could be wrong," the Secretary of State said.

"Yes, I could be wrong," John said. "But tell me...can we afford to take the chance?"

"No," the Prime Minister said. "And we won't."

John felt a flicker of sympathy for the Prime Minister, politician though he was, as the meeting began to break up. It was clear that the Secretary of State was one of those who believed that *he* would make a better Prime Minister—and, with the prospect of another alien war on the horizon, he might have a chance to unseat the Prime Minister. And the Colonial Secretary would back him, if only to make it clear that he didn't approve of the mere *concept* of surrendering British territory. He shook his head in wry amusement as he rose himself, remembering one of his predecessor's more cynical remarks. Only in Britain could bureaucratic infighting be more dangerous than enemy fire.

"We'll have a private meeting tomorrow morning," the Prime Minister said, before John could make his escape. "And then, depending on what the other world leaders say, we'll know how to proceed."

"Yes, Prime Minister," John said. He met the Prime Minister's eyes. "Do you think they'll see sense?"

The Prime Minister sighed. "A lot of political pressure has been building up over the last fifteen years, Admiral; a great many issues have been left to fester, rather than being resolved by diplomacy or force. And now we may not be able to keep the lid on any longer."

"With an alien force of unknown power at the edge of explored space," John said.

"That's a very long way away," the Prime Minister said. "The economic and diplomatic crisis? That's right here on Earth."

CHAPTER TWENTY

"THOSE ARE OUR ORDERS from the admiralty," John said, addressing the room at large. "Does anyone see a problem with carrying them out?"

His gaze swept the room. Commander Newcomb and Major Parkinson would both understand the military necessities, but Ambassador O'Neil and the contact team—the *international* team—might have different ideas. Poking the hornet's nest might, to them, seem dangerously unwise, even if it didn't mean taking them away from Wensleydale.

"I think our orders have to be carried out," Simon Benton said. The xenospecialist—he specialised in alien technology—leaned forward. "If our analysis is accurate, the invaders possessed technology roughly equal to ours...a hundred or so years ago. God alone knows how far they've advanced in the interim. I'm honestly surprised they haven't crossed paths with us a long time ago."

"A couple of the tramlines between us and Alien-One are alien-grade," Newcomb said, quietly. "It's possible they are simply unable to cross them."

"Or they're waiting for us to blunder into their system," Parkinson said. "They might not be *inherently* aggressive unless they know there's something worth taking."

"The Haddocks didn't have interstellar flight," Benton countered. "They couldn't have stumbled across the invaders."

"The *Ha-Hah-Docks*," Ambassador Tiara O'Neil corrected, tartly. "It isn't *that* difficult to pronounce."

Stephen hid his amusement. It had taken two weeks to convince the newcomers to tell the humans more than the bare minimum about themselves...and *nothing* they'd shared had been of particular value. Stephen had read a dozen xenospecialist reports that speculated that the aliens had taboos about talking about themselves, even to the point of being reluctant to share their names. He'd met enough braggarts to be pleased at the thought of a race that considered bragging to be taboo, but still...refusing to share their *name* was odd. And yet, he reminded himself once again, they were alien. They might appear more human than the Tadpoles, but their mentalities might be very different.

"The point remains," Benton said. "They did *not* have the tech to explore the tramlines. *Ergo*, the invaders stumbled across them and attacked."

"The...however you pronounce their name...were presumably broadcasting radio signals into space," Parkinson pointed out. "Someone a little closer to Alien-One than Wensleydale might have picked them up and traced the signals back to their source."

"It's all speculation at the moment," Stephen said. He took a sip of his tea. "Does anyone see any problems with carrying out our orders?"

"I'd be happier with a larger fleet backing us up," Newcomb said, dryly. "But that's not going to happen, is it?"

Stephen shook his head. The briefing from the First Space Lord—and the encrypted message from Duncan—had made it clear that there would be no reinforcements. Convincing the Great Powers to dispatch six fleet carriers, four battleships and nearly fifty smaller starships had been difficult, even though there was at least a *potential* threat lurking near Alien-One. It might have stopped the Great Powers from contemplating a suicidal war, at least for the moment, but it also put a great deal of strain on interstellar shipping. Keeping the fleet in being for more than a few months would be incredibly difficult.

And the main body of the fleet will remain at Falkirk, where it can cut off any enemy strike, he thought. *At least it'll make their logistics a little simpler.*

He sighed, inwardly. That was whistling in the dark and he knew it. Falkirk didn't have the infrastructure to support the fleet. It would take time to build up a logistical support base, time Stephen knew they didn't have. He'd half-expected to be ordered to delay his mission until a base had been established, even though it would have taken months. But the First Space Lord had good reason to want to dispatch the survey mission as quickly as possible.

"We'll be departing this evening," he said, pushing his doubts to one side. "Madam Ambassador, can you do the switchover by then?"

"Yes, Captain," Tiara said. If she was annoyed at passing her work to another ambassador, it didn't show on her face. "I'll be transferring a couple of my personnel to the dedicated contact team, but I don't believe there will be any major problems. The *Ha-Hah-Docks* have not shown any particular attachment to me or any of my personnel."

"They haven't shown much interest in us at all," Parkinson pointed out. "You'd think they'd want to figure out what makes us tick."

"They *are* concentrating on establishing their settlement," Tiara countered. "Winter is coming, Major, and they're the last of their race. Even with our help, they're going to have a tough time of it until the colony is properly grounded. There are a *lot* of gaps in their capabilities."

Stephen nodded. Human colonies tended to be low tech, at least for the first generation or two. Their technology might be primitive, but at least it could be easily repaired. The Haddocks hadn't had the time to plan their colony mission properly. It was a minor miracle that they'd done as well as they had. Stephen couldn't help being impressed. He wasn't sure humanity could have done so well if they'd faced a similar challenge.

"We can concentrate on cultural exchanges and suchlike later," he said, firmly. "Right now, keeping them alive is a priority. The contact team can handle that, surely?"

Tiara nodded. "They've brought a collection of supplies and tech, Captain," she said. "It will be tight, I think, but the aliens should have enough time to establish a colony and make it self-sufficient."

"One hopes so," Stephen agreed. "Do you have any concerns?"

Doctor Percy Ganymede frowned. "They have been reluctant—very reluctant—to allow us to perform any kind of medical examination, Captain," he said. "We don't think there *is* a biohazard—and we've actually learned quite a bit through waste analysis and remote scans—but I strongly feel that we should push them on the issue. If we *are* meant to take an alien team with us, back to their homeworld, we should know how to heal them if necessary."

"They definitely don't like talking about themselves," Stephen said, wryly. He caught Tiara's eye. "Madam Ambassador?"

Tiara looked irked. "From a practical point of view, I agree; we need to know what makes them tick. But from a moral and ethical point of view, we should not be trying to force them onto the examination table. How would you feel if a little grey alien insisted on performing invasive medical examinations on *you*?"

"I'd question the point of rectal probing," Ganymede said. "Although yes, examining someone's wastes can tell us a great deal about their health—and diet."

He met Stephen's eyes. "I understand that there are concerns about accidentally alienating the aliens," he added. "But from a health and security perspective we need to know how to provide medical care if necessary. Something that would help a human get better might well *kill* the aliens and we wouldn't know until it was too late. And besides, we need to know what they can tolerate. If high-g harms them...sir, we have to know about it."

"We can make their participation in the mission contingent on a medical examination," Parkinson suggested. "I assume they'll want to see their homeworld again."

"It might be doable," Tiara said. "But, so far, they have been reluctant to provide us with any medical data."

"You could always authorise more...*invasive* covert scans," Ganymede said. "With all due respect, Madam Ambassador, screening refugees for health risks has been an accepted medical procedure for the last two hundred years."

Stephen resisted the urge to rub his forehead in frustration. "Madam Ambassador, please inform the aliens that they have to submit to a medical examination if they wish to accompany us to their former homeworld," he said. "I understand the concerns, but we do have to know how to treat them."

Tiara frowned, but said nothing.

"We'll be passing through the tramlines and heading straight for Alien-One," Stephen said, into the silence. "Once there, we will carry out a covert survey of the alien system, with particular interest in its military and economic potential. Ideally, we will withdraw without being detected and allow our superiors to decide how best to proceed."

He took a breath. "We will do everything in our power to avoid contact," he added. "But if they do stumble across us, we will attempt to establish communications as quickly as possible. And if that fails, we will attempt to break contact and slip into interstellar space before crossing the tramline. We are not embarking on a mission to liberate Alien-One from its invaders."

Parkinson smiled, humourlessly. "And if we can't escape?"

"We will be operating under strict Quiet Storm protocols," Stephen said. "Our first priority will be to make sure that the enemy doesn't learn *anything* useful about the Human Sphere, particularly its internal astrography. The datacores are to be prepared for self-destruct at a moment's notice, just in case we cannot blow up the ship herself."

He winced at the thought. A Great Power—a *human* Great Power—would take prisoners and treat them decently, but no one knew how an alien race would handle prisoners. The Tadpoles hadn't been kind to their human captives, even though they hadn't been openly malicious. Not, he supposed, that it mattered. *Invincible's* hull would tell the aliens far too much about human technology, even if the datacores were destroyed. He hated to even *think* about triggering the self-destruct, but he knew he might have no choice. A hostile alien race could *not* be allowed to get their hands on humanity's most advanced starship.

Although she may not be that advanced by their standards, he reminded himself. *A hundred years...they could be so far ahead of us that resistance would literally be futile.*

"This will be a uniquely challenging mission," he told them. "But I have faith in our ability to execute it."

"It will certainly be a change," Parkinson agreed, deadpan.

Stephen nodded. *Invincible* had spent the last two months in orbit, watching the Haddocks systematically unload their mothership and establish their colony. It had been boring...and while he was experienced enough to appreciate boredom while he had it, he knew it was starting to get to him. There was a limit to the number of drills that could be carried out to keep the crew alert, while there was little in the way of shore leave facilities on the planet itself. The early colonists had never seen the need to set up bars or brothels or anything else the spacers might want. There simply wasn't much to do on their world.

"Check with the aliens," Stephen told Tiara. The ambassador nodded, shortly. "If they want to accompany us, they can board this evening and settle into their quarters."

"As you wish, Captain," Tiara said.

Stephen felt a flicker of annoyance, which he rapidly suppressed. He understood her concerns, even though he didn't share them. But there were limits to just how far he was prepared to risk his ship, crew and passengers, including the aliens themselves. Maybe the aliens didn't like talking about themselves. That didn't absolve him of his duty to keep his people safe.

"Thank you," he said. He raised his voice. "Dismissed!"

He took a moment to gather his thoughts as his Ready Room emptied, then rose and strode through the hatch. There was work to do.

. . .

"Well, at least they were willing to tell us *something* about themselves now," Ganymede said, five hours later. "They even agreed to let themselves be scanned."

Stephen frowned as he peered into the alien quarters. The Haddocks seemed to like the atmosphere to be warmer and moister than the average human, once they'd been shown how to set the temperature for themselves; he couldn't help wondering if they knew they were under observation. There were five aliens onboard *Invincible* and they comported themselves as if they were in enemy territory. They didn't even *speak* to each other.

"I suppose that's progress," he said. A dull quiver ran through the ship as she prepared for departure. "Did you learn anything useful?"

"Their biochemistry is more adaptable than ours, although that *might* be the result of genetic engineering," Ganymede said. "We're currently decrypting their DNA-analogue, Captain, but at the moment we don't know enough to say for sure. They can eat everything we can and quite a bit more besides, I think. I don't think they'd have any trouble living and thriving on any Earth-compatible world."

He shrugged, expressively. "We may have been worrying for nothing," he added, after a moment. "There's nothing stopping them from devouring plants and animals on Wensleydale. I think they'll be fine, too, unless they require trace elements we've missed. I had a look at their rations, though, and I'm inclined to believe that they won't have any trouble."

"Good," Stephen said. He dreaded to think what the Colonial Office would say if they discovered they had to start shipping emergency food supplies to Wensleydale. Nothing good, he'd be bound. "And from a military point of view...?"

"We haven't tried to stress-test them, of course," Ganymede said. "They're fast, but overall I'd say we're stronger. They don't seem to have so much vulnerability to gas and similar attacks, but I suspect they are vulnerable to sonic or light weapons. I haven't had a chance to assess their brain structure, sir, yet I'd bet that they will have issues when they work in groups. Their eyes seem to be randomly scattered around their heads."

Stephen smiled. "That must cause problems."

"I'm not sure, sir," Ganymede said. He sounded perplexed. "I imagine it must have evolved for a reason, but I don't know what."

He looked at the display for a long moment, as if he wasn't sure what to say. "I'll tell you something else odd about them, sir. Their blood is unusually thick. If they were human, I'd be afraid of blood clots. I'd go so far as to say there are traces of internal organisms within their bloodstreams. But we are reaching the limits of what our scans can tell us."

"And we don't have a body to dissect," Stephen said. "Do they pose any threat?"

"I'm fairly sure, now, that there isn't a biohazard," Ganymede said. "But I'd advise caution, sir. This race is close enough to us, biologically speaking, that cross-species infection is a very real possibility. They may not be aware that they're carrying diseases, Captain, but they may pose a threat anyway. I'm keeping them under quarantine for the moment."

"But if we want them to come out and participate in the mission, we'll need to be sure that they're not contagious," Stephen said. "Do you think we could put them in spacesuits?"

"Their spacesuits are cumbersome," Ganymede said. "I've got the machine shop working on shipsuits for their bodies, sir, but they'll still be cumbersome."

"Understood," Stephen said. "Keep me informed."

He studied the aliens for a long moment, unable to suppress the tingle of unease that ran down his back. The Haddocks had every right to be concerned about travelling on an alien ship—and *Invincible* had to seem like something out of their nightmares—but still...his instincts were insisting, loudly, that something wasn't quite right. Maybe it was just the looming awareness that the aliens were not human. God knew the Tadpoles and Foxes had done things that had surprised and confounded their human enemies.

And these aliens have to be struggling with an inferiority complex, he reminded himself. *The Vesy nearly tore themselves apart when they realised just how far advanced we actually were.*

A question occurred to him. "Do we know anything about their society yet?"

"Very little," Ganymede admitted. "Their society appears to be extremely hierarchical, but that may be an artefact of spending the last century on a generation ship. It will be interesting to see if the frozen aliens have the same attitudes, when they wake. They may not be inclined to submit to a rigid structure calibrated for racial survival in deep space."

He smiled, rather thinly. "That's a long-term study program, of course," he added. "We know nothing about their take on matters like gender equality or social change. They may be as fluid as the Tadpoles or as rigid as the Vesy. We simply don't know."

"Yet," Stephen said.

"Yet," Ganymede agreed. "There are too many points we won't be able to ask them about until we deepen our understanding of their language. The hard sciences are relatively easy, Captain. Two plus two is always four, regardless of who does the counting. But questions about social science are far less easy to get across. They just don't share our assumptions about how the universe works. Even now, it's quite hard to discuss philosophy with the Tadpoles."

"And all too easy to destroy Vesy society," Stephen said. He wouldn't mourn for the brutal aspects of a primitive world, but the good would be lost along with the bad. "We have to be very careful not to damage this society too."

"Yes, sir." Ganymede looked pensive. "That said, I don't think they're in *that* much danger of being overwhelmed."

Stephen's wristcom bleeped. "Captain," Newcomb said. "We have completed our checks and handed local system command over to *Pathfinder*. The remainder of the crew have returned to the ship. We are ready to depart on schedule."

Stephen nodded, allowing himself to feel a flicker of anticipation. They were *finally* heading into the unknown. The prospect of encountering a dangerously-advanced alien race wasn't enough to put a damper on his feelings. He'd joined the navy to see the universe, after all, but he hadn't been anywhere *new*. Now...

"Understood," he said. "I'm on my way."

CHAPTER TWENTY-ONE

"THE FLEET HAS WISHED US LUCK," Morse said, as *Invincible* made her way across the Falkirk System. "They're looking forward to our safe return."

"Glad to hear it," Stephen said. The international fleet was holding position near the tramline, ready to respond to an emergency in the next system or block any alien thrust towards Earth. It was not the most efficient of formations, but he couldn't see any alternative until they knew what they were facing. "Inform them that we will do our duty."

He leaned back in his command chair. "Have *Pinafore* and *Dezhnev* checked in?"

"Yes, Captain," Newcomb said. "They're ready to jump."

Stephen nodded. "Inform *Pinafore* that she is to have the honour of jumping first," he said, calmly. "And we are to proceed on the assumption that the next system is hostile."

"Aye, sir."

The display updated again, a second later, as they approached the tramline. Civilians wouldn't understand how the military *didn't* know what was waiting on the far side, but civilians rarely appreciated the difficulties of interstellar travel. The second tramline out of Falkirk led to a dull red star, one that was almost certainly alone in the dark; no one, save perhaps for rogue colonists, had any reason to give the system more than a brief glance. Nothing hostile had ever come *out* of the tramline and that, as far as the Royal Navy was concerned, was enough to put survey efforts on the backburner. The Admiralty had been far too concerned by the Second Interstellar War to bother devoting resources to exploring a tramline chain that they knew wasn't going to be exploited for decades...

If at all, Stephen thought, grimly. *The economic problems back home might cut down on the colonisation program—or cancel it completely.*

His heart started to race. This was it, a jump into unexplored space. *Anyone* could be lurking on the far side, anything at all. The mystery invaders might have secured the system and turned it into a bastion, although he found it hard to understand *why*. If they'd known nothing about humanity, why worry about securing their borders?

"Message from *Pinafore*, Captain," Morse said. "She's ready to jump."

"Understood," Stephen said. He braced himself, once again. The odds of being intercepted were staggeringly low, as always, but it was hard to escape the sense that *something* nasty was waiting on the far side. "Tell them they can jump when ready."

Pinafore vanished from the display. Stephen silently started to count the seconds in his head, feeling an uneasy sensation of *déjà vu*. They'd taken equal care with the jump to Wensleydale, but here...here there was a *good* reason to believe there might be a welcoming committee on the far side. He let out a long breath when *Pinafore's* icon snapped back into place, five minutes after her jump. There was nothing on the far side but a dull red star.

"Take us through," he ordered, calmly. "And tell *Dezhnev* to follow us in ten minutes."

He gritted his teeth as *Invincible* crossed the tramline and vanished. The display blanked, just long enough for him to feel a twinge of alarm before the system rebooted itself and started to display the live feed from the ship's sensors. A red dwarf hung in the centre of the display, alone save for a couple of comets. There was literally nothing to draw attention from a spacefaring race.

And yet, the system isn't useless, he thought, as the dwarf's other tram-line snapped into existence on the display. It was alien-grade, too weak to be used by any race that hadn't figured out how to use the Puller Drive to enhance the tramline's natural gravimetric resonance. *We can use it to get to the next system.*

"Captain," Sonia said. "It will take us nine hours to reach the tramline unless we break stealth mode."

"We'll take our time," Stephen said, shaking his head. The system looked empty, but that was meaningless. An entire fleet could be hidden in the interplanetary desert, completely undetectable as long as it radiated no betraying emissions. "There's no point in allowing anyone to get a look at us."

"Aye, Captain."

Stephen glanced at Newcomb. "Did our guests have any problems when we jumped?"

"No, Captain," Newcomb said. "They didn't feel *anything*, as far as the scanners could tell."

"Interesting," Stephen mused. Every known race reacted, in some way, to jumping through a tramline. The groundhog boffins might swear that jump-shock didn't exist, but every spacer knew better. "And something that might be potentially worrying, for the future."

He shrugged. "You have the bridge, Mr. XO," he said. "Alert me the moment anything changes."

"Aye, sir."

· · ·

Stephen had half-expected something—anything—to happen, but *Invincible* and her two consorts seemed to be alone in the dull red system. He catnapped in his Ready Room and scanned reports from the xenospe-cialists, trying to get some additional insight into the aliens before it was too late. But nothing happened. By the time he returned to the bridge, a few short moments before the jump into the next system, he felt tired, worn and cranky.

"*Dezhnev* can take the lead, this time," he said. The Russians had insisted on it, probably hoping to get the inside track on claiming any useful real estate on the far side. "We'll jump through as soon as we confirm local space is clear."

"Aye, sir," Morse said. "She's jumping...*now.*"

Stephen exchanged a sharp glance with Newcomb as the Russian ship vanished from the display. The Russians *should* have waited for his order before jumping, even though there had been no suggestion that it wouldn't be forthcoming. He couldn't help feeling annoyed at their presumption. It might be very dangerous if they anticipated orders during combat.

They shouldn't run into any trouble, he told himself, as the icon flickered back into existence on the display. *We're too far from the primary for any hostiles to have eyes on the tramline.*

"Captain," Morse said. "The Russians discovered an Earth-compatible world."

Stephen leaned forward. "Any artificial emissions?"

"None, sir," Morse said. "They're saying the system is empty."

Stephen shook his head slowly. That didn't make sense. The new system—he made a note to register a name for the system as soon as possible—was prime real estate, only one jump from Alien-One. Logically, the aliens *should* have claimed it. They certainly should have made sure that no one *else* could claim it. And yet...he checked the data download from the Russian ship, searching for the slightest hint the system was inhabited. But there was nothing. The system was as silent as the grave.

A chill ran down his spine. Maybe the entire system *was* a graveyard. The invaders who'd driven the Haddocks from their homeworld might have exterminated the unlucky ones who'd been left behind, then exterminated every other alien race they'd encountered. Or...he shook his head, dismissing the thought. For every life-bearing world that evolved an intelligent race of its own, there were fifty life-bearing worlds that developed no life forms more intelligent than a large dog. But...it was still odd. Why would a spacefaring race with access to the tramlines *not* colonise and develop the system?

"Take us through the tramline," he ordered, tersely. It was quite possible that the Russians had missed something. "And keep us in stealth."

The mystery only deepened as *Invincible* jumped through the tramline and glided into the system. It *was* prime real estate. A G2-star: four planets in the habitable zone, one of which wouldn't need any terraforming before the first body of settlers arrived. And yet, the system was utterly silent. No radio signals, no artificial emissions...there didn't even seem to be a colony station orbiting the habitable world. He frowned, again, as the stealth probes slid past the planet, their passive sensors peering down into the planet's atmosphere. If there were any settlements on the surface, they were very well hidden.

"I'm picking up two additional tramlines," Lieutenant Alison Adams reported. A new line appeared on the display. "Both of them should be in use."

"Either they use stealth systems to hide themselves, even when they think they're alone, or the system is empty," Newcomb said. "It makes no sense."

Stephen nodded in agreement. The invaders *should* have made use of the system, particularly as they didn't have to actually *fight* anyone for it, or...or what? They might not have access to the alien-grade tramlines—they might not even realise that the tramlines existed—but that should have made the system *more* attractive, not less. What did *that* mean? Did the invaders not have access to the tramlines after all? Or...or did they simply not think that there was any point in claiming an uninhabited world? Stephen had heard of human empire-builders who'd thought the same way, but none of *their* empires had ever ended well.

"The system appears to be empty, as far as we can tell," he said, an hour later. He'd called a meeting in his Ready Room, inviting Ambassador

O'Neil as well as Major Parkinson. "Can either of you think of an explanation for this?"

"No, sir," Parkinson said. "You'd expect the world to be claimed without delay."

"The Russians want to claim it already," Tiara said. Her voice was irked. "They've already stated that they'll file a formal claim with the World Court, on the grounds that their ship was the first to enter the system and the first to discover a habitable world. Legally speaking, they have a point."

"They'll also be right next door to an alien race of unknown power," Stephen pointed out, dryly. "Is that what they really want?"

Major Parkinson cleared his throat, loudly. "The Haddocks might also have lied to us," he said. "They may have fled a civil war, not an interstellar invasion."

"Their records stood up to analysis," Tiara pointed out. "Or do you feel that a pre-FTL race would be able to create a *fake* set of records that defy all attempts to prove it wrong?"

"Human writers got a lot right," Parkinson said. "We still mine pre-space literature for technological ideas."

"They also got quite a lot *wrong*," Tiara said. "Starships the size of small moons, warships that could devastate entire planets if they coughed, FTL drives that don't depend on the tramlines, artificial intelligence... even technology that might as well be magic. The simplest explanation, which is usually the *best* explanation, is that the *Ha-Hah-Docks* were telling the truth."

"And yet, any race with *our* level of technology should have colonised this system," Parkinson said. "Why didn't they?"

"The Tadpoles settled Heinlein nearly forty years before the human settlers arrived," Tiara reminded him. "And what happened when the settlers *did* arrive? They saw no sign of settlements on the surface, so they assumed that the planet was uninhabited. It never occurred to them to look below the waves."

"To be fair, they also didn't know that there *was* such a thing as intelligent, non-human life," Stephen said. "Do you believe we should proceed?"

"Yes," Major Parkinson said. "There's no way we can complete the mission unless we make the next jump into Alien-One."

"Agreed," Tiara said. "If nothing else, sir, that is where we *know* we'll find the invaders."

"Assuming they exist," Major Parkinson grumbled.

Stephen held up a hand before another argument could break out. "We will proceed on the assumption that there *is* a potential threat," he said. "And we will take every precaution when we jump into Alien-One."

He took a long breath. The perfectionist in him wanted to take a month or two to survey the unsettled system, perhaps with an eye to challenging the Russian claim, but he suspected it would be pointless. If the invaders had claimed the system, he doubted the Royal Navy would be inclined to challenge it; if they hadn't, the Colonial Office wouldn't be keen on taking on new responsibilities. And besides, it would only be delaying the inevitable. They *had* to jump into the next system.

The weight of command settled around his shoulders. "We'll jump in two days," he said, firmly. "That will give us enough time to complete the basic survey *and* prepare to jump some distance from the primary. We really do *not* want to be watched as we make the jump."

"Yes, sir," Parkinson said.

"See if you can stall the Russians for the moment," Stephen told Tiara. "We don't know if the remainder of the Great Powers will back their claim to this system."

"No," Tiara agreed. "It's likely to become a very small issue if we manage to make contact with the invaders."

• • •

"They're really quite odd-looking," Corporal Roger Tindal commented.

"Stow that chatter," Alice snapped. She didn't blame Tindal for finding the aliens a little odd—and unearthly—but they were on duty. "Keep an eye on them."

She glared at the display, wishing they'd been allowed to take up positions within the alien quarters themselves. It would have made monitoring them so much easier. But that hadn't been allowed. The aliens were guests, not prisoners. Alice had no illusions about how carefully their quarters were being monitored—the aliens were being watched closer than some prisoners in jail—but none of it was particularly obvious. The aliens might not realise just how closely they were being watched.

And it will be a diplomatic incident if they ever figure it out, she thought, feeling a swell of boredom. The endless drills had turned monotonous—they'd practiced everything from boarding and counter-boarding to providing emergency assistance to the civil authority—but at least they weren't as tedious as watching the aliens. *Unless they just don't see it the same way as us.*

She kept her face under tight control, even as her mind began to wander. Jeanette's latest message had caught up with her as *Invincible* passed through the Falkirk System, although Alice hadn't had a chance to review it before it had become too late to reply. Jeanette was very insistent that the farm should be sold, to the point where Alice was growing increasingly convinced that her sister was in desperate need of money. But...she wasn't exactly *poor*.

Jeanette probably overextended herself in the stock market, Alice thought. She'd seen how much Jeanette made—and how much money passed through her company, day after day. The farm could be sold for its full market value and it would only be a drop in the ocean. *And she wants money to keep herself afloat.*

"I wonder how they manage to mate," Tindal said. "Which one of them is female?"

"I have no idea," Alice said. The aliens all looked alike to her, save for their eyes. No doubt they thought the same about humans. "Does it really matter?"

"No, Captain," Tindal said. "But it seems to me that they've been very incurious. Remember Captain Hiller?"

Alice nodded, slowly. Captain Hiller had been an American USMC pilot who'd been attached to her unit, back when she'd been a lieutenant. "Yeah," she said. "I remember him."

"He wanted to fly everything," Tindal reminded her. "He'd go into the cockpit or squadron office and beg to be allowed a shot at the controls. And when they'd say yes, he'd hog the controls as long as he could. I heard he did the same when he was attached to the French Foreign Legion."

"I remember him," Alice repeated. She was all too aware she was allowing her irritation to show, but she was too tired to care. "So *what*?"

"The aliens are travelling onboard a starship that has to be fantastically advanced, by their standards," Tindal said. "Why haven't they asked for a tour? Or even a copy of the *Child's Guide to Spacecraft*? Instead, they're just sitting in their quarters...doing bugger-all. They're not even reading their own books, let alone ours."

Alice frowned. Tindal had a point. *She* would be curious if *she* was onboard an alien craft, even if it was primitive compared to human technology. And the Haddocks *had* given the humans a tour of *their* ship. Did they believe that such requests were somehow impolite? Or did they expect *humanity* to take the lead and offer a tour? She'd been in places where the actions of her fellow humans were incomprehensible, let alone aliens. And yet...

It might be rude to ask about the toilet in some parts of the world, she told herself. *But if you needed the toilet desperately, why would you refuse to ask?*

"You should mention that to the intelligence officer," she said, after a moment. Logically, the aliens *should* want a tour. And it wouldn't be hard to give them a tour that would be both fascinating and utterly uninformative.

It wouldn't be the first time a civilian guest had been carefully misled by naval minders. "And I'll make sure to mention it too."

She turned her attention back to the aliens and studied them, thoughtfully. Perhaps they simply weren't comfortable on *Invincible*. The giant assault carrier had to be hellishly intimidating to a race that had needed over a century to cross a mere fifteen light years. Its mere existence told them things about humanity's prowess they probably hadn't wanted to know. FTL drives, artificial gravity, energy weapons...*Invincible* was a clear warning that their race had a long way to go.

And yet, there was something about the aliens that bothered her. Something...something she was missing, something that nagged at the back of her mind. She just wished she could put her finger on it.

A low drumbeat echoed through the ship. It was time to jump.

"We should get some answers soon," she said, softly. "And until then, all we can do is be wary."

CHAPTER TWENTY-TWO

"LOCAL SPACE IS CLEAR, CAPTAIN," Lieutenant Alison Adams reported. "There's no sign that we have been detected."

Stephen nodded, slowly. They were right on the edge of the Alien-One system, so far from the primary that they could be reasonably sure of remaining undetected even if they weren't so deeply in stealth mode that he was nervous about coughing. And yet, there was a quiet nagging doubt about just how powerful the alien sensors might be. The unknown was more worrying than known dangers.

"Hold us here," he ordered, quietly. Each second felt like an eternity. "Do we have a solid link to the destroyers?"

"Yes, sir," Morse said. "Laser links are up and running."

"Good," Stephen said. If something happened to *Invincible*, one or both of the destroyers would flee back to the Human Sphere. The Royal Navy would know that the aliens were hostile and do something about it. "Lieutenant Adams, start deploying the passive sensor arrays."

"Aye, sir," Alison said.

And hope to God they can't pick up what little emissions we're radiating, Stephen added, in the privacy of his own mind. His precautions were excessively paranoid, by human standards, but he really had no idea how good the alien sensors were. His imagination suggested technology straight out of a science-fantasy universe, where starships could be unerringly tracked two light years away. *This could go very badly wrong.*

He forced himself to relax as the sensor arrays came online. The boffins had assured him that they were incredibly sensitive, capable of picking up the merest flicker on the other side of a solar system. Stephen hadn't found that particularly reassuring—the giant sensor arrays protecting Sol might have their counterparts in Alien-One, watching for *Invincible* and her comrades—but there was no help for it. They'd just have to pray the aliens didn't have something so advanced that they could detect a starship jumping through the tramline.

"The system is inhabited," Alison said, quietly. "I'm picking up *thousands* of emission sources, right across the system."

Stephen leaned forward as the display slowly began to fill with icons. Alien-One was fairly typical, as star systems went; three planets within the habitable zone, two more rocky planets *outside* the zone and four gas giants, one large enough to rival Jupiter. And it had been exhaustively developed. There were stations orbiting each of the rocky planets, asteroid settlements in free orbit around the primary and cloudscoops orbiting the gas giants. Smaller icons flickered into existence a moment later, cones of light reminding him about the time delay. The starships and interplanetary spacecraft they represented were moving. It was impossible to say *precisely* where they were.

"Transmit the live feed down to the analyst deck," he ordered. "How advanced is this system?"

"I'm picking up drive fields, sir," Alison said. "They're roughly comparable to our own..."

She paused. "Sir, I'm also picking up fusion torches."

Stephen blinked. "As well as the drive fields?"

"Yes, sir," Alison said. "And quite a few other things. This whole system is very odd."

Newcomb leaned forward. "Do they know about the tramlines?"

Alison hesitated. "I believe so," she said, finally. "They're sending ships towards Tramlines Beta and Charlie. But not Alpha and Delta."

Stephen studied the display for a long moment. There was no way to know where Delta went, not without sneaking a great deal closer, but Alpha...Alpha led to an empty planet, just waiting for settlers. It was odd, to say the least. Alpha didn't *look* to be weaker on this side of the jump. The one-way tramline might be beloved of science-fiction fantasists—it was a fairly common plot device—but no one had ever stumbled across one in real life.

Although there is that tramline that eats every ship that tries to jump through it, he reminded himself. It had taken the various Great Powers several months to realise that there seemed to be no way back for anyone who jumped through, assuming they survived the jump. *Maybe it can only be accessed from one end.*

His eyes narrowed. Alpha wasn't like that, was it? "Why not Alpha?"

"Unknown," Alison said. "They must feel the system is worthless."

Stephen shook his head. The aliens *might* have got unlucky when they'd peered through Tramline Alpha and missed the habitable world, but they should have been able to detect it, simply through its effect on the primary star. And even if they hadn't, the system had quite a few other attractions. The asteroid belt alone should have interested any spacefaring race.

"Odd," he said. "Keep a close eye on that tramline."

He felt his concern start to deepen as more and more data flowed into the system. The aliens seemed to be deploying technology ranging from the modern to the very primitive, more primitive than the alien generation ship. Drive fields rubbed shoulders with simple rockets, even gas jets. Half their shipping fleet seemed dependent on using planetary bodies for gravity-assist, manoeuvring around the gravity wells to hurl themselves across the system; the other half seemed to be comparable with *Invincible* herself, moving freely across the system with no regard for the laws of physics. There were radio transmission everywhere, but they were completely incomprehensible. The translation software couldn't make heads or tails of them.

"The system could be under occupation," Newcomb said, quietly. "Not allowing the locals to possess modern technology might be one way to keep revolutions from succeeding."

"It's possible," Stephen agreed. "But so little of this makes sense!"

The display updated, again. This time, it picked out a number of asteroid settlements that were barely radiating anything. Stephen wondered if they were trying to hide, although it didn't seem likely. They would be a great deal more detectable if someone passed within a few hundred kilometres of their position.

"We'll keep watching them," he said, after a moment. "There's no immediate danger, so we can afford to take our time. And then..."

He shrugged. In truth, he didn't know what they'd do next.

Collect all the data we can, then sneak out of the system and return to the international fleet, he thought. He'd feel better about attempting First Contact when there was a sizable fleet handy to cover the contact team. The aliens were clearly *capable* of building warships...and the Haddocks had made it clear that they *had* built warships. *And then we can decide what to do next.*

• • •

"Well," Tiara said. "They're not limited to just one system, are they?"

She allowed her eyes to sweep the compartment. Two of the Haddocks—the *Ha-Hah-Docks*, she reminded herself sharply—were standing in front of the table, wearing shipsuits that bulged in odd directions when they walked. A handful of marines stood at the rear, keeping an eye on the aliens; the remainder of her team, and the captain, were seated at the table. It was, quite possibly, the oddest meeting she'd ever chaired. And, perhaps, the most important.

"No, Madam Ambassador," Simon Benton said. "It's fairly clear they do have access to the tramlines."

"Except they don't make any use of Alpha and Delta," Tiara said. "Does anyone have an explanation for *that*?"

"No," Captain Shields said. "Our best projections say that Delta leads to another G2 star, so they *should* be making use of it. We don't understand why they seem disinclined to use two of the tramlines."

Tiara made a face. She'd studied dozens of possible scenarios—ranging from two races evolving in the same system to alien renegades being forced to run for their lives—but a multi-system alien empire was perhaps amongst the worst. There was no way to predict how the newcomers would react to humanity, let alone what they'd do when they discovered that humanity had encountered refugees fleeing their tyranny. She simply didn't know what to make of it.

She looked at the captain. "Is there any sign they're more advanced than us?"

"Not as far as we can determine," Captain Shields said. "But we may be missing the signs."

"Or this might be the very edge of their territory," Benton offered. "For all we know, Madam Ambassador, all their *really* advanced stuff is on the other side of the galaxy."

"That would be bad," Tiara agreed, dryly. "Do we have any *proof* that this is one small outpost of empire?"

"No," Captain Shields said. "But we don't have any proof it isn't, either." He leaned back in his chair. "We have two choices," he said. "We can remain here, for the moment, and continue to monitor them. Given time, we might be able to crack their language and start listening to their communications. Or we can sneak back out and whistle up a few reinforcements."

"Like a few thousand ships," Benton said. "Madam Ambassador, if this system is all they have, they'd still pose a significant threat. And if they have more systems on the same scale, they may be considerably more dangerous than we think."

"And yet, this system may be under occupation," Tiara said. She looked at the lead alien. "What do you think?"

"We do not know," the alien said. The voder stripped his voice of all emotion. "We are unaware of what has transpired in our absence."

Captain Shields frowned. "Can you understand the transmissions we piped through to you?"

"No," the alien said. "None of them were understandable."

Which means...what? Tiara didn't care for the implications. *Was there a physical genocide or a cultural one? Or are we misunderstanding what we're seeing?*

"Captain," she said, slowly. "What do you recommend?"

"I think we should continue to gather information, for the moment," Captain Shields said. "If we don't crack their language or discover anything else useful by the end of the week, we slip out again and report back to Earth."

Tiara nodded to herself. It wasn't as bold or as daring a plan as she might have expected from a military officer, but she couldn't fault the logic. They were already pushing the limits of what could be learnt from long-range sensors, yet there were few other options. Going closer raised the odds of being detected considerably, but there might be no other way to find out more. And yet...

We really need more ships out here, she thought. *If nothing else, we might need to make it clear that we won't be pushovers.*

"Very well," she said. "We'll stay here for a few days, then withdraw."

Ganymede coughed. "I think we should withdraw now," he said. "We know enough to convince Earth to take the threat seriously. I'd be happier making contact *after* we've fortified Falkirk and a handful of other worlds."

"The odds of being detected are quite low," Captain Shields said. "But it might be wise to send *Dezhnev* back to Falkirk."

"Send *Pinafore*," Tiara advised. "We don't want to risk any...political issues...creeping into the report."

Captain Shields looked displeased, but nodded anyway. "Very well."

"This is our system," the alien said. "Can we watch with our own eyes?"

"I believe so," Tiara said. "Captain?"

"We can give you access to the observation blister," Captain Shields said. "But it may be a long time before you go home."

• • •

Stephen was more used to boredom than he cared to admit. Someone—he'd forgotten who—had once pointed out that military service was ninety percent boredom mingled with ten percent sheer terror and his experience had tended to bear that out. Cold logic told him that the odds of being detected were very—very—low. And yet, as *Invincible* lurked at the edge of Alien-One, he couldn't help feeling as though he was just waiting for the other shoe to drop. He stood watch on the bridge, visited every compartment time and time again to make sure the crew was alert, then slept fitfully...half-convinced that, every time he closed his eyes, he'd be awakened by the alarm.

He made a point, every day, of reviewing the latest sensor records—and analyst reports—but none of them could tell him anything really useful. They'd picked up alien ships he was *sure* were cruisers, carriers and even battleships, but he had no feel for the alien mentality behind them. What would they consider acceptable tactics, if push came to shove? And how far were they prepared to go to get what they wanted? He couldn't really disagree with the assessment that indicated that the entire system was under occupation. It just didn't seem very logical to him.

In the long-term, taking slaves and working them to death just isn't economical, he told himself. That had been proven true, time and time again, for any society that developed technology. The effort involved in enslaving people could be better used elsewhere, not least because the slaves themselves didn't like being enslaved. Slave revolts rarely succeeded, but they could be thoroughly disruptive. *So how has this occupation lasted for so long?*

It made no sense to him. The aliens surely wouldn't give their best if they weren't benefitting from it. Collaborators had to get *something* out of collaboration, something more than merely being given a little power to abuse their fellows. Human experience insisted that *true* integration only worked when the conquered were shown a path to equality with the conquerors. But here...it looked as if the invaders *had* successfully crushed any opposition from the conquered, then put them to work. Unless they were misinterpreting the data, of course. *That* was all too possible.

He shook his head slowly, wondering if today was the day he'd override his concerns and dispatch stealth probes to the alien homeworld. The odds of being detected were still very low, although if they *did* get detected the aliens would know that *someone* was watching them. He'd read a dozen proposals for getting a little closer to the aliens without being detected, but none of them were as flexible as the stealth probes. And yet...he sighed out loud. There were risks, inherent risks, whatever he did. He just had to accept it and move on.

Who would want to be in command, he asked himself, *if he had to make a call that might start an interstellar war?*

His door buzzer rang. He looked up, surprised. Very few people would visit his cabin, not when he held most of his meetings in his Ready Room. His cabin was *his* place, the place he went to rest after a long day. It wasn't somewhere he cared to be interrupted.

"Enter," he ordered.

Ambassador Tiara O'Neil stepped into the room, looking as calm and composed as ever. Stephen frowned—she could easily have called ahead to say she was coming—and then straightened his tie. She'd probably seen worse than a middle-aged naval officer without a jacket in her career. Besides, she'd never struck him as someone likely to make a fuss about pointless protocol.

Which is an asset, in her position, he thought, as he stood. *Aliens might not take our protocol very seriously.*

"Madam Ambassador," he said. "What can I do for you?"

"Very little, I suspect," Tiara said. She gave a smile that took the sting out of the words. "Unless you have all the answers we seek...?"

"I'm afraid not," Stephen said. He motioned her to a chair, then walked over to the drinks cabinet. "Would you like something to drink?"

"Just tea, if you please," Tiara said. "I have to keep a clear head."

Stephen nodded as he tapped the water heater. "Good thinking," he said. Two of his crewmen were in trouble because they'd drunk more than they should. They were still on punishment duty, no doubt thanking their lucky stars that they hadn't tried to report for duty while drunk. Men had been *hanged* for being drunk on duty. "I've got some Jamaican Leaf Tea."

He dropped the teabags into mugs, then filled them with water. "Do you have any new insights?"

"Very little," Tiara said. "I just have the feeling that I don't understand what I'm seeing, which is very frustrating. Unravelling the secrets of the Russians or the Chinese would be easier, I'm sure."

"They're human," Stephen commented. He poured milk into the mugs, then passed one to her. "And the aliens are...well, *alien*."

He met her eyes. "Do you have any specific concerns?"

"We're going to have to make contact with them," Tiara said. "What happens to the *Ha-Hah-Docks* when we do?"

Stephen winced, openly. Human history showed a wide range of precedents, few of them good. Refugees were rarely welcome when they returned home...if, indeed, they *were* allowed to go home. It was quite likely that, for most of the refugees, Wensleydale would be the only home they'd ever know.

"We'll have to see what the diplomats say," he said. "Who knows? Maybe the invaders and the invaded have formed a partnership."

"Perhaps," Tiara said. "How much would you bet on it?"

Stephen opened his mouth to reply, but his wristcom bleeped before he could say anything.

"Yes?"

"Captain, we've detected an alien starship near the outermost gas giant," Newcomb said. "It appears to be dead, as far as we can tell. There's no sign of life."

Stephen exchanged glances with Tiara. "Launch two stealth probes to make a very close-range inspection," he ordered, as he brought up the in-system display. He couldn't help a thrill of anticipation. If the alien ship was truly abandoned—and derelict—they might have had their lucky break. "And prepare a boarding party."

"Aye, Captain," Newcomb said. "I'll launch the probes at once."

"I'll want to send some of my experts along," Tiara said, quietly. "They're familiar with alien tech."

"Then send them to join the marines," Stephen said. "And warn them that this is a very delicate operation."

"Of course, Captain," Tiara said.

CHAPTER TWENTY-THREE

IN SPACE, ALICE HAD HEARD, no one can hear you scream.

Her lips twitched. *Unless you have the comlink on, in which case* every-one *can hear you scream.*

It didn't make her feel any better as she slowly glided towards the alien ship, feeling her heart starting to thump in her chest. It was easy to for-get just how *big* space was inside a starship, with metal bulkheads and few portholes. She could pretend she was in an underground complex, one where she could step out into the light at any moment. Now, inside a Mobile Combat Suit, she couldn't hide from the truth. She was very small—tiny, really—and space was very, very big.

The suit turned slightly, allowing her to see the derelict alien ship. A pair of stealth probes had hung next to the alien craft for hours, watching for the slightest hint that the aliens might actually be alive. But the alien ship was as dark and cold as the grave. Alice wasn't sure what to make of it. An older ship might be outdated now—there were some ships in naval service that wouldn't last very long if they had to fight a modern battle—but surely the aliens could have stripped the hulk of anything useful and then reprocessed the hull to provide raw materials for another starship. There was literally nothing to be gained by leaving the hulk in an orbit that would eventually, inevitably, decay. It worried her more than she cared to admit. If the aliens were prepared to simply write off a starship, just how many ships did they have?

She sucked in her breath, feeling very alone as the alien ship took on shape and form. The boffins had assured her, during training, that microburst transmissions were almost impossible to detect except at very close range, but the boarding party had orders to maintain radio silence anyway. She didn't really blame Major Parkinson and Captain Shields for insisting on it. The system was teeming with alien life. A single transmission might be enough to lead the aliens right to them.

The alien craft looked...odd. It reminded her of a human starship, rather than the more organic designs flown by the Tadpoles, but...there was something odd about it. The ship appeared to be modular, like most human ships, yet...the hull—too—appeared to be modular, put together in a manner that was oddly familiar. It nagged at her mind until she put her finger on it. One of her boyfriends, years ago, had been an avid modeller, purchasing modelling kits and putting them together with his bare hands. Once, he'd bought a handful of incomplete sets and mingled them together to create a unique design. It seemed to Alice, as the alien ship drew closer, that the alien designers had done the same. Their ship looked to have been put together from a multitude of parts.

It looked almost like an assault shuttle, she thought, as if the designers had *wanted* to suggest that it could enter a planet's atmosphere. She would be astonished if it *could* and outright flabbergasted if it could actually take off again. The hull didn't *look* strong enough to survive a trip through a planet's atmosphere, and the wings were little more than decoration, although she had to admit that was meaningless. Alien technology might be capable of getting a ship down to the surface and up again without problems. If they could...

They may think this ship is primitive, she thought, grimly. *And they didn't even think she was worth breaking down for scrap.*

She braced herself as the alien hull grew and grew until it dominated the horizon, her perceptions twisting until the hull was below her. Her magnetic boots snapped on automatically as she touched the hull, so gently that she was *sure* she hadn't triggered any alarms. She waited anyway, watching her suit's sensors carefully. If the aliens had detected them...but there was nothing. The alien ship remained dark, cold and utterly silent.

The hull was pitted with *something*, she thought, as the boarding party started to search for a hatch. It was hard to escape the sense that the alien ship had been in space for a very long time. The paint was almost completely gone, leaving flakes of metal exposed to vacuum and bathed in surges of radiation. She kept an eye on her suit's sensors, half-expecting to discover that the ship's power plant was dangerously radioactive. But if the hulk had been genuinely dangerous, surely it would have been pushed towards the local sun. It was how humanity had cleaned up nuclear waste dumps after the orbital towers had been completed.

A marine held up a hand, signalling her. Alice walked over and saw a gash in the hull, leading into the darkness. She shone her light into the hole, picking out what looked to be a fairly standard interior design. The decks appeared to be made of something thin and flimsy—she couldn't help thinking of aluminium—that hadn't stood up well to whatever had hit the hull. It looked as though the impact had devastated the interior.

A mass driver? It was possible, although she would have expected a mass driver to destroy the entire ship. *Did one of the defenders score a lucky hit?*

She took a breath, then slowly lowered herself into the alien ship. The darkness rose up around her, seemingly reluctant to retreat as she shone her light around. There was something about the interior that sent a chill down her spine, something she couldn't put her finger on. It was alien, yet...almost human. The bulkhead hatches looked as if they were designed for something akin to humans.

Although they're bigger than they need to be, Alice thought, slowly. *Maybe the aliens are bigger than us.*

She pushed the thought aside as the remainder of the contact team joined her. The marines fanned out, watching for threats, while the xenospecialists deployed a handful of sensors and started to inspect the bulkheads. They'd wanted to deploy research drones, back when the mission had been planned, but Alice had flatly vetoed it. The drones *would* make it easier to survey the alien ship, yet they would also increase the risk of detection. She was damned if she was going to let the aliens see they were there until it was too late.

Or at all, she told herself. *Ideally, we want to go in and out before it's too late.*

Doctor Simon Benton leaned over, pressing his fingers against her suit's contacts. "I can't find a computer node within the hull," he said. He sounded remarkably calm, for a civilian inside an alien ship. "We'll have to go further into the ship."

"Understood," Alice said. The aliens clearly didn't believe in distributed datanets. Or maybe the contact team simply hadn't been able to find a local node. She rather doubted the nodes would be particularly useful, not after they'd been exposed to vacuum and radiation for hundreds of years. "We'll go in a moment."

She took a second to shoot a report back to *Invincible*—if the aliens could detect a laser transmission, humanity was in deep shit anyway—and then used hand signals to communicate her orders to the platoon. A pair of marines would guard the hatch while the remainder of the boarding party started to explore the ship. Given time, Alice suspected, they'd have to set up living quarters on the alien ship, somewhere the contact team could take off their suits and relax for a few hours. She'd slept in her suit before, but she had to admit it wasn't a pleasant experience. There was a reason suits were rarely used on active service.

The interior of the alien ship was creepy. It was just human enough, she decided as she peered into darkened chambers, to be disconcerting. She expected to see bodies, every time she turned a corner; she expected to see pieces of debris drifting in zero-g. And yet, the air was clear. The aliens might have swept the hulk for anything useful before abandoning her, but...she shook her head. It made no sense at all. Maybe they'd declared the hulk a tomb, or a war memorial. *Ark Royal's* grave—really, nothing more than an expanding field of debris—was sacred, as far as the Royal Navy was concerned. Scavengers would never be permitted to remove even a single plate of armour from the site.

And that means we might have trodden on their feet, she thought, grimly. She'd heard stories from Vesy. The natives were generally respectful of humans, but they went utterly berserk when their sacred ground was violated. *They may see our presence here as a deliberate affront.*

She kicked herself, mentally, for not thinking of that earlier. It probably wouldn't have been enough to keep Captain Shields from ordering them into the alien hulk, but...he should have kept the possibility in mind. Perhaps he had. Alice was hardly one of his confidantes. Major Parkinson presumably had a good relationship with the ship's captain—traditionally, the CO and the senior marine were meant to be close—but she didn't know for sure. Captain Shields had always struck her as being someone promoted slightly above his level of competence.

He'll grow into the role, she told herself. *Didn't you have problems when you were promoted too?*

She pushed herself around a corner and stopped, dead. *Something* was floating in the air...blood? She leaned forward, trying to peer through the haze. Was that an alien body on the far side? It was hard to be sure. She'd seen horrific sights when the marines had raided terrorist or insurgent lairs—they treated their prisoners terribly—but this was worse. The body looked like a hunk of meat. It looked as though the alien had been systematically flogged to death before the body froze.

Her gorge rose. She swallowed, hard. Throwing up inside a suit would be thoroughly unpleasant. And besides, she couldn't afford to show weakness.

"I'm picking up traces of alien biomatter," Doctor Hammond said, as he touched her suit's contacts. The xenospecialist sounded sick. "And...I'm not sure what happened to him."

"Bag up the body," Alice ordered, sharply. "Get it back to the waypoint."

She didn't want to watch. The body had been flogged so thoroughly that it was impossible to tell what the alien had looked like, when it had been alive. It was deeply disturbing. She had no compunctions about using torture to make a suspect talk, if they were pressed for time, but this...this was pointless sadism. No one could have inflicted such horrific injuries without some degree of hatred being involved. She didn't think she wanted to talk to the aliens unless humanity held a very definite advantage...

Benton caught her eye. "There's an access point over here," he said, as the xenospecialists carefully manoeuvred the body back to the gash. "I should be able to get inside."

"Do it," Alice ordered. "We'll concentrate on searching the rest of the ship."

The alien ship slowly gave up its secrets as the marines probed its bowels. There were a dozen or so bodies, all treated so violently that no one could swear to just how many bodies there actually were. Alice couldn't fathom just how badly they'd been treated in their last moments of life. She'd been warned of just what she could expect, if she fell into enemy hands, but...but this was worse. The aliens had to be monsters.

Perhaps we should sneak out of the system, fortify the tramlines and then make contact with the entire navy behind us, she thought, as she peered into yet another compartment. She *thought* they were heading towards the bridge, but it was impossible to be sure. The engineers weren't making much progress on tracing the power linkages running through the ship. *These aliens are dangerous.*

Her head started to ache as they slowly made their way towards the ship's prow. She was going into alien-shock, she suspected. The alien ship was getting to her. The proportions were subtly wrong. It was close enough to human for the differences to start wearing away at her mind. She felt sweat beading on her forehead as she turned and led the way back to the gash, making a mental note to set up a relay system as quickly as possible. It would be a great deal easier to cope if they could talk to their fellows.

At least I'm not the only one having problems, she thought, as the marines regrouped. *We simply don't have any way to train for alien contact.*

Benton waved for her attention. "I think I found a computer node," he said. "The tech doesn't look that advanced, compared to ours, but the interior has been thoroughly fucked. I don't think we're going to be able to draw anything from it."

Alice wasn't surprised. Wiping datacores and then destroying them was standard procedure, even when dealing with alien enemies. God knew *these* aliens were perfectly aware that they weren't alone in the universe. They even appeared to have enslaved their victims, something the Tadpoles or the Foxes had never done. And that would give their slaves an excellent chance to learn about them too. Alice couldn't recall a slave revolt that had actually succeeded, but it only had to happen once.

She leaned against a bulkhead. It felt oddly soft against her back, as if one good push would be enough to bring it crashing down. "Can you tell us anything *useful* about the ship?"

"Very little," Benton said. "Technologically, she's not particularly advanced. I'd say she was on the same level as *Ark Royal*, back when she was new. There's nothing to suggest the presence of any super-technology here. But she might well be outdated, as far as the aliens are concerned."

Alice nodded, ruefully. There was no way the aliens would leave a *useful* ship floating around uselessly. Surely, repairing her would be cheaper than constructing a whole new starship. But...she shook her head, crossly. She was sure they were missing something, she just didn't know *what*.

"The bodies are on their way back to *Invincible*," she said. "Hopefully, they'll tell us something useful about the aliens."

"Hopefully," Benton agreed.

Corporal Hammersmith pulled himself into the chamber. "Captain," he said, touching his hand to her suit. "We found the bridge!"

Alice pushed herself away from the bulkhead. "Where?"

"It's right at the front of the ship," Hammersmith said. "And it appears to be intact!"

Alice puzzled over it as Hammersmith led her and Benton down a dark corridor. No one in their right mind would put a starship's bridge somewhere *vulnerable*, not unless they had a death wish. A civilian ship might be *designed* to suggest that the bridge was at the top of the hull, but the *real* work would be done elsewhere. *Invincible's* bridge and CIC were deep within the carrier's hull, protected by layer after layer of armour. The ship was designed to take one hell of a pounding before the command network failed.

But Hammersmith was right. The alien bridge *was* at the prow of the ship. It made absolutely no sense. A single laser warhead would be enough to cripple the ship, unless the armour was better than she thought or there was another bridge—a real bridge—further inside the hull. But they were steadily putting together a map of the ship's interior, their suits trading pieces of data and blending them into a whole. There simply wasn't much room for a secondary bridge.

Perhaps they planned to fly the ship from engineering, she thought, as Benton set up a local communications network. *But even that would be chancy.*

She surveyed the alien bridge for a long moment, wondering just what the aliens had been thinking. The bridge was smaller than she'd expected, consoles and chairs scattered around the compartment seemingly at random. There didn't seem to be a command chair, or anything that suggested that one of the aliens was actually in charge. She didn't think there was a hierarchy at all. Unless the alien captain stood...it was possible, she supposed, but unlikely. The compensators might have problems at an awkward moment and send the alien sprawling.

"The command network appears to be intact," Benton reported, as he bent over one of the alien consoles. "We should be able to hack into the system."

Assuming there's anything left to find, Alice thought. The aliens wouldn't have needed to destroy the entire ship to render her effectively useless. Merely wiping or removing the datacores would be enough to do *that*. *They might just have left us nothing to find.*

She shook her head, sourly. She was starting to suspect they were wasting their time. The alien bodies *might* tell the xenospecialists something useful about the aliens and their biology, but the ship wouldn't tell them anything about modern alien technology. And yet, they had to keep exploring the ship. It might tell them something useful.

We know they're roughly humanoid, she told herself. The ship had clearly been designed for humanoid life forms. *But then, every alien race we've encountered has been humanoid.*

She looked up as Sergeant Radcliffe entered the compartment. "Captain, we've finished surveying the engineering section," he said. "It's surprisingly advanced for such a primitive ship."

Alice lifted her eyebrows. "Can we learn anything from it?"

"The engineers seem to think so," Radcliffe said. "The ship's drive is outdated in some ways, they say, but more efficient in others. It might be worth duplicating."

"That's something," Alice said. She felt a flicker of amusement. "There'll be a finder's fee, won't there?"

"I dare say," Radcliffe said. She *heard* the grin in his voice. "That will encourage the engineers to work harder."

"And us too," Alice said. "I could do with the money."

CHAPTER TWENTY-FOUR

"YOU'RE NOT GOING TO BELIEVE this, captain," Doctor Percy Ganymede said. He stood on one side of the quarantine field, looking down at his console. Stephen stood in the observation chamber, watching through the surveillance monitors. "The bodies...there are three *different* races amongst the bodies."

Stephen blinked. "You mean...we're dealing with a multiracial polity?"

"I'm not sure," Ganymede admitted. "Captain, these bodies are in *awful* condition. I think someone actually used a cell disrupter on the bodies before they froze. Their biomatter has been ripped to shreds. But I've been able to recover enough to indicate the presence of three different races, only one of which is known to us."

"The Haddocks," Stephen said.

"Yes, Captain," Ganymede agreed. "The problem is that all three bodies have something in common. Their DNA-analogues contain fragments of a *fourth* DNA-analogue, the same in all three cases. It's pervasive enough that I might suspect that they were actually hybrids, were that not extremely unlikely. The three races do not appear to be actually related."

Stephen frowned. "Are you saying that three races somehow managed to interbreed?"

"I'm not sure," Ganymede admitted. "It's biologically impossible. I don't think that it would be possible even with extensive medical intervention. I've certainly not heard of any projects to crossbreed humans with Tadpoles, or Foxes, or...or any non-human race. It would be a great deal of effort for no appreciable purpose."

He shrugged, expressively. "It's also possible that I might be misinterpreting the data," he added, after a moment. "These bodies are very badly battered, sir. I may be completely wrong."

"I hope so," Stephen said. If Ganymede was right...it didn't bode well for the future. "It could be just a misinterpretation."

"They may be light-years ahead of us in biological science, sir, if they *can* interbreed two wholly separate races," Ganymede warned. "We can enhance human senses to some degree, or splice in gills and bone reinforcements for mermen, but we can't even begin to splice in alien organs. I don't think that any doctor worthy of the name would be willing to try. It would be against the code of conduct."

Stephen nodded, slowly. He knew, all too well, that secret facilities *did* carry out research into biological warfare—and alien DNA—but such work almost never went mainstream. And he couldn't imagine the researchers trying to combine human and alien organs to produce...to produce what? The very thought was sickening. And yet...he thought he could see the logic. An invader might start biologically assimilating a conquered race to prevent them from retaining a separate culture of their own. Human conquerors had tried to do the same, time and time again. It even worked, sometimes.

"Keep me informed," he said, finally. "I'll be on the bridge."

He scowled to himself as he turned and walked out of the compartment, heading to the intership car. The engineers had started dissecting the alien ship's drive, making a number of interesting discoveries... but none of them justified risking his ship. *Invincible* was far too close to an overwhelmingly powerful alien race for comfort. The destroyers were receiving copies of everything *Invincible* discovered, and they were in position to flee if the aliens stumbled across the carrier, yet...they were running an awful risk. It wouldn't be long before he'd have to decide if he wanted to stay, and risk contact, or sneak out of the system and whistle up reinforce-ments. He didn't want to make contact with the aliens without a sizable force at his back.

But we know next to nothing about them, Stephen told himself. *We don't even know how to talk to them.*

It wasn't a comforting thought. An interstellar empire that included at least three races *should* know how to establish communications—there was no point in issuing orders to one's subjects if the subjects couldn't understand them—but it might take time to build up a common language. Again. Who knew how they'd react if they heard humans speaking in the language of one of their slave races? If, of course, the Haddocks were slaves. A hundred years had passed since the generation ship had fled into inter-stellar space. The slaves might have become partners in empire by now.

And yet, we can't understand their messages, Stephen thought. *And they seem to be using tech from a dozen different eras simultaneously.*

He strode onto the bridge and checked the main display. It seemed crowded now, filled with hundreds of icons representing everything from alien starships and spacecraft to asteroid settlements and mining sta-tions. He found it hard to believe that the aliens wouldn't stumble across *Invincible* sooner rather than later, although cold logic told him that the odds of detection were still quite low, as long as they were careful. *Invincible* was doing her best to pretend to be a hole in space. No one would know any different as long as they kept their distance.

"Captain," Newcomb said. "The latest report from the boarding party is in your console."

Stephen nodded. "Any change?"

"Nothing new, sir," Newcomb said. He sounded more than a little frus-trated. "They've searched the ship from top to bottom."

"Yes," Stephen said. "And they've found very little."

It didn't quite make sense. He knew crewmen who kept diaries and per-sonal logs, even though it was officially frowned upon. Officers had been busted down to crewmen—or even kicked out of the navy completely—for recording classified data in their logs. And yet, humans *liked* to make their space personal. They put posters on the bulkheads, family photos beside their beds... Everyone had a datapad, loaded with eBooks or videos; there were text-mails, v-mails, even collections of porn. But the aliens seemed to live in barren compartments that were completely impersonal. He'd been in *prisons* that were kinder to their residents.

They're just not human, he reminded himself. *Or maybe they just stripped the ship bare of personal items before abandoning her.*

"The engineers think they will be finished in a day or so," Newcomb said. "What do we do then?"

"Withdraw, as silently as we came," Stephen said. He didn't think they'd be able to find out much more about the aliens from stealth. They'd have to sneak out of the system and plan first contact before they returned. It wasn't going to be easy. "And make sure they never knew we were here."

And then the alarms started to howl.

• • •

Corporal Sandy Loomis was bored.

It wasn't something he wanted to admit, certainly not to Sergeant Johan. And yet, he was bored. He'd joined the Royal Marines for action and adventure, not riding herd on spacers or escorting aliens around the ship. And while he'd been excited, at first, to watch the aliens, the thrill had worn off very quickly. The Haddocks were boring too. They rarely spoke to each other, let alone their human hosts; they never went anywhere, save for the observation blister and the washroom. Sandy had shadowed them and the xenospecialists for an hour—it felt like days—and none of them had ever spoken a word to him.

I should have tried out for SAS Selection while we were on Earth, he thought, as he watched the alien make his—or her—way down the corridor. There was something about the aliens that creeped him out, although he tried to tell himself that it was just nerves. *I might have seen real action if the transfer had been approved.*

He smiled at the thought, even though he knew that mere approval for SAS Selection didn't guarantee anything. SAS Selection was the toughest training course on Earth, even for an experienced Royal Marine Commando. He'd known men go to Hereford for Selection and then get sent back to their unit shortly afterwards, men he'd been certain would waltz through the course and claim the famous badge. And other men had been invalided out of the military altogether. It said a great deal about their injuries that they hadn't had a few months in hospital before being returned to their unit. Modern medical science could handle almost anything that wasn't immediately lethal.

The alien's hand darted over the sensor, opening the hatch. Sandy followed him—or her—into the observation blister, silently wondering why the aliens bothered. Yes, *technically* they were in the alien home system, but *practically*...they couldn't see their homeworld with the naked eye. Sandy had checked, just to be sure. The alien homeworld was on the other side of the system primary. *Invincible* might be a hundred light-years from their homeworld, for all the aliens knew. But they seemed to like staring into interplanetary space.

At least they're happy, Sandy conceded, privately. Nothing short of some action would make *him* happy. They'd been able to go hiking on Wensleydale, and conduct a few drills, but there had been bugger-all else to do there. No bars, no women—at least none of negotiable virtue—and nothing else. *I need something to do.*

His pocket sensor screamed an alert. Sandy blinked at it, just for a second. The alien swung around with terrifying speed, his arm seeming to grow longer and sharper an instant before it slammed into Sandy's chest. Sandy stumbled, feeling knives stab into his very soul. The pain grew stronger...

...And Sandy, helplessly, blacked out.

. . .

"Report," Stephen snapped, as his crew rushed to battlestations. "What happened?"

"Unauthorised transmission," Lieutenant Thomas Morse reported. "Sir, it was sent from the observation blister!"

Stephen felt his blood run cold. The aliens! He'd let the Haddocks go to the observation blister, day after day. Had they been lulling him into a false sense of security? Or had they made a mistake? They might not have known...

He shook his head. No one sent a transmission by accident, particularly when they'd been *warned* to keep all signals to the bare minimum. He'd made a dreadful mistake and his ship was suddenly in very real danger.

"Jam it," he snapped, although he knew it might be too late. No, it *was* too late. "Major Parkinson, take the aliens into custody!"

He forced himself to think. The alien homeworld was a *long* way away, and out of direct line-of-transmission, but it didn't matter. There were installations—and starships—scattered right across the system. How long would it take for the message to reach someone capable of doing something about it? He didn't know. Hell, what did the message actually *say*? Was it a datapacket containing everything the Haddocks had been able to find out about their hosts or...or was it just a scream for attention? Not, he supposed, that it mattered. The cat was very definitely out of the bag.

"Commander, contact the boarding party," he ordered. "They are to make their way back to the shuttles at once."

"Aye, sir," Newcomb said.

"Helm, prepare to take us away from here," Stephen added. He briefly considered destroying the hulk, once it was abandoned, then dismissed the idea as unnecessarily provocative. The aliens were likely to be angry enough when they realised *Invincible* had been spying on them for the last week. "As soon as the boarding party is safely back, get us out of here."

"Aye, sir," Sonia said.

Stephen leaned back in his chair, forcing himself to project calm. And yet, inside, his thoughts were racing. The Haddocks had betrayed them. Why? Had they been quislings all along? Had one of them been a traitor to his own kind? Or...or what? It didn't matter, he told himself again. To hell with treating them gently. They would all have to be neutralised and securely confined, at least until humanity figured out which ones could be trusted. If any of them could be trusted...

They could have been lying to us all along, he thought grimly. *And if that's the case, what is really going on here?*

• • •

Lieutenant Fredrick Spode braced himself as he keyed the hatch, holding his rifle at the ready. Three other marines took position behind him, ready to back him up if the shit hit the fan. The alien *should* be trapped within the section—every hatch had been automatically sealed when the alarms sounded—but they couldn't take anything for granted. An alien who had somehow managed to smuggle a communications device onto the ship was one who might also have managed to smuggle a weapon too.

The hatch hissed open, revealing empty corridor. He snapped out a quick report to the major, then hurried down the passageway, checking each of the side hatches as he moved. They were all sealed, locked tight. He didn't think the alien could have gotten in—and the bastard was trapped, if he *had* gotten in—but he had to be careful. The alien had already proven that it was a devious bugger.

Maybe this is a nightmare, he thought, as he keyed the next hatch. *And I'll wake up soon.*

The smell struck him as the hatch hissed open, a faint stench of pollen—and blood—that had no place on a starship. He tensed, snapping his mask into place. *Something* was clearly loose in the air. A bioweapon? He peered forward, looking at the hatch leading into the observation blister.

It was open, even though it should have sealed automatically. Ice flickered down his spine. It wasn't right. Something was very badly wrong.

"Cover me," he hissed.

He inched forward, trying to move as quietly as possible. The briefing had made it clear that the aliens might hear better than humans, but there was no point in taking unnecessary chances. He wanted to throw a stun grenade into the compartment as he reached the hatch, yet he didn't dare take the risk. There was supposed to be a marine in the compartment too, one who hadn't responded since the alarms had sounded. He might be on the verge of death, if he wasn't dead already. Corporal Sandy Loomis was a responsible marine. Fredrick couldn't imagine anything less stopping Loomis from responding to the call.

Gritting his teeth, he threw himself into the compartment. Loomis was leaning against the bulkhead, his body practically folded in two. One look at the blood was enough to tell Fredrick that Loomis was beyond all help. The injury was just too savage. Fredrick glanced around, looking for the alien, and saw a mangled body lying on the deck. He looked to have been tortured to death.

Loomis couldn't have done that, Fredrick thought, as he checked the alien warily. The body *looked* dead, although he knew from bitter experience that that might be meaningless. He'd seen insurgents and terrorists fake it, hoping to have a chance to strike a final blow when the marines turned their backs. *What the hell hit him?*

He keyed his radio. "Sir, the alien appears to be dead," he said. "I think he committed suicide. This whole compartment is biologically contaminated."

"Understood," Major Parkinson said. "I'm dispatching a recovery team now."

Fredrick nodded, then examined Loomis quickly. It looked as though the alien had struck him with a sword, although he'd been unable or unwilling to literally cut the poor bastard in half. Whatever the alien had hit Loomis with must have had some kind of anticoagulant effect. He'd bled out much more than he should, even considering the sheer scale of the damage. His blood didn't seem to have clotted at all.

Fuck, he thought. His throat was burning. He hoped it was just his imagination. *What the fuck are we dealing with here?*

. . .

"The remainder of the aliens committed suicide too," Parkinson reported. "They must have had some form of suicide implant, a particularly nasty one."

Stephen gritted his teeth. "How did we miss it?"

"I think we weren't looking for it," Ganymede said. He sounded badly shaken. "Sir...the aliens who committed suicide...sir, their bodies look exactly like the bodies we pulled from the alien ship."

"I see," Stephen said. "Did those aliens commit suicide too?"

"I don't know, sir," Ganymede said. "But they seem to have gone to a lot of trouble to make their corpses unrecognisable."

"They also scattered a *lot* of biomatter around," Parkinson added. "We're going to have to purge the entire section."

"Keep everyone who might have got a whiff of it under quarantine," Stephen ordered. He forced himself to think. Ganymede had a point. The aliens didn't *need* to literally rip their bodies apart just to commit suicide. They were hiding something, but what? The process wasn't good enough to destroy all traces of their DNA and they knew it. "We'll check them out thoroughly before we allow them to rejoin the crew."

He looked at Newcomb. "Commander, how long until the boarding party is retrieved?"

"They're heading for the shuttles now," Newcomb said. "I think..."

"Captain," Lieutenant-Commander David Arthur interrupted. "We have incoming..."

The display flared with red icons. Stephen leaned forward, badly shocked. The aliens had responded with terrifying speed. Even if they had something akin to the flicker network, they shouldn't have been able to react so quickly. Had the boarding party triggered a silent alarm? Or...

"Communications, bring up the first contact protocols," he snapped. The aliens were already spreading out, their active sensors searching space for *Invincible*. There was no longer any point in trying to hide. "Transmit them, now!"

"Aye, sir," Morse said.

"They're locking targeting sensors on our hull," Arthur said. "They've got us."

Stephen gritted his teeth. "Stand by point defence," he ordered, sharply. He was trapped, torn between two priorities. He had to keep his ship safe, but—at the same time—he needed to retrieve the boarding party. "Communications, any response...?"

"No, sir," Morse said. "They..."

"Missile separation," Arthur snapped. "They've opened fire!"

Shit, Stephen thought.

He raised his voice. "Launch fighters," he ordered. "All batteries, commence firing!"

CHAPTER TWENTY-FIVE

"GO, GO, GO!"

Wing Commander Richard Redbird braced himself as the starfighter was hurled into interplanetary space. The onboard display was already starting to fill with red icons, each one a potential threat. He heard the CAG wittering in his ear, telling him that the aliens had simply opened fire. They'd opened fire! They hadn't even bothered to take a moment to evaluate the potential threat before they'd opened fire.

They're mad, he thought, grimly.

He pushed the thought to one side as his display refocused. The aliens were already launching starfighters, smaller and nimbler craft than his own Tornado. Behind them, there was a mass of gunboats and a handful of mid-sized starships his warbook pegged as purpose-built escort carriers and destroyers. They didn't seem to be keeping their distance though, he noted; they seemed suicidally determined to come within reach of *Invincible's* guns. It didn't make any sense at all.

Maybe we stumbled into sacred territory, he told himself. *Or maybe they just reacted badly to discovering an alien warship within their system.*

"They're opening fire," the CAG said. "You have permission to engage. Weapons free; I say again, weapons free."

Richard nodded as the squadron formed up on him, ready to engage the alien fighters. The aliens were definitely fast little buggers, buzzing around like angry hornets and snapping off plasma bolts even though the human starfighters were technically out of range. Or perhaps not. Their plasma guns seemed to have longer range than their human counterparts, the magnetic containment field lasting long enough for the plasma bolt to travel quite some distance. Thankfully, their targeting didn't seem to be any better. But they were filling space with so much fire that hardly mattered.

Being blown out of space because I steered into the path of one of those bolts would be very embarrassing, he thought, wryly. The alien craft were zipping backwards and forwards, evading plasma bolts that hadn't—yet—been fired. It wouldn't be long before they realised they had a significant advantage. *But they'll have to close the range if they want to engage the carrier.*

"Keep them off the ship," he ordered, shortly. "And if they want to retreat, let them."

An alien starfighter lunged at him, spitting fire in all directions. The pilot seemed to be rotating his craft randomly—either that, or the starfighter was actually a miniaturised gunboat with rotating turrets. Richard was reluctantly impressed. The alien craft *had* to be balancing two separate drive fields, allowing it to perform impossible tricks. He wondered, as he returned fire, just how the alien engineers managed to get the trick to work. He'd always assumed that two drive fields simply *couldn't* be made to work together. One would either overpower the other or both drive fields would be torn apart.

"They're dodging well," Flight Lieutenant Monica Smith said. Her voice was grim. "This one thinks he's going to stick something up my arse!"

"Hold on," Flight Lieutenant Ryan Loyn said. "I'll cover your arse."

Richard gritted his teeth as the alien starfighter reversed course, slashing back towards Richard's starfighter so violently that Richard was *sure* the alien wanted to ram him. He'd never heard of two starfighters actually *colliding*, not outside bad novels and worse movies, but the alien seemed to *want* to ram. He snapped off a shot and had the satisfaction of watching the alien craft vanish from the display, bare seconds before he would have had to evade sharply or let the alien crash into his starfighter. There wouldn't have been a hope in hell of surviving *that*.

These bastards are mad, he thought, as the communications systems filled with similar complaints. The aliens fought like madmen. They didn't seem to have any sense of self-preservation at all. Their pilots seemed quite willing to throw their lives away just to take a shot at the human ships. *What the hell are we fighting?*

Another alien starfighter shot past him, so close that he thought he could have seen the alien craft with the naked eye. He barely had a second to evade before the alien whooshed past him, then zipped around and resumed firing. The aliens seemed to *like* knife-range dog-fighting. He blew the alien craft to dust and flew into a clear space, just for a second. The human starfighters were taking one hell of a beating. They seemed to have an advantage in discipline, but the sheer madness of the aliens told against them.

"They're sending in the gunboats," the CAG said. "Alpha Squadron, move to intercept."

Richard nodded, feeling sweat trickling down his back. Gunboats were bigger targets than starfighters, but they made up for it by being covered in plasma guns. They could shoot in all directions, making it hard to dive into their blind spot and engage from the rear. Worse, they carried bigger missiles. A plasma or nuclear-tipped warhead could do immense damage to *Invincible*. He didn't dare assume that the aliens had missed that trick.

"Acknowledged," he said. "Alpha Squadron, form up on me."

He glanced at the overall display as his remaining pilots formed up on him. Three starfighters were gone...he felt a twinge of guilt that he hadn't even seen them go. He wouldn't know what had happened to them until he reviewed the records afterwards, if there *was* an afterwards. A fourth starfighter appeared to be damaged, although he had no idea what had clipped the starfighter's wings without destroying it. He ordered the pilot back to the carrier as he led the way towards the enemy gunboats. There was no point in giving them an easy target.

The battle seemed to be turning into a maddened frenzy, as if the aliens were lashing out instinctively rather than following any sort of battle plan. They'd clearly deployed some kind of quick-reaction force—the lack of anything bigger than a destroyer suggested that the alien squadron hadn't been too far away when they'd heard the signal—and they had been caught by surprise, but they should have had *some* kind of plan. Or at least procedures to maximise their striking power. Instead, they were flailing around randomly. A handful of alien starfighters made a run at *Invincible*. He wasn't surprised to see two of them ram the starship, although they barely scratched the armour. He supposed it was proof they weren't armed with antimatter or something else that exploded on contact. Antimatter had been created in the labs, but—so far—no one had found a way to mass-produce it, let alone turn it into an effective weapon.

He clenched his teeth as the alien gunboats drew closer. Like the starfighters, their plasma guns seemed to have an extended range...not that it mattered. He'd have to close to engagement range if he wanted to kill them before they got too close to the carrier. The Old Lady was their only way home, after all. He didn't think the destroyers would be able to pick up the starfighter pilots, even if they weren't already heading back to Falkirk. The international force *had* to be warned.

And if this is an enemy quick-reaction force, he asked himself, *how long will it be before they send in the battleships?*

"Engage at will," he ordered, as the enemy gunboats entered range. "Give them hell."

. . .

"Four starfighters rammed our hull," Newcomb reported. "The armour is intact."

Stephen nodded in relief. The aliens were advanced—that much was clear—but at least they weren't *frighteningly* advanced. Their weapons were good—and they seemed to have some advantages—yet they weren't powerful enough to blast *Invincible* to dust with a handful of shots. And yet, he knew it was just a matter of time before something larger showed up to do battle. The enemy's big guns were probably already on the way.

And they deployed their quick-reaction force in record time, he thought, as another enemy starfighter was blown out of space by the point defence. *How the hell did they get here so quickly?*

Major Parkinson's face appeared in the display. "Sir, the boarding party is assembling now, but they're going to have problems getting back to the ship."

"I know," Stephen said. A couple of shuttles would be sitting ducks with the alien starfighters looking for targets. And with the aliens refusing to respond to hails, there was no way he could negotiate a ceasefire. "Tell them to sit tight for the moment."

He rubbed his forehead. *Invincible* could *not* stay where she was, not for long. He had no idea how the enemy had managed to scramble a quick reaction force so quickly, but whatever they'd done could presumably be used to deploy a battleship or two as well. And if something larger and nastier than *Invincible* showed up, he would have no choice but to retreat immediately. *That* would mean abandoning the boarding party to its fate.

"Enemy gunboats are entering attack formation," Arthur reported. The Tactical Officer didn't look up from his console. "They're targeting our drive section."

Stephen gritted his teeth. The drive section was heavily armoured, but there were limits. A handful of nukes would be more than enough to cripple the ship, leaving her stranded in alien territory. He'd have to trigger the self-destruct and pray the aliens didn't manage to comb anything useful from the wreckage. And that they didn't manage to take the boarding party alive.

"The point defence is to cover the drive section," he ordered, as the enemy gunboats began their attack run. "Do *not* let them get a shot into our drives."

"Aye, sir."

Stephen took a long breath, trying to consider his options. But none of them appeared to be any good. He couldn't stay where he was indefinitely—he knew he was pushing their luck now—and he couldn't simply abandon the boarding party. And yet, he couldn't get the boarding party back to *Invincible*. He briefly considered ordering the boarding party to get into the shuttles and escape on a low-powered ballistic trajectory, but he had a nasty feeling it wouldn't work. There were too many active sensors in the vicinity for a pair of shuttles to escape detection.

"Gunboats firing...now," Arthur reported. "Point defence is engaging the missiles."

Their missile tech doesn't seem to be that much better than ours, Stephen thought, as the analysts updated their projections. *They don't even seem to have penetrator ECM warheads.*

He shook his head, sharply, as the last missile vanished from the display. There was no way he could *count* on the enemy not having modern— or post-modern—warheads. If the enemy force was their idea of a local guard force, rather than a front-line combat squadron, they would probably be last in line for modern equipment. God knew the Home Guard or the Coastal Patrol received whatever funding and equipment was left, after the army and the navy had taken their colossal portion of the defence budget. There was a good chance that the enemy reinforcements would have more advanced weapons.

"The gunboats are regrouping," Arthur reported. He broke off. "Sir, the enemy destroyers are moving into attack formation."

Stephen cursed under his breath. *Invincible* could handle a squadron of destroyers, but every death—every destroyed ship—would make it harder to negotiate afterwards. The aliens didn't seem to be interested in negotiation, yet...how would humanity react, if they detected an alien starship poking around Sol or Britannia? Try to make contact...or shoot first and ask questions later? There were places in Britain—and, he assumed, the rest of the Great Powers—where trespassers would be very lucky if they were merely arrested, rather than being shot on sight. He didn't think the

Sol Guard would be very pleased if it detected an alien starship far too close to Earth for comfort.

He glared at the display, feeling hopelessly out of his depth. He knew how to handle hostile ships—and he *wanted* to unleash *Invincible's* full power on the aliens—but he couldn't help being indecisive. What should he do? He could take out the alien ships, only to make future negotiations impossible. *Humanity* would demand blood, if a handful of ships were destroyed by an alien intruder. How could he blame the aliens for feeling the same way?

"Order the starfighters to intercept their missiles," he ordered. Standard tactics called for launching strikes against the destroyers, hoping to keep them away from the carrier, but that would escalate the situation beyond repair. He didn't want to be responsible for starting a war. "Stand by point defence."

"Aye, Captain."

Stephen nodded. The alien starfighters were drawing back, a handful surrounding the alien derelict as if they were protecting it. Their mere presence was dangerous, he knew; there was no way the boarding party could risk jumping into space as long as the alien starfighters were watching them. Did the aliens *know* they'd trapped a group of humans? He suspected they did, if only because they should have seen the shuttles attached to the alien hull. And that left him with another problem...

"Order Alpha and Beta Squadron to clear the alien starfighters away from the derelict," he said, flatly. "Once local space is clear, they are to escort the shuttles back home."

"Aye, sir," Newcomb said.

The display spangled with red light. Stephen sucked in his breath as the alien missiles roared towards his ship. The analysts went to work, throwing a dozen different projections up in front of him. Multistage missiles, apparently; unless, of course, the aliens had somehow managed to *really* slim down the drive section. Stephen suspected it was the former. He doubted that anyone could afford to produce missiles with starship-grade drives. The fact the aliens were deploying a *lot* of them was worrying enough.

They must have shot all their beancounters, he thought. Each multistage missile cost about ten times as much as a starfighter, something that caused all sorts of headaches during budget debates. *Or they're so rich they don't have to care about expending so many missiles so casually.*

"They're not deploying penetrator ECM," Arthur said. "I request permission to deploy decoys of our own."

"Granted," Stephen said. If nothing else, they'd learn something about alien warheads. Were they tracking *Invincible* on their own or were they being directed by a master warhead? If the former, there was a good chance they could be decoyed away; if the latter, they probably wouldn't be fooled by the deception. "And engage the enemy missiles with point defence as soon as they enter range."

He leaned forward, watching—grimly—as the point defence opened fire. A dozen enemy missiles vanished from the display, but the remainder kept coming...he gritted his teeth in frustration as he realised they were slipping into very slight evasive manoeuvres. They were nowhere near as elaborate as a starfighter would do, but they were good enough to throw off his point defence. For every shot he fired that scored a hit, a hundred missed their targets and zipped uselessly into interplanetary space. The alien missiles were coming closer...

Invincible shook, violently. "Report!"

"Direct hit, port armour," Arthur reported. "They're firing laser warheads!"

"Damage control teams to section Theta-Rho-19," Newcomb ordered.

Stephen glanced at the display, just as his ship rocked again. A nuclear strike...*Invincible's* armour had kept the blast from penetrating into the ship, but it had wiped out a number of point defence clusters and sensor nodes. If the aliens knew what they'd done—and it was quite likely they did, as their technology was clearly similar to humanity's—they'd know the carrier now had a blind spot. They'd do everything in their power to fly missiles and starfighter torpedoes through the hole and hammer them into *Invincible's* hull.

"Deploy probes to cover the gap," he snapped. The alien starfighters weren't budging from the derelict. Worse, two of their destroyers were on their way to help. He had no choice, but to engage them. "Tactical, target the enemy destroyers and prepare to open fire."

"Aye, sir," Arthur said.

Stephen forced himself to think. Should he seek to close the range by taking *Invincible* into direct contact with the alien ships? He should have the advantage, unless the aliens really *did* have a superweapon of some kind, but it ran the risk of losing his ship. It would also tell the aliens far too much about humanity's weapons. The destroyers would take warning back to Falkirk, if *Invincible* was lost, but...

New icons flared into existence. "Captain," Lieutenant Alison Adams snapped. "I'm reading four—no, *five*—new starships! Warbook calls them a battleship, a fleet carrier and a trio of heavy cruisers!"

Fuck, Stephen thought. *Invincible* might be able to deal with the fleet carrier—at least if she managed to get into engagement range—but the battleship probably packed enough firepower to deal with her. *I...fuck.*

"Recall the starfighters," he ordered, grimly. "Helm, roll us over and take us out of the system. We'll slip into cloak as soon as we are out of active sensor range."

Newcomb looked up, surprised and horrified. "Sir...the boarding party doesn't have time to get out!"

No, they'll just be vaporised if they try to get to us now, Stephen thought. *And we don't have time to wait any longer.*

"I know," he said. He hated himself in that moment, hated himself for daring to fail. The Royal Navy did *not* leave people behind. Everyone knew what happened to people who were unlucky enough to be captured by terrorists or insurgents. The aliens might be more civilised, but there was no way to know. He had no choice. He had to retreat. "The responsibility is mine."

He took a final look at the display. "And launch ghost probes and mines to cover our retreat," he added. "We might as well make life difficult for them."

CHAPTER TWENTY-SIX

"THEY'RE LEAVING?" Benton asked. "They're...leaving? They're abandoning us?"

"They don't have a choice," Alice snapped. She didn't blame Benton for being shocked—he was a civilian, not someone who knew just how quickly a situation could devolve into an utter nightmare—but she'd had a nasty feeling that it was coming the moment the aliens showed up. *Invincible* couldn't hope to fight five capital ships and survive. "And now they'll be coming for us."

She tongued her mouthpiece, silently grateful that everyone had managed to get into their spacesuits as soon as the alarms sounded. The shuttles would be targeted the moment the aliens finished chasing *Invincible* across the system—she refused to consider that the aliens might manage to actually run the assault carrier down and blow her to atoms—and the boarding party would be in serious trouble. She had no idea if surrender was an option or not. She'd sooner trigger her suicide implant and die than allow herself to fall into terrorist hands, but who knew how the aliens would treat prisoners? Standing orders were to attempt to make contact with alien captors—she'd brushed up on the protocol during the voyage—but these aliens worried her. They hadn't made any attempt to communicate with the human intruders. They'd simply shown up and opened fire.

Which suggests they're not worried about retaliation, she reminded herself, as she opened the hatch. *And that means they might not be willing to take prisoners.*

She gritted her teeth. The alien derelict was as airless as ever—thankfully, the captain had vetoed the suggestion to repressurise parts of the hull—and they *should* be able to hide, at least for a while. And then...and then what? The civilians were sitting ducks. They had firearms—and they'd all passed the level-one firearms test—but that didn't make them soldiers. There was a good chance they were all about to get killed.

"Get into the hulk," she ordered. The shuttle's active sensors were offline—there were few better ways to commit suicide than radiating a signature in the middle of a combat zone—but its passive sensors were tracking the alien ships. They were already dispatching shuttles of their own. "We have to stay out of sight."

"They'll be coming here first," Sergeant Radcliffe said. "They can see the shuttles."

Alice nodded. "Program the shuttle computers for a complete wipe-and-destroy the instant the aliens set foot on them," she ordered the pilot. They'd be able to use the live feed from the shuttles for a wee bit longer. She doubted it would last very long at all—the aliens would probably pick up the transmissions—but it would give them a slight edge. "And then we hurry further into the ship."

The civilians didn't complain as they made their way along the corridor. It was easier than it would have been in gravity, Alice supposed. They'd have no trouble accessing places that would normally have been out of reach. She'd wondered, after the boarding party had found no trace of a gravity generator, if the aliens preferred to live in zero-g, like belters. But the starship definitely *looked* as if its designers had understood the concept of *up* and *down*. It didn't have the random design of a belter craft.

She accessed the feed from the shuttle through her suit and frowned as she saw the alien craft come in to dock beside the gash in the hull. Their hatch opened a moment later, revealing a handful of humanoid forms in spacesuits. They were carrying rifles that looked uncomfortably large, suggesting unpleasant things about their physical strength, although she supposed heavy-duty weapons weren't quite such an encumbrance in zero-g. She wasn't sure what type of weapons they were, either. Something that large could easily be a plasma weapon—the Tadpoles had successfully miniaturised plasma guns, but humanity had never managed to duplicate the trick—or even a gauss rifle. *She* wouldn't have been particularly happy about firing either inside a confined space, but the aliens might have different ideas.

"I make it fifteen of them," Radcliffe muttered. "Anyone differ?"

"No, Sergeant," Alice said. She hoped the microbursts were as hard to track as the boffins swore. "But there'll be other shuttles on the way."

She cursed under her breath as she realised how alone she was, now *Invincible* had retreated into interplanetary space. The old farts had always complained about micromanagement from the MOD—and she'd read books from the Troubles where soldiers insisted they couldn't take a shit without permission in triplicate—but now she would have killed for orders from some higher authority. If she fought the aliens—if she set traps—would she merely pour fuel on the fire and make all-out war inevitable? Or was it inevitable already? She *really* didn't like the implications of the aliens opening fire, without making any attempt to open contact first. They hadn't even tried to assess their potential opponent before opening hostilities.

"Rig mines along the access corridor," she ordered, grimly. It was chancy, but it was remotely possible that they'd be able to hold out long enough for *Invincible* to return. The starship might be able to evade her foes, then sneak back quickly enough to grab the boarding party and run. It wasn't much, but it was all she had. "And then scatter sensors around too."

Alice linked back into the shuttle's feed, just in time to see the lead alien cut his way into the shuttle. The alien had gone through the airlock, slicing away at the armour with what looked like a monofilament blade. Alice was unsure if she should be impressed, worried, or both. The alien had clearly had no trouble *recognising* the airlock. They were just too close to humans for comfort. A second later, the connection broke as the shuttle wiped and destroyed its datacores. Alice sucked in a breath as she checked the handful of sensors near the gash in the derelict's hull. The aliens didn't seem to have noticed anything was wrong.

And let's hope they can't put the computer back together after we turned it into a pile of dust, she thought, as she watched the aliens start to flow into the derelict. Another alien shuttle landed and disgorged another cluster of alien soldiers. *If they can do that, we might have a problem.*

"I've got the civilians in a hidey-hole," Hammersmith reported. "Want me to come back up?"

"Not yet," Alice said. She wished she knew—again—how the aliens would treat prisoners. "I want you to guard them as long as possible."

She came to a halt at the edge of an access corridor and settled down to wait. The aliens didn't seem to be launching probes, at least as far as her sensors could tell...although she had to remind herself, again, that that might be meaningless. She'd been told about the Royal Marine who'd been smart enough to hack into the surveillance system monitoring a particularly complex exercise and use it to guide his men into a perfect position for an ambush. If the aliens could bring the derelict's systems back online, they could presumably track the humans without making it obvious. And whatever alien came up with *that* idea would be feted for his intelligence, instead of being summarily demoted for giving himself an utterly unfair advantage.

I bet his company loved winning, though, she thought. *They just wouldn't be able to do it on a real battlefield.*

The aliens advanced slowly into the ship, gliding forward in a formation that was surprisingly familiar. One alien moved forward while two more covered him, then a second alien joined him while the third advanced another step. It wasn't easy to tell which of them was actually in charge, if indeed *any* of them were in charge. Their spacesuits were completely identical, as far as she could see. But then, she supposed that wasn't surprising. Her spacesuit didn't carry rank bars either.

And being in combat is the only place you can get away with not saluting a senior officer, she reminded herself, dryly. *You don't want to accidentally tell an enemy sniper who he needs to shoot.*

Her lips twitched at the thought, an instant before the first mine detonated. The aliens stumbled backwards, a couple firing a handful of rounds down the corridor before catching themselves. Alice smirked to herself. If nothing else, the aliens would be a lot more careful before heading further into the derelict. But they'd also not be in the mood for taking prisoners.

"They're watching for traps," Radcliffe commented, as the aliens resumed their advance. "And we didn't have much room to hide them."

Alice nodded. Given a few hours—and an unlimited supply of materials—they could have turned the entire ship into a death trap. Royal Marines were *trained* to leave booby traps in their wake, making life difficult for anyone who came after them. But her platoon simply hadn't had the time to set more than a handful of traps. She wished, again, that they'd been able to get the civilians off the ship. The marines would have hundreds of other options if the civilians were gone.

We could just jump off the ship and hope for the best, she thought. A suit could keep its wearer alive indefinitely, with the right cocktail of suspension drugs. Her father, damn the man, had put himself and his whore of a lover in suspension for years and *survived.* It would have been an impressive feat, if he hadn't been *him. But the civilians wouldn't be able to endure a long wait.*

She glanced at the dark bulkhead, wondering just what was going on outside the hulk. The alien warships could be clustering around the derelict or, more likely, they could be trying to hunt down and destroy the assault carrier. She had no doubt the aliens would throw everything they could muster at *Invincible,* particularly if they thought the carrier had come alone. They wouldn't want her to get back to Falkirk with a priceless cargo of tactical data.

But the destroyers are probably already on their way home, Alice thought. There was no flicker network between Alien-One and Falkirk. *Once they get there, the Royal Navy will know what's happened here.*

Radcliffe nudged her suit. Alice looked at him. He held up three fingers, then nodded down the corridor. Alice followed his gaze, checking the sensors automatically. Three aliens had appeared at the end of the corridor, advancing towards the human position in a manner she could only call *calm*. She couldn't help thinking that the aliens were a curious mixture of extremely professional and staggeringly careless. But then, they might be having problems adapting to the new environment. Zero-g wasn't for everyone.

She moved her hand, silently counting down the seconds as she unhooked a grenade from her belt. She'd kept it back, rather than using it to prime another booby trap...now, she thought it had been one of her better decisions. The aliens were getting closer and closer...she reached zero and lobbed the grenade down the corridor, her suit sending the detonation signal as it flew past the aliens. She glanced away instinctively as the grenade exploded, then ran forward. The three aliens were—somehow—still alive. Their suits had taken the brunt of the blast.

They'll be dead soon, she thought. She felt a stab of pity, despite herself. *The air is already leaking out of their suits.*

"Get their weapons," she ordered, sharply. There was no time for hand signals—and besides, the other aliens would have heard the blast. "Hurry!"

She knelt beside the closest alien and yanked his helmet away. A face— a Haddock face—stared up at her. The alien was clearly still alive, despite having suddenly been exposed to vacuum. Alice had heard of enhancements that helped a person survive vacuum, at least for a few extra moments, but she hadn't thought any of them were actually workable. But the alien seemed to have survived longer than humanly possible...

It twitched, stabbing out at her with a blade. Alice cursed and threw herself backwards as red lights flared in her HUD. The blade had sliced right through her suit! She punched the alien as hard as she could, smashing his head into a bloody pulp, then checked her suit's auto-repair functions. Whatever the alien had stabbed her with had somehow sliced right through the suit's tendons. She'd have to patch the suit the old-fashioned way.

"Let me," Radcliffe said. "The other two are dead."

"Watch them," Alice ordered, harshly.

She kicked herself, mentally, as Radcliffe slapped a patch on her suit. Her instructor would have booted her out of commando training if she'd made such a mistake under his supervision, if he hadn't beasted her to within an inch of her life first. The arsehole had always been threatening to beast his trainees, although she'd never actually heard of him actually doing it. But now...she probably deserved a kick up the arse and a long digression on why she was the sorriest wannabe marine in the entire history of the Royal Marines. It had been a very stupid mistake.

"That's the suit patched," Radcliffe said. "Did he cut your skin?"

"I don't think so," Alice said. She saw the alien knife, turning slowly in the vacuum, and caught hold of the hilt. It reminded her of a K-BAR...maybe not a monofilament blade, but sharp enough to slice through a great many things if there was enough power behind the stroke. She was fairly sure she would have felt it if the blade had actually touched her bare skin. "I..."

She looked up, sharply, as she saw movement at the end of the corridor. "We have to move!"

The aliens opened fire a second later. Alice pushed herself down to the deck, then hauled herself into a side-corridor before they got their bearings. Radcliffe followed, hurling another grenade towards the aliens as he moved. The explosion seemed bigger, somehow, in vacuum, but Alice had no way to know how effective it was. A chunk of the sensor network was gone.

They must be destroying it, piece by piece, she thought, as she led the way down the next corridor. There was no time for a gallant last stand, not when they could keep the aliens busy for a few hours longer. *And we have no way of knowing how many aliens have been brought onto the ship.*

She keyed her mouthpiece. "Hammersmith?"

"Here, Captain," Hammersmith said. "No contact yet..."

"We've had the contact," Alice said, dryly. Another report flashed up in her HUD. Corporal Patel had dropped out of the network. She hoped that meant he'd simply lost contact, but she feared the worst. The communications network wasn't *that* fragile. "Are the civvies coping?"

"A little panic," Hammersmith said. "But we're safe for the moment."

Alice nodded to herself. "We'll try to keep them chasing us," she said. What *was* happening outside the ship? She wished she knew, even if it was bad news. At least she'd *know*. "I..."

She swore as she rounded the corner and came face-to-face with an alien patrol, already lifting its weapons. Alice opened fire, spraying the aliens with bullets. Thankfully, their armour wasn't *that* strong. It didn't look as though the aliens had built combat suits...she shook her head. They might not have had them on hand, or simply thought better of bringing them to the party. Deploying a mobile combat suit inside a regular starship was asking for trouble. She allowed herself a second's amusement at the concept of one of the world's most formidable weapons stuck in a too-small corridor, then dismissed the thought. There just wasn't time for humour. Her sensors were insisting that there were more aliens on the way.

"There's another bunch coming up behind us," Radcliffe said, as he opened a hatch. A long corridor—an alien Jefferies tube—led further into the starship. "Captain, take the lead."

Alice blanched. "Sergeant..."

"Hurry," Radcliffe said. "You're faster than me."

Alice gritted her teeth, then clambered into the tube. It would have been impossible in a gravity field, at least when she was wearing the spacesuit. Even in zero-g, she couldn't help feeling a little claustrophobic. The bulkheads were uncomfortably close. She was uneasily aware that the aliens might even get the last laugh, if the bulkheads narrowed any further. In a training exercise, she'd have to put up with jokes about being fat; in real life, the consequences would be far worse...she forced herself to scramble up the tube. Her perceptions kept twisting, she wasn't sure if she was going up or down...

"Shit," Radcliffe said, quietly.

Alice tried to glance back. Radcliffe was half-inside the hatch, but the aliens were trying to pull him back. She forced herself further into the tube, hoping to win him time, yet...yet it was already too late.

"Captain, keep moving," Radcliffe said. It was an order, however phrased. "Keep moving!"

He threw himself backwards, slamming the hatch closed behind him. A second later, there was a single explosion on the far side. The hatch seemed to bend inwards, then jammed. Alice knew, without having to check, that Radcliffe had triggered his suit's self-destruct. He'd given his life for her...

It won't be wasted, she promised herself. If she was lucky, the aliens would assume that she'd been killed by the blast too. The blast had certainly been big enough to take out two humans, suits or no suits, along with any alien unfortunate enough to be near the explosion. *I swear, it will not be wasted.*

Gritting her teeth, she forced herself to keep moving.

CHAPTER TWENTY-SEVEN

"I THINK WE'RE ALONE NOW, CAPTAIN," Lieutenant Alison Adams said. "There's no trace of pursuit."

Stephen allowed himself a moment of relief. The combination of decoy drones, projecting a small fleet of sensor ghosts, and *Invincible's* sheer speed had allowed them to break contact, barely. He doubted the Admiralty would be pleased when they found out that he'd revealed the assault carrier's top speed, but there had been no choice. The alien ships hadn't been able to keep up with them.

Which is good news, he told himself, firmly. *At least we have one advantage.*

He looked at Morse. "Did the destroyers make it out?"

"*Pinafore* acknowledged, sir," Morse told him. "*Dezhnev* did not."

Stephen frowned down at the display. "Did the aliens kill her?"

"Unknown, sir," Morse said. "But I don't see how they even *found* her."

"I don't see how they found *us*," Stephen said. "We have to assume their sensors are very good."

He worked the problem, turning the different angles over and over in his mind. The radio transmission hadn't gone *that* far, surely. Unless the aliens had known where they were all along...he shook his head. They must have been very certain of being able to mousetrap and destroy *Invincible* if they were prepared to allow her crew to spend four days dissecting the derelict before showing themselves. It made no sense. But then, if the derelict was actually two hundred years behind their modern ships, they might not care...

Then we shouldn't have had a hope of getting away, he told himself. *Their weapons weren't particularly better than ours.*

"We'll hold position here," he said. "Deploy a shell of recon drones around us to watch for any turbulence. I want to know if there's even a *tiny* flicker of energy anywhere near us."

"Aye, Captain," Sonia said.

"And launch two stealth probes towards the derelict," he added. "We need to know what's happening to our people."

He gritted his teeth. He'd abandoned a mixed military and civilian team to the tender mercies of the aliens, aliens who'd already shown themselves willing to simply open hostilities without even *trying* to open contact first. Was the derelict that important to them? Or did they merely lash out, instinctively, at anyone who came within range? God knew that humans—and Tadpoles and Foxes—had taken their instinctive behaviours into space as well as everything else. The new aliens might be no better.

Or we might have stumbled into the wrong side of a civil war, he thought. *Or...*
He dismissed the thought. "Damage report?"

"Damage control teams are on site now," Newcomb reported. "They're reporting that our inner armour integrity is barely compromised. They figure they can patch up the outer armour and replace the destroyed protuberances in an hour or so."

Stephen let out a long breath. *Invincible* had faced her first major combat test and flown through it with flying colours. The damage could have been worse, a great deal worse. And it would have been if they'd stayed to engage the enemy. But he couldn't help feeling that he'd turned and fled, abandoning his people to an unknown fate. He had no reason to believe the aliens would treat prisoners well. If nothing else, they'd have to force the humans to talk so they could build up a common language.

If they're even interested in trying to talk, he thought. He really didn't like the implications of the aliens simply opening fire without warning. A *smart* race of conquerors would *surely* take the time to assess their enemy before invading...unless there had been more data in the rogue transmission than they thought. The contact team would have to dissect it, section by section, to find out what the Haddocks had told their conquerors. *They must have found a way to issue orders to the Haddocks...*

He cursed under his breath. *Nothing* about the scenario made sense. Three different alien races, seemingly linked together; a refugee, betraying *Invincible* to the aliens who'd chased him from his home...Stephen could understand someone betraying the ship because their friends or family were being held hostage, but the generation ship had been in flight for a hundred years. There was no way to communicate with any refugees, not in real-time. The hostages might be long dead by now.

And we seem to have lost one of the destroyers, he reminded himself. *What happened to her?*

He glared at the display. The Russians were meant to stay in stealth at all times, passively monitoring the laser links to the stealth platforms and recon drones. It was possible that Captain Danilovich had simply jumped the gun and headed home the moment he realised that *Invincible* was under attack—and Stephen wouldn't fault him for doing so—but he hadn't sent any message to *Pinafore*. Stephen had no idea if he should be searching Alien-One for the Russians or assuming that they were already on their way to Falkirk.

His console bleeped. "Captain, this is Foote in Tracking," a voice said. "I've been working the data, sir. I think I know how they jumped us."

Stephen leaned forward as a datapacket unfolded in front of him. "Go ahead."

"There's a weak tramline between Planet Seven and Planet Four," Foote said. A red line appeared on the display, linking the two planets together. "It's very weak, sir, but with the right technology someone could use it to send a message, even jump a small fleet across the system in a heartbeat. If there was a flicker station positioned near that tramline, the message would have been relayed to Planet Four very quickly indeed."

"While we assumed we still had hours before the aliens could respond," Stephen mused. It *sounded* good, although jumping through such weak tramlines tended to be difficult. The Royal Navy discouraged it unless the situation was dire. "Do you have any hard data to back up your conclusions?"

"The alien ships were on a vector that suggests they came from the tramline when they revealed themselves," Foote told him. "And the timing is consistent, sir. They would have jumped out almost at once."

Terrifyingly quickly, Stephen thought. The Royal Navy kept a handful of detachments on instant-readiness at all times—as did the other Great Powers—but it tended to put unacceptable wear and tear on the crews and equipment. He wasn't sure *humanity* could scramble such a formidable force in less than an hour or two, even if the ships were constantly on alert. *These aliens are very territorial indeed.*

He leaned back in his chair, feeling his body ache. Now the fighting was over, he wanted to catch some rest, but he knew that wasn't possible, not yet. His place was on the bridge. And yet...and yet...he'd need to rest soon, before something else happened. He needed to decide what to do, damn it. *Pinafore* was already on her way out of the system—and the Russians might be on their way too—and the Royal Navy would know that *something* had happened, but he wasn't sure what *he* should do. Try to rescue his people or head straight back to Falkirk?

We have a duty to our people, he told himself. *But we also have a duty to preserve our fighting power.*

Angrily, he dismissed the thought. "Do we have a tactical analysis?"

"Yes, Captain," a new voice answered. "Ah...this is Simpson. I've completed the preliminary analysis."

Stephen nodded. He'd met the young man during the shakedown cruise. Simpson was a good analyst, but nowhere near suitable for command track. He simply didn't have the ability to make decisions in a split second. Stephen knew from bitter experience that being decisive wasn't as easy as it sounded, but it didn't matter. The ability to make a call within seconds, without waiting to see what might happen in the next few minutes, was a vital command skill.

And one that can't be learnt by doing, he thought. *But then, all our emergency drills leave out the emergency.*

"Go ahead, Mr. Simpson," he ordered.

"From what we've seen, Captain, I'd say that they have a slight edge over us," Simpson said, "although it's possible we could have fought a reservist unit instead of a front-line force. Their multistage missiles were marginally faster than ours and, I might add, deployed in vast numbers. On the other hand, their penetrator technology—at least the technology they showed us—is actually inferior to ours. They make up for it by firing hundreds of missiles at their target.

"Their starfighters, too, are somewhat more agile than ours. I think they've definitely managed to integrate two separate drive fields, allowing the starfighter to rotate its guns and fire to the side without actually altering course. On the other hand, again, their starfighters also appear to be more fragile than ours. A single hit is enough to destroy them."

And thank God for that, Stephen thought.

"We don't have anything like enough hard data on their warships," Simpson said, "but they didn't try to run us down as we retreated, so we stand by our original belief that we have a slight speed advantage. Anything fast enough to catch us isn't strong enough to kill us...but they might score a lucky hit. We don't want to wind up like *Vanguard*."

"No," Stephen agreed, wryly amused that Simpson seemed to have forgotten who he was talking to. "That would be awkward."

He studied the display for a long moment. *Vanguard* had been hit by an enemy missile during the Second Interstellar War's final campaign. It had left her stranded long enough for the enemy to bring considerable force to bear against her, although it hadn't been enough for them to actually *destroy* her. He'd studied the records, back when he'd been expecting to serve on a battleship himself. *Vanguard* was a heavily-armoured ship, yet she'd been very lucky to survive. It could easily have gone the other way.

"We've run some projections, based on our observations about their speed and apparent tonnage, but we simply don't have enough hard data to make solid statements about their warships," Simpson said. "We think their battleships actually have more missile tubes than ours—and fewer turrets for plasma guns—yet we won't *know* until we actually see them in action. Their armour may be considerably better than ours if they're disdainful of heavy energy weapons."

"Or they may not have the tech to make them," Stephen mused. "How long did it take us to move from small plasma cannons to battleship heavy guns?"

"They had plasma weapons a hundred years ago, sir," Simpson said. "Scaling them up is just a matter of time. I find it hard to believe they are unaware of just how dangerous plasma weapons can be."

"True," Stephen agreed.

He considered it for a long moment. Naval doctrine, rewritten after the First Interstellar War, stated that the missile would rarely, if ever, get through an active defence grid. Even firing vast numbers of missiles was no guarantee of scoring a hit. It was why starfighters closed to minimum range before launching their torpedoes and battleships carried heavy plasma cannons instead of stuffing their hulls with missile tubes. Even the latest penetrator warheads couldn't guarantee a hit. Starships carried energy weapons because they were impossible to shoot out of space or decoy away...

They must know what plasma weapons can do, he thought. *We dare not assume otherwise.*

"I see," he said. "Anything else?"

"Not as yet, sir," Simpson said. "There were a number of other oddities in their systems, but we're not prepared to make definite statements about them yet. About the only thing I want to mention now is that our analysis computers insisted that we were facing a multinational force. The technology levels were roughly equal, but there appeared to be several different...ah, takes on how theory should be translated into reality. But the...

ah...*takes* weren't particularly consistent. It was as if someone had taken a Russian targeting computer and used it to fire Chinese missiles, which carried American and British warheads."

"Curious," Stephen said. "Let me know when you have a definite report."

For what it's worth, he added silently, as he closed the channel. *We haven't seen anything like enough to make any definite statements about what we're facing.*

He rose. "Commander Newcomb, inform Ambassador O'Neil that I want to see her in my Ready Room," he said. "You have the bridge. Alert me immediately if there is even the slightest *hint* of an enemy presence."

"Aye, sir."

. . .

There will be four empty bunks tonight, Richard thought, as he undressed and stepped into the shower. Warm water cascaded down, washing away the sweat and stress of battle. *And we won't have a hope of recovering their bodies.*

It was a morbid thought and so he dwelt on it for several seconds, even though starfighter pilots *knew* there was little hope of their bodies ever being recovered and returned home. It was rare for a starfighter to be so badly damaged that the pilot was killed, without his body being blown to atoms. He knew the risks—and the dead pilots had known the risks too—but it still felt like he was betraying them. He'd gotten too close to his squadron and he knew it.

We're the twenty-minuters, he told himself. It was an old joke, one that had stopped being funny the moment it had sunk in what the joke actually *meant. The average life expectancy of a new pilot, when he enters combat for the first time, is twenty minutes.*

He scowled, silently promising himself that he'd punch the next person who made that damn joke. It was true, all too true, and he knew it. *None* of his pilots had seen real combat, save for the mad descent into Terra Nova's atmosphere. It shouldn't have surprised him that four of them hadn't survived their first true combat experience. And yet...those who had survived had better odds of completing their term. A pilot who survived his first two weeks of actual combat, if the wartime stats were to be believed, had an excellent chance of surviving the entire war.

"At least we gave as good as we got," Loyn said, from behind him. "Didn't we?"

Richard said nothing. The young men and women wanted—*needed*— to believe that they'd done well. And they hadn't done badly, despite flying inferior starfighters. He was going to have *words* with whoever was in charge of assigning starfighters when they got home, telling him in no uncertain terms that the Tornadoes were not suitable for engagements against enemy starfighters. Hell, they weren't suitable for engagements against jet fighters either.

He scrubbed himself down and turned to allow the water to run down his back, hastily looking away when he caught a glimpse of Monica's breasts. His body was suddenly intent on reminding him just how long it had been since he'd slept with a woman...he gritted his teeth, reminding himself—sharply—that Monica was his subordinate. He shouldn't be thinking of her as a young woman, or anything—really—apart from a pilot he had to send into danger on a regular basis. And yet...he hurriedly rinsed himself and stepped out of the communal shower. He'd been told that pilots felt horny—hornier—after surviving their first real mission, but it would just have to be left unsatisfied. There were too many other things to do.

"Briefing room in thirty minutes," he called back, after checking the display. "And then we'll hit the sleep machines."

Richard ran his eye down the display. *Invincible* was safe, for the moment. The flight crews had already replenished their starfighters and moved them to the launch tubes, ready for immediate launch. Delta Squadron—the poor bastards—were already sitting in their starfighters, just in case the enemy showed up without warning. They were tired, he was sure, after the last battle, but there was no choice. *Someone* had to be ready to meet an enemy attack and delay it long enough to win everyone else time to scramble.

He pulled on his flight suit, then stepped into the sleeping compartment. Four bunks remained untouched, their owners missing...he sighed, feeling their absence like a punch in the gut. He'd read stories written by men and women who'd survived the first two wars and wondered, at the time, how they could be so unfeeling. He thought he understood now. If they'd allowed themselves to become attached to the new meat, to pilots fresh out of training, it would only hurt more when they finally died. There would be time for friendship later, if they survived...

I'm sorry, he thought. He'd have to bag and box their possessions, then return them to their families. Their families wouldn't get anything else. They might not even get clear answers about when and where their sons had died. *I'm very sorry.*

He didn't want to do it. Privacy was so limited in the starfighter compartment that it felt like a violation to open their drawers, even though the four men were dead. He *knew* it wouldn't hurt them and yet...and yet he didn't want to do it. And he didn't have to do it immediately, either. It could wait. There was no guarantee that the ship herself would manage to make it back to Falkirk, let alone to Earth. They might all be dead by the end of the day.

"No," he said, out loud. It wouldn't get any easier. "It has to be done."

Gritting his teeth, he retrieved a box and went to work.

CHAPTER TWENTY-EIGHT

"THE GOOD NEWS," Doctor Percy Ganymede said, "is that I think I've figured out what we're facing. The bad news is that I don't think you're going to like it."

Ambassador Tiara O'Neil took a sip of her tea to calm her nerves as she sat in the captain's Ready Room. She'd run through hundreds of possible scenarios when she'd accepted the post, but she'd never really *expected* the aliens to simply open fire. Or for the refugees to send an alert to the aliens hunting them and then commit suicide. She knew, better than anyone else on the ship, that aliens were not human and their behaviour couldn't be predicted easily, but it had still been a shock. Her role on the ship had suddenly been rendered completely useless.

Captain Shields tapped the table impatiently. "Get to the point."

Ganymede didn't look offended as he took control of the display. "We found the same...ah...biomatter in each of the alien corpses," he said. "The cellular disruption level was quite high, as I believe I told you, but we were still able to pull enough from the remains to confirm that there were two *separate* strands of DNA-analogue within the bodies. It was why we thought they might be hybrids."

He grimaced. "It's worse. Much worse.

"We found traces of the same alien biomatter in all of the aliens who committed suicide, Captain. The stuff was threaded through their

DNA-analogue. My guess is that the cellular disrupter implant—or whatever they used to kill themselves—wasn't as powerful as the one used by the derelict's crew. Or...it's possible that it's a natural effect and...and that they simply didn't have the power to make it work. We found enough evidence to prove..."

His voice trailed off. "We also found traces of the biomatter in the remains of Corporal Loomis," he added. "It was already adapting to his biochemistry..."

"You're waffling," the Captain said, sharply. "Get to the point!"

Ganymede looked up at him. "We're dealing with a sentient virus," he said. "Well, it's not really a *virus*, but the name stuck. The invaders aren't an alliance of three races, Captain. They're three races that have been... turned into hosts for the virus, for the true enemy. I think the generation ship's crew was already infected by the time they cast off and fled. By the time they reached us, sir, they might well have lost their independence once and for all."

Captain Shields sucked in his breath. "You're talking about a cross-species infection on a massive scale. Is that even possible?"

"The virus *was* trying to adapt to Corporal Loomis's body," Ganymede said. "I...I ran some tests, under strictest quarantine. My best guess, based on the results *and* what we pulled from the alien corpses, is that the virus takes root in a host, then starts multiplying rapidly until it can take over the body. It probably builds up an alternate control network and then stabs into the brain, hacking into...well, the body's command and control system. I'm not sure if it can read memories, or operate the body without betraying its presence, but it might be possible."

Tiara took another sip of her tea, trying to come to terms with what she'd been told. A living *disease*? No, all diseases were *living*. An *intelligent* disease? Or perhaps a disease—a virus—that merely wanted to propagate itself as widely as possible. But...if it was a virus that saw all other forms of life as nothing more than hosts, it was...it was going to be impossible to talk to it. They might not even recognise humans and their allies as intelligent.

Captain Shields pressed his fingers together for a long moment. "Can they...can they take over a body and walk into our positions without being detected?"

"A simple blood test should be enough to reveal their presence," Ganymede said. "I'm not sure how long it takes to proceed from the moment of infection to complete takeover. It does seem to happen very fast, but building up internal structures may take longer than merely multiplying the base biomatter. Loomis...it's at least vaguely possible that they might have been able to reanimate Loomis's body. We just don't know."

"This is a nightmare," Tiara said. "Can we...can we *cure* the victims?"

"I don't know, not yet," Ganymede said. "The infection is extremely vicious. It's possible that something in our regular immunisations will give it trouble—or that an enhanced immune system would be able to eat it for breakfast—but I have a feeling that it will be unstoppable once it starts attacking the host's brain. I'd have to study an ongoing infection to be sure."

"Shit," Captain Shields said. "The marines who found the bodies...did they get infected?"

"I don't think so," Ganymede said, after a moment. "They went straight into quarantine, sir, where they were carefully monitored. So far, we haven't seen any trace of alien biomatter within their blood. The virus may not be airborne, sir, or their masks were sufficient to keep it out. Or it may be lying low within their bodies. We simply don't know."

"Which means we may never be able to let them out of quarantine," Captain Shields mused, grimly. "If the virus does become airborne..."

"We might be in some trouble," Ganymede said.

He tapped the table. "There's two other points I need to bring to your attention," he said, carefully. "First, the alien virus may be capable of using something smaller than a human as a host—a mouse, for example. I'd actually like to try infecting a small animal, just so I can see how the infection progresses. Second, the alien mentality is likely to be very different from ours. They may see themselves as fragments of a greater whole—a hive mind, in essence, rather than a society of individuals. It may explain their tactics, sir. They showed a complete lack of regard for their survival."

"So we must expect more suicidal tactics in the future," Captain Shields said.

"Which may not be suicidal from *their* point of view," Tiara said. She looked down at her hands. "They may see their lives as...as nothing more than flakes of skin, to be shed and discarded at will."

"Or they may not be intelligent at all, as we understand the term," Ganymede said. "We may need to infect a prisoner on death row and see what happens."

Tiara felt sick. "Out of the question!"

"It wouldn't be the first time medical experiments were performed on prisoners awaiting death," Ganymede said. "And we *do* need answers."

Captain Shields held up a hand. "Enough," he said. "Doctor, I want a full report on my desk by the end of the day. And then I want you to devote every effort to finding a cure, something we can use to save anyone who might have been infected."

Ganymede stood. "Yes, Captain."

Tiara watched him leave the cabin, then turned back to Captain Shields. "I need a drink."

"I feel the same way too," Captain Shields said. He sounded oddly amused. "But we could be attacked at any moment."

"It wouldn't matter if I was howling drunk or not," Tiara said, dryly. She'd been taught that the only thing she could do, when the bullets started flying, was to keep her head down and let the military handle it. "Do you think we can make peaceful contact?"

"If they see us as little more than hosts, they may not have any reason to listen to us when we try to talk to them," Captain Shields said. "We don't talk to horses or dogs, do we?"

"No," Tiara said. "But neither horses nor dogs are intelligent creatures. The virus...if that's really what we're dealing with...must be aware that its hosts are intelligent creatures."

"Humans have always sought to dehumanise their enemies," Captain Shields pointed out, grimly. "Chattel slaveowners shrank away from the prospect of the slaves being human, let alone equal, because that would make their enslavement morally wrong. The virus may feel the same way about its hosts, if it bothers to think about it at all. Or it may consider itself a superior form of life."

He shrugged, expressively. "Or it may be nothing more than a bundle of instinctive behaviours, reading the host's mind and using its memories for instruction. Or it may be so alien that its thoughts are completely beyond our understanding."

Tiara nodded, impatiently. "So...what do we do now?"

The captain didn't seem to hear her. "We know that some of the infected boarded the generation ship," he said. "And they were careful—very careful—to keep us from getting a good look at their biology as they landed their colony. By now, they may have infected the remainder of their population—and the human colonists."

"That would set off alarms, wouldn't it?" Tiara leaned forward, alarmed. "There's a whole contact team on the planet, very aware of the dangers of cross-species infection."

"A danger few of us believed to be real," Captain Shields said. "All the stories about plagues from interstellar space, or the common cold exterminating an entire alien race...they never played out. But now, we have something that actually *does*. And all it would take are a few moments of carelessness for the colonists to get infected, then start infecting the contact team too."

"Contact teams do run regular blood tests," Tiara reassured him. "And there are starships in the system with strict orders not to make direct contact with the planet, or the aliens, or the contact team."

The captain didn't look convinced. "But, you see, we have a problem. We don't think we can make peaceful contact with the aliens, although we should probably try. And a number of our people have either been taken prisoner or killed—and if they've been taken prisoner, they might already have been infected. And if *that* happens..."

Tiara felt her blood run cold. "They don't know *that* much, do they?"

Captain Shields winced. "Doctor Benton knows a *lot* about our technology," he said flatly, "as do many of his fellows. And the marines know a great deal too. And while they are trained to resist interrogation, none of the Conduct After Capture courses included the possibility of being infected by a sentient virus. They may not be able to keep themselves from revealing everything the aliens want to know."

"Like our internal astrography," Tiara said.

"Correct," Captain Shields said. "Madam Ambassador, we were wondering why they didn't claim the world on the other side of Tramline Alpha. Perhaps the *reason* they didn't claim it is because there's no intelligent race to turn into hosts...but now, they know about us and the others. They might launch an invasion within the next few weeks."

Tiara stared at him. "And we have no idea just how big their space is, really."

"No," Captain Shields said. He nodded towards the in-system display. "We know they've overwhelmed three races—and that's only the races we've seen. Their space could be vast, with thousands of star systems and millions of starships. If we take out a single ship, we will have no way of knowing just how badly we've hurt them. Preventing them from learning *anything* useful about us becomes our highest priority.

"We have a dilemma. If we attempt to rescue the captives—or, failing that, make sure they have no chance to tell their secrets—we risk *Invincible*. Worse, we risk losing everything we've discovered. We *may* have a chance to send a communications probe after *Pinafore* before she transits out of the next system, but if not...humanity will have to relearn everything we've discovered if we don't make it home. Worse, they'll have no warning about what might be happening on Wensleydale. If they aren't careful, the aliens will have a chance to covertly spread deeper into the Human Sphere."

"And yet, if we *don't* attempt to rescue the captives, the aliens can dissect their brains at leisure, all the while readying their invasion fleet. Who knows what titbit of information will give the aliens the clue they need to hammer us back into the Stone Age? And we would be condemning the captives to a fate worse than death."

Tiara met his eyes. "We don't have a cure, yet," she said. "They may be condemned by now already."

"I know," Captain Shields said. "But how long does it take before the infection becomes irreversible?"

Tiara had no answer. They needed to know, but there was no way to know...short of finding someone willing to let himself be infected for the greater good. The thought was sickening, yet the logic was overpowering. She'd had been taught to regard morality as flexible—aliens often had different standards to humans—but there were limits. Using a human as an experimental animal was beyond the pale.

She looked at the captain and knew he was seeking her advice. He was caught between two fires, between a grim awareness that *Invincible* had to take her discoveries home and a very valid concern about what the aliens might extract from their captives. They couldn't risk getting destroyed, hundreds of light years from home, but...they couldn't risk letting the aliens interrogate the captives either.

"Can we rescue them?" Tiara asked. Not for the first time, she wished she knew more about military matters. "Do we even know where they are?"

"I don't know, Madam Ambassador," Captain Shields said. "We left a handful of recon platforms behind, but they'll have problems tracking the aliens. All the aliens would have to do is move the prisoners onto a ship and we'd lose track of them completely. Rescue missions are always tricky, even on the ground. In space..."

He winced. "And it might make matters worse if we do."

"I don't think that's a problem," Tiara said. It galled her to admit it, but she'd *also* been trained not to hide from the truth. "These aliens—or, rather, their viral masters—are clearly hostile. There's no hope of organising peaceful contact."

Captain Shields gave her a surprised look. "Do you not want to *try*?"

"Yes, we should try," Tiara said. "But there comes a time, in diplomacy, when you're stretching out your hand—further and further, in the hope that someone will take hold—until you suddenly find yourself falling on your face. These aliens have shown no inclination to meet us halfway, Captain. They didn't even try to *talk* to us. I think the only way we'll get them to take us seriously is by giving them a bloody nose."

"Humans have been hurt and killed by cattle," Captain Shields pointed out. "Does that stop us from eating roast beef?"

"No," Tiara said. She considered the analogy for a long moment. "But how often does it happen? If cattle killed humans *every* time we tried to eat them, and the price of a roast beef dinner was a few lives, how long would it be before we did stop?"

She leaned back in her chair, feeling frustrated. She was definitely excess baggage now; there was nothing for her to do, at least until they got back home. Yes, they *could* try to talk to the aliens, but she was growing increasingly certain it was pointless. The virus hadn't shown any signs of wanting to talk. It wasn't a failure on her part, she told herself firmly. She'd done everything she could reasonably do. There was no way she could open communications with an alien mentality that regarded humans as nothing more than hosts.

At least I didn't screw up like Douglas, she thought, remembering one of the cautionary tales that had been drilled into her head during basic training. Ira Douglas had wanted to get a deal so badly that he'd practically given away everything, for nothing. And then the Troubles had started anyway. *They never even gave me the chance to screw up like him.*

Captain Shields keyed his wristcom. "Mr. XO, is local space still clear?"

"Yes, Captain," Newcomb said. "There's no trace of enemy activity."

"Then take us to Tramline Alpha, best possible speed commensurate with stealth," Captain Shields ordered. "Once we cross, we'll send a signal to *Pinafore* and then return to Alien-One once they reply."

"Aye, Captain."

"And then meet me and Major Parkinson in my Ready Room at 1700," the captain added, firmly. He sounded a little more enthusiastic. "We have a rescue mission to plan."

"Yes, sir."

Tiara looked up. "You intend to get them back?"

"If we can alert *Pinafore*," Captain Shields said. "It will take some time for them to respond, Madam Ambassador. They might not receive the signal before crossing the next tramline or...they might not receive it at all. If not"—he bit his lip—"we may have to head back to Falkirk ourselves, leaving the prisoners behind."

"I don't envy you," Tiara admitted. She had never really understood, not until now, just how much rested on the captain's shoulders. The power to issue any orders he pleased was matched with the responsibility to issue the *right* orders—and, if necessary, lead his crew to their deaths. If he made the wrong call, the entire ship would be lost. "What will the Admiralty say?"

"I suspect they'll probably want to court-martial me," Captain Shields said. Tiara gave him a surprised look. "I made mistakes, Madam Ambassador, and my crew are likely to pay the price. But this time, at least, it should be easier."

"How so?"

"We know the aliens are hostile now," Captain Shields said. "And that lets us be hostile right back."

CHAPTER TWENTY-NINE

"OFFER NO RESISTANCE," the marine ordered, as the aliens slowly advanced into the chamber. "Don't do anything threatening."

Doctor Simon Benton barely heard him. He was too scared. The nineteen humans were trapped, facing aliens who'd just appeared out of nowhere and opened fire. They were humanoid, but that didn't mean they had anything in common with humanity. He didn't even know which particular alien race he was dealing with. Their helmets hid their features behind a white mask.

He fought to control his breathing as the aliens slowly, very slowly, collected every piece of removable equipment in the chamber. Weapons, portable sensors, even a couple of datapads...they all went into the alien bag. Their guards kept their guns levelled at the prisoners, as if they expected the prisoners to suddenly burst into life and tackle them with their gloved hands. It wasn't going to happen. Simon knew, all too well, that the spacesuit wouldn't stand up to a bullet. The aliens didn't need grossly oversized guns to slaughter their captives.

Perhaps they're compensating for something, he thought, as he eyed the alien guns. It was a weak joke, but it helped to calm his mind for a second or two. *Or maybe they thought we were bigger and nastier than them.*

He forced himself to concentrate on the weapons, trying to assess them. They were bigger than the aliens carrying them. Either they'd devised some new material, he told himself in a desperate attempt to stave off panic, or they were designed for zero-g. He hadn't done much shooting in his life—he'd barely passed the firearms certification course—but he knew that rifles were heavy. The alien weapons had to be heavier still. It might be some kind of gauss rifle, perhaps, one with relatively little recoil. *That* would be an important consideration in zero-g operations.

The nearest alien took his arm and shoved him to the hatch. Simon didn't offer any resistance, allowing the aliens to push and prod him down the corridor and up the intership shaft. The alien ship seemed very alien, all of a sudden; the aliens had replaced the human lights and sensors with lights of their own, casting odd shadows in all directions. And yet... he couldn't escape the sense that the aliens hadn't actually *built* the ship. Maybe it was just a trick of the light, or zero-g, but they didn't seem to fit into the vessel.

But we know there's more than one race involved, he thought, as they were pushed towards the gash in the hull. *One of the others might have built this ship.*

He gasped, feeling a moment of sheer terror, as he was shoved through the gash and into space. He was alone...they'd spaced him...no, the alien was right next to him, navigating space with the ease of a native. A mid-sized spacecraft was hovering just outside, so blocky and angular that it could almost pass for a *human* ship. The aliens, it seemed, had the same lack of concern about aesthetics as the naval designers. Simon understood that practicality came before elegance, but he still found it sad that humanity felt no need to emulate the Tadpoles when it came to designing starships. *Their* starships were alien, very alien...and yet, they also had a certain elegance. There could be no doubt who'd designed them.

The alien craft came closer with terrifying speed. He wanted to catch himself, but he doubted the aliens would let him. Instead, he was shoved into the hatch and slammed into a net. The others joined him moments later, the hatch sliding closed as the gravity field slowly asserted itself. Simon fell towards the deck, trying not to think of the implications. The aliens clearly had far more precise control of their gravity fields than humanity.

Unless they actually have a weaker system, he told himself. *Or if they simply turned it off long enough for us to board, then turned it back on again.*

He shook his head as he picked himself off the deck. *That* was nothing more than whistling in the dark. The aliens had no obligation to make their prisoners comfortable—and they'd certainly shown no inclination to try. They could have opened communication when they'd faced *Invincible*, not simply opened fire. The combination of naked hostility and technological superiority—in at least one element—didn't bode well for the future.

An icon popped up in front of him. The aliens were pumping air—breathable air—into the airlock chamber. His suit analysed it quickly. The air was warm and moist, but breathable...it was close, very close, to the air in the alien generation ship. He felt a pang of bitter regret, wondering why he'd volunteered to remain with the contact team when he could have stayed on Wensleydale. But then, the generation ship might have been impressive—and it was—but it couldn't tell him anything *new*. The tech was little more than a hugely scaled-up version of technology humanity had surpassed long ago.

He jumped as an alien touched his arm, hard enough to sting. Its faceless mask seemed to peer at him for a moment, then the alien carefully unlatched the helmet and pulled it free. Simon felt his heart start to pound as he stared into a blue alien face, with fishy skin and big yellow eyes. The mouth was terrifyingly fish-like, twitching constantly; it was all he could do to look at the alien face and not recoil. A wash of complete unreality—alien-shock—cascaded over him. It was impossible, utterly impossible, to tell himself that the alien was a man in a suit. He—if it was a he—was just too real.

The alien continued to disrobe, removing the remainder of the suit and then the handful of underclothes. Simon, too far gone to feel shock or terror, couldn't help thinking that the alien was wearing *lingerie*. But he supposed it made a certain kind of sense. The aliens liked it hot and wet, which suggested they were comfortable wearing almost nothing. He tried to study the alien body calmly, trying to pick out details that would help him understand the aliens. And yet, there were almost no clues. If the alien had genitals—or anything relating to genitals—they were concealed.

They may not have sex like us, he told himself. *They may have more in common with the Tadpoles...*

The alien tapped Simon's spacesuit meaningfully, then gestured to the pile of discarded clothes. Simon swallowed, hard. The alien wanted him to undress? He wanted to resist, to refuse to remove the suit, but he knew he had no choice. The aliens wouldn't find it *that* hard to undress him by force, if they wished. They might simply take a monofilament knife to the suit if they couldn't figure out how to undo the latches. The designers had intended to make it easy to remove. It wasn't as if he'd been given a marine combat suit to wear. He hesitated, then—reluctantly—started to remove his helmet. The aliens watched him like hawks. He told himself, firmly, that they wouldn't have any prurient interest in his body. They were alien.

He took a breath and regretted it, instantly. The air was warm, very warm. It smelt weird, like a jungle combined with a barnyard. Droplets of water—and something else—brushed against his tongue. He was breathing it in...his heart raced, his fingers slipping over the lower latches. If the alien air was poison, if the suit's sensors had missed something nasty, he was dead. He was dead...

Stop panicking, he told himself, firmly. *You're not dead.*

He forced himself to take another breath. The air felt oddly thick, and it tasted as though he was breathing in wet dust, but it seemed to be breathable. He gritted his teeth, then removed the rest of his clothes. The aliens swept in and picked them up, the moment he was finished undressing. He tried not to think about the others, let alone look at them. They were all naked too.

The lead alien—the naked alien—signalled for Simon to follow him. Simon braced himself, then padded through a hatch and down the empty corridor. He looked from side to side, hoping to see something that might be useful later on, but saw nothing. The bulkheads were bare metal, without anything that might have passed for decoration. They didn't even have directions embedded in the walls. It made sense, he supposed, if they'd been collected by a prisoner transport ship, but still...even *military* ships had more decorations lining their bulkheads than *this*.

Another hatch opened, revealing a single large compartment. The alien pointed inside; Simon shrugged, then followed the finger into the room. It was bare, save for something that *looked* like a toilet. He groaned inwardly, realising that none of them would have any privacy, then glanced back at the alien as the last of the prisoners were ushered into the compartment. The hatch hissed closed a moment later, sealing them inside. They were trapped.

"Be careful what you say," the marine said, very quietly. "The walls will have ears."

Simon nodded, although he was more than a little perplexed. The aliens had made no attempt to talk to them. How could they possibly interrogate their prisoners without being able to talk to them? And...they didn't appear to have provided food or water or anything else. Did they suck nutrients out of the air? Surely they wouldn't assume their captives would do the same, even if humans *could* eat their food. They'd conquered the Haddocks, after all. The Haddocks ate like humans.

He glanced around the compartment. His team looked frightened, but grimly determined to keep it together. The prospect of being taken prisoner *had* been covered in their training, although the aliens didn't seem willing to let them put their communications training into practice. Maybe they were just giving their captives a break before the torture started. Or maybe they just didn't care about what their captives could tell them. And yet, if they were that unconcerned, why hadn't they all been shot the moment they'd been taken prisoner? It made no sense...

It seemed hopeless. The aliens had confiscated their tools, along with their clothes. There was no way they could cut through the bulkhead and escape, even if they had somewhere to go. He could feel dull quivers running through the ship, suggesting that it was about to depart. *Invincible*—or any other rescue mission, if it was dispatched—wouldn't know where to find the captives. Despair threatened to overwhelm him. They were a very long way from home.

Wait and see what happens, he told himself, firmly. *And then we can try to talk to them.*

· · ·

Alice took a moment to inspect her suit, as soon as she found a place she could manoeuvre without the risk of getting stuck, but it wasn't good news. The alien who'd stabbed her had definitely managed to take out the self-repair elements. Radcliffe's patch seemed to be holding, for the moment, but she knew she couldn't count on it. The patches weren't designed for long-term use.

She pulled a roll of duct tape out of her pouch and wrapped a line around the patch, hoping to keep it firmly fixed to the suit. Ideally, she'd go straight back to the ship and get a replacement, but that wasn't a possibility. She checked her weapons automatically, then tried to patch into the sensor network. It was a risk, but one that had to be borne. She couldn't keep moving blind.

Shit, she thought, as she saw the aliens herding their prisoners through the ship. *They're taking them somewhere else.*

She shut down the connection to the sensors before the aliens could detect her presence, then forced herself to move up the shaft as quickly as possible. The aliens could *not* be allowed to remove the prisoners, not without her coming along for the ride. If someone could hide every human and alien starship in existence within a solar system—and be reasonably sure they would not be detected—it would be piss-easy to hide nineteen humans. *Invincible* wouldn't have the slightest idea where to even *begin* looking. Alice didn't think the aliens would make it easy, either. Alien prisoners were worth their weight in gold.

And everyone who takes an alien prisoner has the right to claim a bounty, she reminded herself. Prize money was an old naval tradition. Anyone who captured an alien *starship* would be set up for life. *The aliens may have the same custom.*

She reached the top of the shaft, glanced in both directions, then pulled herself down to the nearest gash in the hull. The aliens didn't seem to have bothered to place guards on the smaller gashes, as if they believed they'd killed or captured every last one of the human intruders. It seemed sloppy—and made her suspicious—but she suspected the aliens hadn't really had time to muster and deploy a sizable force to sweep the derelict from one end to the other. Or they were more concerned about getting their captives off the derelict before *Invincible* returned.

If she does, Alice thought. *They wouldn't have left us in the first place if there hadn't been a clear threat to the entire ship.*

She peered through the gash, allowing her passive sensors to sweep local space for anything that might be dangerous. A handful of alien starships were clearly visible, one of them large enough to be a battleship. Alice cursed under her breath—a battleship would be a fair match for *Invincible*, particularly if there was a fleet carrier in support—and then glanced towards the abandoned shuttles. A team of aliens was swarming over them, slowly uncoupling them from the derelict. Beyond them, another set of aliens were escorting their human prisoners to an alien ship.

Shit, Alice thought. The alien ship looked to be a small cruiser, but it was impossible to tell for sure. She had no idea what sort of sensors it carried. *I need to get over there too.*

She watched, grimly, as the aliens finally managed to shove the shuttles into their cruiser's hold. Alice doubted they'd learn anything useful—the command and control system was already fried—but she knew there was no way to be sure about that either. She considered sending the self-destruct command, before reminding herself that the resulting explosion would probably destroy the alien ship and kill the prisoners. Instead, she braced herself as the aliens slowly abandoned the derelict and, when the alien craft was preparing to move, launched herself after it.

Her HUD flashed up a series of alarms, warning her that there were active sensors in the vicinity. Sweat ran down her face as she twisted her suit, using gas jets to angle her flight towards the alien ship. She was tiny on an interplanetary scale, so small that she would be dwarfed by the average missile or mass driver projectile, but if they saw her she was dead. A single burst of plasma fire would be more than enough to vaporise her completely. Or they might dispatch a welcoming committee. *She* wouldn't have let an alien ride on her hull, not if she knew the alien was there. The aliens would be wise to assume she was carrying a nuke.

Which I'm not, she thought. *That was a dreadful oversight.*

She landed, gently, on the alien hull and ducked down. It was surprisingly human, although there was a sloppiness about how the armour plates had been installed that bothered her. The aliens didn't seem to have been very concerned about appearances. She'd once been told that there were good-*looking* military units and *good* units—the two would never be entwined—but there was definitely something slapdash about the alien hull. It didn't seem to weaken the ship, as far as she could tell. Any hope she might have had of climbing *into* the ship and mounting a single-handed rescue mission had been thoroughly dashed.

So I wait, she told herself. *And signal for help.*

She slipped her suit's sensors into tracking mode and scanned the stars, locating the stealthed relay platform. *Invincible* should have left it behind, unless the captain had tripped the self-destruct system before retreating. Alice didn't think he would have cut them off from all hope of contacting the ship, but the captain *did* have standing orders not to risk letting certain pieces of technology fall into enemy hands. Or the aliens themselves might have stumbled across the platform, triggering the self-destruct anyway. It was possible, even though it would have required a massive stroke of luck. The aliens *had* detected *Invincible* poking around the derelict, after all.

Her HUD bleeped. *Platform located.*

Alice nodded to herself, then transmitted her suit's memory core towards the platform, then hastily gabbed out a message. *Invincible* would be able to track her, she hoped. She'd keep sending messages as long as she could. And yet...there was no reply. She hadn't expected one—the platform would hardly have betrayed its location so easily—but it still felt as though she was alone. Her suit would keep her alive indefinitely, but...

She shivered as the alien craft started to move, carrying her along for the ride. If the aliens didn't find her, she'd be able to keep track of their position until the carrier arrived...if it ever did.

It will, she told herself firmly. She clung to the thought, even though she knew the odds were strongly against it. *All I have to do is wait.*

CHAPTER THIRTY

"JUMP COMPLETED, CAPTAIN," Lieutenant Sonia Michelle reported.

"No enemy contacts detected," Lieutenant Alison Adams added. "We appear to be alone."

Stephen nodded, curtly. The system—the inhabitable system—was as dark and silent as the grave. He didn't understand why the enemy—the *real* enemy—hadn't bothered to claim the planet as a breeding ground for more hosts, but it hardly mattered. Right now, the only real concern was signalling *Pinafore* before it was too late.

"Communications, send the signal," he ordered. There was no hope of *detecting Pinafore* either. They'd just have to hope that Captain Corcoran had obeyed orders and followed a least-time course to the other tramline. "And copy all of our logs, including tactical combat reports, to five drones."

"Aye, Captain," Morse said. There was a long pause. "Logs are copied, sir. The drones are ready for launch."

Stephen looked at the display, then nodded. "Dispatch the drones," he ordered. "Standard ballistic trajectories, as planned."

"Aye, Captain," Morse said. New icons appeared on the display, just for a second. "Drones dispatched, sir."

"Very good," Stephen said.

He cursed under his breath. If *Pinafore* received the message—or one of the drones made it to the other tramline—*Invincible* would have managed to get word out to the rest of the Human Sphere. He could take his ship back to Alien-One and attempt to rescue his people with a clear conscience. But if something had happened to *Pinafore*—there was still no sign of *Dezhnev*—and the drones didn't spot human ships emerging from the tramline, whoever came looking for them would run into a nightmare. Cold logic told him that he should abandon the prisoners and hurry back to Falkirk, but cold logic wouldn't help him sleep at night. The Royal Navy did not abandon its people, ever.

We should have brought extra destroyers, he thought, grimly. *Or even a courier boat or two.*

He pushed the thought aside. "Helm, take us through the tramline," he ordered. "Tactical, be on full alert."

"Aye, sir."

Stephen braced himself as *Invincible* reversed course and returned to the tramline. His stomach clenched savagely as the universe darkened, an instant before the display blanked completely. It was suddenly very hard to convince himself that they had not jumped into a trap, that there *weren't* a million alien warships on the far side, just waiting for a chance to tear his ship apart. The display lit up again, showing an ever-expanding sphere of empty space. Nothing appeared to be within engagement range.

Unless they're in stealth mode too, he reminded himself. The thought didn't make him feel any better. If the aliens had caught a sniff of *Invincible* as she jumped out the first time, they might have cloaked as they slipped closer to the tramline themselves. *They might be watching us now.*

"Local space appears clear, sir," Alison said. "The closest active emitter is four light-minuters away."

"Noted," Stephen said. He glanced at Newcomb. "Do we have the latest download from the recon platforms?"

"Aye, sir," Newcomb said. "They don't appear to have abandoned the derelict."

Yet, Stephen added, silently. The time delay made it impossible to know what was going on in real time. *They could have evacuated—or slaughtered—everyone by now and then headed back to their fleet base.*

"Helm, set course for the derelict," he ordered, quietly. "Keep us in stealth mode. I don't want to have to turn tail and run because they caught a sniff of us."

"Aye, Captain," Sonia said.

Stephen gritted his teeth. It was going to be slow, very slow. But they didn't have a choice. A single betraying emission might bring the aliens down on them like the wrath of an angry god—or, worse, give the aliens a chance to plan an ambush. HMS *Warspite* had crippled—and practically destroyed—INS *Viraat* during the Anglo-Indian War. Stephen had taken part in war games where a fleet carrier had to sneak through hostile space, *without* meeting the same fate. It had been surprisingly difficult.

And we're a very long way from help, he reminded himself. *Invincible* was designed to operate on her own, like the famed *Ark Royal*, but a handful of escort ships would have been very reassuring. *A single hit might be enough to do real damage.*

He felt sweat trickling down his back as they glided further and further into the alien system, his sensors tracking alien craft buzzing around like a swarm of angry bees. The aliens appeared to be assembling a fleet, although it was hard to be sure. Their drive systems were just different enough to make it impossible for the analysts to say anything for certain. But if they were assembling a fleet, what did they have in mind? An immediate push through the tramlines to Falkirk? Or merely a defensive stance until they decided what to do next?

If we're right about their true nature, they'll go on the offensive, he thought, grimly. *And even if we're not, they'll want to take up blocking positions in the next system just to keep us away from their industrial nodes.*

The display updated, time and time again. Stephen watched, silently calculating the system's industrial potential. It was odd—like their starships, the alien tech base appeared to be at a number of different levels simultaneously—but it was definitely a fair match for Earth's. Perhaps more so, if the aliens were as united as he'd been led to believe. Earth's industrial base was, in theory, immense, but it wasn't remotely united and there was a great deal of duplication. None of the Great Powers would allow themselves to become dependent on another nation for anything.

On the other hand, it does give us a great deal of redundancy, he thought, wryly. *Do they have so much redundancy built into their industrial base?*

He ran his eye down the reports as the analysts tore into the material. The theory about the gas giants supporting a tramline—a number of tramlines—appeared to be correct. A handful of alien craft were hopping across the system, using the tramlines rather than making the transit in realspace. It wasn't particularly economical, but it had definitely proved its tactical value. He studied the list of potential targets of opportunity, feeling numb. They weren't going to do any more damage than strictly necessary, yet...there were a *lot* of potential targets. He couldn't help thinking that *Invincible* was badly outgunned.

"Sir," Alison said. "I've managed to pull a more up-to-date download from the latest set of recon platforms."

Stephen nodded. "Show me."

He leaned forward as the brief, but intensive engagement was replayed by the drone. *Invincible* had held her own—he couldn't help a moment of pride—until the alien reinforcements had arrived. And then...the aliens had dispatched shuttles and something that looked like a light cruiser to the derelict, swarming the ship. The final report, relayed from one of the marines, stated that the civilians were trapped and about to surrender.

Damn it, Stephen thought. *If only we knew how they treated prisoners...*

He shook his head. He already knew the answer. The prisoners would be infected, then the aliens would simply wait until their virus—even *that* was still hard to believe—took over the host and, presumably, gained access to the host's memories. Stephen couldn't help wondering how such a life-form had evolved in the first place, if it had truly evolved at all. It was quite possible that *someone* had devised the virus as a biological weapon and then simply lost control of it. Humanity had come very close to the brink when biological weapons were deployed on a large scale. It was the one genie the Great Powers agreed had to be kept, very firmly, in the bottle.

Or they might not have lost control at all, he speculated. *They might still be in full control of the virus.*

The thought made him shudder. He'd watched horror stories where rogue nanotech got loose—or was deliberately released—and turned the human race into zombies or slaves. It was a hopeless kind of slavery, the worst possible kind; resistance was not only futile, but unthinkable. He wondered, grimly, if the aliens who'd been infected *knew* they'd been enslaved, if there was something of the original personality still alive and screaming inside their bodies. It would be a hellish nightmare, particularly for the children. They would presumably never have a chance to live before they were infected...

Slaves to the virus or slaves to whoever created the virus, it hardly matters, he told himself, savagely. *It has to be stopped.*

"They moved the prisoners onto the ship," he mused. "What happened afterwards?"

"Unknown as yet, sir," Alison said. "That report is about forty minutes out of date."

"Then keep us moving," Stephen ordered. "We'll pick up the latest report from the platforms closer to the derelict."

And hope they haven't taken the prisoners elsewhere by now, he added, grimly. Seven hours had passed since *Invincible* had retreated to the tramline. The aliens had had plenty of time to head elsewhere—and access to a tramline, if they wanted to jump right across the system. *We might never be able to find them.*

He forced himself to think, considering his options. But they were far too limited. The prisoners had to be rescued, quickly. They *had* to be recovered before the virus overwhelmed them. Benton alone knew far too much about human technology for Stephen to be sanguine about what would happen if the aliens gained access to his knowledge. The man had a suicide implant, but he might not trigger it. Worse, he might not realise he *needed* to trigger it. The captives would be expecting everything from simple questioning to outright torture, not an alien infection. They wouldn't realise that they were under attack until it was too late.

We have to find out what happened to the prisoners and rescue them, or admit that they now know far too much about us, he told himself. *And if that happens, we may have lost the war before it even begins.*

• • •

Tiara was feeling thoroughly useless.

She knew, without false modesty, that she was good at understanding the alien viewpoint and finding ways to translate ideas and concepts from one race to the other. And yet, she didn't know how to begin to talk to a sentient virus. If, indeed, it *was* a virus. The xenospecialists seemed unsure what it actually was, dropping words and medical technobabble as if they either expected her to keep up or—more likely—they were actually trying to confuse her. Or, perhaps, trying to hide the fact they didn't know what they were talking about. Men and women who'd built careers out of knowing more than anyone else were often reluctant to admit that there were limits to their knowledge. It might cast their abilities into doubt.

As if we didn't know that already, she thought, wryly. All the experts had sworn blind, twenty years ago, that humanity was alone in the universe and, if there *were* aliens, they would be peaceful. They'd been wrong, tragically wrong. *And we wouldn't have held it against them if they had admitted their ignorance.*

Her lips quirked. *Always listen to the experts,* her father had told her, years ago. It had taken her quite some time to realise he was quoting a famous pre-space philosopher. *They'll tell you what can't be done. And then you go do it.*

"It's really quite a fascinating little structure," Doctor Percy Ganymede said. He held out a datapad. "Would you like to see the live feed?"

Tiara took it and frowned. The alien virus was almost beautiful, in its way. It reminded her of coral reefs and crystals growing in crystal...and yet, it was incredibly dangerous, growing at terrifying speed. Ganymede had fed the alien virus a diet of human blood, cultured in sickbay, and the results had been striking. The alien virus was already building the structures it needed to take over a body.

"I've actually been dissecting its DNA-analogue," Ganymede said. "You know how there's a vast amount of data contained within our DNA? The alien DNA is much more compressed, designed to build itself up into an alternate command structure for the victim's body. Each level contains the seeds of the *next* level and, I suspect, it can simply drop down a level if something prevents it from manifesting quickly."

Tiara nodded, impatiently. "Do you have a cure?"

"Not as yet," Ganymede said. "I've tried a number of simple broad-spectrum antivirals and antibiotics, but none of them have been particularly successful. It's quite an aggressive little piece of work, Madam Ambassador. It adapts quicker than anything I've seen in the wild. We can slow it down—we *have* slowed it down—through dialysis, but I don't think we can drive it out of someone's body yet. And...I don't think it's a natural virus at all."

"Someone made it," Tiara said. "*Why?*"

"To take over the universe, perhaps," Ganymede said. "Or maybe it had some other purpose and it simple mutated out of control."

He took the datapad and focused on the alien virus. "There's always something strikingly *irregular* about naturally-evolved DNA," he said. "The human genome contains a *lot* of junk DNA that serves no useful purpose, as far as we can tell. There are proposals put forward, every so often, to try to remove some of the junk, but they rarely get anywhere outside the Belt. We simply don't know enough to predict what will happen if we remove the junk on a large scale."

"There might be other negative effects," Tiara mused.

"Correct," Ganymede said. "*Artificial* DNA, the...ah, *improvements* we splice into our genome, always looked regular, even after it is passed down from parents to children. It doesn't evolve on its own, as far as we can tell"—he shrugged—"yet, I should add. There are people who speculate that any improvements will cause problems further down the line, but—so far—nothing's surfaced."

"But we don't do it on a grand scale," Tiara said. She looked up at him. "What if we *did*? I mean, what if we boosted everyone's immune system?"

"I don't think we can boost our immune systems to the point we can keep the alien virus from gaining a foothold," Ganymede told her. He smiled, thinly. "Like I said, it's a ruthless little...ah, bugger."

Tiara smiled, rather wanly. "I *have* heard worse, Doctor."

"Right now, we don't have a cure," Ganymede said. "We *do* have a workable blood test—that's actually fairly straightforward—and we *can* use ultraviolet light to kill it. I'm fairly sure that it can't survive exposure to vacuum, although we should probably be careful about taking that for granted. We've been storing frozen viruses—and embryos—for centuries."

"Make sure the captain knows about this," Tiara said. "Do you have any other concerns?"

"So far, I haven't been able to figure out how they managed to trigger the cell disruption effect," Ganymede said. "My best guess is that they actually build up a kind of electric organ—like an electric eel—which generates a power they can use to destroy their own bodies. I don't think we missed any implants when we scanned our guests, although I could be completely wrong. It may be nothing more than an implanted weapon...a biological implanted weapon."

Tiara frowned. "Is that likely?"

"I don't know," Ganymede said. He nodded at the datapad. "The virus does build up very rapidly, Madam Ambassador. It's possible that it can and it does generate enough power to destroy itself, or to serve as a weapon. But it's also possible that I am completely wrong."

"So you said," Tiara reminded him. "Keep trying to find a cure."

Ganymede met her eyes. His voice was quiet, but firm. "Given how... savage this virus is, Madam Ambassador, I don't believe we can save anyone once it reaches their brain. There is no way it can be removed without... without killing the host. Euthanasia may be our only viable option."

"I can't accept that," Tiara said. "There has to be another option."

"I've reviewed the literature on mind-control implants," Ganymede said. "There were quite a few experiments performed during the Age of Unrest and before, Madam Ambassador. And all of them were quite chancy procedures at best. Putting an implant in someone's head, for whatever the reason, was pretty much impossible to undo. The risk of brain damage was incredibly high. This virus...it's going to be far worse than any implant. Flushing it out of the host's brain will almost certainly kill the host."

Tiara swallowed. "And so...we have to kill our own people?"

"If someone cut off his arm, if his arm was infected, he might keep the virus from taking his entire body," Ganymede said. "But if he was too late, or he didn't have the nerve, or...yes, killing our own people may be the only realistic option. We will keep looking for a cure—nanotech, perhaps, or perhaps a weakened version of the alien virus—but I don't know if we can succeed."

He took a long breath. "Madam Ambassador, this war is going to be very different from anything else we've ever faced," he added. "This war is going to be for survival, fought against a foe that can infect our very bodies and turn them against us. And if we make a single mistake, we could lose everything."

Moments later, the alarms began to howl.

CHAPTER THIRTY-ONE

ALICE JERKED AWAKE, BREATHING HARSHLY.

For a long moment, she wasn't entirely sure where she was. It wasn't the first time she'd slept in a spacesuit, or caught a short nap while on exercise, but this...she was in a spacesuit, trapped on an alien hull. She knew that a handful of alien ships had been boarded during the wars, but she couldn't remember if anyone had stowed away on one before. It would go down in the history books...

Sure, she told herself. *Probably under the heading of how not to do it.*

She felt weird, she reflected, as she slowly checked her surroundings. Her forehead felt sweaty and hot, as if she were running a temperature. She'd dreamed...she'd dreamed weird dreams, dreams where she'd alternated between a strange misgiving about the future and a horniness that had been almost overpowering. It was rare for her to dream while she was on deployment—normally, she was kept too tired to do anything other than throw herself into her bunk and black out for a few hours—but now... she felt *very* weird.

Probably too much breathing in my own farts, she thought, sourly. The suit's air recycler could keep the air reasonably clear, but there were limits. Just being trapped in the suit for hours on end was thoroughly unpleasant. *And I still have no idea where we're going.*

She tongued the keypad and brought up the list of options, then scanned the stars to provide a precise location. The alien spacecraft had left the derelict far behind and headed into interplanetary space...she wasn't sure where it was going, but she rather suspected it would be pretty much impregnable. Her suit automatically locked onto the recon platform—or where the platform should be—and transmitted an update. Once again, there was no reply.

So, she asked herself as she took a sip of nutrient solution. *What the hell do I do now?*

She rolled over and sat upright, scanning the alien hull for signs of life. Nothing was moving, save for a distant communications dish that was apparently beaming signals into the inner system. There didn't *seem* to be any aliens on the hunt, looking for her...of course, she reminded herself, they might be happy to leave her where she was until they could quietly evacuate the remainder of the ship. Her sensors reported a handful of escort units, including the battleship, holding position near the cruiser. The aliens were clearly determined not to run any risk of the humans escaping.

Which leaves me with a problem, she thought. *What do I do?*

There weren't many options. She might be able to get into the ship, which wouldn't be that hard, but she didn't think she could do it without setting off hundreds of alarms. And even if she *did* manage to sneak into the ship, she'd never be able to take control of the cruiser and send it flying back to the tramline...assuming, of course, it did have tramline jump capability in the first place. Prisoner transport ships back home rarely did. The only option that seemed practical was to try to cripple or destroy the alien ship, but even that would be difficult. She simply didn't have anything like enough explosives to do real damage.

She leaned back, staring up at the unblinking stars. If *Invincible* was nearby, she *should* be able to mount a rescue...but there was that damn battleship. Her mind formed a mental picture of a team of marines carrying a nuke onto the ship and detonating it before the battleship tore *Invincible* apart, yet she knew it wouldn't be likely to work. The odds of getting through the alien point defence were very low, particularly if the aliens realised what they were doing. And besides, they'd need to get the nuke *into* the ship to be sure of doing real damage.

And if Invincible *is nowhere nearby, I'm screwed,* she thought. *And not in a good way.*

She giggled, despite herself. The odds of survival were terrifyingly low. Her concerns about the farm—and her sister's sudden desire to sell it—were meaningless. There was no way she could hope to get home, not unless she got very lucky. And the longer she stayed on the alien hull, the greater the chance of being spotted...or suffering a catastrophic suit failure at the worst possible time. Shaking her head, unable to dismiss the sense of faint *wrongness* that plagued her mind, she forced herself to think. If her life was already lost—and she knew the odds of survival were almost zero—she might as well sell it dearly.

And if I can make the aliens pay, she told herself, *I will.*

●　●　●

"Captain—ah, *Major*—Campbell apparently survived and remained undetected," Major Parkinson said. If he was annoyed at the courtesy promotion granted to his subordinate, he didn't show it. "As of her last message to the stealth platform, she was still undetected."

Stephen leaned forward as the display updated itself. "Where is she now?"

"The enemy convoy is apparently proceeding towards Planet Four," Parkinson said. "It's moving at a very slow pace indeed."

His voice sharpened. "The data she sent us included a warning that her suit was slashed," he added, darkly. "She might be...compromised."

Or dead, Stephen thought, grimly. *And that might be preferable.*

He didn't blame Parkinson for being pissed at the thought. The Major was a formidable man. He wouldn't have accepted Alice Campbell as one of his subordinates if he wasn't entirely sure he could trust her with his life—and the lives of his men. The thought that she might have betrayed them, willingly or not, wasn't something he'd want to consider. But they had no choice. If there was even the merest possibility that Alice Campbell was no longer in her right mind, they had to assume the worst.

"The alien squadron should be going a great deal faster," Newcomb said, nodding to the display. "They're taking days—weeks, even—when they should be taking hours. Why didn't they just jump through the tramline?"

"Assuming Planet Four is their final destination, it would actually add a few hours to their trip," Lieutenant-Commander David Arthur said. The Tactical Officer looked thoroughly unconvinced. "That said, Captain, my considered opinion is that this is a trap. They're tempting us with a very tempting target indeed."

Stephen could see the logic, but he wasn't so sure. The enemy ships would be grossly unwise to assume they could overwhelm *Invincible* and whatever reinforcements the carrier might have scraped up at short notice. They didn't *know* *Invincible* was alone. Or did they? If they'd already infected and overwhelmed some of the captives, they might know that the carrier was completely alone. They'd certainly be able to calculate how long it would be until *Invincible* could receive reinforcements.

Assuming they were ever dispatched, he thought, coldly. *The international fleet has more important priorities than recovering a handful of prisoners who may be already lost to us.*

He studied the enemy formation for a long moment. A cruiser, carrying the prisoners; a battleship, four destroyers and a single ship that didn't seem to have any analogue in the warbook. The analysts suspected it was a freighter, according to their latest updates, but they didn't know for sure. Stephen rather figured it was an escort carrier or something along those lines. The alien fleet carrier appeared to have vanished.

It is a very tempting target, he thought. *But that battleship is too much for us to handle on our own.*

He keyed his wristcom. "Helm, take us in pursuit," he ordered. "But be sure to stay well out of detection range."

"Aye, Captain."

"We need to get rid of that battleship," Stephen said. The analysts had told him things he hadn't wanted to know about the alien ship's firepower. "Or at least lure it out of position."

Parkinson frowned. "We could try to board her..."

"You'd be cut to ribbons," Newcomb said, bluntly. "We might be able to take her if we got close enough to bracket her with our first shots."

Stephen shook his head. There was no way the aliens would fail to notice *Invincible* if she closed to kissing range. Their sensors were nowhere near weak enough to miss something right on top of them. The first volley *would* damage the alien ship, he was sure, but not enough to cripple or destroy her. And then...her guns would tear *Invincible* apart. And that would be that. He couldn't take the risk.

"They'd see us," he said.

"Then we get in front of them and pretend to be a hole in space until they're at point-blank range," Newcomb said. "It should work."

"Too risky," Stephen said. *Warspite* and her sisters could get away with it—and the Royal Navy wouldn't be grievously weakened if the enemy blew them out of space instead—but *Invincible* was too noticeable. "We don't want to give them a free shot at our hull."

"We could leave a mine in space," Arthur said. "Let them impale themselves on the nuke."

"It would have to be a pretty big nuke," Newcomb said. "Unless we got very lucky, we might not even scratch their paint."

Stephen nodded. "We need to lure that battleship away from the convoy," he said. "And I think I have an idea."

• • •

Doctor Simon Benton felt...he wasn't sure *how* he felt. He'd slept, he thought; he'd gone to sleep and woken up on the alien deck. He should have felt refreshed, if hungry. And yet, his body felt as if he hadn't slept at all.

The gravity seemed to be shifting rapidly, leaving him feeling heavy one moment and light as a feather the next. He wasn't sure if the aliens were having problems with their gravity generators or actually trying to torture their prisoners, but either way...he had to fight to stumble to his feet.

There was no food or drink. The prisoners were lying on the deck, looking very much the worse for wear. He caught sight of Doctor Sandy McGhee, as naked as the day she was born, and felt nothing. It was all he could do to drag his eyes away. Not because he was staring at her breasts, but because his body felt like a sack of potatoes. The light was too bright, his head was starting to ache and he could hardly force himself to move. What was happening to them?

We can survive without food for a few days, he thought. God, he wished he'd paid more attention in survival classes now. Or joined the Scouts or the Cadet Force or *something* that might have prepared him for hell. *But how long can we survive without water?*

No answer came to his mind, but...he didn't think it was very long. Hours? Or days? He kicked himself, mentally, for not drinking enough water to drown a submarine before the aliens took his spacesuit. Or eating a few dozen ration bars...or something, as long as it kept him alive for a few minutes more. It wasn't as if he hadn't had the *chance* to stuff himself before it was too late. But now...his stomach growled, warningly. It wouldn't be long before hunger got the better of him, once and for all.

He peered around the room. The marine—Loomis, he thought—was lying on the deck, utterly unmoving. His body was shivering violently, as if he'd caught a cold. Simon remembered the...the flakes of alien biomatter in the air and shivered himself. What had they eaten? The alien food might be deadly poison, as far as the human race concerned...or something worse, something that would merely make them very ill. Perhaps it was a deliberate scheme to wear down their resistance. God knew he wouldn't be able to hold out for very long.

The hatch opened. He managed to turn, just in time to see a pair of aliens stride into the room. They picked up the marine, pressed some kind of sensor against his forehead, then put him back down again. Their movements were surprisingly gentle, but very firm. Simon gritted his teeth, then forced himself into their path. They seemed not to notice him until he was right in front of them.

"Food," Simon managed, somehow. It was hard to talk. His mouth felt as if it was crammed with gunk. He was too dry to spit. "We need food and water."

The alien regarded him inscrutably, then pressed something into Simon's bare chest and *pushed*. His body collapsed to the floor, suddenly utterly unable to move. The alien looked down at him for a long moment, its big eyes studying Simon with what looked like polite interest, then simply walked on. Simon wanted to scream and shout after the alien, but his mouth refused to work. He seemed to have lost all feeling below his neck.

They're not interested in interrogating us, he thought, numbly. His mind was spluttering helplessly, his thoughts breaking up into incoherent splinters. He felt as though his head was about to explode. *They're just interested in hurting us.*

It made no sense. Were the aliens so arrogant, so unconcerned with the looming war, that they didn't feel they *needed* to collect intelligence? Or were they simply more interested in watching people suffer? Or...it just made no sense! He didn't understand what he was seeing. The aliens...what had the aliens *done* to them? Perhaps they didn't even realise that their prisoners were sickening.

Or maybe they regard anyone who allows himself to be taken prisoner with utter contempt, he thought. The Japanese had done that, back in the Second World War. The Russians had done the same...they still did, if he recalled correctly. *They may think little of us...*

His body shuddered. The pain became overwhelming...

...And, helplessly, Simon Benton plunged into darkness.

• • •

"We've got a solid lock on them now," Alison said. The alien ships were clearly visible on the display. "They haven't changed course."

Stephen nodded. "At least they haven't collected reinforcements," he said. "But continue to monitor local space anyway."

"Aye, sir, Alison said.

Stephen studied the display for a long moment. He'd ordered a number of drones flown near the alien formation, watching for ships hidden behind cloaking devices. The aliens didn't *seem* to be using the prisoners to bait a trap, although he was all too aware that the aliens might *want* the prisoners recaptured. They had no way to know how far the infection had spread on *Invincible*, if it had spread at all. Letting the humans recover their lost personnel, unaware of the biological Trojan Horse...it made a great deal of sense. But it depended on the aliens realising that *Invincible* would come back to recover the prisoners.

They may care very little for each individual host, he told himself. *And if they assume we don't give a damn about our people too, they may not expect us to launch a rescue mission.*

He scowled at the bitter thought. It made sense, sure, but it was also what he wanted to believe. And that worried him. Seeing what he *wanted* to see would be a good way to get himself killed and the entire ship destroyed. He needed to be careful. There were just too many things that could go wrong.

And yet, we're running out of time, he thought. *If we let them get much closer to Planet Four, they're going to be getting reinforcements out here before we're done.*

He looked at Morse. "Communications, do you have a laser link to the drones?"

"Yes, sir," Morse said. "They're ready for deployment when you give the command."

Stephen sucked in his breath. "And the message for Campbell?"

"Programmed into the alien contact matrix," Morse assured him. "Her suit should pick the message out of the background easily."

And the aliens should not, Stephen thought. The aliens certainly hadn't bothered to pay any attention to the First Contact package. *Or so we have been assured.*

He gritted his teeth. An alien virus that was capable of burrowing its way into a host's brain and taking over—presumably reading the host's memories as well as everything else—would be capable of understanding the host's mentality. Or, at least, it *should* be capable of understanding the host's mentality. They might be able to decipher messages written to confuse someone who didn't share the right cultural background...if, of course, they cared enough to try. *He* found it hard to comprehend an alien mentality that didn't want to understand its enemies, but he thought he understood. The virus—whatever it really was—wouldn't want to start thinking there was something *wrong* with overwhelming its hosts.

That might cause an existential crisis, he thought. *And whoever is behind the virus, if its creators are still alive, might face a revolution.*

Stephen dismissed the thought, angrily. There was no more time. They couldn't wait any longer, not when their people might be losing their individuality. And if they could not be saved...at least they could be put out of their misery. It wasn't a thought he wanted to dwell on—modern medical science could cure almost anything that wasn't immediately fatal—but he had no choice. He was the captain. The buck stopped with him.

"Send the signal," he ordered. "The drones are to go active in ten minutes."

"Aye, Captain," Morse said.

And now we're committed, Stephen thought. *And we might be flying right into a trap.*

CHAPTER THIRTY-TWO

THE SUIT BLEEPED AN ALARM.

Alice jumped, one hand reaching automatically for the rifle she'd stowed beside her. She'd found a hiding place on the hull, somewhere she *thought* she'd be out of eyeshot, but the aliens might decide to sweep their ship for stowaways at any moment. God knew the marines did the same, during wartime. Who knew *who* might manage to land on the hull and betray the ship's location to its enemies?

Sweat prickled on her forehead as the message scrolled up in front of her eyes. *Invincible* was out there, closing in on the alien ship. She looked up, her eyes searching automatically for the alien battleship. It was lost in the darkness, invisible to the naked eye, but her suit's sensors had no trouble picking it out. She wondered, absently, just how *Invincible* intended to deal with the alien ship. The assault carrier's full specifications were classified well above her pay grade—she'd been told that there were compartments on the ship she was *not* to enter without permission—but she didn't *think* the carrier could take a battleship. Maybe Captain Shields thought his starfighters could kill the battleship before their target blew *Invincible* to dust. A long-range engagement *might* just work.

She finished reading the message, then forced herself to relax. Her orders weren't very specific—she was to join the marines as soon as they boarded the alien cruiser, keeping her spacesuit on at all times—but that was no surprise. Smart commanders knew that the people on the ground had a much better idea of what was going on; they had to be allowed the freedom to improvise, without having their superiors issuing impractical orders from a distance. Captain Shields seemed willing to let Major Parkinson have his head, thankfully. It spoke well of him.

Pressing her lips against the helmet's nozzle—she tried to forget how many marines called it a *tit*—she took a long drink. The mixture normally tasted slightly unpleasant—the energy drugs could be dangerously addictive, if overused—but this time it tasted thoroughly disgusting. She frowned, checking the suit's telltales for any hint the life support system had been damaged. The energy drink was separate from the water reserve, but it was normally blended with water before being funnelled into her nozzle and then into her mouth. Nothing appeared to be wrong...maybe she just had a bad batch. Or all the horror stories about men who'd drunk themselves into an early heart attack had taken a baleful toll on her subconscious. She'd heard of two men who'd had to retire after overusing the energy drinks.

And now, I wait, she thought. She still felt unwell—as if she had a nasty cold—but the prospect of actually *doing* something made her feel better. Not, she supposed, that it would have mattered if she hadn't felt any better at all. She was a marine and she had her duty and she was damned if she was proving all the doubters right by letting a little sniffle get the better of her. *They won't be able to doubt me after this.*

A dull quiver ran through the alien hull. She glanced up, just in time to see the stars shimmer as the alien ship picked up speed. Their drive field was getting stronger, suggesting that they were trying to make a run for it. She had a nasty feeling that that wasn't a good sign. The cruiser was small enough, perhaps, to outrun the assault carrier. But there was no way it would be able to outrun her starfighters.

I might have to figure out a way to cripple their drive, she thought, as she gingerly rose to her feet. Her legs felt oddly weak, as if she'd been lying immobile for hours. *And if I can't, the entire operation might fail.*

. . .

"The drones are active, Captain." Alison sounded impressed. "I *know* they're fake, sir, and I still can't tell the difference between the sensor ghosts and *real* ships."

Stephen nodded, grimly. The aliens, not knowing that *Invincible* had deployed drones, had to be seeing a handful of ships coming up behind them. Their battleship was the only vessel in the vicinity—he hoped— that could block the human ships before they entered engagement range. They would *have* to send the battleship away from the convoy, ordering her to intercept the sensor ghosts...unless they didn't give much of a damn about the prospect of a human squadron running rampant in their system. Or, maybe, their sensors were good enough to realise that they were being spoofed. Either way, the navy would get some good data from the engagement.

Come on, he thought, trying not to let the tension show on his face. *Take the bait, you arseholes.*

"The alien convoy is picking up speed," Alison reported. "I think they're making a run for it."

They'll never build up enough speed to escape, Stephen thought. *Invincible* was actually in *front* of the enemy convoy, keeping pace with the carrier. *And they have to know it too.*

"We could still try to take out the battleship, sir," Newcomb said, over the private communications link. "The fighters could give her a battering."

Stephen shook his head. The alien battleship's full capabilities were unknown, but he would have been astonished if she wasn't carrying enough point defence to give his starfighter pilots a very hard time. He couldn't justify sending them into a maelstrom when he knew he'd need them later, when the time came to retreat. Risking the marines was quite bad enough.

"Captain," Alison said. "The battleship is altering course!"

"Hold position," Stephen ordered. If the battleship had caught a sniff of *Invincible's* true position, the carrier would have to alter course rapidly. A cunning battleship CO might quietly note *Invincible's* position, then wait until there was a chance to sidle into range without making it look obvious. "Let's see where they're going."

The enemy battleship didn't seem to be any faster than her human counterparts, he noted, as the battleship reversed course. She wasn't remotely nimble. Slowly—yet moving at a speed most humans would consider unimaginable—the battleship advanced towards the sensor ghosts. A pair of destroyers accompanied it. Stephen silently calculated the vectors in his head, trying to figure out how long it would take the ships to return to the convoy. The destroyers could presumably return far faster than their bigger brother, but they would be no match for *Invincible* and her fighters. He rather hoped they'd have the sense to stay out of the fighting.

And yet, every lost ship will hurt them, he told himself. *If it really does come down to war...*

He shook his head as the battleship moved further and further away. The aliens would need roughly twenty to thirty minutes to get close enough to the drones to realise that the human fleet was nothing more than sensor ghosts. And yet, there was no way to be sure...it struck him, suddenly, just how much guesswork they'd worked into the operations plan. If the marines failed to locate the prisoners within ten minutes, *Invincible* might find herself caught between the devil and the deep blue sea. He could easily wind up making things worse for himself...

...Or even having to abandon the marines as well as the captured contact team.

The distance between the convoy and the battleship is widening in both directions, he reminded himself. *Unless she's capable of pulling a far higher rate of acceleration than she's shown us, she should need at least thirty minutes to get back to us.*

Sweat trickled down his back. Timing was everything. They had to wait until the battleship was out of the picture, yet...the longer they waited, the greater the chance the aliens would realise they were being spoofed. And then...Stephen didn't know what the aliens would do, but he knew what *he* would do. He'd reverse course at once, before it was too late. Perhaps it wouldn't be too late after all.

"The battleship is now fifteen minutes away," Alison reported.

"Prepare to launch starfighters," Stephen ordered. It was an unnecessary order. The starfighter pilots were already waiting in their launch tubes, counting down the seconds to launch. "On my mark...launch all fighters."

The minutes ticked away. He gritted his teeth, cursing—again—the sheer lack of intelligence on their new foe. If he had a good—or at least reasonable—idea of just how their sensors worked, he might have been able to make a better prediction of precisely when they'd realise that the sensor ghosts were nothing more than ghosts. But no prediction could be completely accurate. A power fluctuation at the worst possible moment would be all too revealing, if one of the ghosts vanished for a second or two. Battleships and fleet carriers generally didn't vanish off the scopes unless they went into cloak. And now...

"Launch starfighters," he snapped. "Helm, bring us about. Tactical, prepare to engage the enemy!"

"Aye, sir."

Stephen braced himself as the two enemy destroyers slid forward. They had to know they were badly outgunned, but they were coming at *Invincible* anyway. Behind them—well behind them—the battleship was already reversing course again. Thankfully, her destroyers appeared to be continuing the hunt for the sensor ghosts. She wouldn't be able to interfere for a while, but...he didn't dare forget her presence. And—of course—an alert would already be spreading across the system. The aliens might be mobilising a full-scale fleet to hunt the assault carrier down and kill her.

"Starfighters away, sir," the CAG reported. "Assault shuttles are ready to deploy."

"Deploy," Stephen ordered. There was no time to clear local space before sending in the marines. They'd just have to hope the enemy ships had too many other things to worry about. "Engage at will. I say again, engage at will!"

"Aye, sir!"

• • •

Richard sucked in his breath as the starfighter was catapulted out of the launch tube, a faint shiver running through his craft as the drive field came to life and propelled the starfighter into deep space. Two red icons flared to life on his display, both marked as priority targets; a third, a little behind the first two, was marked down for disabling shots only. The CAG was very determined not to accidentally kill the captives they were trying to rescue. Richard didn't blame her. There would be no way to *know* if the captives were truly dead or stashed away in an alien base somewhere in deep space.

We'd know they were dead if we recovered their bodies, he told himself. *Let's go.*

"Form up on me," he ordered, as the alien destroyer swept closer. The craft was loaded with point defence, its gunners firing out in a pattern a civilian would have unhesitatingly called *random*. Richard knew better. The aliens were trying to break up the human formation and make it harder for his pilots to launch their torpedoes into the alien hulls. "Engage on my mark."

The formation shifted backwards and forwards, the starfighters jerking around to make their precise location utterly unpredictable. Richard gritted his teeth as the aliens focused their fire, trying their damnedest to pick off one or two of his craft; he cursed as a pilot was blown out of space, their starfighter vaporised so completely that there was no hope of recovering a body. The alien ships seemed *designed* for anti-starfighter operations.

He hoped that meant they weren't packing anything that might threaten the carrier.

They could just ram the carrier, he reminded himself, grimly. *Invincible* was heavily armoured, but Richard doubted she'd survive if an enemy destroyer rammed her. Even if the hull remained intact, the damage would be so severe that there would be no hope of survival when enemy reinforcements arrived. *We can't let them past us.*

The enemy destroyer grew on the display as the starfighters zoomed closer, dodging wave after wave of plasma fire. She was a blocky, ugly thing; her hull bristled with weapons and sensor blisters, each one trying to locate and target a human starfighter before it was too late. Richard couldn't help wondering if the aliens had thrown the destroyers together in a hurry, taking components off the shelf and slamming them into a mishmash rather than taking the time to put the starship together properly. And yet, he had to admit the design was alarmingly effective. The alien craft was hard to approach without running the risk of being blown out of space.

"Launch torpedoes on my mark," he ordered. The enemy destroyer came closer, its weapons firing madly. "Mark!"

He pressed down on the firing key, hard. The starfighter jerked as it unleashed its torpedoes, launching all four in a single volley. His wingmen followed suit, each one launching a full volley of torpedoes. They didn't dare run the risk of *not* taking out the destroyer. He yanked the starfighter away as the enemy ship refocused its fire, trying to take out the torpedoes before they slammed into the hull. But the torpedoes were tiny, compared to the starfighters, and very fast. Only a handful were picked off before it was too late.

"Direct hits, multiple direct hits," the CAG said. "The enemy vessel has been damaged..."

The enemy destroyer vanished from the display. "The enemy vessel has been destroyed," Richard corrected. A handful of torpedoes had detonated *inside* the ship. It would take a *much* larger starship to take that sort of battering and survive. "I say again, the enemy vessel has been destroyed."

"Scratch one destroyer," Monica cheered. She paused as new icons flashed into life. "Sir, the enemy carrier is launching starfighters!"

"Delta and Beta Squadrons, return for rearming," the CAG ordered. More enemy icons appeared on the display. "Alpha, Charlie, Echo and Foxtrot, give them hell!"

"Understood," Richard said. The enemy carrier had only deployed two squadrons of starfighters. He had the numbers, even if the enemy craft were far more agile. "Alpha Squadron, form up on me. We're going in!"

"Aye, sir!"

. . .

"The second destroyer has been taken out, Captain," Arthur reported. "I believe their escort carrier is attempting to make a run for it."

Stephen considered it, briefly. There was little to be gained—immediately—by destroying an alien craft that was clearly trying to retreat. Shorn of her starfighters, the escort carrier was no threat unless she got close enough to ram. And yet, in the long term, it might work out in humanity's favour. There seemed to be little hope of *peace*. If they took out the escort carrier now, they might not have to face her later. It was an opportunity he could ill-afford to waste.

"Target her with missiles," he ordered, briskly. The alien starship was still within missile range, *without* the destroyers who would have normally protected her from incoming threats. "Fire."

"Aye, sir," Arthur said. "Missiles away!"

Stephen turned his attention to the starfighter engagement. *Invincible's* squadrons had a very definite advantage in numbers, but the alien starfighters were holding their own. He hoped that they were facing a front-line unit, rather than alien reservists. If the reservists did so well, how much better would the front-line units be? They were doomed—and they had to know it—but they were bleeding the humans badly.

We need to switch out the Tornados for space-only starfighters, he resolved, making a mental note to raise the issue with the Admiralty. The Tornados weren't bad craft, but they simply weren't designed to engage other starfighters. *And then we need to transfer the Tornados to a marine landing craft. They'd do better when they're not expected to be space-superiority fighters as well as ground-attack fighters.*

"Sir," Arthur reported. "The enemy carrier has been destroyed."

"Very good," Stephen said. "Order two of the deployed squadrons to return for rearming. We may need them."

"Aye, sir."

He allowed himself a moment of relief that the missiles hadn't been wasted. It had been a long shot, literally, but it had paid off. The enemy ship's point defence hadn't been good enough to keep his missiles from slamming into her hull. She didn't look to be anything more than a converted freighter, something that nagged at his mind. The Royal Navy had only converted freighters because it had had a sudden, desperate need for starfighter-launch platforms. Who were the aliens fighting?

Probably everyone they encounter, Stephen thought. *If they really are nothing more than a sentient virus, their economy might be all screwed up. They might think nothing of diverting freighters and turning them into warships... they might not even have an economy, as we understand the term.*

He put that aside for later consideration as the marine shuttles moved towards the enemy cruiser, the starfighters flying out ahead to take out the cruiser's point defences. It was a risk—a single unlucky shot might be enough to kill the prisoners or blow up the entire ship—but there was no choice. He didn't dare risk sending assault shuttles into the maelstrom of point defence if it could be avoided. They were already taking far too many risks as it was.

"Sir," Alison said. Stephen could hear alarm in her voice. "The enemy battleship is picking up speed."

Shit, Stephen thought, as new vectors appeared on the display. The battleship's acceleration curves were higher than predicted. And that meant...

the marines had less time than they'd thought. Unless...Stephen dismissed the handful of possible options. They had too great a chance of ending badly. *We need to move fast.*

"Update Major Parkinson," he ordered. "And then"—a dozen alternatives ran through his head—"tell him to use his best judgement."

"Aye, sir."

CHAPTER THIRTY-THREE

ALICE'S RADIO BUZZED. "CAPTAIN," Major Parkinson said. "Are you there?"

"Yes, sir," Alice said. She really didn't feel well now, but...she was damned if she was letting the side down. "Where are you going to land?"

"Here," Major Parkinson said. An icon flashed to life in front of her. "Come through the airlock and join us."

"Yes, sir," Alice said.

Her lips quirked as her suit's sensors reported incoming plasma fire. The starfighters were picking off the enemy ship's point defence weapons, clearing the way for the marines. There was a chance they'd accidentally hit Alice instead, she knew, but the risk would just have to be borne. She'd already done her duty by leading the rescue party right to their location.

I really didn't let the side down, she told herself, scrambling to her feet. She knew she'd face some pretty hard questions about what had happened to the remainder of her platoon, once she was back on *Invincible*, but she'd recovered nicely. *Madam Goat would be proud of me.*

Her lips quirked. Madam Goat—she'd forgotten the wretched woman's real name—had been her sports mistress, back at boarding school. Alice had loved sports, but she'd hated the old biddy. Madam Goat had combined an enthusiasm for sports with a hatred of teenagers and a complete lack of scruples about punishing any of her students who didn't come

321

up to her high standards. Alice hadn't been surprised to hear that Madam Goat had been fired two years after she'd left school. Too many parents had eventually complained...

She shook her head, hard. The memories of being ordered to run around the sports field in her underwear, icy water splashing around her bare feet, seemed to have come out of nowhere. Madam Goat had been punishing her for *something*...but Alice had forgotten what terrible crime she'd committed. No doubt it had been something minor. Madam Goat could be relied upon to fly off the handle at the merest pretext. Commando training had been easier to bear, somehow, after enduring school sports.

Her forehead prickled with sweat. She wanted to wipe it away as she made her way towards the LZ, but she couldn't get her hand up inside the suit. Instead, she forced herself to keep going despite a wash of sensations. She was tired and ill and her legs were wobbly...she told herself that she had to keep moving. There was no way she was going to faint in front of Major Parkinson. He'd never respect her again if she let him down in the middle of a combat zone.

The shuttle materialised out of the darkness, dropping down to land on the alien hull. Alice saw a flash of white light as a plasma torch burned into the hull, atmosphere whooshing out before the airlock was firmly secured in place. She grinned to herself as she ran closer, the airlock hatch opening invitingly. The armoured marines were already filing into the alien craft, launching probes ahead of them. Her suit linked into the command net, the communications grid filling with greetings. She felt as though she'd come home.

"Stay with me," Major Parkinson said. There was something oddly... *off* about his voice, as if he didn't quite trust her after all. "Do *not* take off your suit."

"Yes, sir," Alice said, fighting down a hot flash of resentment. She was *definitely* not in her right mind. "How long do we have?"

"Ten minutes, if that," Major Parkinson told her. "We might have to leave in a hurry."

Alice swallowed. "Yes, sir."

The alien gravity field reached up and caught her as she plunged into the alien ship, her perspective spinning around madly as she landed on the deck. Her suit's sensors bleeped a warning, telling her that the air was breathable...but teeming with flakes of alien biomatter, just like the generation ship. Alice wondered what it meant as the marines made their way deeper into the ship, their suits putting together a picture of the alien craft's interior. Had the Haddocks built the ship? Or had they been tricked, right from the start? Her head started to pound as she forced herself onwards, old memories flashing into her mind. Maybe she should have reported herself unfit for duty.

A trio of aliens—unarmed aliens—appeared at the head of the corridor. Alice sucked in her breath as she saw them, their big yellow eyes peering back at her. A moment later, the aliens ran forward, their arms extended. The marines shot them down, instantly. Alice blinked in surprise as the alien bodies hit the deck. The marines hadn't just shot them, they'd put bullets through their arms and legs too. There was no way the aliens could have stopped them.

She looked at Parkinson. "Sir...?"

"Later," Parkinson growled. "For now, make sure you put them all down so they can't get up again."

Alice stared at him in surprise. What was this? Some kind of zombie movie? But there was no time to argue. A timer had appeared in her HUD, warning her that they had less than eight minutes to find the captives and get them back to the shuttle. Alice had no idea what would happen when the timer reached zero, but she doubted it would be pleasant. The alien battleship was still out there, somewhere.

The gravity field fluctuated, growing stronger for a brief second before weakening again. An attempt to slow them down? Or a brief power failure? The lights, the too-bright lights, were slowly starting to dim, dimming so slowly that she didn't realise it was happening for several moments. She looked from side to side, glancing into empty compartments and a handful of rooms of indeterminate function. The alien cruiser didn't *look* very active. Perhaps it was nothing more than a glorified prison barge. She'd seen a couple, back during her enhanced training. The ships were designed to limit the damage the prisoners could do if they broke out of the cells.

"Down here," Corporal Pastor snapped. "I've got a lock on the captives!"

Alice followed him down the corridor, feeling an odd air of unreality falling over her. The aliens didn't seem to be offering much resistance, save for barricading a handful of hatches further into the ship. It was possible that they simply didn't have a very big crew—prison barges also limited the number of potential hostages—but it still worried her. Did the aliens *want* the marines to recover their captives? She couldn't help thinking that they'd had plenty of other options. They could have simply tried to *communicate* with the human race.

The hatch hissed open. She heard Pastor swear over the communications link. Ice ran down her spine as she hurried forward, peering through the hatch. The prisoners—all of the prisoners—lay on the metal deck, clearly ill. Corporal Loomis appeared to be utterly unmoving. She would have thought he was dead, if her suit hadn't picked out faint signs of breathing.

"They're naked," Pastor said. He sounded disgusted. "And they soiled themselves..."

"Help them get back to the shuttle," Parkinson ordered. Alice could hear the suspicion in his voice. She knew what he was thinking. He thought the whole mission had been far too easy too. "And then make sure they go straight into quarantine."

"Aye, sir."

Alice felt a stab of guilt as she bent over Doctor Benton, picking him up and throwing his limp body over her shoulder. Benton had been a scientist, a civilian...he was the sort of person the Royal Marines existed to *defend*. He'd known the dangers, a quiet voice pointed out at the back of her head, but...he hadn't deserved to suffer. And *she'd* been in command when he'd been captured. She didn't think her heroics—and the death of most of her subordinates—would make up for his suffering. There was no way to escape the simple fact that she'd failed in her duty.

Guilt washed at her mind as she picked up one of the younger assistants too, relying on the suit's muscles to carry them. The young girl—it bothered her that she couldn't remember the young research assistant's name either—had been on her first real mission. Reading between the lines of what she'd told Alice, during some brief downtime, she'd somehow managed to pull strings to get herself assigned to the contact team. And now...her body felt too light to be real. She had practically starved in less than a few hours.

The gravity flickered again. "Take anything that isn't nailed down," Parkinson ordered, curtly. "And then get them back to the shuttles."

Alice nodded, allowing her eyes to sweep around the compartment before she turned to hurry through the hatch. The air was so hot and misty that it was hard to see. And yet, she could see enough to tell that the compartment was bare, utterly bare, save for something that looked like a toilet. She didn't think it had been designed for humans, although its designers had clearly been *humanoid*. It also didn't look to have been used. The prisoners had practically collapsed as soon as they'd arrived.

A disease of some kind? She puzzled it over for a long moment. *Or were they deathly allergic to something in the air?*

She tapped her suit's sensors, forcing them to analyse the air again. There had to be something they'd missed, but what? The sensors were designed to sound the alarm if there was even a *hint* of something dangerous floating in the air. But the sensors found nothing, save for flakes of alien biomatter. The biomatter appeared to be inert, as far as the sensors could tell, but there was nothing else particularly odd about the alien atmosphere. It was hot and moist, Alice supposed, yet she'd endured worse. She'd been on deployment to Malaysia.

"Move," Parkinson snapped.

The aliens still hadn't organised resistance, Alice noted, as she carried the two captives back to the shuttles. The marines spread out, holding a dozen potential chokepoints...but the aliens made no attempt to challenge them. Her suspicions deepened. The aliens wanted them to recover the prisoners. And that meant...what? They were naked. There was no way they could smuggle a nuke onto *Invincible* without having it spotted. They'd certainly be subjected to all sorts of tests before they were even allowed to see the shuttle.

Benton groaned. Alice turned her head so she could see his face, wondering if he was waking up, but he seemed to be trapped in a nightmare. His eyes were twitching under the eyelids, his face forming a multitude of expressions...each one odd, as if he could no longer quite remember how to smile or frown. Or, perhaps, as if he simply wasn't used to his face...

Curious, she thought, putting her concerns aside. *What did they do to them?*

"They might have been conditioned, sir," she said, out loud. "I've never heard of it being done so quickly, but it is a possibility."

"Yes, it is," Parkinson said. His voice was flat, so flat that she *knew* he knew something he wasn't going to tell her. "Keep a wary eye on them."

Alice felt a hot flash of irritation as she reached the shuttle. She knew there would always be secrets she didn't need to know, although—like most combat soldiers—she didn't trust high-ranking officers to judge what she did and didn't need to know. And yet...she hadn't thought *Parkinson* would keep something from her. It was just from her, too. The other marines would have joined in the conversation if they hadn't already known what was going on. She felt an uneasy wave of suspicion. She hadn't felt so paranoid since she'd gone to boarding school and found herself the butt of the queen bee's jokes. The sense that everyone was watching her was overpowering.

Silly bitch should have realised that I was used to using my fists, Alice thought, remembering the expression on the idiot's face. It had been worth the punishment to teach the smug bitch a lesson. *I didn't get sent to boarding school because grandma and granddad thought it would make a lady out of me.*

She stepped into the shuttle, feeling the gravity field twist around her, and passed the two bodies to the medics. The light was suddenly very bright; her HUD flashed up a warning, informing her that the shuttle's interior was bathed in ultraviolet light. The medics were in full skinsuits, completely disconnected from the atmosphere...Alice felt another twinge of unease as they eyed the patch Radcliffe had slapped on her suit. What was happening? What had they discovered while she'd been clinging to the alien ship for dear life? She wanted to know...

A nasty thought struck her. She'd been on the ground in Sierra Leone, after a massive flood had led to colossal social unrest. The Royal Marines had had to help pull bodies out of the mud, dumping them by the side of the river until they could be cremated with lasers and the ashes buried in a pit. They'd used ultraviolet lights there, too; they'd sterilised the bodies, hoping to prevent another disease outbreak. She shivered, helplessly. Were the aliens using biological warfare against the human race?

But they'd need to do a lot of research before they managed to come up with something truly dangerous, she told herself. Her training had included quite a bit of focus on biological weapons, something the old sweats insisted was largely a waste of time. Royal Marines didn't need to know the details to seal off entire city blocks and quarantine them until the disease had either been cured or run its course. *They couldn't have devised a bioweapon in less than a day or two, could they?*

"You have to stay in the airlock, for the moment," the lead medic said. "Do *not* get out of your suit."

"Do as she says," Parkinson said. The other marines were filing into the shuttle, carrying the remainder of the captives with them. "Alice, I mean it. Do *not* leave the airlock."

"Yes, sir," Alice said.

She stepped into the airlock, fighting down a wave of childish emotions that threatened to overwhelm her. Tears prickled at the corner of her eyes, as if she was going to cry...even though she hadn't cried in years. Something was very definitely wrong. She sat down, leaning her suited back against the bulkhead as the shuttle disengaged from the alien craft and flew into space. The aliens still made no attempt to keep them from leaving. Alice felt her suspicions harden into certainty. The aliens had *allowed* them to recover the prisoners.

There must be a bioweapon—or something—involved, she thought, pressing her armoured hands against her helmet. The prisoners had looked seriously ill. Coming to think of it, she felt unwell herself. She looked down at the patch on her chest, where she'd been stabbed by the alien blade. Had there been something nasty on the blade? *Am I infected?*

Panic yammered at the corner of her mind. She knew how to cope with everything from fistfights to all-out firefights in the midst of a nuclear war, but she had no idea how to deal with an alien bioweapon. It certainly wasn't the common cold. The medics might never let her out of the airlock, they might never clear her to return to duty...they'd never *know*, for sure, if it was safe to allow her to re-enter the world. She felt sick. She had to swallow hard to keep from throwing up in her suit. If they didn't dare let her out of quarantine...

She let out a long breath. There was no way she was going to end her days as an experimental animal, watching helplessly as the doctors poked and prodded her body. And yet, she might have no choice. If her suffering let the doctors find a way to prevent *others* from suffering...she considered, briefly, terminating her own life. It wouldn't be that hard, even without a suicide implant. The dreaded Conduct after Capture course had suggested a number of ways she could take her own life, if captivity became too much to bear. Her trainers had dwelt on the horrors that might await her with almost ghoulish glee. She understood why they were concerned—a woman could expect no mercy if she fell into enemy hands—but she'd never really believed it could happen to her.

Or that I could be broken, she thought, grimly. *If Madam Goat couldn't break me, what hope do insurgents or terrorists have?*

It was a silly thought. Madam Goat might have been a sadistic bitch, always happy to punish her students for every little mistake, but she was no terrorist. There were limits to her powers, even though they hadn't been very evident at the time. Terrorists would starve her, brutally beat her, rape her...she had no illusions. She'd told herself she could endure, but she didn't know for sure. The Conduct after Capture course couldn't put her through *absolute* hell, just a simulation of it. She'd passed, but there would always be a question mark over her abilities until she faced captivity for real.

But this was different, she knew. The enemy was *inside* her...if, of course, she was correct. Maybe she was just unwell...no, that wasn't particularly likely. She was in the peak of physical health. Her body even had an enhanced immune system. She could have laughed at the common cold. But whatever the aliens had infected the prisoners with seemed to be laughing at her immune system. She knew, in her heart, that she was right. She'd been infected with an alien bioweapon...

...And her life would never be the same again.

CHAPTER THIRTY-FOUR

"THE PRISONERS HAVE been recovered, sir," Morse reported. "The marines are on their way back now."

Stephen nodded. "Helm, alter course," he ordered. The alien battleship was *still* accelerating, damn it. Her CO—if the aliens *had* a CO—had to be on the verge of burning out her drive nodes. Maybe the aliens had their own version of court martial proceedings. Stephen knew what the Admiralty would say to any captain foolish enough to let prisoners be snatched back under his nose and it wouldn't be remotely pleasant. "Tactical, prepare to launch missiles."

"Aye, sir."

Newcomb caught his eye. "The marines will be back onboard in seven minutes," he said, grimly. "The prisoners don't look good, sir. The full quarantine procedures have already been prepared."

We may have been too late, Stephen thought. *And now there's a risk of infecting the entire ship.*

"Make sure they stay in quarantine," he ordered, coldly. "The marines are to shoot to kill if there's even the slightest prospect of them getting out."

"Aye, sir."

Stephen leaned back in his chair, considering the vectors. The alien battleship would enter missile range in five minutes, unless it was packing multistage missiles an order of magnitude more powerful than the missiles he'd already seen. It was possible, he supposed. The NGW program had been working hard, trying to find ways to scale up the multistate missile system so it could strike targets well out of standard missile range. But they'd been running into an increasing number of hard technological limits.

And they'll be impaling themselves on our missiles, he told himself. *But their armour can probably take a number of glancing blows before they're forced to break off pursuit.*

"The starfighters have rearmed, sir," the CAG said. "They're ready for an antishipping strike."

Alison looked up as more red icons materialised on the display. "Sir, I'm picking up a number of smaller ships incoming," she said. "They'll be on us in thirty minutes."

"They must have been scrambled as soon as they heard about the engagement." Newcomb sounded disturbed. "That's very fast, even if they were on alert."

"They won't get here in time to make a difference," Stephen said, with a confidence he didn't entirely feel. The alien battleship seemed to be faster than he'd realised. Perhaps their smaller ships were faster too. "Analysis, do we have a revised set of projections for the alien battleship?"

"Yes, sir, but they're based only on what we can see," the analysis officer said, through the intercom. "They may be faster still."

Stephen nodded as he studied the projections. The alien battleship *shouldn't* be able to match *Invincible's* speed, unless it had some kind of drive technology no one had ever heard of. If it did—if it could—they were in deep shit. They'd have to take the bastard out, somehow, or get run down and blown to atoms. The aliens would probably want to board *Invincible*—he was sure of it—but he'd hit the self-destruct before he let them take his ship. They'd learn too much from her battered remains.

And I'd be condemning my people to a fate worse than death, he reminded himself. *Better to end it cleanly.*

"Captain," Arthur said. "Do you want to destroy the alien cruiser?"

"Yes," Stephen said. He had no idea how much the aliens had learned from their captives, in the few short hours they'd held them, or how far the information might have spread, but it was worth some effort to try to prevent it from spreading any further. "Take the bastard out."

"Aye, sir," Arthur said.

"Enemy ship will enter missile range in one minute," Newcomb said. "They're locking tactical sensors on our hull."

Stephen sucked in his breath as the seconds ticked down to zero. "Deploy starfighters," he ordered. "The CSP is to provide additional point defence; the remaining squadrons are to attempt to slow the battleship."

"Aye, sir."

The display sparkled with red lights. "Missile separation," Alison snapped. "I say again, missile separation!"

"Point defence is to engage at will," Stephen said. He couldn't help being impressed. The enemy battlewagon had a *lot* of missile tubes. Either that, or they'd rigged external racks onto the hull. The Royal Navy only did that during wartime. "Deploy drones and ECM countermeasures, all levels."

He smiled, grimly. They had orders to refrain from using their most advanced technology if it could be avoided, but now...if they didn't use it, there was a very good chance of losing the entire ship. The enemy was clearly trying to smother them with missile fire. He wondered, grimly, if that meant the alien battleship was weak in heavy energy weapons. It might not matter. Long-range sensors insisted that it *did* carry turrets, like a human battleship, but they would only become important if the range closed sharply.

Not that it matters, he reminded himself. *If they cripple us, if they slow us down, we'll be overwhelmed and destroyed.*

"The starfighters are outbound, sir," the CAG reported. "They'll be engaging the enemy ship in two minutes."

Stephen nodded, coldly. The starfighters were going to take *massive* casualties. There was no way to avoid it. Something *clutched* at his heart as he realised he'd sent three squadrons of young men and women to die. He had no choice, he told himself again and again; he *had* to send them out to buy time. And yet...he knew they'd known what they were signing up to do, but...

We have no choice, he told himself, once again. *We have got to keep them off our backs for a few minutes longer.*

He took a breath. "Ramp up our drives to full power," he ordered. "Open the range as quickly as possible."

"Aye, sir," Sonia said. "Do we make a run for the tramline?"

Stephen hesitated. The aliens had to know where they'd come from, didn't they? It was impossible to tell. Just because they hadn't settled the unpopulated planet didn't mean they hadn't surveyed the system. No *human* commander would be happy with an unsurveyed system right next door, let alone a tramline chain that led into the unknown. Even if the virus couldn't use the weaker tramlines—and the analysts seemed unsure if they could or couldn't use them—they still should have picketed the system...

Another set of red icons appeared, between *Invincible* and the tramline. Ice ran down his spine. Enemy cruisers, four of them. The aliens *did* know where they'd come from, then. It couldn't be a coincidence. *Invincible* was going to have problems evading the bastards as long as the battleship behind her kept firing missiles up her tailpipe. He sucked in his breath, savagely. The alien missiles weren't any more effective than their human counterparts, but there were a *lot* of them.

"No," he said. "We'll make a break for deep space."

"Aye, sir."

"Missiles entering engagement range," Arthur snapped. "Point defence going live...now."

Stephen braced himself, watching the live feed from the analysis deck as the team struggled to understand what they were seeing. The alien missiles didn't seem very smart, not compared to their human counterparts; they seemed to rely on sheer weight of fire, rather than penetrator warheads and ECM tricks. They were dumb...ironically, they were almost *too* dumb to be fooled by some of his countermeasures. Only a couple of missiles expended themselves uselessly on his decoys. The remainder kept boring in for the kill.

They're using some kind of stealth system to conceal their exact position, he thought, as the point defence opened fire. Dozens of alien missiles blinked out of existence; others, somehow, survived shots that should have killed them. Stephen wasn't surprised. The point defence computers were taking their best shots, but there were too many targets for them to give their full attention to a single missile. *They may score hits simply by overwhelming our defences...*

The ship rocked, violently. "Laser hit, rear section," Newcomb snapped. "Damage control teams are on the way!"

Stephen glanced at him. "Damage report?"

"The armour took the brunt of the strike," Newcomb said. "No significant damage..."

The ship shuddered, again. "Nuclear hit, upper port armour," Newcomb said. "The hull is intact, but our sensors and point defence have been severely degraded."

"Deploy drones to compensate," Stephen ordered. A missile flashed across the screen and vanished, its drive system failing before it reached its target. "Tactical, deploy mines to slow them down."

"Aye, sir."

Newcomb looked up. "Sir, the marine shuttles are docking at the quarantine airlock," he said. "The medics and xenospecialists are waiting for them."

"Understood," Stephen said.

He took a long breath, promising himself that, if he ever set out on another contact mission, he was going to take an entire fleet with him. *Pinafore* had been sent back to Falkirk and *Dezhnev* was missing, presumed lost. Two destroyers weren't anything like enough for a contact mission. If he had another ship, he could have transferred the former prisoners to her without having to risk *Invincible*. A specialised xenoresearch ship would have come in very handy.

And yet, the politicians keep cutting the survey budget, he thought. *Getting them to fund a specialised ship would be difficult.*

Another shudder ran through the ship. "Direct hit, lower starboard hull," Newcomb reported, grimly. "They took out more of our sensors."

"Keep us going," Stephen ordered. The alien acceleration curve appeared to have topped out, thankfully. *Invincible* would eventually out-run her tormentor, if she managed to stay alive and reasonably intact. "And deploy additional drones to confuse them."

"Aye, sir."

They probably won't be fooled again, Stephen thought. *Their sensors will have a solid lock on our hull, now. They won't believe that we've suddenly changed position in the blink of an eye. But we have to try. There's nothing else we can do.*

Alarms howled. "Laser hit, deck eleven," Newcomb said. "Armour plating in that section is ruined! We're venting atmosphere!"

"Seal that section," Stephen snapped. There were crew quarters in that section, if he recalled correctly. They'd have to double up, later, but right now it wasn't a problem. "And keep us moving!"

"Aye, sir."

We just need to hold out for a few minutes longer, Stephen told himself, firmly. *It won't be long now.*

He braced himself, feeling sweat trickling down his back. The alien starship was firing rapidly now, spitting out missiles so frantically that her tubes *had* to be overheating. They were ignoring all safety precautions in their desperate bid to smash *Invincible* before she could get away, reloading their tubes so rapidly that there was a very real chance of a disastrous accident. And yet, the range was already starting to widen. The alien ship was on the verge of losing her chance to kill *Invincible*.

Just a few minutes longer, he told himself, again. *We can make it.*

. . .

"She's a big monster, isn't she?" Flight Lieutenant Anders Parham said. "And she's packed with point defence!"

"That sounds like one of my exes," Monica said. "*Big monster* describes him perfectly."

Richard scowled as the alien battlewagon came closer. She was pumping out missiles at a terrifying rate, but—somehow—her crews were finding time to fire their point defence weapons at the approaching starfighters. Space was practically *burning* with plasma fire, each little flicker more than enough to blow his tiny starfighter to atoms. They didn't even have much of a blind spot behind their drive section, he noted. They'd crammed point defence into the hull around the drives, just to keep someone from engaging them from the rear.

"Go for their drives," he ordered. "Fire on my command."

Space became a maelstrom of light as he darted into engagement range, jinking the starfighter randomly from side to side. The aliens fired savagely, blasting away at the human starfighters as if there was no tomorrow. He saw a pair of icons vanish from the display, one of them taking out in the middle of what should have been an evasive manoeuvre. The aliens—damn them—had scored a lucky hit. A third starfighter pilot died a moment later. Richard suspected, as he glanced at the remainder of the live feed, that he'd actually steered *into* the path of a plasma bolt.

We're lucky they didn't bring any more escort ships to the party, he told himself. *The battleship alone is quite bad enough.*

He sucked in his breath. The enemy destroyers seemed to be holding their positions, rather than trying to join the party. They were probably still trying to find the drones. He doubted they'd have any luck—the drones were designed to destroy themselves if there was a risk of being taken intact—but he was grateful for small mercies. The starfighters would have had a far worse time of it if they'd had to run a gauntlet of fire from escort ships or waste time clearing the escorts out of the way before they could engage the *real* targets.

"Entering engagement range now," he said. "Firing...now!"

The starfighter jerked as he launched all four torpedoes, then threw himself out of the path of yet another plasma bolt. The aliens seemed a little confused, as if they weren't certain if they wanted to engage the missiles or the remaining starfighters; he took advantage of their brief disorientation to hurl his craft back out of engagement range. Maybe the aliens thought they had enough point defence to tackle *both* the starfighters and their missiles. He'd shot his torpedoes and they were *still* trying to kill him.

He smiled, humourlessly, as the torpedoes slammed into the alien hull. The alien craft seemed to shudder, a handful of drive nodes badly damaged or destroyed...given how hard they'd been pushing their drives, the impacts alone might have done serious damage. He watched, hoping to see their drive field dissipate entirely, but they hadn't done anything *like* enough damage. The alien craft had been slowed down, yet it hadn't been stopped.

"Return to the ship," the CAG ordered. "I say again, return to the ship."

"Understood," Richard said. He glanced at his display. Thirty-two pilots had charged into the teeth of alien fire, nineteen pilots had made it out again. The hell of it was that it was a favourable exchange rate. Slowing the alien battleship down might just have given *Invincible* a fighting chance. "We're on our way."

"The alien destroyers are moving," Monica said. "You think they'll be trying to track the Old Lady?"

"Probably," Richard said. He'd been told, time and time again, that the assault carrier could outrun anything that could actually *kill* her. The destroyers couldn't kill *Invincible*, unless they managed to *ram* her, but they could keep track of her position for the bigger ships. It wouldn't be long before the aliens managed to mobilise an entire fleet. "And that means we'll just have to kill them."

• • •

"The starfighters managed to disable some of the alien drive nodes," Alison reported. "She's losing speed rapidly."

Stephen let out a breath he hadn't realised he'd been holding. It had come with a cost, an immense cost, but the starfighters might just have saved their mothership. They hadn't taken out the alien battleship, yet they hadn't *had* to take the battleship out to save their bacon. All they'd had to do was slow it down.

We'll mourn later, he told himself, savagely. The analysts were already wittering about the alien point defence and how it might be weakened next time. *Right now, we have to save the entire ship.*

The alien battleship belched one final wave of missiles, then cut her drives completely. Stephen had no idea how the aliens thought—if they even thought at all—but he suspected it was a tacit admission that *Invincible* had managed to make good her escape. It wasn't perfect—the destroyers were rapidly catching up—yet he'd take what he could get. And yet...the aliens seemed very...*alien*. He simply didn't understand their thinking at all. If they wanted to keep the prisoners, or prevent them from being recovered, they could have done more; if they'd *wanted* the humans to recover the infected prisoners, they could have done *less*. They just didn't seem to be behaving logically.

They're alien, he reminded himself. *They may not think like humans.*

It wasn't a pleasant thought. If humans were bad at predicting how their fellow humans would react, when confronted with unpleasant surprises or outside context problems, how could they predict how *aliens* would react? The Tadpoles and the Foxes occasionally did things that made no sense to human observers...

He pushed the thought aside. *We'll figure them out*, he thought. *And then we will understand how to proceed.*

"Captain," Alison said. "The enemy destroyers are maintaining a solid lock on our hull."

Stephen nodded. The destroyers were out of missile range. He *could* deploy starfighters to kill them, but they'd simply back off long enough to escape the starfighters, then follow the ships back to their mothership when their life support packs began to run down. There was no way he could cloak a starfighter, not unless...he shook his head. He'd lost too many starfighters to risk his pilots on a desperate gamble. The aliens were going to know where his ship was for the next few hours and there was nothing he could do about it.

As long as we can stay ahead of them, it doesn't matter, he told himself. *And once we get through the tramline, we should be able to hide.*

"Keep an eye on them," he ordered. "And keep a careful watch for turbulence. There's no point in trying to hide now."

He looked at Newcomb. "Quarantine report?"

"They're being moved into the secure bay now," Newcomb said. "It doesn't look good."

"No," Stephen agreed. "It doesn't."

CHAPTER THIRTY-FIVE

ALICE COULDN'T HELP FEELING as though she was in prison.

The airlock wasn't a bad place to sit, even though she was still in her suit. It was far from comfortable, but she was used to discomfort. And yet, the sense she was trapped—that she had no way to escape without being shot—nagged at her mind. No one had *said* anything to her, beyond telling her to stay in the airlock and keep her helmet firmly in place, but she knew the quarantine procedures as well as anyone else. A person infected with a potential biohazard would not be allowed to leave. Their guards were issued orders to shoot to kill if there was no other choice.

She rested her back against the bulkhead, feeling sweat beading on her forehead. Her head hurt, her vision was starting to blur...she blinked, angrily, and felt it clear. Electric shocks seemed to be running all over her skin, poking her at random. She hadn't felt so bad since she'd caught a nasty cold, back in one of the refugee camps. *That* had felt like her first real brush with death. She knew she'd been lucky to survive.

The communications channel was quiet, even the short-range micro-burst transmitters were silent. She knew the shuttle wouldn't want to do anything to attract attention—the aliens could blow the shuttle out of space and never even notice what they'd done—but it still bothered her. She was practically a pariah, like she'd been when she'd been sent to

Coventry at school. Her dormmates had refused to speak to her for a week, after she'd been banned from playing netball when her grades had started to slip. It had been a silly moment of schoolgirl politics that had left a lasting impression. And it had never crossed her mind that the marines would act the same way.

They're not ignoring me out of spite, she told herself, savagely. They were *not* allowed to make radio transmissions unless it was urgent. Better she sat in her suit and wilted than draw enemy attention to the shuttle. *They're doing the right thing.*

But it didn't *feel* that way, she reflected, as her arms started to shiver. She hadn't felt so bad since she'd crawled through the muddy pond as part of her early training. The Royal Marines had started life as naval infantry and their instructors had never let the recruits forget it, even though the vast majority had gone on to serve in space. Wading through rivers and sneaking through mud had seemed a little pointless, but she had to admit it built character. And besides, the thrill of knowing that they'd *won* some of those exercises had made up for the discomfort.

A low quiver ran through the shuttle, the gravity field shivering slightly. They'd docked at an airlock, rather than landing in one of the shuttlebays. She didn't think that was a good thing, not now. Normally, getting the prisoners—the *former* prisoners—out of the shuttle would be a priority. But if there was a biohazard...she leaned against the bulkhead and told herself to wait. There was no point in getting stroppy. She would just have to wait and find out what was going to happen when it happened.

The hatch slowly hissed open. Bright light—the suit informed her that it ran all the way up to ultraviolet—poured in. She winced, her helmet's visor darkening automatically. Her eyes started to hurt again. Two figures stood in the light, both little more than dark shadows. It was suddenly hard, very hard, to stumble to her feet. They came forward, but she waved them away and forced herself to stand. She was damned if she was letting them *carry* her through the ship. Her legs felt wobbly, but she managed to inch forward anyway. The gravity field seemed to be rising and falling at random. She thought—she hoped—that it was just her imagination. If the gravity field really was failing, *Invincible* had taken more damage than she'd thought. Just how close had they *been* to that damned battleship?

Her radio crackled. "Come forward, step by step."

Alice nodded—she couldn't muster the energy to say something— and stumbled through the airlock into a sealed compartment. The lights seemed to grow brighter, sending stabbing pains deep into her eyes. She cursed the helmet under her breath—it should have darkened still further—and held up a hand in front of her eyes. It helped, a little. The two figures walked beside her, both wearing heavy-duty suits. They looked ominous in the bright light.

Water—no, a chemical bath—splashed down over the suit. Alice nearly slipped as alerts flashed up in front of her, then forced herself to keep going. A complete decontamination, then. She hadn't been through one since she'd endured the chemical and biological warfare drills, years ago. The liquid cleared, washing the remnants of the chemicals away. Water, she told herself. She hoped the makeshift patch would survive the decontamination treatment. It had been a long time since she'd had to undergo the procedure, but she seemed to recall that most of the decontamination chemicals were very dangerous to bare skin. She might wind up being accidentally killed by her own side.

The water stopped as she stepped through another hatch. Her radio buzzed a moment later.

"Alice," a voice said. An *unfamiliar* voice. "Can you remove your suit or do you require assistance?"

Alice scowled. She *shouldn't* need help to remove a spacesuit, but...her fingers were refusing to obey her commands. They felt short and stubby, almost as if she'd regressed back to babyhood. She felt as if she were trapped in a nightmare, as if she couldn't move no matter what was looming in the distance. She hated to admit that she needed help—she'd always been reluctant to show anything that could be taken as weakness but she had no choice. It was all she could do to unlock the suit's inner fastenings.

"Yes, please," she said. God, she hoped the rest of the marines never heard about it. No one would *say* anything to her face, save perhaps for her peers, but everyone would know and think less of her...God, she hoped she'd see the rest of the marines again. It would be worth being busted all the way back down to private to know she hadn't been infected after all. "I..."

The armoured figures closed in and began attacking her suit with surprising delicacy. Alice had to fight to keep herself still—she was all too aware of just how badly someone could be hurt by enhanced muscles—as her suit and clothing were removed, piece by piece. Her clothes felt wet, utterly sodden with sweat. She looked down at herself and grimaced. Her skin almost looked mottled. There were faint marks and bruises everywhere, as if she'd been in a bare-knuckle fistfight. When had *that* happened? She was sure she would have noticed if she'd gone a few rounds in the ring with one of the company's unarmed combat experts.

"Move forward," the lead figure ordered. His voice sounded harsh in her ears, as if it was slightly atonal. "And remain calm."

Alice stepped through the airlock, straight into another chemical bath. She kept her eyes and mouth firmly closed as she stumbled forward, wondering just how many eyes were watching her. They were probably laughing their arses off at the naked woman slipping and sliding through the airlock. It felt like a prank, but it was deadly serious. Warm water cascaded down as she reached the far end, washing the chemicals away. She hoped they hadn't made her hair fall out. She'd cropped it close to her scalp—long hair would merely have got in the way—but she didn't want to shave herself completely.

The next room was an examination chamber. She couldn't help thinking that it looked more like a torture chamber, complete with leather straps on the bed. Anyone who lay down might not be able to get up until they were released. Paranoia bubbled at the back of her mind—they could do *anything* to her—until her legs started to buckle. She was *not* in a good state, she told herself firmly. And, if there was anything she could do to help others who might be in the same boat, she had to do it.

She lay down and submitted, without complaint, to what felt like an endless swarm of medical tests. Some were understandable—she had no difficulty in recognising blood and urine tests—and others seemed to have been made up out of whole cloth. The suited figures never seemed to speak, although she was sure they *had* to be communicating. They were probably using implanted radios, if their suits didn't have radios. Her mind was threatening to start wandering again by the time they pushed a straw into her mouth. She sipped gratefully, tasting the thin orangey taste of an energy drink. It didn't taste quite right, but she drank it anyway. She hadn't realised how thirsty she was until they'd given her something to drink.

Her mind seemed to clear as the medical staff retreated to the far bulkhead, no doubt to assess what they'd discovered so far and decide what to do next. Alice scowled at their backs, then carefully tested the straps. They refused to break, even when she started to tug on them...panic yammered through her thoughts as she realised she might have to break her own wrists to escape. But the straps might be designed to tighten automatically...

...And she didn't *need* to escape. She was on *Invincible*, not an enemy ship. She was not a prisoner, even though she *felt* like a prisoner. Where had *that* thought come from?

"Hey," she managed. The medical staff seemed to jump. "What's going on?"

The suited figures turned to face her. Their faces were completely hidden behind their helmets, giving the whole scene an increasingly surreal appearance. The bright lights didn't help. She didn't *feel* like she was in hospital, wherever she was.

"We'll explain shortly," a voice said. It didn't seem to come from any of the figures. "Until then, please remain calm and wait."

Alice growled in frustration, but there was nothing she could do. The medical staff completed their consultation, then attached a set of life support equipment to her arms and a pair of tubes between her legs. Alice cursed the indignity, wondering precisely why they thought her urine was so dangerous. She hadn't felt so humiliated in her entire life. Did they expect her to stay in the bed forever? Or did they think she couldn't make it to the toilet on her own?

Probably, she thought. She felt as if she was slowly regaining her strength, but her head was still pounding. *And they might be right too.*

The air beside her started to shimmer. Major Parkinson appeared out of nowhere, wearing nothing more than his BDUs. Alice stared at him in shock, her tired mind taking far too long to realise that he was nothing more than a hologram. It dawned on her, suddenly, that Major Parkinson was looking down at her...she was strapped down, naked, tubes attached to her orifices...a wash of shame threatened to overcome her. He would never look at her in the same way again. She might as well hand in her resignation now and save time.

"Alice," Major Parkinson said. "How are you feeling?"

"Sir," Alice said. Her voice sounded raspy, even to herself. "What's happening to me?"

Major Parkinson studied her for a long moment. "What do you *think* is happening to you?"

Alice felt her temper snap. "I don't have time for fucking guessing games, *sir*," she snapped, pulling at the straps. "What is *happening* to me?"

"You were infected," Major Parkinson said. He was being gentle. It had to be very bad news indeed. "When they cut your suit, they infected you with..."

"A bioweapon," Alice finished. She sagged back onto the bed. A bioweapon. She was a dead woman walking. There was no hope of finding a cure in time to save her. And she knew the procedure for anyone who couldn't be saved. She wondered, morbidly, if they'd let her have a gun with a single bullet or if they'd simply put something nasty into her chemical drip. "I'm dead."

"Maybe," Major Parkinson told her. "Alice...they didn't infect you with a bioweapon, not in the sense you mean. They...they infected you with themselves."

Alice blinked. "Sir...what do you mean?"

"The aliens *are* a bioweapon," Major Parkinson said. "We're calling them an intelligent virus, although the boffins insist that they're not *actually* a virus. Alice...some of them got into you. They're trying to take control."

"...Shit," Alice said. She wasn't sure how to process what she'd been told. Things *didn't* get into her against her will. She'd promised herself, long ago, that she'd castrate anyone who tried to violate her...to *rape* her. And now...she'd practically been raped by a bunch of aliens so tiny she couldn't see them with the naked eye. "I..."

She swallowed, hard. "How long do I have?"

"We're not sure," Major Parkinson told her. "How are you feeling? I mean...mentally?"

I can handle it, Alice thought, defiantly. She hated to admit weakness, damn it. And yet, she knew she *had* to tell him what she was feeling. *But can he trust anything I say?*

It wasn't a pleasant thought. She knew she was still in control, for the moment, but how could he take her word for it? Could *she* take her word for it? She didn't know if she could trust her own thoughts any longer. Her body was slowly becoming an alien puppet...she swallowed, again. Her throat was suddenly very dry. How would it happen? Would she shut her eyes and never wake up? Or would she be a prisoner, trapped in her own mind, as an alien used her body?

"Strange," she admitted, finally. "My mind was wandering...a lot. I kept having strange sensations and feelings and...old memories kept resurfacing."

Major Parkinson cocked his head. "Anything of military significance?"

"No, sir," Alice said. "I was remembering my old sports mistress."

"Odd," Major Parkinson said.

Alice felt her cheeks heat. "I might have been a little delirious."

"Probably," Major Parkinson said. He smiled, although it didn't quite touch his eyes. "That's the only time *I* remember *my* old sports master. The old fart kept telling us that he'd been in the army."

"And he was done for lying about military service?" Alice guessed. "Or was he allowed to retire quietly?"

"He wasn't lying, *technically*," Major Parkinson told her. "He'd really been in the army, you see. Only...he'd been a cook. Someone let the secret slip during my final year. And then Gellibrand Minor started cracking the old joke about the army guy who'd killed ten men, the guy who'd been in the Catering Corps and poisoned them. The bastard was not amused."

"Poor Gellibrand," Alice said. She'd met her fair share of Walts, even though it was definitely illegal. Every man thought less of himself for not being a combat soldier. "Just how badly was he caned?"

"Oh, he got away with it," Major Parkinson said. "He was a laugh and a half. His father had been a general, so he had a habit of pointing out the holes in the exaggerated war stories we got from the masters. And then he joined the army and got killed in some godforsaken hellhole. I don't know what they told his father."

Alice leaned back, resting her head against the bed. "What are they going to tell my...my sister?"

"I don't know yet," Major Parkinson said. "Alice, the doctors think the infection hasn't managed to overwhelm you yet. If they're lucky—if they and you are very lucky—they may be able to devise a cure, a way of flushing it out of your bloodstream. And if that happens..."

"I don't think I'll be leaving this bed," Alice predicted, grimly. The alien biohazard was a complete unknown. They might *never* feel confident that she was free of the infection. And how could she blame them? She would never see her sister again. "Major, when the time comes, give me a gun. Please."

Major Parkinson rested an insubstantial hand on her shoulder. "If the time comes, I will see to it personally," he said. "Until then, I want you to keep fighting. Do *not* let the bastards win."

Alice nodded. "Yes, sir."

"I'll try and make sure you get some entertainment," Major Parkinson told her. "Something that will keep your brain functioning. Or maybe something mindless...? *Stellar Star and the Supernova Explosion?*"

"Anything," Alice said. Stellar Star was definitely mindless. No one watched her adventures for good storytelling and realistic social commentary. She took a raspy breath. "Sir...I want Sergeant Radcliffe and the others put down for medals. They did their duty."

"I understand," Major Parkinson said. "I'll see to it personally."

"And I need to write a report," Alice added. She tried to pull her hand free, again. "Can I sit up?"

"I'll ask the medics, but I don't think they'll want to let you loose just yet," Major Parkinson said. "You may have to record your report. I'm sorry."

"I know," Alice said. She didn't blame him—or the medics—but it was still humiliating as hell. They couldn't trust her any longer. It hurt, even though it wasn't her fault. "I'm sorry, too."

CHAPTER THIRTY-SIX

"**DEAR GOD,**" Ambassador Tiara O'Neil breathed. She sat on the Ready Room sofa, her face pale as she studied the live feed from the quarantine chamber. "What are you *doing* to her?"

Commander Newcomb, sitting beside the ambassador, gasped in horror. Stephen was inclined to agree. Alice Campbell was lying on an examination table, straps wrapped around her hands and feet. She was completely naked, but there was nothing erotic about her condition. A set of tubes ran into her arm; another rested between her legs. He felt sick just looking at the sight, as if he were transgressing a social norm. It was unpleasantly voyeuristic.

"We're attempting to cleanse her bloodstream," Doctor Percy Ganymede said. His voice was disturbingly clinical. "So far, the results have been...mixed."

"Mixed," Stephen repeated. How could Ganymede be so calm? "What is the virus *doing* to her?"

"Right now, we believe it is attempting to survive *our* attempts to extract it," Ganymede told him. "We're drawing her blood through a filtering machine, steadily removing all traces of the alien biomatter. Thankfully, it doesn't seem to have managed to build any command and control structures or we would have a far harder time of it. However...it *may* have managed to influence her mind to some extent. Her brain chemistry appears to be in flux."

Stephen looked up at him. "And she's the lucky one."

"Yes, sir," Ganymede said. "The nineteen former captives have all been overwhelmed, more or less. The virus was able to establish itself very quickly—we think because the captives were kept deliberately weak through lack of food and water—and right now it is very definitely in control. They've even started breathing out chunks of the virus, just like the common cold. I don't think we can save them, sir."

"We failed, then," Stephen said. He'd lost over forty people during the brief engagement, forty people who might have died for nothing. "They were already lost to us."

"Perhaps not, sir," Ganymede said. "We *have* been able to learn a great deal about the alien virus in the last few hours. I believe we may be able to use what we've learnt to keep it from spreading further."

"And they might not have been able to access their host's memories before the hosts were recovered," Major Parkinson added. "If so, we kept them from learning what Benton and the other boffins knew. That isn't something to sniff at."

"I hope so," Stephen commented. Intellectually, he knew they were right. But emotionally...it was hard to believe that his people had died for *something*. "Do you believe you can develop a cure?"

"Not as yet," Ganymede admitted. "I believe, based on the differences between Alice Campbell and Simon Benton, that Campbell received a less *aggressive* form of the virus. It's possible that the aliens didn't *mean* to infect her, or at least they didn't plan it. The virus currently overwhelming the liberated captives seems to have been supercharged. It may actually kill the host instead of taking it over."

He paused. "There should be ways to muster a biological response," he added. "Once we unravel the alien DNA-analogue, we can devise a countermeasure of some kind. It may even be possible to rewrite the milder form of the alien virus and use it as a vaccine."

"Or just make our eventual destruction inevitable," Major Parkinson growled. "For all we know, the virus is capable of adapting to counteract vaccines."

"We know it doesn't think much of our broad-spectrum antibiotic and antiviral treatments," Ganymede agreed. "It's simply an order of magnitude more dangerous than anything *natural*. But we may be able to devise something more fitting."

"Or a technological solution," Stephen mused. He didn't want to start injecting himself with *anything* based on the alien virus. It struck him as far too dangerous. "Some form of nanotech, perhaps."

"Perhaps," Ganymede agreed. "But we would be letting a very nasty genie out of the bottle."

Stephen took a long breath. "That's a decision for someone higher up the food chain," he said, grimly. The Admiralty—no, the Cabinet—would need to make that call. Nanotech was carefully regulated, with reason. "Right now...what do you want to do with the recovered captives?"

"Keep them under observation and watch how the virus progresses," Ganymede told him, flatly. "I don't think we can do anything for any of them now, short of a mercy killing. It might allow us to talk to them, sir, or even to learn what we may expect later on. We still know very little about their mentality."

Stephen nodded. "And Campbell?"

"She's probably the only one with a realistic chance of survival," Ganymede said. His voice was cold. "I'd like to keep trying to save her."

"Don't even think of *stopping*," Major Parkinson said. "She deserves a chance to fight."

Ganymede glanced up at the display. "I can't promise anything," he told him. "But we should be able to give her a fighting chance."

"Make sure you keep them all—every last one of them—under very tight security," Stephen said. He met Ganymede's eyes. "Are you certain the virus cannot get through the quarantine precautions?"

"I'm not entirely sure of *anything*," Ganymede admitted. Stephen silently gave him points for admitting it. "We know that high-intensity ultraviolet light kills the alien biomatter, which is definitely a point in our favour, as do certain chemicals within the decontamination procedures. I've got everyone who enters or leaves the quarantine zone passing through a Level Five decontamination process, sir, and we're monitoring their condition constantly. It may seem paranoid, but...I'm not sure we're being paranoid enough."

Stephen winced. The alien virus was *nasty*. A single mistake—a single droplet of alien biomatter getting through the decontamination procedure—would be enough to contaminate his entire ship. He didn't want to *think* about what would happen if the alien virus got loose on a planet's surface. Biological warfare wasn't quite as easy as some movies and books suggested, but it was still pretty damned unpleasant. The alien virus might get firmly established within a planetary ecosystem before anyone realised it was there.

Major Parkinson was clearly thinking along the same lines. "What would happen if they bombed a planet with the virus?"

"I'm not sure," Ganymede admitted. "The virus was clearly present within the atmosphere, in both the generation ship and the alien cruiser, but in both cases there were also elements that might have fed and supported the virus. It's possible that an atmosphere that *lacked* such elements would be hostile territory, as far as the virus was concerned. It really is quite fragile, in so many ways. But on the other hand...it's also possible that they could enslave an entire planet just by carpet-bombing the cities with the virus."

"It's like a nightmare," Major Parkinson said. "Or a bad movie."

"It wouldn't be that easy, Major." Ganymede sounded as though he was *trying* to be reassuring. "We do have some hard data from attempts to deploy biological weapons on Earth. They'd have to get the virus through the planetary atmosphere first, I think, and then they'd have to get it into a host. And they'll have to do that while contending with ultraviolet light put out by the sun. I don't think the virus will survive long in the open air."

"Which could be nothing more than whistling in the dark," Major Parkinson pointed out, darkly. "Maybe they bred up a version *designed* to survive in the open air."

"We know that even relatively *low* doses of ultraviolet light kills the virus," Ganymede said, patiently. "I will have to run more tests, Major, but I'm fairly sure that it won't survive long in the open air."

Fairly sure, Stephen thought. *I don't think...*

He shook his head. Ganymede was right, damn him. There was no such thing as a certainty, not any longer. The virus might have already escaped quarantine. Or it might be biding its time and waiting for a chance to escape. Or...he shook his head. They had no choice, but to assume the worst. They might already be on the verge of losing their minds to a remorseless alien foe.

"I hope you're right," he said. "Did you find anything to suggest that the virus was *reporting* to someone higher up the food chain? Or even anything to suggest that the creators are still alive?"

"If indeed there were creators," Major Parkinson rumbled.

"Nothing," Ganymede told him. "We simply don't know."

He paused. "We *don't* know anything about their society, but we think we can make some deductions," he added. "For one thing, the infected—once the virus starts actually taking over their bodies—start breathing out a great deal of alien biomatter. It's possible that this is simply another infection vector, sir, but it's also possible that this is a form of communication. They may have a hive mind, roughly akin to the distributed intelligence devised by the bigger corporations."

"I was under the impression that distributed intelligences aren't actually *intelligent*," Newcomb said. "They're really nothing more than a distributed computer network."

"They're not, unless they're being very quiet about it," Ganymede said. "But the aliens may share data through breathing biomatter in and out. It's possible that information spreads quite rapidly through their society."

"It seems to me that bombarding their worlds with ultraviolet light might impede their communications," Parkinson said. He sounded vindictive, as if he wanted to start tearing into the aliens with his bare hands. "It might even cut down on their reproduction."

"It might," Ganymede agreed. "On the other hand, they're clearly capable of using radio to communicate too. Except...they may find it rather crude. That might explain some of their odder actions. Fragments of their hive mind must fall in and out of contact with the whole on a regular basis."

"The fog of war, only worse," Parkinson observed. "Far worse."

Stephen nodded. He knew, all too well, the sort of chaos that could erupt when the communications network broke down. A well-ordered battle squadron could suddenly become a number of individual ships, some trying to carry out the original plan—whatever it had been—while the remainder hastily tried to improvise. Reforming a communications network was difficult enough at the best of times, but it was almost impossible to do it quickly while under enemy fire. It was why Royal Navy doctrine focused on keeping the communications datanet active at all times.

And why we route communications through multiple ships, he told himself. *We don't want to risk losing the datanet because we lost the flagship.*

He leaned back in his chair. "Thank you for the briefing, doctor," he said. "You'd better get back to work."

Ganymede rose. "Thank you, Captain," he said. "I'll inform you if anything changes."

"I believe Alice can pull through, sir," Parkinson said, once Ganymede had left the compartment. "She's a strong woman."

"She's also been infected by a virus bent on taking over her body," Tiara said. "She will have a very hard time of it."

"With all due respect, Madam Ambassador, she has *already* had a very hard time of it," Parkinson said. "We have faith in her ability to recover."

Stephen exchanged glances with his XO. He didn't fault Parkinson for being loyal to his subordinates—and Alice Campbell had done extremely well, considering the circumstances—but they would never be able to let her out of quarantine, not until she could be transferred to a biological research lab. Even if she was pronounced cured, who knew if she could ever be trusted again. Stephen's heart pounded with rage at the unfairness of it all. He understood treason—and the kind of muddy thinking that would eventually *lead* to treason—but this was different. Alice Campbell hadn't set out to be a traitor. Indeed, she hadn't *been* a traitor.

But we'll have to treat her as one, just the same, he told himself. *And she deserves much better.*

"Let us hope so," he said, firmly. He tapped the display, switching it back to the near-space view. The two pulsing red icons, close enough to track *Invincible* but too far away to be caught easily, almost looked *better* than the dying marine. "It is my considered opinion that there's nothing to be gained by lingering in this system any further. Do any of you disagree with that?"

"No, sir," Newcomb said. "I think we've outstayed our welcome."

Stephen nodded. He hadn't known Newcomb *that* long, but he was confident that the younger man would have disagreed—privately—if he felt Stephen was wrong. It was a pity that they hadn't had *much* time to build up a rapport, but they'd endured their first combat mission together. He figured that meant they were on the right track.

"And we have little hope of making contact with them," Tiara said. The Ambassador sounded frustrated. "They're just bent on overwhelming every race they encounter."

"Sometimes, you just have to give people a bloody nose before they'll talk to you," Major Parkinson said. "The aliens haven't really been given a *reason* to talk to us."

Stephen wasn't so sure. Logically, an alien race bent on conquest should have made an effort to figure out who they were trying to conquer before starting something they might not be able to finish. For all the aliens knew, the human race might rule half the galaxy and *Invincible* might be a thousand years out of date. But if the virus was literally incapable of seeing other intelligent races as little more than hosts, it might not realise that it needed to talk to them. And yet, if the alien virus *did* take memories from its hosts, it *had* to know that its hosts were thinking creatures...

They don't eat us, he thought, grimly. *They assimilate us.*

It was a terrifying thought, something right out of a science-fiction nightmare. The human race would be both enslaved and destroyed if the virus won. Infected humans would give birth to other infected humans, children who would never have the chance to grow into adulthood before their individuality was stripped away and destroyed. No, they'd never really be individuals at all. Humanity's cities would become hives for the virus, while humanity's starships carried it across the stars. How long would it be before the virus reached the Tadpoles? Or the Foxes and Cows and Vesy?

Something created this nightmare, he told himself. *What the hell were they thinking?*

It was madness. The virus *might* have a kill-switch built into its genetic structure—he *hoped* the creators had programmed a way to kill it quickly, if necessary—but there was no way it could take out *all* the virus. Had it mutated out of control, killed its creators and gone on a rampage? Or were its creators simply waiting for their creation to take the galaxy before they showed themselves? Or...were they such absolute xenophobes that they'd designed and launched a weapon capable of exterminating all other forms of intelligent life?

They must have been out of their minds, he thought. *Or maybe they were just monsters.*

He shook his head. There was no way he could claim the moral high ground. For all humanity's claims to morality, humans had done some truly awful things to one another over the years. Mass slaughter and genocide, cultural destruction and enslavement...human history was written in blood. The strong did what they wished, while the weak bent over and took it...and waited for their chance to be strong too. Humanity had advanced in many ways, over the last two hundred years, but it had also regressed. And yet, the weaknesses of the previous societies had led to their destruction...

And even if we did claim the moral high ground, it wouldn't matter, he thought. *Might may or may not make right, but it sure as hell determines what happens.*

"They're blocking our path to the tramline," Newcomb said. Stephen dragged his attention back to him with an effort. "And as long as those bastards keep their distance, there's no way we can evade contact long enough to escape."

"Then we're going to have to deal with them," Stephen said. The two destroyers were watching—carefully—for any hint that the human ship was about to reverse course and try to come to grips with them. They'd have plenty of time to alter course themselves before *Invincible* could get into weapons range. "And then we're going to have to make a run for the tramline."

He studied the display for a long moment. The enemy had mobilised hundreds of ships, gathering half of them into powerful battle squadrons and deploying the remainder to act as beaters. He could keep them out of weapons range, if he tried, but as long as they knew where he was going they'd always be able to keep themselves between *Invincible* and the tramline. And, if they got bored of waiting, they could always chase *Invincible* across the system in a bid to wear her down.

Or put a cloaked carrier or battleship in our path, he thought, grimly. He might have given them the idea himself. *Given time, they can find quite a few ways to make life difficult for us.*

"All right," he said. "First, we're going to make sure the crew gets plenty of rest. We should be safe enough for the moment, as long as we don't get too close to one of their capital ships. And then..."

He had a plan. It was risky, particularly given the circumstances, but it would have to do. He *had* to get rid of those destroyers. "This is what we're going to do..."

CHAPTER THIRTY-SEVEN

"**PREPARE FOR BALLISTIC LAUNCH,**" the cag said. "Alpha leader?"

"Ready, Commander," Richard said. He'd managed to catch a few hours of sleep since the engagement, but he felt as though he hadn't slept at all. His squadron wasn't in any better state. They'd had to hastily absorb pilots from two of the other squadrons, without any time to exercise together. They'd have to learn on the job. "Deploy at will."

He braced himself as the magnetic catapult picked up the starfighter and hurled it into open space. The drive remained silent, powered down even as the passive sensors searched for enemy targets. Two red icons appeared on the display, both keeping their distance from *Invincible*. Richard felt a flicker of glum admiration. He wasn't sure how much of the scuttlebutt running through the ship he should actually believe, but he had to admit that the aliens were doing an excellent job of tracking the carrier. They were close enough to follow her into stealth and far away enough to avoid anything the humans might throw at them.

But they shouldn't be able to track us, Richard thought, as the laser links flashed into existence. The squadron hung in the darkness of interstellar space, radiating nothing that should draw the enemy's attention. A short-range active sensor would probably pick them up—the starfighters were too small to carry a cloaking device—but the enemy would have to get a lot closer before such a sensor could be considered reliable. *They shouldn't have the slightest idea we're here.*

His eyes slipped to the display as *Invincible* turned away, slowly bringing up her drives in a bid to outrun the enemy destroyers. She was fast, perhaps the fastest carrier in active service, yet she seemed to be moving at an almost *ponderous* pace. Richard patted his starfighter's display, unable to resist a smile. No carrier—no *starship*—ever built could hope to outrun a starfighter. And no carrier could hope to outrun a *destroyer* either. The enemy—whatever they truly were—would be counting on it.

He eyed the enemy ships carefully, waiting for them to react. They'd have to pick up speed themselves soon, if they didn't want *Invincible* to simply outrun them. They might not know *precisely* when human cloaking technology could be activated, allowing *Invincible* to slip away from them, but they'd have to err on the side of caution. They'd *have* to start to move sooner rather than later or risk losing their sensor locks. He wondered, idly, what would happen if the enemy destroyers *did* let *Invincible* go. It would be very difficult for the carrier to recover its fighters if she had to stay under cloak.

They'd do us a great deal of harm and never know it, he thought, with a touch of gallows humour. The aliens *shouldn't* have been able to see *Invincible* launch her starfighters. If they had, they could afford to play cat-and-mouse until the starfighters ran out of life support. *I wonder how much harm we've done them without knowing it.*

His console *pinged*. The alien ships were moving, prowling after *Invincible*. Richard sucked in his breath as the aliens brought their active sensors online, focusing them on the escaping carrier. If it occurred to them to sweep local space, they *might* detect hints that the starfighters were present. But then, that would also reveal their *precise* location. It might endanger them if *Invincible* launched missiles at them on ballistic trajectories. And yet, it probably wouldn't put them in *much* more danger.

He sucked in his breath, feeling his heart to pound as the alien ships drew closer. The starfighters had to go active, but they had to time it perfectly. Going active too soon would give the aliens a chance to escape, going active too late would give the aliens a clean shot at them before they could start evasive manoeuvres. His eyes traced the vectors on the display, his mind racing to calculate the best possible time to go active. The timing had to be as close to perfect as possible.

His gaze slipped to the squadron status display. Everyone was waiting, ready to bring their drives and weapons online. And yet...he wouldn't know how well they'd perform until they actually went active. Every starfighter pilot had the same training—and no one would have been allowed to go on active duty without going through thousands of hours of simulations and live-fire exercises—but half his squadron pilots were practically strangers to the other half. They didn't know how their wingmen would react, let alone what they should do if the shit hit the fan. In hindsight, perhaps their time would have been better spent in the simulations than in the bunks. But tiredness was the last thing they needed when they were about to fly into combat.

Not that it matters, he told himself. He'd heard the horror stories from the old hands, the ones who'd gone out time and time again during the most intense battles of the war. *They'd* never had a chance to rest between missions. They'd been too busy trying to keep enemy starfighters off their carriers or attacking alien starships before they could deal out death and destruction to their human enemies. *We have to make do with what we have.*

The alien destroyers slowly took shape on the display. They were just like their sisters; boxy, looking almost as if they'd been thrown together at random. He couldn't help finding their appearance oddly irritating, as if the aliens had *deliberately* copied human styles when they'd designed their ships. It was a silly feeling—and he *knew* it was a silly feeling, because the aliens probably put practicality ahead of aesthetics too—but it refused to go away. Their starship designs felt like deliberate insults.

"Stand by," he ordered, quietly. The range was closing rapidly now, their window of opportunity starting to open. "Prepare to go active."

The final seconds ticked away. He braced himself, praying silently that the enemy destroyers weren't unnaturally fast. If they were fast enough to evade the starfighters, or at least widen the range significantly before the starfighters powered up completely, they *might* be able to survive and maintain contact with *Invincible*. There was no proof the aliens had access to vastly superior drive technology, but no proof they didn't either. *Invincible's* rumourmongers seemed unable to decide if the aliens hadn't realised that the carrier would come back for the captive humans or if the aliens had deliberately allowed them to be recovered. Richard wasn't sure which one was worse. If the latter, he assumed the aliens had some *method* in their madness. Alien prisoners were important, very important. They were rarely traded back until after the war was over.

If we even manage to talk to them, he thought, sourly. *We can't trade prisoners until we can actually tell them we want to trade.*

The alien starships entered range. "Go active," he ordered, slapping the button to flash-wake his starfighter's drives. "I say again, go active!"

A low hum echoed through the starfighter as the drive powered up. He felt sweat on his forehead, but there was no time to wipe it away. The aliens had a brief—very brief—window of opportunity themselves, if they reacted in time to take advantage of it. They could lunge at his ships and kill as many of them as possible before their drive fields stabilised. If they thought of it...he cursed as the aliens ramped up their drives, throwing themselves forward with grim determination. They'd thought of it.

"They're opening fire," Monica said. Her voice was calm, but Richard could hear an undercurrent of alarm. No one wanted to be caught helpless and immobile in space when an enemy ship opened fire. It was very much their worst nightmare. "I say again, they're opening fire."

"Noted," Richard said. The enemy ships were technically out of range, but they were spewing plasma bolts anyway. It cost them nothing and it might just be effective, if a bolt lasted long enough to strike one of their targets. "Stand by to engage..."

The drive powered up. He took control of the starfighter and hurled it forward, spinning into a series of desperate evasive manoeuvres as a hail of plasma bolts blasted through his former position. The aliens hadn't killed any of his pilots, but not for lack of trying. They were still desperately trying to blow his craft out of space as they converged on their targets, firing like madmen. A single hit would be more than enough to kill any of his ships.

"Alpha Squadron, take Target One," Richard ordered. "Beta Squadron, take Target Two."

The alien craft grew larger and nastier on the display as he corkscrewed towards it, his targeting sensors already picking out possible weak points. He ignored its recommendations, firing his torpedoes straight into the enemy hull. His wingmen followed suit a moment later, giving the aliens something else to worry about as they flipped over and flew away from the alien ship. The aliens took out nearly two-thirds of the torpedoes—Richard couldn't help being a little impressed—but it was nowhere near enough to save their ship. A chain of explosions blew it into dust.

"Target destroyed," he said. "I say again, target destroyed."

"Target Two destroyed," Wing Commander Wilkins said. "We ripped her apart."

"Very good," the CAG put in. "All starfighters, return to the Old Lady. I say again, return to the Old Lady."

"Understood," Richard said. He reversed course, the remainder of the squadron falling in around him as they rocketed back home. "We're on our way."

He glanced down at his display for a long moment. Local space was clear, but his long-range sensors could pick up power signatures all over the system. Some of them would be starships heading towards the human ship, the time delay ensuring that neither he nor the Old Lady's sensor crews knew *precisely* where they were. Others would be harmless, either asteroid mining stations or interplanetary ships. There was no way to tell the difference until they got a great deal closer.

And we may have started a war, he thought, numbly. *How long will it be until they come boiling out of the tramlines, bent on revenge?*

He shook his head. The aliens had fired first. They'd certainly shown no interest in communicating with their human foes. And that meant... trouble. If the aliens were truly alien, completely beyond comprehension, there was no hope of peace. It was humanity—and its allies—or the new aliens. The war had barely started, if indeed it was a war, and it was already shaping up to be worse than anything humanity had ever experienced. Even the *Tadpoles* hadn't aimed at enslavement or genocide.

It doesn't matter, he told himself, firmly. *Right now, all that matters is getting home.*

• • •

"The starfighters have returned to the ship, sir," the CAG said. "They're being rearmed now."

"Good," Stephen said. The two enemy destroyers had been blown away, but they'd probably had time to get a message out. Even if they hadn't, enemy sensors would note their sudden disappearance and draw the right conclusion. "Sensors?"

"Local space is clear, sir," Alison said. "The probes have not picked up any trace of cloaked ships."

Which may be meaningless, Stephen thought. If a cloaked alien ship had had the presence of mind to track the destroyers, rather than *Invincible* herself, they *might* manage to escape detection long enough to keep a sensor lock on the human ship. *And if their cloaking technology is better than ours, they may not be radiating any turbulence either.*

He pushed the thought aside. That way led to paranoia—and indecision. He couldn't allow himself to freeze up as he tried to determine what, if anything, he should do. His ship was in the middle of a war zone. He had to extract *Invincible* and her crew before it was too late.

"Tactical, take us into cloak," he ordered. "Helm, plot a path to the tramline."

"Aye, sir."

Stephen leaned back in his command chair and watched the alien ships as they took position in front of the tramline. There was a *lot* of them. A handful were even heading towards *Invincible's* last reported position, although they'd never get there in time to pick up the carrier again. Most of the alien ships were small, no match for *Invincible* alone, but they'd be able to whistle up bigger warships if they got a sniff of *Invincible's* position. The larger ships appeared to be clustering around the tramline, as if they couldn't decide which way they were going. He allowed himself a moment to contemplate the prospect of the international fleet breaking into the system to cover their retreat, then dismissed it. They couldn't count on anything. The international fleet had orders not to abandon Falkirk unless the situation was dire.

It is dire, he thought. His lips thinned. *But only for us.*

"Captain," Sonia said. "I've plotted out a course that should minimise our chances of being detected."

Stephen considered it for a long moment, then nodded. "Engage," he ordered. "Keep us as far from any alien contacts as you can."

"Yes, sir." Sonia worked her console for a long moment. A dull tremor ran through the ship's hull. "We'll cross the tramline in four hours."

Stephen looked at the display. "Very good," he said, as the red icons kept deploying in front of them. "Tactical? Status?"

"Weapons are charged, ready to engage the enemy," Arthur said. "The starfighters have rearmed and are ready for deployment."

"Keep one squadron on alert for immediate launch, but give the others some downtime in their squadron rooms," Stephen ordered. "They'll need to be ready to take to their craft at five minutes' notice."

"Aye, sir."

"The damage control teams have done what they can, sir," Newcomb said. "However, there are parts of our hull that really need a shipyard."

"As long as it's patched up," Stephen said.

He pulled up the engineer's report on his display and scanned it, rapidly. It was more optimistic than he'd expected, under the circumstances. The hull *should* hold up long enough to get them back to Falkirk, where they could link up with the fleet train's mobile shipyard for more permanent repairs. Unless, of course, the mobile shipyard had been diverted. It wouldn't be the first time the beancounters had objected to deploying one of the most expensive ships in the Royal Navy into a potential war zone. Normally, Stephen would even have agreed with them. The mobile shipyard was nothing more than a very big target if—when—the shit hit the fan.

And anyone who really wants to impede our deployments will know to blow it away, he told himself. *Hitting our logistics would slow us down without exposing their ships to significant risk.*

He looked up at his XO. "How's the crew holding up?"

"Very mixed, sir," Newcomb said. "We won the last engagement, which was great for morale, but they know we're still at risk. And there are all sorts of rumours about the alien threat. Very few people know what's actually happening in this system."

"The internal precautions probably don't help either," Stephen agreed. The engineers had rigged ultraviolet lamps everywhere they could, but they couldn't cover every last compartment. If the infected aliens boarded the ship, they might lose even if they drove the boarding party back into space. He rather suspected they'd have to rewire the shipboard lighting to produce ultraviolet light too. They weren't designed for it. "I'll speak to the crew."

He keyed his console. "All hands, this is the captain.

"We entered this system in the hope of making peaceful contact with a new alien race and, if we were unable to establish peaceful contact, to learn as much as we could about them before the war started. We have failed to establish peaceful contact and, given what we've learnt about the aliens, we now know that war is practically inevitable. Our duty has narrowed down to escaping this system and returning home, carrying what we've learnt with us."

Stephen took a breath. "We now know that the alien enemy—the true enemy—is a virus, a virus that leaps into a host and turns an innocent victim into a deadly enemy. It is a nightmarish foe, utterly without precedent. It has already consumed three races; worse, it has proven it can infect and consume humans too. We face a war for survival on a scale none of us had ever dared contemplate. Our engagements here, in this system, are merely the first shots in a terrifying war.

"But we *have* engaged the aliens. They are an advanced race, and they have a unique means of attack, but we know they can be beaten. I have faith that, if we have to engage the aliens one more time before we leave, that this ship and crew will be up to the task. We *will* get home, we *will* make sure that humanity knows what it is facing, we *will* ensure that the human race will survive. Good luck to us all."

He closed the connection and leaned back in his command chair. Telling the crew everything...there were commanding officers who'd disapprove. And REMFs too, who'd want to try to keep the information under control. There would be panic when word got out. The mere prospect of a disease outbreak was quite bad enough, but this was worse. People would be shooting their neighbours out of fear they were infected, even though the alien virus hadn't reached Earth...

Yet, he thought. *We have no idea what's happening on Wensleydale.*

"Keep us moving," he ordered quietly. "It's time to go home."

CHAPTER THIRTY-EIGHT

THE TENSION ON THE BRIDGE was so thick that one could cut it with a knife.

Stephen could *feel* it growing as *Invincible* made her slow way towards the tramline. The aliens were searching for the carrier, deploying starfighters and gunboats in a desperate attempt to quarter space to find her before she could make the jump. Hundreds of sensor platforms, some of them dangerously advanced, were coming online, filling space with thousands upon thousands of active sensors. Behind them, a sizable fleet—one easily large enough to swat *Invincible* out of existence—lurked, waiting for a shot at his ship. It wouldn't be long before one of the hunters came too close for comfort.

"They're starting to approach our position." Arthur's voice was very quiet, even though there was no way the aliens could *hear* them. The tactical display glowed with alien gunboats, sweeping closer to *Invincible*. "I suggest altering course."

"Helm, alter course as gently as possible," Stephen ordered. "Tactical, stand by to engage."

He checked the firing plans, time and time again. If the gunboats *did* get a sniff of *Invincible*, they would have to be wiped out as quickly as possible. He didn't dare let them get into position to intercept his starfighters as they were launched into space. And yet...he watched the red icons moving closer, unknowingly hopefully unknowingly—crossing *Invincible's* path. He could take out most of the active sensor platforms with long-range railguns—he doubted they were any less fragile than their human counterparts—but it probably wouldn't matter. The bigger ships would have plenty of time to bring up their own sensors before *Invincible* managed to take out her tormentors and slip back into cloak.

And then they'll have a solid lock on our position, he told himself. *It won't be hard for them to run us down after that.*

The alien gunboats made their closest approach—Stephen held his breath—and then flashed off into the distance. Stephen eyed them suspiciously, wondering if the gunboats *had* caught a sniff of them after all and quietly signalled for backup instead of altering course and boring in for the kill. It would be the smart move. The gunboats would be wiped out, even if they *did* report *Invincible's* location. It didn't jibe with their previous lack of concern for their lives.

Perhaps they think we're a far more dangerous opponent than they believed and wasting gunboats would therefore be a bad idea, he thought, wryly. *Or perhaps they didn't get a sniff of us after all.*

He reminded himself to be careful—it was what he wanted to believe—and then leaned forward as *Invincible* continued to crawl forward. The enemy sensor platforms were still active, sweeping space for the slightest hint of the carrier's location, but they weren't the real threat. There could be hundreds of *passive* sensor platforms out there too, covertly listening for the faintest betraying emission. *Invincible* could be slipping past one now and he'd never know about it. The aliens might have designed their platforms to be as stealthy as their human counterparts.

"I'm detecting seven or eight cruisers, sweeping up the tramline," Alison added, as a new set of icons popped into existence. "The warbook calls them medium cruisers."

Stephen nodded tersely, feeling sweat trickling down his back. Human navies hadn't built many medium cruisers, beyond proof of concept ships that had never been turned into anything more than training vessels. They lacked the speed of light cruisers and the flexibility—and weapons load—of heavy cruisers. Hell, even *cruisers* were a relatively new concept. It wasn't until human and alien technologies were merged together to create a whole new set of possibilities that humanity had started building cruisers in earnest. Before then, they'd been nothing more than bigger targets.

"Keep an eye on them," he ordered. The cruisers *probably* couldn't take *Invincible*, but they could make life difficult long enough for the battlewagons to catch up. "Inform me if they change course."

"Aye, sir."

Arthur muttered a word under his breath. "Captain, one of the drones is reporting a hint of turbulence, directly ahead of us," he said. "It might be a cloaked ship!"

Stephen seriously considered—just for a second—throwing everything he had at the hazy icon on the display. A cloaked ship, caught by surprise, would take immense damage from his missiles even if she wasn't blown out of space. But it would reveal *Invincible's* presence...and might even prove useless, if the cloaked ship wasn't actually there. The turbulence could be nothing more than a random flicker of energy or...or a decoy, designed to trick *Invincible* into doing something stupid. He wanted—he needed—to get closer to the tramline before the aliens got a hard lock on his presence.

He cursed under his breath. If they continued on their present course, the odds of being detected—assuming there was anyone to do the detecting—would rise sharply. But if they altered course, they'd cause more turbulence themselves...which would also increase the odds of being detected. He could cut his drives completely and pretend to be a hole in space, but they wouldn't get them any closer to the tramline...and besides, they might already have been detected. Their mystery opponent—and he had no idea if there actually *was* an opponent—might already be whistling up reinforcements.

"Helm, alter course," he ordered, quietly. They'd have to circle around the alien ship and hope for the best. "Tactical, continue to monitor the turbulence."

"Aye, Captain." Sonia's fingers danced over her console. "We're altering course now."

And let's hope there isn't another set of watching eyes out there, Stephen thought. The aliens *couldn't* have enough ships to blanket their entire system, could they? They might know where *Invincible* had to be going, but they were still faced with sweeping an impossibly vast segment of space. *If they have enough ships to patrol the entire region...*

He shook his head. There was no point in dwelling on it. They had to get closer...

"Captain," Alison said. "The gunboats are returning!"

Stephen tensed. "Do they have a lock on us?"

"I don't think so," Alison said. "But they're sweeping space for us."

They may have caught a sniff of something, Stephen thought. *Or our mystery watcher caught a sniff of us and summoned the gunboats.*

He studied the vectors for a long moment. "Increase speed," he ordered. "Time to the tramline?"

"One hour, assuming we maintain a steady course and speed," Sonia said.

"Captain," Arthur said. "They're massing other ships near the tramline."

Stephen nodded, curtly. It wasn't as if he couldn't take *Invincible* out into deep space and jump through the tramline there. But there were so many alien ships in the region that he'd have to go *very* far out, delaying his report to the international fleet. He had no way of knowing if *Pinafore* had actually received his message before she jumped further along the tramline chain. If she hadn't—and *Invincible* never made it home—the first the human race would know of its new enemy would be when their starships came boiling out of the tramline, looking for new hosts to infect. He couldn't afford to delay any longer.

"Then..."

An alarm rang. "Captain, the gunboats are altering course towards us," Alison snapped. "I think they've seen us!"

"It certainly looks that way," Stephen agreed. Oddly, he felt calm. "Prepare to launch starfighters!"

"We've got another ship decloaking, right on top of us," Arthur added. "Sir, she's a light cruiser!"

"Drop the cloak," Stephen ordered. The alien ship was far too close, but that wasn't exactly in her favour. She should have tried to sneak close enough to ram or remain in hiding until the bigger ships arrived. "Engage her with missiles!"

"Aye, Captain!"

"Launch starfighters," Stephen added. "And then commence the railgun firing sequence."

"Aye, sir!" Arthur tapped his console. "Railguns firing...now!"

And let's hope we manage to poke out a few of their eyes, Stephen thought. The gunboats were tightening up their formation, plunging towards *Invincible* in a steady stream of death and destruction. *They'll have the bigger ships on us soon.*

"Launch a shell of probes," he ordered, as the alien light cruiser died. "If there's anything else trying to sneak up on us, I want to know about it."

"Yes, sir."

• • •

Richard barely had a moment to catch his breath before his starfighter was hurled into interplanetary space. The gunboats were picking up speed, no doubt hoping to slam shipkiller missiles into the carrier before the CSP wiped them out. He yanked his starfighter around, one finger resting on the trigger as he swept towards the gunboats, the remainder of his squadron following him into the fire. The gunboats opened fire at once, tiny turrets spitting plasma fire in all directions. He moved the joystick from side to side, weaving through the enemy fire as the range narrowed sharply.

The gunboats might have a significant advantage in firepower—there was no point in trying to deny it—but they were bigger targets.

"Engage at will," he ordered, as the enemy formation came into range. "Switch guns to automatic."

He pulled the joystick back, hard, as a flash of plasma fire blasted past his ship, his guns firing automatically whenever the targeting sensors had a clear shot. The gunboats were slipping and sliding all over the place—he was tempted to make a joke about their pilots being drunk—their movements clearly random. It was a more effective tactic than he cared to admit. The missiles they carried might be larger than starfighter torpedoes, but they could also be fired from further away.

A gunboat vanished, followed quickly by two more. The others opened fire, launching their missiles towards *Invincible*. Richard bit off a curse as his automatic systems blasted four of the missiles out of space—the other pilots picked off a dozen themselves—but the remainder kept going. The gunboats kept going too, rather than trying to back off. Richard swore out loud as he realised the aliens intended to ram *Invincible*. A direct hit, particularly to the drives or launch tubes, would cripple the carrier.

"Take them out," he snapped. He wondered, vaguely, why the aliens hadn't simply tried to ram *before* firing their shipkillers. But then, if the gunboats had been wiped out before they could ram the carrier, they would have saved the missiles for nothing. "Now!"

Another enemy gunboat vanished from the display, followed by two more. The aliens were diving into the maelstrom of point defence without a care in the world, practically overloading their drives in a bid to ram the carrier before they could be killed. Richard gritted his teeth as he picked off another gunboat, then cursed as he saw two missiles strike the ship. Neither one appeared to have inflicted serious damage, but losing sensors and point defence would be just as dangerous in the long run. The last of the gunboats made a suicide run, only to be picked off a heartbeat before it would have slammed into the hull.

"We got them all," Monica said, delightedly.

"Splendid." Flight Lieutenant Anders Parham sounded sharp—and tired. "There's only a few million or so to go."

"We'll hold position on the carrier," Richard said. Parham was right, but as long as the other gunboats were light-hours away they weren't going to be an immediate threat. "And prepare for the next onslaught."

. . .

"Minor damage, upper hull," Newcomb reported. "The damage control teams are on the way."

"Deploy drones to fill the gaps in our coverage," Stephen ordered, automatically. They were on the verge of running out of sensor drones. Offhand, he couldn't recall any single starship deploying and losing so many in a single engagement. "Tactical?"

"The enemy is forming a blocking force," Arthur reported. "And they're mustering ships to engage us."

Stephen nodded, grimly. The enemy cruisers were blocking *Invincible's* path to the tramline, while two battle squadrons were rushing into position to support them. And there might be others under cloak, too. Stephen eyed the enemy blocking force grimly, wondering if it was just the bait in a trap. It wasn't something *he* would do, but the aliens had shown a frightening lack of concern for their own lives. They might not see anything wrong with expending nine cruisers just to get *Invincible* where they wanted her.

Not that we have much choice, but to spring the trap, he told himself. The alien battle squadrons had a solid lock on the carrier now. He might be able to evade contact with most of them, but probably not *all* of them. And even if he managed to blast his way past one, it would run the risk of crippling his ship. *We need to jump through the tramline and they know it.*

"Ramp up our speed as much as possible," he ordered, sharply. If they were lucky, they *might* be able to punch their way through the blocking force before the other alien ships could intervene. But it would also give the aliens a chance to ram his hull. "And take us on a least-time course to the tramline."

The display sparkled with red lights as more and more enemy gunboats came into sensor range. They had an impressive top speed, he noted, and an endurance starfighters couldn't match. The Royal Navy hadn't paid too much attention to the gunboat concept, even after nearly losing a battleship to enemy gunboats, but that might have been a mistake. They certainly seemed to offer their users the chance to rush additional firepower into the combat zone.

But they can't hop through the tramlines on their own, he reminded himself. *They simply cannot be deployed outside their home system without a carrier.*

"Enemy gunboats will be on us in ten minutes," Alison reported. "The medium cruisers are targeting us with long-range missiles."

"Order the CSP to intercept the gunboats," Stephen said. The aliens would probably try to time their launches so the missiles arrived at the same time as the gunboats. It was what *he* would have done. "And keep us moving towards the tramline."

He looked at the tactical display. "As soon as the range drops, I want to hit those cruisers with everything we have, up to and including the main guns," he added. "They are *not* to be allowed a chance to ram us."

"Yes, sir," Arthur said.

"New contacts," Alison said, sharply. "A third battle squadron...behind the blocking force!"

Stephen hastily recalculated the vectors in his head. The aliens had messed up the timing, he thought. Not by much, but *just* enough. *Invincible* should be able to get through the tramline before the third squadron could engage her. Barely. The odds weren't good, but they were better than zero. Unless the aliens had something else up their sleeves...

"The blocking force is opening fire," Alison reported. "And the gunboats are making their final approach."

"Order the point defence to engage," Stephen ordered.

He forced himself to remain calm as the damage started to mount. The alien gunboats were throwing themselves into the teeth of his defences, a handful making it through to slam into the hull. He'd been fearful of some hitherto unknown weapon, something that would allow a single gunboat to take out the entire ship, but nothing materialised. And yet, with the damage growing steadily, it might be only a matter of time before his ship was battered into a useless hulk...

"Enemy ships entering weapons range," Arthur reported. "Opening fire...*now*."

Stephen braced himself as the big plasma guns started to fire. The Royal Navy had taken a lot of flak from armchair admirals, when the plans had been announced, for outfitting a carrier with battleship guns, even though they gave *Invincible* more teeth than the average fleet carrier. Carriers weren't *meant* to engage the enemy at knife-range, the critics had argued; carriers simply lacked the armour to stand up to a short-range energy weapons duel. And yet...

The aliens didn't expect us to be packing so much heat, he thought, as a pair of enemy cruisers were ripped apart. They really *wouldn't* have closed the range if they'd known how dangerous *Invincible* could be. *And if they try to ram us, they'll be making themselves easy targets.*

A shockwave ran through the hull. "Direct hit, starboard flight deck," Newcomb said, grimly. "Captain, we won't be able to launch and recover fighters from that deck for a while."

"Understood," Stephen said. He felt a surge of vindictive pleasure as a third alien ship vanished from the display. The tramline was coming closer. "Order the fighters to prepare for an emergency jump manoeuvre..."

"Sir," Arthur snapped. "The enemy battle squadron has opened fire!"

Stephen gritted his teeth. The enemy ships were firing at the extreme limits of their range, even with multistage missiles...he *hoped* they were firing at the extreme limits of their range. If he was wrong...

"Take us through the tramline as soon as we cross it," he snapped. They *should* be able to make the jump before the enemy missiles arrived. "Have the fighters latched themselves to the hull?"

"Yes, sir," the CAG said. "They're ready."

"Then take us through," Stephen said. He braced himself. Jumping at speed was going to *hurt*. "Now!"

The universe dimmed, just for a second. Stephen doubled over, feeling as though someone had punched him in the gut. He heard someone vomiting behind him, but didn't turn to see who. His stomach was churning so badly that he thought he was going to throw up too...

...And then the display sparkled with red icons...

...And he knew he'd made a terrible mistake.

CHAPTER THIRTY-NINE

"GUNBOATS," MONICA SAID. "They followed us through the tramline!"

For a long moment—too long—Richard's mind refused to believe what he was seeing. A tiny little craft like a gunboat could *not* transit the tramlines without a carrier. It was impossible, flat-out impossible. And yet it had happened. The aliens were already swooping down on *Invincible*, seemingly unbothered by the jump shock. Richard's chest felt like an elephant had jumped up and down on him for a few minutes, but the aliens...

Shit, he thought. *If they can overcome the jump shock so quickly, what else can they do?*

"Disengage from the ship," he snapped. *Invincible's* automated defences were already moving to cover the hull, but they'd have problems coping with the gunboats. "Take the bastards out!"

He felt woozy as he guided the starfighter away from the hull, his sensors already seeking out enemy targets. Half the gunboats seemed to have already shot their missiles on the other side of the tramline—it was the only explanation he could think of why they weren't launching missiles as they neared their target—but the remainder were firing shipkillers right into the teeth of *Invincible's* defences. His starfighter picked a handful of missiles off as they flashed passed him—as did the other pilots—yet a number survived to strike home. Richard could almost *hear* the carrier screaming in agony as the missiles tore into her hull.

And if she dies here, none of us will get home, he thought. The long-range sensors weren't picking up any trace of human or alien starships outside the combat zone. It didn't look as though the international fleet had deployed to save *Invincible. No one will ever know what happened to us.*

An enemy gunboat flashed past him, its turrets blazing with fire. He blew it to dust with a single shot, then evaded a hail of plasma bolts from its wingman. Two more followed, firing their missiles as they closed in on *Invincible.* Behind them, he saw the first enemy capital ships start to transit the tramline. They were already far too close to *Invincible* for comfort, well within multistage missile range. He hoped—he prayed—that they'd already shot their magazines dry, but he doubted *Invincible* could be so lucky. The battleships had probably already reloaded their missile tubes.

"Keep the bastards off the carrier," he ordered. Thankfully, there didn't *seem* to be any more gunboats passing through the tramline. "And..."

He forced himself to consider his options, knowing that it was pointless. There just weren't enough human starfighters left to mount an assault on even *one* of the battleships, let alone all three. All they could do was hold out as long as possible, covering the carrier while trying to put as much distance as possible between themselves and the alien ships. Who knew? They might make it.

Sure, he thought, wryly. *And perhaps the horse will learn to sing.*

• • •

"Direct hit, multiple direct hits," Newcomb snapped. "Upper port hull!"

The internal armour held, Stephen thought, relieved. *They didn't manage to get into our innards.*

"Helm, take us towards the second tramline, best possible speed," he ordered. The enemy gunboats had been a nasty surprise. But who would have expected small craft to be capable of transiting the tramline? There was no way any *human* gunboat could accomplish such a feat. "Tactical, deploy full ECM; I want them to be unsure of our exact position."

He gritted his teeth as the three red icons on the display began to glide forward, heading straight for *Invincible*. Three battleships...any one of them more than powerful enough to turn the carrier into dust. He thought his ship could outrun them, given time, but he didn't dare take that for granted. The aliens had already shown a willingness to overstress their drives, just to come to grips with their enemies. Statistically, one of the three battleships would lose too many drive nodes to continue...

...But he didn't dare count on that either.

"Captain," Arthur said. "The enemy ships are opening fire."

"Return fire," Stephen ordered. He had very little hope of scoring a hit on one battleship, let alone three, but it might *just* upset the enemy enough to make it harder for them to keep solid locks on his hull. It was whistling in the dark, yet...he had a shortage of other possible options. "Order the starfighters to shield our hull."

"Aye, Captain."

The last of the enemy gunboats vanished from the display. Stephen let out a sigh of relief, then checked the damage assessment. The gunboats hadn't done *that* much damage to his hull, but they *had* wiped out nearly a third of his point defence weapons. Their sacrifice had made it easier for their bigger brothers to get missiles through Stephen's defences and slam them into his hull. *Invincible* was going to take one hell of a battering before she managed to pull away from the alien ships, if she ever did. Stephen would have aimed at the target's drives, if he'd been in command of the alien fleet; he rather figured the aliens felt the same way too. Taking prisoners would be a priority for them.

They have ways to make us talk, he thought. He'd have to hit the self-destruct if *Invincible* was crippled badly enough to ensure her capture. There was no way he could risk letting the ship and crew fall into enemy hands. *And I can't condemn my crew to a fate worse than death.*

He studied the alien ships as his missiles entered their point defence envelope. Their point defence datanet didn't seem to be *quite* as efficient as its human counterpart, but the battleships had enough point defence *weapons* that it hardly seemed to matter. All but one of the missiles were wiped out of space before they could reach their targets; the last, a laser warhead, inflicted a tiny amount of damage before it too was gone. Stephen cursed under his breath as the analyst deck updated their projections. *Invincible* simply didn't carry enough missiles to have a reasonable chance of getting something through the enemy defences.

And we don't have enough starfighters left to mount an attack either, he told himself. *I'm not throwing them away for nothing.*

"Enemy missiles entering point defence range," Arthur reported. "Engaging...now."

Stephen braced himself. The starfighters fanned out, taking pot-shots at missiles as they roared past. A hundred vanished, picked off before they flashed past the starfighters and bored towards *Invincible*; a hundred more disappeared as they were picked off by the point defence or veered away from the carrier as they locked onto the decoys instead of the real ship. It looked as though the enemy hadn't bothered to launch command-and-control warheads, even though they had the capability. Stephen didn't dare take that for granted. It was quite possible that the aliens *had* launched such warheads, only to lose them to the starfighters.

And they may have decided to try to soften us up first, he thought, as the missiles closed in on his ship. *They might...*

Invincible shuddered, violently. Red icons flashed up all over the display, so many that Stephen felt an icy hand clutch at his heart before half of them vanished. The aliens had pounded *Invincible* hard, two of their missiles exploding *inside* the hull. It looked as though the inner armour had held, for the moment, but a number of crewmen had already been reported missing. Stephen didn't give much for their chances. No shipsuit ever designed could stand up to a nuke at close quarters.

"I'm getting a damage report now," Newcomb said. "They shot out two of the drive nodes."

"Shit," Stephen muttered. *Invincible* had multiple redundancies built into her drive system—and everything else, as far as possible—but there were limits. Losing a couple more nodes would mean losing speed, which would mean being overwhelmed and destroyed. He raised his voice. "Alter our position to make it harder for them to hit the other nodes."

"Aye, sir," Sonia said.

She didn't sound very confident, Stephen noted. He didn't blame her. *Invincible* could not afford to alter course, not unless she wanted to give the aliens a free chance to kill her. But that made it harder for Sonia to ensure that they *didn't* give the aliens a shot at the other drive nodes. The aliens knew just where to hit, too. They'd have no difficulty estimating the rough locations of the active nodes.

"Do the best you can," he added, quietly.

He looked at Arthur. "Deploy laser warheads on ballistic trajectories," he ordered. "Turn them into makeshift mines."

"Aye, sir," Arthur said.

He didn't sound very confident either. There was rarely any point in trying to mine open space. The enemy ships wouldn't follow a predictable path, normally. Hell, keeping one's *precise* location unpredictable was pretty much the first lesson in the tactical manuals. But now...the alien ships *would* be following a predictable course as they chased *Invincible*. The mines might *just* catch an alien ship. And even if they didn't, they might convince the aliens not to chase *Invincible* too closely. Who knew what *else* they might run into?

"The enemy ships are launching a second salvo," Alison said. "It seems a little weaker than the first."

So are our point defences, Stephen thought, grimly. *And they've presumably had time to assess the results of their first strike.*

"Order the starfighters to move to intercept," he said. "And stand by all remaining point defence."

He kept his eyes on the display as the alien missiles roared towards his ships. The aliens didn't seem to be trying to be subtle, but they didn't *need* to be subtle. They were trying to overwhelm his defences through sheer weight of numbers and...he had to admit it was working. His engineering crews were doing what they could, even trying to replace the destroyed point defence weapons while *Invincible* was fighting for her life, but the damage was mounting rapidly. They weren't losing speed, thankfully, but they weren't accelerating fast enough to leave the battleships behind.

They damaged too many of our nodes, he reminded himself. *Our acceleration curve has been shot to shit.*

He gritted his teeth. The engineers were working on getting one of the nodes back online, but it was really a job for a shipyard. He didn't think anyone had managed to repair a drive node while the ship was underway, let alone under heavy fire. The whole edifice really needed to be stripped out and replaced. There was no way they were going to be able to do *that* while they were under fire.

Another shockwave ran through the ship. "Direct hit, starboard flight deck," Newcomb said, tiredly. "They don't seem to have realised they hit it already."

Stephen nodded. It wasn't good news...but it *was*, in a way. The starboard flight deck had been knocked out of commission before *Invincible* had jumped through the tramline. There hadn't been any hope of repairing the damage even before the *second* missile had struck home. The aliens probably didn't know it, but they'd wasted a missile that could have done some real damage if it had struck elsewhere.

"Order the entire section evacuated," he said. The entire structure was a mess. It would probably have to be rebuilt completely. The starship was designed to be modular, but even so...it was going to be a nightmare. "We'll concentrate on repairing..."

One of the enemy icons flashed, then vanished from the display. "We got the fucker," Arthur screamed. "We got him!"

Stephen opened his mouth to reprimand the younger man for his language, then thought better of it. "What happened?"

"He impaled himself on our laser warheads," Arthur said. "We ripped him to pieces at practically point-blank range!"

"Very good," Stephen said. The laser beams must have hit something vital, although he had no idea what. The missile tubes, perhaps. If one of their warheads had been induced to detonate it might have set up a chain reaction that would take out the entire ship. It was supposed to be impossible, but he'd been in the navy long enough to know that *nothing* was impossible. "And the other two battleships?"

"They're altering course," Arthur said. "I think they're being a little more careful now."

Stephen nodded. Taking out one of the enemy ships was good news, even though there were still two left. At least the enemy knew they'd been in a fight...he shook his head, even as his crew celebrated. They'd bought themselves some more time, but not enough. *Invincible* simply wasn't picking up speed fast enough to save herself.

"Bridge, this is engineering," Chief Engineer Theodore Rutgers said. "We think we have the drive node back online, but we'll have to power her up and synchronise with the others before we know. I request permission to cycle the drives."

Stephen exchanged a glance with Newcomb. They had no choice. They *had* to resynchronise the drive field. And yet, if something went wrong, there would be no time to reboot the system before the aliens caught up with *Invincible* and blew her into dust. The slightest flicker in the drive field might be enough to bring the entire system crashing down.

"Do it," Stephen ordered.

A low quiver ran through the ship. He felt the deck shudder under his feet, the gravity shimmering faintly before stabilising...he let out a sigh of relief as he realised it had worked. They might just have a chance to escape after all...

"The drive field is intact, Captain," Sonia reported.

"Then ramp up our speed as much as possible," Stephen ordered. "And take us out of their range."

He leaned back in his command chair as the background humming of the drives started to grow louder. The aliens were in hot pursuit, but...they suddenly had much less time to destroy *Invincible* before it was too late. And they'd know it too. They'd see the carrier's drive field grow stronger...

"Deploy all of our remaining drones," he ordered. "We need to buy time."

"Aye, Captain," Arthur said.

"And launch more missiles on ballistic trajectories," Stephen added. "If we can slow them down, even for a few seconds, we might just be able to open the range..."

The alien ships seemed to go mad with rage, pushing their drives forward even as they belched salvo after salvo of missiles. Stephen watched their drive fields fluctuating, hoping that the aliens would lose too many nodes and find themselves suddenly crippled in interplanetary space. They'd probably have multiple redundancies built into their systems too, but...

They have limits too, he told himself, as the first wave of missiles crashed into his point defence. *They cannot hope to catch us if we manage to put enough distance between us and them before we lose the drive node again.*

He kept a wary eye on the endless stream of reports from engineering. The remainder of the drive nodes were holding up well—they'd been thoroughly tested during the shakedown cruise—but the repaired node was fluctuating madly. Normally, he would have ordered it powered down for the duration, yet he *needed* it. He prayed, silently, that it would hold out long enough for the ship to get away. The aliens...

"Captain," Alison said. "One of the alien ships is falling out of formation!"

"Confirmed," Arthur said. "She lost her drive field."

"Good," Stephen said. There was no time to enjoy it. *Invincible* was on the verge of losing part of her drive field too. "Deploy our remaining missiles towards the third alien craft."

"Aye, sir," Arthur said.

There was a long pause. "Captain, they're breaking off!"

Stephen blinked in surprise. It was the one thing he hadn't expected. The alien battleship *could* have continued the pursuit, at least until *Invincible* outran her so completely she could slip back into cloak and crawl to the other tramline. There was a reasonable chance of the carrier losing another drive node and the aliens knew it, too. And yet, the alien ship was slowly turning away...

"Keep us on our current course, but launch a probe ahead of us," he ordered. The aliens would have needed precognition to prepare an ambush—or a great deal of luck—yet he couldn't afford to rule it out. "And keep us on a direct course for the tramline."

"Aye, sir," Sonia said.

Stephen let out a long breath as the distance between the two ships widened. "Recall the starfighters," he added. It didn't look like he had more than a single squadron left. "I want them rearmed, then ready to deploy the moment we encounter more enemy ships."

"Aye, Captain."

He forced himself to remain calm, to be aware of possible traps even as *Invincible* slowly made her way towards the tramline. And yet, the aliens seemed to have given up the pursuit altogether. Had they decided that it had already proven too costly? Losing one battleship and crippling another *had* to have put a dent in their fleet. Or were they mustering a fleet to invade the Human Sphere? They might have calculated that humanity wouldn't have time to react before the invasion began...

Or perhaps they don't know we can use the weaker tramlines, he thought. It was probably wishful thinking, but it was tempting nonetheless. *They may think we're flying into interstellar space, like the generation ship.*

"Local space is clear, Captain," Alison said, quietly. "There's no sign of any cloaked ships."

"Remain on alert," Stephen ordered, firmly. His head was starting to pound. He needed rest, but he didn't dare leave the bridge. "We have to assume the worst."

Five hours later, *Invincible* crossed the tramline and jumped into the next system.

The aliens made no move to pursue.

CHAPTER FORTY

"THIS IS ONE HELL OF A REPORT, Captain," Admiral Weisskopf said. The American studied the datapad for a long moment. "I don't think it will please our political lords and masters."

"No, sir," Stephen said. His report was already winging it home to Earth via the flicker network. He doubted *anyone* would be pleased to read it. "On the other hand, we now know about a very deadly threat."

"Alien viruses infesting intelligent races and turning them into puppets," Admiral Weisskopf mused. "I suppose you'll be lucky if they don't try to have you committed."

"They'll have to have the xenospecialists committed as well," Stephen said, bluntly. Admiral Weisskopf, thankfully, was an experienced combat vet. He wouldn't make the mistake of dismissing a report out of hand because he didn't want to believe it. "Their reports are quite detailed."

He shook his tired head. The Admiralty might find reason to be displeased with his performance—particularly if the media started blaming the navy for fouling up first contact—but they couldn't deny the nature of the threat. He'd risked his ship and crew in a bid to save the contact team, yet...they were infected so completely that the doctors had ruled out all hope of saving them. They might as well be aliens. Alice Campbell was the only one who seemed to have retained her mind and even *she* was still fighting for her life.

"Unfortunately so," Weisskopf agreed. "*Pinafore* did get through to us, Captain."

Stephen looked up at him. "And *Dezhnev?*"

"Missing, presumed lost," Weisskopf said. "The Russians don't appear to be *that* concerned, yet, but they'll want answers sooner or later."

"Yes, sir," Stephen said. "We *have* combed our records. We simply don't know what happened to her."

"We may never know," Weisskopf said. "It's a big universe, Captain. She wouldn't be the first ship to vanish."

He leaned back in his chair. "The bad news is that the alien virus *did* get loose on Wensleydale. A number of ships and crews were infected, it seems, before we got the warning and slapped the whole system into quarantine. Fortunately, the warships had strict orders to avoid all contact with the ground—just in case—and they were able to round up most of the civilians."

"Shit," Stephen said. He thought, briefly, of the aliens he'd met. They'd fled, unaware that they were carrying the enemy with them. And they'd gone into suspension, never realising that it made them vulnerable. The *Ha-Hah-Docks* might no longer exist, save as alien hosts—and slaves. Their culture had been totally destroyed. "What about the remainder?"

"A couple of ships might have made it past the blockade," Weisskopf said. "We've passed a warning up the flicker chain, but...we don't know what will happen when they reach an inhabited world. It could get very bad."

"Yes, sir," Stephen said. "What now?"

"You will probably be ordered to take your ship back to Earth or Britannia," Weisskopf said, bluntly. "My engineers have assessed the damage and they feel that it would be better to carry out the repairs in a shipyard. We can patch up the hull and a few other things, Captain, but the majority of the work needs to be done elsewhere. I, on the other hand, will be deploying a blocking force in hopes of keeping the enemy from penetrating to Falkirk. If, of course, they *can* use the weaker tramlines."

"They're more advanced than us in some ways," Stephen said, quietly. "I feel it would be unwise to assume they can't get to us."

Weisskopf nodded. "My analysts predict that they can find a way to the Human Sphere even without using the weaker tramlines," he said. "Of course, we don't know how much they know about our internal astrography. They may have to waste a great deal of time surveying useless tramline chains before finally stumbling across us once again."

"Let us hope so," Stephen said. It felt dangerously optimistic. "We really don't know how much they might have extracted from the prisoners before they were rescued."

"Or how far that information spread," Weisskopf agreed. "You took a hell of a risk, Captain, but under the circumstances I'm quite happy to underwrite it. Leaving captives in their hands is pretty clearly a no-no."

He cleared his throat. "Overall, I think you did pretty well," he added. "The aliens made no move to respond to any of your attempts to open communication, even before you discovered their true nature, and—as such—you were justified in treating them as hostile and attempting to recover the captives. In hindsight, we should have sent more ships with you—and I'm sure *someone* will try to make political hay out of that mistake—but hindsight is always clearer than foresight. I'll advise your superiors of my feelings on the matter."

"Thank you, sir," Stephen said, recognising the dismissal. "I'll inform you when I receive my final orders."

He stood, saluted, and left the compartment. The Admiral's aide—a dark-skinned woman with a curiously intent expression—smiled faintly at Stephen, then led him down the corridor and back to the airlock. The shuttle was already waiting for him, the pilot sitting in the cockpit. Stephen was ruefully impressed. The Americans clearly didn't want to keep him on their ship any longer than necessary.

But then, we might be attacked at any moment, he thought. *And then they'll need me on my ship.*

He sat back in his chair and tried to relax, taking a deep breath to calm himself as the shuttle disengaged from the American battleship and returned to *Invincible*. Admiral Weisskopf was right, unfortunately. Stephen's ship was too badly damaged to remain at Falkirk, even though her crew were the only people with any experience of fighting the new threat. He would have to take her home, where he'd probably find himself wasting most of his time giving evidence at various boards of inquiry. Someone probably *would* insist that the Royal Navy had messed up the first contact mission, starting a completely unnecessary war. The Royal Navy—and the government—would have to expend a great deal of effort proving that there had been no chance to open *real* communications with the aliens.

With a virus that thinks of us as hosts, Stephen thought. The more he thought about the concept, the more frightening it became. *It has no reason to think of us as anything else.*

He took another breath. The coming war—the war he believed to be inevitable—was going to be utterly nightmarish. It was impossible to be sure, but...the virus might be able to devote far more of its system GNP to its war machine than any human power. The virus might deploy a fleet of ships a hundred times larger than anything humanity could deploy. There were over a hundred starships clustered around Falkirk—Stephen could see them on the display—and he knew, with a sick certainty, that they wouldn't be enough. If the virus could jump through the weaker tramlines, it was only a matter of time...

And they saw us jump, he reminded himself, as the shuttle docked. *They know it's possible now, even if they didn't know before...*

He dismissed the thought. There was work to be done. *Invincible* had to be readied for her return to Earth...

...And for war, if the aliens arrived before she left.

We'll be fighting them again soon, Stephen thought. *It's just a matter of time.*

· · ·

"What a fucking mess," Monica said. "I'm sorry, sir."

Richard swallowed several nasty responses that came to mind. "I suppose it is a fucking mess," he said, as he picked up the box. "But how would you feel if someone treated your possessions as nothing more than a nuisance after you died?"

"I'd be dead," Monica said, practically. "I think I'd be beyond caring."

"Hah," Richard said. "But do you care now?"

He checked the name on the bunk, then opened the drawer to reveal a handful of uniforms and civilian clothes. The former went into the washing basket, where they'd be reassigned to other pilots; the latter went into the box for eventual shipment to the poor bastard's family. A small datapad was hidden underneath the clothes, along with a handful of datachips and a leather-bound diary. He sighed—keeping a personal diary wasn't against regulations, but he'd have to run it past the security officers before it could be returned to his family—and dropped all three of them in the box. The datachips were unmarked, which probably meant they were porn. That too was technically against regulations...

I should probably make them vanish before they get sent home, he thought. It wouldn't be the first time something embarrassing had been revealed when a dead pilot's possessions were returned to his family. Pilots rarely bothered to think about their long-term futures when the odds of surviving their deployments were not high. The dead pilot might easily have been cheating on his partner or...or something worse. *But the intelligence staff will have to have a look at them too.*

There was nothing else in the drawer, save for a pair of woman's panties. Richard wondered, idly, if the pilot had worn them under his flight suit—he would hardly be the first pilot to wear a memento of his wife or girlfriend as he flew into battle—and then added them to the box. The pilot's relatives could keep the panties, along with everything else, or throw them out. It was their choice to make.

"Put a label on the box," he ordered, as he pushed down the lid. "And then mark it for immediate dispatch."

"Yes, sir," Monica said. She looked around the compartment, empty save for the two of them. "What's going to happen to the squadron?"

Richard shrugged. Alpha Squadron had three pilots left; the remaining squadrons barely had nine pilots between them. He doubted they'd be reconstituted easily, not when so much institutional knowledge had been blown away by alien weapons. It was quite likely that the carrier's squadrons would be decommissioned, their remaining pilots reassigned to other squadrons as the starfighter component was rebuilt from the ground up. Alpha Squadron *might* survive. He didn't think the others would.

"We'll see," he said. "I don't think they'll make a decision until the time comes for us to leave."

He looked at her. "Why do you ask?"

"There are too many rumours flying around," Monica said. "I wanted to know what *you'd* heard."

"Nothing authoritative," Richard told her. "I just heard a lot of rumours too."

Monica smiled, wryly. "Do you want to jump in a privacy tube?"

Richard blinked. "What?"

"You, me, no strings attached...some *glad to be alive* sex," Monica said. "It isn't as if we have many other opportunities."

She leaned forward. "Interested?"

Richard's mouth was suddenly dry. He was her immediate superior. He shouldn't even be *thinking* about fucking her, even though there was a very good chance that they'd both be reassigned to new units as soon as they returned to Earth. They'd both seen the enemy craft at knife-range. He shouldn't be considering it. And yet, part of him was very tempted. His cock stiffened at the thought. They were alive...she was attractive and willing and people might be prepared to turn a blind eye...

"No," he said, finally. His cock twitched, angrily. "We shouldn't."

Monica raised an eyebrow. "Are you sure?"

No, Richard thought.

"We'll regret it in the morning," he said, instead. "And, right now, we really don't want to be caught in bed together."

Monica studied him for a long moment, then turned and walked out of the hatch, deliberately swinging her hips. Richard had to force himself to look away. A year ago, when they'd had the same rank, he would have said *yes* without a second thought. Their superiors would have definitely turned a blind eye, as long as they didn't let their personal relationship affect their professional duties. Part of him still wanted to call her back, if she was still willing. But he knew it would be a bad idea.

Fuck it, he thought. *It really is a bad idea.*

But there was a part of him that simply refused to believe that that was true.

• • •

"This is the last will and testament of Alice Campbell," Alice said. She felt...unsteady, as if the only thing keeping her alive was a constant dose of foul-tasting medical cocktails and basic nutrients. She thought she could *feel* the alien virus clawing at her innards, struggling for supremacy. "Being of sound mind and body, I hereby update my will."

She took a long breath. It was being recorded, of course, and there were witnesses...still, she knew it wouldn't be immune to a legal challenge. Jeanette might just challenge Alice's will, if she felt she had a chance to win. The legal officer had been blunt to the point of rudeness about the prospects. Alice could not be said, reasonably, to be of either sound mind or body. The alien virus—damn it—was still trying to turn her into a puppet.

"My shares in the family farm are to go to my nephew and nieces," she said, "with the proviso that they cannot be sold until they reach the age of maturity, unless the family is in serious financial trouble. My savings, such as they are, are to be sent to my sister; my pension is to be paid into the Royal Marine fund for wives and children. My personal possessions in my bunk are to be divided amongst the remainder of the company, save for my family photos; my personal possessions on Earth are to go to my sister."

Her throat ached. She reached for the glass of water with shaking hands, forcing herself to pick it up and take a drink. The alien virus seemed to want to keep her dehydrated, as if it thought she'd be easier prey if she was thirsty. Water seemed to be running through her body quicker than ever before. She hadn't felt so constantly thirsty during a deployment to the Middle East.

"Anything I have that isn't covered by any of the above statements"— she tried to think if she *did* have anything that wasn't covered—"is to go to my sister. She has my permission to do whatever she wants with any of them..."

She took another raspy breath. The legal officer would have to clear the will up, then record it in legalise. Jeanette might try to challenge some of the provisions, if she really *was* desperate for money. What did she have to lose? The law would be massed against her—military personnel enjoyed a great many rights when it came to distributing their property that were denied to civilians—but...perhaps not enough to keep her from winning. Who knew?

Not me, she thought. *I won't be around to see it.*

Major Parkinson had given her a gun, with one bullet in the chamber. He'd told her not to use it unless she'd given up all hope, but...but she was too close to giving up for good. It was unlikely the doctors could save her mind, even if they saved her body. They weren't making any real progress, which meant that all she had to look forward to was the alien virus adapting to the countermeasures and overwhelming her. And then she'd be lost...

She reached for the bedside drawer and opened it. The gun rested there, calling to her. She'd never considered suicide before, not even at school, but now...she wanted to end her life while she still could. The aliens would never let her go.

The air shimmered. A hologram materialised in front of her. Alice glared at it. Doctor Ganymede had always struck her as someone more interested in the alien virus than the patient he was supposed to be treating. He viewed her as little more than a piece of meat...or an experimental animal. And he never entered the compartment himself, even in a suit. It was a wise precaution, she knew, but it still grated. He could at least make an effort to remember she was a human being.

"Doctor," she said, sliding the drawer closed. She could kill herself later. "What do you want?"

Doctor Ganymede met her eyes. "I think we can cure you," he said. "But there's a very good chance that the procedure might kill you too."

Alice snorted. "As long as it gives me a chance, Doctor, it's fine with me."

"Very good," Doctor Ganymede said. "We shall begin immediately."

EPILOGUE

THE SEALED ORDERS had been clear, very clear. Captain Semyon Danilovich knew better than to defy them, even though he thought they were a mistake. Russia might try to keep her borders closed—even after the interstellar wars—but he'd had enough contact with foreigners to know they were human too. He also knew the remainder of the world would see his decision—*Russia's* decision—as little more than treason against the human race. But he knew better than to disobey orders. Someone would be watching him.

His back itched as *Dezhnev* slowly inched further into the alien system. The sour-faced prune of a political officer would be watching him, of course, but who else? The XO? The Tactical Officer? His orderly? Or, perhaps, one of the young female officers who'd joined his crew only a few weeks before deployment. They were perhaps the least likely to be working for the FSB—or reporting directly to the Kremlin—but that very fact made them the most suspicious. Mother Russia expected her women to stay at home and have babies, not go out into a man's world. It was easy to underestimate the women.

And one of them would make an excellent spy, he thought. *Or maybe it's one of the enlisted spacers.*

"Captain," the sensor officer said. "I'm picking up a small squadron of alien ships."

Semyon sucked in a breath. He *had* to try to make first contact, even though the aliens had fired on *Invincible* without warning. He *had* to try to turn them into allies—*Russia's* allies—even though it might cost him his ship. He didn't even know what *Invincible* might have discovered about the aliens, before the running battle that had driven the British ship out of the system. There was even the chance—and it wasn't even a *remote* chance—that the aliens would mistake *Dezhnev* for a British ship and open fire.

"Bring up the first contact protocols," he ordered. If the aliens opened fire, he'd have an excuse to turn and run. It wouldn't be hard to cover their brief absence. "And open communications...now."

To Be Continued in...
Para Bellum
Coming Soon!

A NOTE FROM THE AUTHOR

The first time i wrote in the *Ark Royal* universe, I deliberately put an introduction to the characters first, before plunging them into war. I repeated the pattern in *Warspite* and *Vanguard*, even *The Cruel Stars*. (*The Longest Night*, being an event-driven book, didn't need such an introduction.) This time, I decided to plunge the characters into war straight away, just to try something a little different.

Does it work? Please tell me.
And if you liked this book, please leave a review.
Christopher Nuttall
Edinburgh, 2018

APPENDIX: GLOSSARY OF UK TERMS AND SLANG

[Author's Note: I've tried to define every incident of specifically UK slang (and a handful of military phases/acronyms) in this glossary, but I can't promise to have spotted everything. If you spot something I've missed, please let me know and it will be included.]

Aggro—slang term for aggression or trouble, as in 'I don't want any aggro.'

Beasting/Beasted—military slang for anything from a chewing out by one's commander to outright corporal punishment or hazing. The latter two are now officially banned.

Beat Feet—Run, make a hasty departure.

Binned—SAS slang for a prospective recruit being kicked from the course, then returned to unit (RTU).

Boffin—Scientist

Bootnecks—slang for Royal Marines. Loosely comparable to 'Jarhead.'

Bottle—slang for nerve, as in 'lost his bottle.'

Borstal—a school/prison for young offenders.

Combined Cadet Force (CCF)—school/youth clubs for teenagers who might be interested in joining the military when they become adults.

Compo—British army slang for improvised stews and suchlike made from rations and sauces.

CSP—Combat Space Patrol.

Donkey Wallopers—slang for the Royal Horse Artillery.

DORA—Defence of the Realm Act.

Fortnight—two weeks. (Hence the terrible pun, courtesy of the Goon Show, that Fort Knight cannot possibly last three weeks.)

'Get stuck into'—'start fighting.'

'I should coco'—'you're damned right.'

Kip—sleep.

Levies—native troops. The Ghurkhas are the last remnants of native troops from British India.

Lorries—trucks.

MOD—Ministry of Defence. (The UK's Pentagon.)

Order of the Garter—the highest order of chivalry (knighthood) and the third most prestigious honour (inferior only to the Victoria Cross and George Cross) in the United Kingdom. By law, there can be only twenty-four non-royal members of the order at any single time.

Panda Cola—Coke as supplied by the British Army to the troops.

RFA—Royal Fleet Auxiliary

Rumbled—discovered/spotted.

SAS—Special Air Service.

SBS—Special Boat Service

Spotted Dick—a traditional fruity sponge pudding with suet, citrus zest and currants served in thick slices with hot custard. The name always caused a snigger.

Squaddies—slang for British soldiers.

Stag—guard duty.

STUFT—'Ships Taken Up From Trade,' civilian ships requisitioned for government use.

TAB (tab/tabbing)—Tactical Advance to Battle.

Tearaway—boisterous/badly behaved child, normally a teenager.

Walt—Poser, i.e. someone who claims to have served in the military and/or a very famous regiment. There's a joke about 22 SAS being the largest regiment in the British Army—it must be, because of all the people who claim to have served in it.

Wanker—Masturbator (jerk-off). Commonly used as an insult.

Wank/Wanking—Masturbating.

Yank/Yankee—Americans

BONUS PREVIEW

If You Liked *Invincible*, You Might Like *The Hyperspace Trap*:
The first Angel in the Whirlwind *spin-off.*

A year after the Commonwealth won the war with the Theocracy, the interstellar cruise liner Supreme is on its maiden voyage, carrying a host of aristocrats thrilled to be sharing in a wondrous adventure among the stars. The passengers include the owner and his daughters, Angela and Nancy. Growing up with all the luxuries in the world, neither sister has ever known true struggle, but that all changes when a collision with a pirate ship leaves the cruiser powerless and becalmed in hyperspace. And they're not alone.

Now, the mysterious force that's living on this floating graveyard is coming for Supreme's crew and passengers. As madness starts to tear at their minds, they must fight to survive in a strange alien realm.

And there's no way out...

PROLOGUE

It was hard, so hard, to think.

The drain was all-consuming, tearing at his mind as if they wanted to pluck his thoughts from his brain-sac. Tash could barely extend his eyes, let alone rise and crawl forward on his tentacles. The deck felt odd beneath him, as if on the verge of coming apart. His eyesight was flickering and flaring, fading in and out of existence. He had to focus on each motion just to move...his body was betraying him. They were draining him too.

Focus, he told himself. His claws and tentacles lashed the deck, frantically, as he struggled to get to his feet. It should have hurt, but it didn't. His tentacles were numb. *Get to Engineering.*

His mind blurred, just for a second. Or was it longer? He didn't know. Perhaps he was dead and in the seven hells, or perhaps he'd died...perhaps they'd *all* died. Maybe the others had suffered enough to be released from their sins, to go onwards...he wanted to believe it, even though he knew it was nonsense. He was a rationalist. The seven hells didn't exist. *They* existed. He knew *they* existed, but they were not demons. They were...

He stumbled over a body and nearly fell. For a moment, he thought the body had reached out to grab him before realizing that his tentacles were spasming. Shame gripped him as he stumbled backward, an embarrassment that tore at his soul. He hadn't lost control of himself like that since he'd been a child, dozens of solar cycles ago. Oddly, the shame gave him an opportunity to focus his mind.

He had to go on.

The body lay there, mocking him. An egg-layer, drained of life. Her tentacles were splayed out, suggesting utter hopelessness. Tash forced himself to look away and crawl onwards despite the looming sense that it was futile. The ship had been trapped long enough for him to lose all hope that they would escape. *They* were watching. He could hear them mocking him as he crawled...

...or was it his imagination? It was hard to be sure.

Time blurred as he moved down the long corridor. The ship was silent, the emergency alarms gone. He'd darted along the corridors until he knew them as well as he knew his own nest, but now they'd taken on a nightmarish aspect, as if he were walking through a dream. The lights rose to blinding levels, then faded until they were so dim he could barely see. Bodies were everywhere, lying where they'd fallen. The entire crew could be dead.

It felt like years before he finally made it to the engineering compartment, decades before he forced the hatch open and crawled inside. Other bodies lay on the deck, unmoving. Tash flinched, despite himself, as his eyes found the engineer. The egg-bearer had been strong in life, respected and feared by the crew. Now his body seemed shrunken, his tentacles spread out in silent supplication. It hadn't saved him from *them*.

Tash's mind ached. He thought he heard someone *howling*. The sound tore at him as he moved over to the nearest console and pressed his tentacles against the reader. There was a long pause, just long enough for him to start fearing that the power was too far gone for the neural link to engage, and then the system opened up to him. A status report blinked into his mind, confirming his worst fears. There were no other survivors. He was alone.

The howling grew louder, mocking him. His thoughts threatened to fragment, either into *their* domain or utter madness. Or both...he couldn't tell if *they* were real or nothing more than a figment of his imagination. Others had heard *them*, hadn't they? He couldn't swear to it. The madness that had gripped the crew, as soon as they found themselves in this cursed place, made it impossible to trust his own mind. He had no idea why he'd survived.

He forced his mind into the computers. They opened, recognizing his authority as the last surviving crewman. It would have been a heady thought—command at his age—if the situation hadn't been so serious. Tash knew it would not be long before he too was dead.

The computers felt sluggish, the neural link popping up constant warnings. A power glitch while his mind was within the computers might kill him, or worse. Tash ignored his fears as he surveyed the command network, tracking the power drain. It was growing worse. The computers, thrown back on their own resources, were trying to compensate, but the maneuver wasn't helping. *They* were draining the ship dry.

That's what they wanted, he told himself. His thoughts were starting to fade. He blanked out, then awoke. *They wanted the power.*

He probed the network, locating the antimatter storage pods. They glimmered in his mind like poisonous jewels, a harsh reminder that their power came with a price. If the containment fields failed, the entire ship would be vaporized. *They* would be pleased. He forced his mind onwards, isolating the storage pods from the rest of the power grid. It might just be enough to safeguard their cargo from *them*. There was certainly no evidence that *they* could just reach out and *take* the antimatter.

The howling grew even louder. Tash flicked his tentacles in satisfaction, disengaging his mind from the computers and slumping to the deck. *They* were angry. His vision was starting to blur again, the world fading to darkness...this time, he doubted he'd recover. His entire body felt sluggish, unable to move. He would join the rest of his comrades in death, but...but at least he'd spited *them*. His mind remained his own. *They* couldn't touch him. Whatever *they* were, *they* couldn't touch him...

...and then the darkness reached out and swallowed him.

CHAPTER ONE

"Well," Captain Paul VanGundy said, "that was a good dinner."

"The cooks are practicing," Commander Jeanette Haverford said. "They'll be passing anything that's less than perfect to us, once we get under way."

"Compared to marine rations," Security Chief Raymond Slater offered dryly, "this is heaven."

Paul smiled in genuine amusement. The three of them sat together in his stateroom, finishing a dinner that had been put together by *Supreme*'s cooks. Paul couldn't have named half the dishes at the table before he'd left the Royal Tyre Navy and signed up with the Cavendish Corporation, but he had to admit they were very good. The dinner hadn't been something he could have afforded off duty. Going to a ten-star restaurant cost as much as he made in a month.

They made an odd trio, he thought as he surveyed his two subordinates. Jeanette radiated calm authority, her short brown hair framing a dark face that betrayed no hint of vulnerability. Her clothes were designed to diminish her form, hiding the shape of her body behind a tailored blue uniform. Beside her, Raymond Slater looked very much like the spark plug he'd been before leaving the Marine Corps. His rugged face had a certain unkempt charm—he'd been ordered to have his scars removed when he'd signed up with the corporation—but he'd never win any beauty awards. Instead, he looked like a man no one would want to mess with. *That*, Paul knew, was a very good thing.

Paul himself looked older than his sixty years. Older men commonly had themselves rejuvenated until they looked to be in their mid-twenties, but the corporation's image experts had insisted that Paul had to look wise and dignified. They'd designed him a look—graying hair, gray beard, blue eyes, strong jaw—and convinced his superiors that he should wear it. Paul had a feeling he'd been lucky to keep his muscle tone. The captain of a cruise liner couldn't go around looking like a bodybuilder, let alone someone who had their muscles touched up every month in a bodyshop.

Blasted image experts, he thought sourly. It wasn't something he'd had to endure in the military. They'd been far more concerned with beating back the Theocracy and carrying the war to Ahura Mazda. *They'll put style over substance any day.*

He cleared his throat. "We'll probably be glad to get ration bars when we're under way," he said. "Right now, we have different problems."

"Yes, sir," Jeanette said.

Paul tapped a switch. A holographic image of *Supreme* materialized in front of them, hovering over the table. As always, the giant cruise liner, a kilometer from prow to stern, took his breath away. The vessel had none of the crude bluntness that characterized military starships, none of the brutal efficiency he recalled from the navy. Instead, there was an understated elegance that made him smile. *Supreme* was no warship. She was practically a work of art.

He leaned forward, drinking in her lines. The starship was a flattened cylinder, studded with giant portholes...practically *windows*. Two green blisters, each one easily larger than a naval destroyer, marked the upper gardens; a third blister, blue instead of green, marked the swimming pool. The bridge, a blister on top of the massive starship, made him smile. It looked good, but he knew it was horrendously vulnerable. A military starship could *not* have such a vital installation in an exposed position.

"We've all written our final reports," he said slowly. He felt nervous, even though he was damned if he'd admit it to anyone. "Is there anything you *didn't* bother to mention?"

"I believe I listed all of my concerns," Jeanette said. "The crew is well trained, but far too many of them are inexperienced. I'd prefer to swap some of them out with more experienced crewers."

"HQ says there aren't many experienced personnel to spare," Paul said. He ground his teeth in frustration. The military drawdown was well under way, despite the chaos pervading the Ahura Mazda Sector. There was no reason the corporation couldn't hire a few hundred experienced spacers. "We're getting some newcomers, but..."

He shrugged expressively. A cruise liner was not a military starship. He had to keep reminding himself of that. There were just too many differences in everything from purpose to training for him to rest comfortably. The months he'd spent learning the ropes had convinced him that all newcomers required training before they could take up posts on a cruise liner. Perversely, someone who hadn't been in the military had less to unlearn.

And most of the hosting staff don't need military experience, he thought. *They're civilians through and through.*

Jeanette pointed at the hologram. "I've got the crew working their way through a series of drills with all the usual actors, sir," she said. "However... there's a difference between training and reality. Most of our junior crewers will still be on probation until the end of the voyage."

"Some of them didn't quite take the training seriously," Slater rumbled. "It wasn't real."

Paul nodded. He'd graduated from the naval academy at Piker's Peak—and Slater had passed through boot camp—but Jeanette and the other crewmen had gone through their own intensive training course. The operations crew were as well trained as many of their naval counterparts, while the host crews had gone through a whole series of simulations and exercises. Indeed, they had endured a surprising amount of cross-training. He could put half the host crew to work on operations if necessary.

He'd been astonished, upon being given access to the corporation's files, to discover just how much trouble civilian crews had to handle. Passengers—some of whom were extremely wealthy and powerful—just didn't know how to behave. The crew had to cope with everything from drunken fights to outright misbehavior, behavior that would have earned a military officer a spell in the brig followed by a dishonorable discharge. He'd watched some of the exercises and come away with a new sense of appreciation for his crew. It took a strong person to remain calm in the face of massive provocation.

"They'll lose that attitude soon enough," Paul predicted. The trainers might not have been able to chew out recruits—he'd never met anyone who could outshout a drill instructor—but they had other ways to deal with wayward students. "Real life will see to that."

"Yes, sir," Jeanette said. She held out a datachip. "Overall, our reaction times to everything from medical emergency to shipboard crisis are well within acceptable parameters. I've ensured that all cross-trained personnel are ready to switch jobs at a moment's notice, just in case we need them."

"Quite right," Paul said. The Royal Navy had taught him that disaster could strike at any moment. *Supreme* might not have had to worry about going into battle, but she did have her own challenges. "Are there any staffing problems I should keep in mind?"

"I don't believe there's anything significant," Jeanette said. Her lips twisted. "Some of our guests *will* be bringing their own bodyguards and servants, of course. They may need some additional training of their own."

Paul kept his face expressionless. "Make sure they get it," he said. "And make sure we have a record of their training. We may need to put them to use somewhere else."

Slater snorted. "Their employers will hate that, sir."

"If we need to borrow their servants, we'll be past caring," Paul countered. *Supreme* had over two hundred crewmen with medical training. A crisis they couldn't handle would pose a severe threat to the entire ship. "Check their firearms licenses too, just in case."

"Yes, sir," Slater said.

Paul looked up at the display for a long moment. "Do you see any security threats?"

Slater took a moment to gather his thoughts. "Internally, no. The basic vetting process didn't turn up any red flags. A handful of yellow flags—a few passengers were marked down for bad behavior on earlier cruises—but nothing else. I don't see any reason to worry about our passengers."

"One of them could be an impostor," Jeanette commented.

"Perhaps." Slater snorted again. "We'll be running basic security checks, of course."

"Of course," Paul agreed.

He kept his thoughts to himself. The corporation ran security checks on everyone, from its senior officers and starship crews to third-class passengers. He'd glimpsed enough of the vetting process when he was being hired to know that it was almost as comprehensive as anything demanded by the government's intelligence services. Passengers who might be a problem would be required to spend the trip in a stasis pod, if they were allowed to board at all. Far more likely, they would simply be denied passage. Lower-grade passenger starships were plying the spacelanes, after all.

"I've also run my security teams through a series of exercises," Slater continued. "If necessary, we can isolate compartments or entire decks and then clear them by force. We'll be as gentle as possible, of course, but by that point we might be far beyond any *gentle* solution. At worst, we can dump knockout gas into any compartment and then pick up the sleeping beauties."

"Which will probably get us all fired," Jeanette said. "Out the nearest airlock..."

"Probably," Slater said. "I should remind you, at this point, that we do not have comprehensive surveillance of the entire ship."

"The passengers would pitch a fit," Jeanette commented.

"Yes," Paul said.

He shook his head in wry amusement. *Supreme* wasn't just a passenger ship. Travel on her was an *experience*. She had everything from a casino to a brothel, just to make sure that her passengers traveled in luxury. Even the third-class passengers, the ones who'd be crammed into tiny cabins on the lower decks, would have access to the entertainments. The thought of being recorded, even for security purposes, would horrify them. They'd be worried about blackmail or worse.

"I am aware of the issues," Slater said stiffly. "It is also my duty to make you aware of the implications. We may not be able to react to a crisis until it is already out of hand."

"I know," Paul said.

Slater didn't look mollified. "A number of our passengers are also prime targets for kidnap," he added. "While I have no reason to suspect internal trouble, I have to warn you that there *is* a prospect of being intercepted. I'd be much happier if we had an escort."

"So would I," Paul admitted. *Supreme* wasn't defenseless, but she was no warship. A destroyer could take her out if a captain had the nerve to close with the target. "I believe that Corporate is still trying to organize one."

"There have been no reports of pirate activity," Jeanette added. "We're not going to fly through the Ahura Mazda Sector."

"A good thing too," Slater said. He looked at Paul. "Captain, I strongly advise you to ensure that we stay well away from any hyperspace storms. Who knows what they're hiding?"

"We will," Paul said. Pirates were a threat. The Royal Navy had driven them out of Commonwealth space before the war, but they'd been on the rise when the navy's attention had been diverted. It might take some time for the navy to resume its patrol routes and drive the pirates back out. "If nothing else, we can probably outrun any pirate ship."

"I wouldn't take that for granted," Slater said. "Robert Cavendish alone is worth a stupid amount of money."

Paul fought hard to keep his face expressionless. Robert Cavendish was one of the richest men on Tyre, perhaps the richest. Only the king and a handful of other aristocrats came close. He should have been a duke, and would have been if he hadn't been more interested in building his empire. *And* he was Paul's ultimate boss. It was a recipe for trouble.

"True," Jeanette agreed. She shot Paul a sympathetic look. "Doesn't he have his own personal yacht?"

"I imagine so," Paul said. Cavendish was rich enough to own and operate a starship the size of a superdreadnaught. Hell, he didn't really need one. A smaller ship could offer as much comfort as a full-sized liner without having to employ over a thousand crewmen. "But there's nothing to be gained by debating it."

"No, sir," Slater agreed. "I suspect there is more to this cruise than simply traveling from place to place."

Jeanette gave him an odd look. "What makes you say that?"

"I read the passenger manifest," Slater said. "It isn't just Robert Cavendish. It's his close family and a number of cronies and hangers-on. *And* a number of smaller businessmen and nobility, enough to occupy an entire deck. I suspect they're preparing a private planning session in between spending most of their time in the casino."

"Joy," Paul said. He rubbed his forehead. Slater was right. *Supreme* would be a magnet for pirates, insurgents, and everyone else with an axe to grind. He'd even raised the issue with Corporate, only to be told to shut up and soldier. Reading between the lines, he'd come to the conclusion that Corporate wasn't happy either. "Keep a close eye on the situation."

"Yes, sir," Slater said.

He took control of the display, adjusting the hologram to show off the weapons emplacements. Paul couldn't help feeling that *Supreme*, for all of her elegance, looked faintly ridiculous. Her design was just too inefficient. But then a full-sized superdreadnaught wouldn't win any beauty awards. All that mattered was smashing her enemies as quickly as possible before they smashed her.

"The weaponry crews are still drilling on the latest tactical simulations," Slater said. "I believe we could hold our own long enough to escape a pirate ship. A regular military ship, however, would eat us for breakfast. Far better to avoid contact."

"And we will," Paul said. "They'll have some problems intercepting us."

"Unless they're trailing us at a safe distance," Slater said. He flipped the display to show a star chart. "And they *do* know where we're going."

Paul exchanged glances with Jeanette. He had some leeway—he could alter course, once they were in hyperspace—but he had to take *Supreme* to her listed destinations. He couldn't refuse to go to a particular world unless he had a *very* good reason. Corporate would be very annoyed with him, even if he could prove the world was under siege. If there was one thing corporations and the military had in common, there was always someone flying a desk who thought he knew better than the man on the spot.

"If we can get an escort, we'll be safe," he said firmly. "And if we can't, we'll fly an evasive course. No one is expecting us to arrive on a precise date."

Jeanette smiled. "How lucky for us."

"Quite," Paul agreed.

He glanced from Jeanette to Slater. "Are there any other matters that need to be addressed?"

Jeanette smiled mischievously. "Mr. Cavendish and his family will be expecting a formal welcome, sir," she said. "You'll have to dress up for it."

Paul tried not to groan. The regular uniform was bad enough—whoever had designed their attire clearly didn't have to wear them—but the dress uniforms were worse. His outfit was covered in so much gold braid that he looked like an admiral from a comic opera navy, while the midshipmen and stewards resembled military captains and commanders. He'd never been able to shake the feeling that people were laughing at him behind his back whenever he wore the dress uniform.

"Select a handful of junior officers and stewards to join the reception," he said. The order was mean of him, but he might as well spread the misery around. Besides, he'd never met Robert Cavendish. The man might take offense if only a couple of people greeted him. "How many others do I have to meet and greet?"

Jeanette made a show of consulting her terminal, as if she didn't already have the information locked away in her mind. "There are three other passengers of sufficient status to warrant a personal greeting from you," she said. "It would also build goodwill if you were to spend some time in each of the lounges."

"I'm sure it would," Paul said. He told himself not to take it too personally. Kissing hands and buttocks—hopefully metaphorically—was part of his job now. Besides, he *did* have a good crew. Jeanette could handle anything that might reasonably be expected to happen while they were in orbit. "Is there anything else?"

"Mr. Cavendish might demand your personal attention, sir," Slater said. "We had a number of high-ranking guests on *Capricorn*. They seemed to believe that Captain Hammond was their personal attendant."

"And he *does* pay the bills," Paul said. "Do we have anything on his previous conduct?"

"No," Jeanette said. She met his eyes. "In his case, sir, that might be meaningless."

Paul nodded stiffly. The host crews kept files on their guests, files that were shared with other host crews. He'd heard they were even shared between corporations, although it was technically against corporate guidelines. An unpleasant passenger would discover that his reputation had preceded him.

And a good passenger would have the same experience, he mused. It wasn't something he wanted to discourage. *But in a better way.*

"It might," he agreed.

He pressed his hands together, tiredly. It was probably a good sign. He'd seen some of the files. A number of people, powerful people, had been marked as everything from being lousy tippers to having wandering hands. Robert Cavendish wouldn't have been spared.

"I think we can hope for the best," he said. "Are there any other matters?"

"We may run out of special ultra-expensive Scotch," Jeanette said. Logistics was her responsibility. "The shipment from Nova Scotia was delayed apparently."

Paul smiled. "Let's hope that's the worst problem we face," he said. "They'll have to drink *expensive* Scotch instead."

"Disaster," Slater said, deadpan. "The end of the world."

"I'm sure some of them will feel that way," Jeanette agreed.

CHAPTER TWO

"Wake up, you lazy bastard," a female voice said. "You're late!"

Junior Steward Matt Evans sat upright, confused. Where *was* he? He'd been out late last night on Downunder Station, barely managing to catch the departing shuttle back to *Supreme*. His head felt as though someone had opened his skull and crammed it with cotton. Several minutes passed before he remembered that he'd made it back to the ship and his bunk before collapsing into blessed sleep. He'd been lucky. A few minutes longer in the pleasure bars would probably have cost him his career.

"Fuck," he muttered. "What *time* is it?"

"Oh-eight-thirty," Carla France said. She was stripping off her night-clothes as she spoke. "The others are already on their way to breakfast."

"Fuck," Matt said again. He'd stuffed a handful of ration bars in his locker, a precaution he'd learned from one of the old hands, but they tasted of cardboard. Not that it really mattered, he told himself as he reached for his water bottle. There was no time to go for a proper breakfast before he was expected on duty. He would just have to make do. "I need a shower."

"And a shave," Carla told him bluntly. "What were you *drinking* last night?"

Matt couldn't remember. The stewards had been granted leave follow-ing an endless series of emergency drills, which had started to blur together in his mind, and he'd spent the day in the pleasure bars. Wine, women, and song...more of the wine than anything else, if his pounding head could be trusted. Carla passed him a sober-up without comment. Matt took the tab and pressed it against his neck, wishing she'd thought to wake him earlier. But he'd only have felt worse.

Carla turned and headed for the washroom. Matt watched her go, silently admiring her nude body. Like him, she'd been to the bodyshop. Corporate insisted on a specific image for its stewards, and neither of them was in any position to object. Carla was twenty-two, the same age as Matt, but her long brown hair, heart-shaped face, and hourglass figure made her look nineteen. Matt felt his cock stir and flushed, embarrassed. Corporate also had very strict rules against stewards winding up in bed together, which had been drilled into him after he'd signed up for the job.

Down boy, he told himself. He wasn't used to casual nudity. His home-world had been a place where men and women were expected to cover themselves from head to toe. The old hands, those who had sailed on *Supreme* and other interstellar cruise liners, had sworn the younger hands would get used to it, but Matt found that hard to believe. It wasn't easy to separate the tall tales from the bullshit. One of the very old hands had claimed, with a straight face, that he'd had a threesome with two very rich girls on *Queen of Space*. Matt hadn't believed a word, although he did have to admit the story sounded more convincing than the incident with the female swimming team...

He stood and opened his locker, silently blessing his superior for insisting that he have everything sorted out before he left the ship. The ration bars were where he'd left them, their brightly colored wrappings silently mocking him. Rumor had it that decent-tasting ration bars existed, but he'd never met them. He unwrapped one and ate it slowly, taking a sip of water with each bite to help it go down. The bar tasted worse than cardboard.

Carla stepped out of the washroom. Matt caught a glimpse of her breasts and looked away, hastily. He didn't have time to get distracted. He kept his eyes on the unoccupied bunks as Carla moved past him, then hurried into the washroom himself. It was a tiny compartment, barely large enough for a single man. He'd been told that the space had been deliberately kept small to limit the chances for hanky-panky, but he suspected a more reasonable explanation was that the corporation wanted to save money. Outfitting Gold Deck alone had probably cost more than the GPP of a stage-two colony world.

The corporation has money to burn, he told himself as he stepped into the shower and turned on the water. Thankfully the cruise liner didn't have to ration water. He'd been told that military starships *did* ration water, although he didn't believe it. There was no reason why water couldn't be recycled or, if worse came to worst, harvested from a passing comet. *They can afford a few minor luxuries.*

He wanted to spend longer in the shower, but he knew he didn't have the time. The drying field tickled over his skin as soon as he turned off the water, flicking droplets all over the compartment. Matt couldn't recall who was on cleaning duty this week—the stewards were expected to keep their own compartments as neat and tidy as they could—but he hoped it wasn't him. He'd been too busy over the last few weeks to keep track of the rota.

"Hurry," Carla snapped from outside. She banged the washroom door. "You do *not* want to be late."

Matt nodded and stepped out of the compartment, as naked as the day he was born. Carla paid no attention to him, for which he was grateful. She was already dressed and applying makeup, as if she needed it. He reached for his uniform and donned it, slowly and carefully. Senior Steward Dominic Falcon wouldn't be pleased if his shirt wasn't tucked in and his jacket brushed clean.

"Don't forget your cap," Carla reminded him. "We're on greeting duty this morning, remember?"

"Yeah," Matt said. He reached for his cap and placed it on his head. "Just give me a moment to check myself."

He inspected himself in the mirror, feeling faintly out of place in his own body. The bodyshop hadn't changed *that* much, but they'd done enough to make him feel as though a stranger was looking back at him. His short blond hair, blue eyes, smooth face, and muscular body were, according to the focus groups, just right for a young male steward. Matt wasn't so sure—the body was a little *too* perfect—but Corporate wasn't interested in his opinions. If the passengers wanted to be surrounded by beautiful people, male and female, the corporation would ensure that was what they got.

The white uniform clung to him, practically glowing under the light. He had enough gold braid to pass for a military officer or member of the command crew, even though he was a mere steward. He had little prospect of climbing any further than senior steward, he'd been warned. Matt didn't mind too much, if he were honest. A few years on *Supreme* would be enough to set him up for life, particularly if he saved his wages or made sure to get a good reference from the corporation. There wasn't *that* much demand for trained stewards outside the cruise liners, but he could take his skills to a hotel on Tyre if he wished.

"Looking good," Carla said. She inspected him. "You've got muscles on your muscles."

Matt did his best to ignore her. Whoever had designed the uniforms was a sadist. Comfort had been sacrificed for sex appeal. Neither of them was walking around naked, but they didn't have to. A person with a little imagination could easily fill in the blanks.

We're lucky we're all reasonably handsome, he told himself. *And we get to keep the look afterwards, if we like it.*

He smiled. Toying with truth, the old sweats had claimed that Corporate had wanted to make sure all the male stewards were as ugly as sin, just so they couldn't compete with the passengers when it came to attracting female attention. Or male attention, if the passengers swung that way. Matt was tempted to believe them. Corporate had inflicted other indignities on its stewards and the rest of the crew. At times he felt that his wages weren't worth having to bow and scrape in front of people who obviously didn't give a damn.

"You too," he said as he reached for his wristcom and put it on. The device bleeped a moment later as it interfaced with his implants, then linked automatically to the shipboard datanet. He'd been warned, in no uncertain terms, not to leave his quarters without it. The wristcom wasn't just for communicating; it gave him access to much of the ship. "Shall we go?"

Carla nodded and opened the hatch. Matt took one last look at the compartment—their superiors might decide to inspect the space at any moment—and then followed her down the starship's bare corridor. The passengers...the guests, he reminded himself...never saw this part of the ship, unsurprisingly. Corporate had decided to save money by ensuring that crew passageways were left barren. The only decor was the corporate logo, visible on every hatch. Matt rolled his eyes in amused disbelief. There was no reason to believe that anyone had forgotten just who had designed and built the giant ship. Matt didn't think there was anything, from the fittings in the staterooms to the gifts in the shop, that hadn't come from the Cavendish Corporation.

A hatch hissed open in front of them, revealing the briefing room. Senior Steward Dominic Falcon was standing at the front, looking down at a datapad. He'd been luckier than his younger subordinates, Matt thought. The bodyshops had given him a more dignified appearance—gray hair, kindly eyes, commanding face—even though they had also made him look remarkably frail. Falcon couldn't be much older than Matt himself, but he looked as if a strong gust of wind would blow him over. He'd been sailing on cruise liners for the last decade.

Matt followed Carla over to join the other stewards, nodding politely to a few of his friends and bunkmates. He hadn't found much time to get to know his new crewmates as they'd spent the last two months either drilling or sleeping, but none seemed to be bad apples. Besides, they'd all been warned to keep their disagreements to themselves. No one would give a damn if a steward spent some time in the brig and then was unceremoniously dismissed when the starship reached the next port of call.

There was little chatter. Matt surveyed the chamber, feeling a chill running down his spine. The stewards didn't look precisely identical—that would have been too creepy, even for Corporate—but they all had the same general appearance. Boyish good looks for the men, blatant sex appeal for the women. Focus groups insisted that they looked attractive to everyone, whatever their orientation. The old sweats hadn't said much about that, on the record, but off the record, the new stewards had had quite a few warnings. It was astonishing what some guests wanted, apparently. And very few of the guests were used to hearing anyone say no.

Even the third-class passengers spent more on this cruise than I can earn in a year, Matt reminded himself. *Corporate considers them more important than me.*

Falcon cleared his throat as soon as the last couple of stewards hurried into the compartment. Matt allowed himself a sigh of relief. Traditionally, the unwanted jobs went to the latecomers...even though they'd *technically* arrived on time. The last thing he wanted was to get noticed. Meet-and-greet duty was bad, but there were worse tasks.

"Three minor updates," Falcon said. He scowled at the newcomers as if they were personally to blame. "First, two of the casino staffers failed to return to the ship. They have not yet been located, but I've been informed that I may have to provide two replacements. This is not a good thing."

Matt kept his face expressionless. The casino staff were technically separate from the rest of the crew for reasons he was sure made sense to someone in Corporate, but they'd had some cross-training. He didn't envy whoever was picked to work in the casino. The tips were high, but so was the prospect of an unlucky gambler turning violent. He wasn't looking forward to having to remove an unruly guest. The exercises had clearly indicated that he could do everything right and *still* get blamed. Corporate would sooner dismiss a steward, hopefully with a decent severance package, than fight a lawsuit in the courts. The bad publicity would override any sense of obligation to their employees.

"Second, the remaining cabins have been sold and the updated guest manifest has been uploaded," Falcon continued. "Take a moment to inspect it. If you have any concerns, please feel free to mention them to me. As always, all reports will be treated in strict confidence."

A flicker of disquiet seemed to echo through the compartment. Matt wasn't surprised. This was his first cruise, but he'd heard the rumors. In theory, reports were private; in practice, the process didn't always work that way. A prospective guest who'd been blacklisted or put on a watch list might sue, particularly if no evidence beyond rumor was presented that he'd been reported for anything. Matt didn't think that Falcon would set out to betray his subordinates—the man was fussy, but decent—yet he also knew that Corporate might not give the senior steward any choice.

"Third, the roster for Gold, Silver, and Bronze Decks has been updated," Falcon added. Two dozen wristcoms bleeped in unison as the roster was downloaded into their tiny brains. "If you have any problems, make sure you let me know by the end of gamma shift. I'll publish the final roster tomorrow."

Matt nodded. Only a brave steward would ask to be transferred. He rather doubted anyone would, unless it was their last voyage. Falcon had had to balance a whole list of priorities when putting the roster together. The best interests of the stewards were right at the bottom. He made a mental note to check the roster as soon as he could, although he knew his diligence hardly mattered. Whatever came his way...well, he'd have to suck it up. He wasn't wealthy enough to afford his own cabin on a cruise liner.

Falcon spoke briefly, assigning duty slots. The latecomers found themselves heading to the casino, not entirely to Matt's surprise. Others were assigned to supervise cleaning crews and inspect cabins, make-work as much as anything else. Matt forced himself to memorize who went where, just in case he needed to find any of his crewmates in a hurry. Stewards weren't encouraged to socialize outside their own little circles.

"Steve, Danielle, Matt, Carla...you're still assigned to meet-and-greet," Falcon finished. "It will be the captain in charge, not I. Reread your protocol briefings; then report to the main shuttlebay for 0930. Do *not* fuck up."

Matt swallowed. "Yes, sir."

The others didn't look any happier, he thought, which didn't bode well. Carla and Steve had served on other liners before transferring to *Supreme*.

They'd presumably gone through the duty already. He exchanged a worried glance with Danielle, who was as green as Matt himself, and then looked down at his wristcom. He'd already reviewed the protocol, but he would make sure to do so again before reporting to the shuttlebay. Fucking up in front of the captain might just get him a one-way ticket out of an unsecured airlock. VanGundy had practically boundless authority on his ship.

Although Corporate would probably be pissed if he upset the guests, Matt thought as Falcon continued to rattle off assignments. *That would get him fired...*

He pushed the thought aside. Falcon had raised his voice.

"The next few days are going to be chaotic," the senior steward informed them. "Those of you who have been on other liners will know this already, but it will be worse here. You'll find yourselves worked to the bone. Please rest assured that things *will* settle down—a little—once we open the vortex and get under way. We'll have time to catch up then."

And go over everything we did wrong, Matt thought. The exercises had been bad. Falcon and the other supervisors, all the way up to the XO herself, had made sure everything that could go wrong *did* go wrong. *Some of us might even be marked down for doing our duty at the wrong time.*

"Report to your assigned stations," Falcon concluded. "And make sure you have a moment to check the duty roster."

Carla snagged Matt as he headed for the hatch. "You did read the alert note, didn't you?"

"Of course," Matt said. Steve and Danielle fell in beside them. "Prostrate ourselves in front of them, never taking our heads off the deck until they walk past—"

Steve elbowed him. "These aren't regular guests," he said. "They're our great...uh...*something* bosses. A hair out of place could get us in real trouble."

"They might tip well," Carla added. "But...better to be very careful."

Matt groaned. "Should I try to take a sick day?"

"Only if you want to spend the next few days in Sickbay," Steve said. "Dr. Mackey isn't kind to malingerers."

"You'd have to take something poisonous to make it convincing," Carla added. "You really don't want a demerit on your record now." She made an unconvincing sickly face. "But we're nothing more than ants to them," she said. "I doubt they'll pay any real attention to us."

"Oh," Matt said, "I hope you're right."

AVAILABLE FOR PURCHASE FROM AMAZON NOW!

Made in United States
Orlando, FL
01 April 2024

45316111R00268